DAFFODILS

by
Alex Martin

Book One
The Katherine Wheel Series

There are those I am told
Don't hear petals unfold
Or the roll of the hills
Or daffodils

(Anon)

This book is dedicated to old Harry, our one-legged, one-hundred-year-old neighbour in Wiltshire, whose vivid anecdotes inspired Daffodils.

The right of A Martin to be identified as the author of this work has been asserted by her under Copyright Amendment (Moral Rights) Act 2000.

This book is a work of fiction. All the characters and places therein are a product of the author's imagination. Any resemblance to people or places is entirely coincidental.

The author has endeavoured to research historical facts accurately. Where they are not so, it is hoped the reader will forgive any anomalies and remember this is a work of fiction and grant the author artistic license. Some dates of real events, such as the start of the Health Visitor Scheme, have been adjusted to fit with the story line. Also, some dates of battles, while approximately correct, have been slightly adjusted for the same reason.

Note on the Front cover: (designed with the expert help of Jane Dixon-Smith of www.jdsmith-design.com)

This photograph, thought to be by Tom Aitken, shows four Women's Auxiliary Army Corps (WAAC) members enjoying a swim on a beach in France in World War One. The WAAC was a voluntary service started in January 1917 when the loss of life among the men in the army was so great that women were needed for non-military roles.

[Original reads: 'OFFICIAL PHOTOGRAPH TAKEN ON THE BRITISH WESTERN FRONT IN FRANCE - WAAC's bathing on the coast somewhere in France.']
Photograph courtesy of: www.flickr.com
FANY stands for First Aid Nursing Yeomanry.
Finding a picture without copyright issues was quite a task. This wasn't my first choice but now I feel it's just right for the story. This is a true photograph of some WAAC girls on the beach in France in 1918 and fits the story like a glove.

The field of daffodils represents the lines of the war dead from the First World War but also renewal and hope, which are important themes in the book. They also signal change and the energy of new beginnings and that also chimes with the story. Narcissi (daffodils) also symbolise vanity. I'll leave the reader to work out where that fits in.

Please go to www.intheplottingshed.com
for further information about The Katherine Wheel Series
and other books by Alex Martin and to obtain a free copy
of 'Trio', a collection of three short stories by the author,
by clicking on the picture of the shed

Follow

Alex Martin, Author

On Amazon

DAFFODILS

CHAPTER ONE

Katy sat on the topmost step of the library ladder, completely absorbed in a book. A tendril of her wavy brown hair had escaped from her maid's cap. She sucked its ends while she lost herself in Jane Eyre's melancholy tale.

Before she left for London, Lady Smythe had ordered her to spring-clean the huge book-lined room from top to bottom and, although Katy knew she shouldn't be reading the books instead of cleaning them, her duster floated unnoticed onto the polished oak floor. She only looked up when insistent tapping on the casement windows broke her concentration.

It took a moment to focus through the dazzling sunlight and see Jem waving his shears in mock salute through the glass. He took off his cap and bowed deeply to her, his chestnut wavy hair and brown eyes forming a perfect camouflage against the fading autumn leaves.

Jem smiled, replaced his hat and returned to clipping the grass verges of the manor house lawn. The curving drive that divided it rolled downhill towards the gabled lodge house, where Katy had been born. Smoke from the lodge's chimney curled erratically in the breeze. She wondered how a little smidgeon of ash could enjoy such freedom while she was stuck here dusting books.

Her younger brother, Albert, was determined to serve his country in the war that had broken out in August. He would boast to anyone who'd listen, "I'm joining up, I am; the first chance I get!" Even if those suffragettes Katy admired so much did get the vote after the war, being female, they would never have the chance to fight for their country. Katy sighed.

A lone horse clip-clopped up the lane towards the manor. She could just make out the ecclesiastical hat of its

1

rider. Her mother, Agnes, had been full of news about the new curate that morning. The old incumbent, Reverend Entwhistle, had died of a seizure six weeks ago. She strained to catch another glimpse. Any newcomer was a welcome diversion from the monotony of village life, but Katy doubted that a churchman would provide much excitement.

Her eyes lingered on the blue haze beyond the hills and the familiar longing engulfed her. Katy had never been further than Woodbury. Her one afternoon off a week did not allow it. A passing train wafted steam across the horizon. If only she could get on it and stay on the iron monster. Who knew where she might end up?

She dragged her gaze back to Jem, toiling away. As he snipped at the drive's edges, the Michaelmas daisies and chrysanthemums nodded and smiled, as if a part of him; a tapestry of colour into which he was somehow woven. Jem would never leave Cheadle Manor. No, he would always be a gardener, content with his patch. She watched his muscular back bend and stretch and bend again.

Jem doffed his cap as the horse and rider ambled into view. The two men exchanged a greeting. The stranger didn't take off his hat to Jem in return. When Jem jerked his head towards the manor, the rider shot a sharp look at the house, before turning his beautiful bay horse around, and trotting briskly back down the hill. He was much younger than Katy had expected, and his long legs looked surprisingly athletic astride his big bay horse.

Katy returned to the refuge of her book and was soon engrossed by Jane Eyre discovering poor mad Mrs Rochester in the attic. Ten minutes later she was interrupted again. Charles Smythe burst in so unexpectedly Katy jumped and the ladder overbalanced, rocking ominously to-and-fro. Charles rushed over to grab it, and Katy's ankle, and steadied both just in time to stop them from crashing down.

"Easy does it!" exclaimed Charles, still gripping ankle and ladder with equal tenacity.

"Sir – you startled me!" Katy noticed his hand on her leg and, blushing scarlet, shook it off. It wouldn't do to be manhandled by the heir to the estate.

"No need to be afraid of me, Miss Propriety. Now, which one of Mother's vast domestic army are you?"

"Katy Beagle, sir."

"Katy Beagle. Hmm, I don't remember you being such a peach."

Charles had been away for a couple of years at university and should have been there still. Katy assumed that his parents, Sir Robert and Lady Smythe, thought Charles was away from home, just like them.

"Tell you what you need after a fright like that. A drop of my father's best whisky. In fact, it's the very thing I came in for. Come on down from your high perch, little bird, and join me in a snifter."

Charles extended his hand to Katy, who was too embarrassed to refuse it.

"What are you doing up there anyway?" Charles poured out two enormous measures of whisky. "Good health," he said, chinking the glasses together.

Katy took a sip of the smoky drink and coughed. It was like drinking liquid fire! She hoped against hope Mrs Andrews, the housekeeper, wouldn't march in and catch her. Charles drank his down in one go and reached for the decanter for an immediate refill.

"Oh, silent one, I repeat - what on earth were you doing up that high ladder in splendid isolation? Educating yourself at my father's expense?"

"Yes, sir, you could say that," Katy said, flattered to be asked, even though her eyes were watering. "I was supposed to be dusting but got distracted reading about Jane Eyre."

The literary reference was lost on Charles. "Are you cleaning the entire library single-handed?"

"Yes sir, normally I'm lady's maid to your sister, Miss Cassandra, but she is away in London for the season." Katy sighed and looked at the floor. "I wasn't needed up there, so Lady Smythe set me to sorting out the library."

She didn't tell him the housekeeper was incensed about it and didn't consider her to be a lady's maid at all. Mrs Andrews - tall, Scottish and forbidding - ruled the house, and her husband, the butler, with a rod of iron. No one, including Mr Andrews, a softly spoken man given to melting into corners, ever dared to contradict her. She and Lady Smythe made a perfect match in that respect and while the lady of the house was away, Mrs Andrews delighted in giving the orders unopposed.

"There's plenty more urgent chores for the likes of you to do, Katy Beagle," Mrs Andrews had said, only that morning. "Cook has a mound of beans to salt for the winter and I have piles of linen to iron and fold, what with the other staff up in London. I don't know what Lady Smythe was thinking getting a dunderheid like you to clean the library with no one supervising you. Don't think for a minute I don't realise you are reading the books more often than dusting them. What use is book-learning to you? You're not even a proper lady's maid, you know."

But Charles, blissfully ignorant of these battles, hooted with laughter, "Why does Mother want the library cleaned? So, Cass can get back to reading every book? I don't think so! You might be her maid, Miss Katherine Beagle, but I'll bet you've read more books dusting this library than Cass ever did. Like reading, do you?"

"I love it more than anything else in the world, sir."

"Do you? It takes all sorts I suppose; can't stand it myself. I'm like my dear sister in that regard. Do you like your whisky? Want a top up?"

"Oh, no, sir. It's fearful strong." Katy had barely touched her drink.

"Think I'll have another for the road. I'm off to Woodbury with commissions from Mrs Andrews later. Do you fancy coming?"

"Me, sir? Into town? With you?"

"Well, why not?"

"I'm supposed to be cleaning," Katy looked around the handsome room. "I doubt Mrs Andrews would think it right for me to accompany you."

"I'll sort out old Andrews – thing is, do you want to come?"

Katy dared another sip of firewater and considered his question. She looked at Charles in a new light. As children they had led separate lives and she had only seen him from a distance. His sandy hair and small frame had inspired many a local boy to mock him when out of earshot and she had laughed at his expense with the rest of them. Now, Charles sported a manly moustache and his well-cut suit made the most of his slender shoulders. As an adult he displayed far more confidence than he had as the puny child she remembered being such a cry-baby. And there was a definite air of fashion about him. It gave him a whiff of style and substance. Slowly she nodded and smiled.

"That's settled then. I need a playmate whilst I'm home. Damned boring with everyone up in London and soon I'll be off to France to search for glory. I've signed up to serve as an officer in the British Expeditionary Force, you know. Got to have a bit of fun before that. We'll set off after a bit of brunch. Be ready at noon."

"But Mrs Andrews, sir," Katy insisted. "The housekeeper's in charge while Lady Smythe's away and I'd have to have her permission, or I might lose my position."

"I'll speak to the old bat right away. Put your best bonnet on – not that silly maid's cap."

CHAPTER TWO

Katy's father, Bert, was an unwitting conspirator in the adventure. As head coachman at the manor, it was his job to hand over the reins of the little gig to his employer's son, but he remained innocent of the identity of Charles' passenger. Had he known his daughter was to accompany his young master, things might have turned out differently. As it was, no one noticed Katy slip out of the kitchen door at midday and hop up into the waiting gig. Soon, they were bowling along, Charles singing at the top of his voice and Katy giggling helplessly beside him. Hens scattered from cottages and heads turned to stare, as the good folk of Upper Cheadle certainly *did* notice who was sitting beside the squire's son.

When the gig, easily recognisable by its livery, swept into Woodbury High Street, Katy revelled in the surprised looks, as they thundered past the townspeople. The whites of Larkspur's eyes showed in frightened rinds as Charles flicked his driving whip along the top of her dappled grey back.

Katy kept her own back ramrod straight and held her head up high when fingers pointed at them as they drove, far too fast, along the cobbled road.

Charles threw back his head and laughed when she nudged his arm and said, "Sir, everyone's staring at us!" He drew up with a flourish outside the King's Head inn and shouted out for the stable boy, who took the horse and gig through its narrow central archway into the yard behind.

Katy didn't dare withdraw her arm when Charles tucked it under his, sailed into the coaching inn and ordered ale for them both. Katy had never been inside the old building before. A bright fire danced in the grate adding its woody aroma to the smell of beeswax furniture polish and stale beer. Wood panelling lined the dark, smoky room and men sat in twos and threes at the tables,

6

discussing the latest news of the war. Charles steered her to an alcove whose bay window overlooked the busy street. Katy sipped her ale and relaxed against her leather armchair, hardly daring to believe she was there.

"Now then," Charles drank his beer down in big gulps, "let's look at the shopping list." He took the single sheet out of his pocket and frowned in concentration.

"Is there much to buy, sir?" Katy felt very important being included in the process.

"Hmm, butcher's, baker's and candlestick makers!" Charles laughed at his own joke and Katy, the ale increasing her confidence, joined in. Some farmers were propping up the bar and they turned to look at the pair by the window. It gave her a ripple of excitement to cause such a stir and she put her hand out to Charles to take the list from him.

She scanned the piece of paper quickly. Mrs Andrew's neat handwriting was easy to read. "We should leave buying the meat until last, then it's less likely to spoil."

"Good thinking, Katy. Trust a woman to know what's what." Charles looked pleased.

Encouraged, she went on, "Yes, I think the chandlers should be first for the candles. Then the grocers for the sack of flour and, oh! Could I choose the ribbons Mrs Andrews wants for the lavender bags?"

"I think you should, Katy. I know I wouldn't have a clue. Tell you what, I'll go to the chandlers and you go to the milliners. I'll meet you at the grocer's in half an hour. How's that suit you?"

Katy's heart skipped a beat. She'd never been allowed off the estate during working hours before, let alone been authorised to buy things for the big house. She knew she could do it though. There was more to her than scrubbing and dusting. If she did this right maybe Mrs Andrews would give her more commissions like this. Eyes bright, she nodded back at Charles. He drank up the rest of his beer in one swift movement. Katy left half of hers. They got up and Charles tossed a couple of coins on the bar counter before steering her, his arm around her waist, back out into the sunlit street. They parted at the milliner's shop.

Katy pushed open the shop door and the little bell clanged her entrance. There was no going back now. Mrs Friedenburg looked up from her lacy bundles. Her eyes narrowed when she saw Katy.

Katy felt herself blush but stepped forward boldly. "Good morning."

"Gut morning, Miss?" The milliner said, in her strong German accent.

"Miss Beagle."

"Ach, yes, Miss Beagle, I know your mother. And vat can I do for you?"

"I work at the manor house and Mrs Andrews has sent me to buy some ribbons for her lavender bags."

"Ah, so? She is late with her lavender this year but I haf just the thing. Come with me." Mrs Friedenburg walked across to the shelves at the rear of the shop.

"Thank you." Katy felt very grown up as she went to join her.

Mrs Friedenburg laid out various narrow ribbons in pastel colours for Katy's inspection. Katy took her time; she was enjoying herself too much to rush choosing. In the end she picked out some blue-grey silk ribbons. The shade was almost a match for lavender stems.

"A very elegant choice, Miss Beagle." Mrs Friedenburg nodded her approval.

The doorbell announced another customer. Katy looked round. Her stomach lurched uncomfortably as Mrs Threadwell and Mrs Hoskins, from Lower Cheadle, entered together. Both women stood stock still at the sight of her.

"Is that you, Katherine Beagle?" Mrs Threadwell ran the Post Office in Lower Cheadle and held full command of the local gossip grapevine.

It would be her, of all people, to see me here, thought Katy and curtsied her assent.

"Well I never!" Mrs Hoskins, housekeeper to the vicar, rolled her eyes at her friend.

The doorbell rang out a third time and Agnes Beagle, Katy's mother, joined the throng. She stepped into the shop. When she saw her daughter, her kindly smile froze and turned it sour.

"Katy!" she exclaimed, "whatever is you doing here?"

"Quite!" Mrs Hoskins said. "We'd all like to know the answer to *that* question."

Katy was grateful Mrs Friedenburg smoothed over the awkward moment. "Ladies, please to come in, come in. How gut it is to haf a full shop. I haf been so quiet lately since the war started. It is not my fault I am German, after all. Tell me, how can I help you?"

Mrs Friedenburg shepherded Mrs Threadwell and Mrs Hoskins over to the counter and kept them chatting.

The two matrons kept looking back over their shoulders as Agnes clutched Katy's arm and hustled her into the darkest corner of the shop.

"Katy, what are you doing?"

"Ow, Mum! You're hurting my arm!" Katy tried to pull away.

"I'll do more than hurt your arm, my girl, if I find out you've been flouting the rules. Why ain't you up at the manor? I thought you was cleaning the library for her Ladyship? Does Mrs Andrews know where you are?"

"Let go of me, Mum!" Katy felt both cross and flustered. The adventure was spoiled now. "Mrs Andrews has sent me on an errand for her. Look. Here's the list."

The written evidence was shoved under Agnes' eagle eye. Though a poor reader herself, she could recognise the housekeeper's distinctive style. "Well, how did you get

9

here then? You never walked? You wasn't on the omnibus, that's for sure."

Katy felt her face grow hot and pink as she answered, "Mr Charles brought me in the gig, didn't he?"

"Mr Charles? On your own? And you thought that was right and proper? I never even knew he was home, what with the Smythes away in London. What was you thinking, Katy? Going with him unescorted and all? We'll never live this down. And there's Mrs Threadwell and Mrs Hoskins too. Everyone'll know about it, sure as eggs is eggs."

"Well, it don't matter if they do. I've done nothing wrong. It's just shopping after all."

Agnes wagged her finger. "I tell you what else too; Jem's mother won't like it. Oh yes, Mary Phipps will have something to say when she gets to hear about your gallivanting. You could lose Jem over this."

"Well I haven't got him yet anyway – we're not engaged or anything," Katy squirmed under her mother's barrage.

"Nor will you ever likely be at this rate," replied Agnes.

The busy doorbell rang out again. Charles Smythe swung the door open wide, nodded at the two ladies sifting through piles of snowy white linen at the counter before spotting Katy standing with her mother at the rear of the shop. Smiling broadly, he strode towards them, saying in a loud voice, "I say, Kate, what's keeping you? I've got the candles and have been waiting for you outside the grocer's for ages. Got lost in the ribbons, have you?"

Katy didn't know which way to look, as four pairs of middle-aged female eyes locked on to her face. All were curious and her mother's were fuming.

Charles appeared oblivious to it all. He turned to Mrs Friedenburg. "What do we owe you Mrs F? Actually, stick it on the tab for Mrs Andrews, would you? Come on Katy, let's finish what we started."

"Just a minute. Er, sir," Agnes said. "I need a word with my daughter first, if it's all the same to you, Mr Charles?"

Charles looked both surprised and annoyed at Agnes' breach of etiquette but said, "Oh, very well. Kate – I'll be at the grocers. Join me there when you can." He slammed the door on the way out.

The little bell trembled.

But her mother didn't seem in any hurry to release her. "Why's Mr Charles home anyway? He should still be up at Oxford, as far as I know."

"It's the war; he's signed up. He'll be away soon enough to France. Said he's got a commission, whatever that is." Katy felt her prior knowledge of this exclusive news regained some of her lost dignity.

"This war! It's got a lot to answer for. I hear of nothing else from our Albert but I'm not letting him go. He's too young. Everyone says it'll be over by Christmas anyway."

"Maybe, Mum, but I must get back to Mr Charles."

"Hmm, go on then but I don't approve, and don't you go thinking that I do!"

Katy, once released from her mother's grip, raced off to the grocers. Charles looked grumpy and remained so for the rest of the trip. The shine had gone off the adventure for them both.

CHAPTER THREE

Katy bumped into Jem in the kitchen courtyard one drizzly morning. He was barrowing in the morning's vegetables to Mrs Biggs, the cook, and Katy had been given the humble task of scrubbing the kitchen steps, despite the rain or maybe even because of it, knowing Mrs Andrews. Katy felt awkward and at a disadvantage, kneeling on the hard cobblestones but she told herself she had nothing to be ashamed of and stood up, lifting her chin, as Jem approached.

"Morning, Jem, how are you?"

"Morning, Kate. I'm fine. Glad to see you at the manor house instead of going out with Mr Charles."

Katy brushed her damp hair from her forehead with the back of her soapy hand. "You're not my keeper, you know."

Katy tried to push past him and get back to the house. Jem's arm shot out to stop her. She turned, eyebrows raised.

Jem let his hand rest on her arm. "Just thought - if you want to go out to places - I could take you."

"You couldn't take me out in the gig though, could you? And you only have Sundays off anyway."

"That's true, Kate, but do you trust Mr Charles?"

"What are you saying, Jeremy Phipps? Just because Charles happens to enjoy my company and wants to spend time with me doesn't mean we're more than just friends."

"Just friends? That's been said before. How can a maidservant be a friend to Sir Robert's son? People of his sort – his class – they don't play by the same rules, especially with their servants."

"Charles doesn't see me as a servant. He sees me as his equal, as a friend, like I said."

"*Mr* Charles," (Katy winced at Jem's emphasis on the mister) "might say that, Kate – he can say what he likes, can't he?"

"You're just jealous, Jem. Just because - *Mr* - Charles sees something in me that you can't."

"I see everything in you, Kate, you know I do. Maybe I am jealous – who wouldn't be? Everyone's talking about you. I'm surprised Mrs Andrews doesn't put a stop to it."

Katy bit her lip. He'd hit a nerve there. "Mrs Andrews can't tell Mr Charles what to do any more than you can!"

"Kate – don't do this. Why won't you marry me and let me look after you?"

"I'm not a child, Jem. I don't need looking after, thank you. I've told you before – I'm not ready to marry anyone. I don't want to get tied down before I've lived my own life."

"I thought you'd say that. You always do."

"Well, seeing as you ask me nearly every week you ought to be used to the answer by now."

Jem laughed. "Kate, Kate! You know I'll be here waiting when this is over, but please, Kate, take care. Don't, don't let him – you know."

"Oh, for goodness sake, Jeremy – what do you take me for?"

"Just take care – that's all." Jeremy's shoulders slumped.

As she turned to go back inside the house to see what other dreary jobs Mrs Andrews had in mind for her, the sound of horse hooves click-clacked over the cobbles. Katy turned to see if it might be Charles back from his ride. Her heart fell when she saw it was the new curate. To her surprise, he dismounted in a single graceful movement, and marched straight up to her.

Imaginary butterflies sprang into life in her stomach. The new curate was tall. He still didn't take off his hat. Was it glued to that extraordinary hair? His golden mane was long, touching his collar in an old-fashioned style that belonged to the last century. He was talking to her, no, *at* her. She stared up at the curate's face, noting his straight nose and startlingly blue eyes under beetle black brows.

13

"Miss Beagle?"

"Yes, sir?" Katy bobbed a curtsey, uncertain of protocol when holding a smelly bucket.

"I was hoping to bump into you."

Katy's astonishment rendered her mute.

Reverend White cleared his throat and began, "Miss Beagle, there has been some gossip about you of which you should be aware. I overheard Mrs Threadwell at the Post Office saying you were, um, consorting with Mr Charles and accompanying him on trips in his gig. Is this true?"

What could she say? She couldn't deny it but what right did this stranger have to interrogate her?

"Well?"

Katy stared back at the cleric with eyes as blue as his own. She knew hers were a deeper, more violet kind of blue but his were the palest turquoise she had ever seen. She imagined the sea being that colour.

She nodded, not trusting herself to speak.

"As your pastor, Miss Beagle, I feel it is my duty to advise against such behaviour. Your position at the manor might be in jeopardy should Lady Smythe discover how you've been spending your days in her absence."

"I'm just doing as I'm told. If Mr Charles asks me to go with him, I can't rightly say no, can I?" Katy said, repeating the words that had worked with her mother.

"Would you like me to speak with him? Is he, um, forcing you in any way?"

Good God, did all men have one-track minds? Anger rose to warm her reply. "Mr Charles and I share similar tastes in music and books, that's all. There's no more to it than that."

The Reverend snorted. How dare he laugh at her! Katy turned to go.

"Books and music? I think you had better remember your station, young woman. And have a regard for your reputation too."

Katy didn't give him the satisfaction of listening. She'd already started walking back to the house, as his last words trailed after her. She looked back over her shoulder before entering the house. How odd, the Reverend was still watching her. When she stared back at him, he turned and clucked his horse towards the stables.

***

Jem pulled up bean poles with a savage lunge. The bean stalks had withered on them, their seeds hard and dry like their old pods. Summer was over. As he worked, his perennial worry nagged at him. What more could he do, or say, to get Katy to come round? He'd told her he loved her, he'd asked her to marry him but no, he wasn't good enough. He was half inclined to believe the old biddies in the village who gossiped that Katy had set her sights on Charles and meant to have him. That was impossible of course. Just wishful thinking in his view. Katy could no more leapfrog the class difference than he could himself, not that he'd ever try.

Trouble was she read too many bloody books. They filled her head with all sorts of silly, impossible ideas. Frustrated though he was, he understood why she wanted more out of life. If he could help her to travel and see the world, he'd do it. He'd thought about emigrating to Australia and asking her to go with him as his wife, but he didn't really want to leave his home. The Phipps had worked this land for hundreds of years and he loved the loamy soil he stood on.

He might understand Katy's restlessness her brother Albert was the same - it was a family trait - but he didn't share it and never would. For Jem it was enough to see the seasons change, to yield the crops from the rich Wiltshire soil and feel a part of the natural rhythm of the countryside that he loved so deeply. He couldn't give Katy the adventure she longed for, but she had his whole heart just the same.

CHAPTER FOUR

Charles might not be a great reader, despite Katy's claims to the contrary but he did love music. The new gramophone was, happily for her, housed in the very library she was spring-cleaning from top to bottom. Whenever he was at home to rule the roost Charles raided every record in his father's limited collection. Katy was transported with delight and listened, rapt with joy, as the music floated over the books she slowly dusted. Charles lounged by the window-seat watching her face respond to the thunder of Beethoven and the strings of Mozart. Vaughan Williams' latest concert piece, 'The Lark Ascending', drew Katy from her ladder in floods of tears. Charles, too moved for words, took refuge in his father's decanter.

One day Charles came in from a shopping trip laden with a parcel of new records. "Katy – look what I've got, a real treat - some Strauss! I shall teach you to dance. Come here. I've only a couple of days leave left before I'm off to my commission. Let's see if you can master the waltz before I go."

Charles wound up the gramophone enthusiastically. Delicate strains from Vienna filled the large room. He slipped his arm about Katy's waist and counted out the beat.

"One, two, three. One, two, three. That's it. You're getting it. Just keep counting and follow me."

Katy studiously counted the beat and watched her heavy boots miraculously follow Charles' polished brogues.

"I could dance with you forever, Katy. Don't you think we make a perfect pair? You know, you'd knock spots off the other debutantes. It doesn't seem right that a pearl like you is buried in the country never to be seen abroad."

Not for the first time, Katy considered the difference in their social status. She'd been reading Pygmalion, the new play by George Bernard Shaw. Charles had bought it for her to supplement Sir Robert's rather conventional library. Eliza Doolittle had only been a flower girl. Katy was the daughter of the head coachman, so she was much more elevated than that. The class divide wasn't such a yawning gap for them. Mrs Andrews could punish her all she liked when Charles was out, but she couldn't control her young master's feelings.

As she waltzed around the library, Katy imagined herself in a ballroom wearing a long evening dress and glowing pearls, her hands and arms encased in elegant silk gloves, just like the ones she used to help Cassandra into. She'd spotted a beautiful white gown left behind by her young mistress who'd claimed it was decidedly passé for London. Maybe she could put it on for Charles.

"Charles?"

"Hmm?"

"Do you think you could meet me up in Cassandra's room this afternoon? I've something to show you."

"We'd be lucky to get away with that."

"It would only take five minutes, but I would really like it," Katy almost whispered her words, barely able to believe her own cheek.

"What fun! An illicit foray into enemy territory? Perfect training for a new recruit, like me. Right-oh, you're on."

"Meet me at three o'clock. Mrs Andrews always has a nap then. She says she's doing the books, but we all know she puts her feet up with a cup of tea and nods off. Even Mr Andrews isn't allowed to disturb her." Katy kept her voice low, just in case.

Charles laughed, "You little minx! I'll be there."

Katy could hardly eat her lunch with the other servants in the big kitchen. Mrs Biggs, the cook, was pre-occupied in taking George Phipps, the head gardener, to task over the lack of early autumn fruit. George was not only Jem's boss but also his father and had sent his eldest son to work

18

a long way out at the edge of the estate, coppicing woodland for the day. When Mrs Andrews joined in the spirited debate there was no Jem to notice Katy murmur her soft thank-you's or see her slipping noiselessly away upstairs.

With trembling fingers, she took the rustling tissue paper off the white ball-gown. She was less well-built than Cassandra but was much the same height. She'd heard Lady Smythe's lady's maid say spitefully that Cassandra had never liked the dress or had even wanted to go to her first ball; adding how unnatural it was for a young lady in her position to prefer setting her hunter to jump a five-bar gate to pirouetting on the dance-floor. Ruth Harrison had even gone as far as to call Cassandra a tomboy. Katie had been sick with envy of them both when they piled into the carriage and set off for London.

On went the silk gloves, left behind because of a powder stain. She had no jewellery to complete the effect, but it would have to do. Katy stood in front of the long mirror in the corner of the room and surveyed herself solemnly.

The hated maid's cap would have to go. She threw it on the bed in disgust. Then she re-arranged her long brown hair into a becoming pile on the top of her head as she had done so often for the owner of the dress. With her stout boots hidden under the silken folds she reckoned she could, like Eliza Doolittle, pass for a lady. She dabbed a little scent behind her ears from the gilt-edged bottle she found on the dressing-table. It smelt of summer roses. A nearly empty pot of rouge had been left behind and she carefully rubbed a little on her high cheekbones. When Charles softly entered the bedroom a little later, he was, for once, dumbstruck.

"You little beauty," he murmured. "Oh, Katy, I could leave home for you."

He gently cupped Katy's chin in his hands and kissed her. Katy gasped in surprise and her mouth opened a little.

19

Charles couldn't help but kiss her properly after that. The embrace lasted so long Katy didn't hear the carriage in the drive or Cassandra's light footsteps up the stairs, followed by Lady Smythe's heavier ones.

CHAPTER FIVE

Neither Katy nor Charles heard Cassandra opening the bedroom door as they carried on kissing in blissful ignorance of their silent witness, standing watching them from the half-opened doorway, aghast at their antics.

Lady Smythe wheezed up the stairs and, on gaining the galleried landing, called out to her daughter breathlessly, "What's the matter, Cassandra? Why are you standing there like a statue?"

"It's nothing, Mother, no need for you to worry," Cassandra said but Lady Smythe swished past her and opened the door wide in order to investigate.

"What on *earth* is going on?" Lady Smythe's breathlessness disappeared in an instant. Her voice rang out as clear and loud as a church bell. "Charles! How could you? And who is this? Katherine Beagle? Unhand my son, you miserable girl!"

Charles and Katy sprang apart and turned as one to face the outraged matron.

"Mother!" protested Cassandra.

"Be quiet, Cassandra. Go downstairs and leave this to me."

Cassandra grimaced at her brother in sympathy and left, her reluctance obvious in every dragging step.

Lady Smythe strode into the room and said, "I demand an explanation! How dare you wear Cassandra's clothes, Katherine? Charles - I shall speak to you separately. Miss Beagle – once you have put on your correct attire – go straight to the library which, I understand from Mrs Andrews, is where you *should* be. First, you must get changed. Then you can await me there. And I want everything in this room put back where it belongs. Woe betide you if anything is missing, young woman. Charles! Come with me, this instant, to your father's study."

Charles mouthed a mortified, "Sorry," to Katy and abandoned her.

She watched him bow to his fate and follow the stiff corseted back of his mother down the sweeping curved staircase. Katy stood on the landing as they descended to the large marbled hall of the manor and disappeared into the study, leaving the door wide open behind them. Only when she heard the raised voices issuing from the study below, did Katy crumple to the floor, regardless of creasing the silk ball dress that became her so well. The angry exchange floated up to her through the open door as she lay in a heap above them. Charles reiterated several times that nothing had passed between himself and Katy except the kiss that his mother had witnessed. Katy squirmed at Charles' feeble responses. It was obvious that his mother remained unconvinced.

Charles' father, drawn by the noise, joined them from across the hall. Katy crouched low behind the banister rail, but Sir Robert didn't look up before entering the study. He too neglected to close the door behind him. When appealed to for his opinion, he barked, "Probably led him on – fetching little thing as I recall."

Katy cursed Sir Robert silently and lay with her ear pressed to the banister, too scared to move in case the rustling silk drowned out the argument. Lady Smythe let Charles mumble on with his protests for five minutes until her patience gave way.

Katy had no trouble hearing his mother's stentorian tones, "And why, Charles, are you home at all? This is an even more important matter. Why are you not at Oxford applying yourself to your studies?"

This time Katy could clearly hear his reply. "I'm off to the war, Mother. Soon be with the British Expeditionary Force in France and out of your way."

Lady Smythe's hectoring suddenly took on a hysterical tone and she ran from the study, sobbing loudly enough for all the servants to hear.

Katy clung to the banisters at the top of the stairs trying to become invisible, but she needn't have worried. Lady

Smythe, crossing the hall below her, looked far too upset to notice anyone.

Charles's father, never one to lower his voice, took up the lecture beneath her. "Unfathomable creatures, women," was the advice Sir Robert gave him, "best avoided. Funds low, are they? Hmm, thought as much. Well, my boy, here's a cheque to tide you over whilst you're serving your country abroad. Don't tell your mother about it and, if I were you, I'd get packing and on the road before lunch. And mind you keep in touch with us once you've enlisted. Good luck, m'boy."

Katy somehow heaved herself off the floor and went back into Cassandra's bedroom. She peeled off the beautiful gown after allowing herself one last, lingering look in the mirror. On went the black maid's dress with its unbecoming pinny and cap.

She trooped down to the library with a heart as leaden as her boots. She knew she could never convince her stern mistress of her innocence. How could she, when all the evidence was against her? She wasn't even confident that Charles had defended her position in the face of both his parents and on their territory. If only he'd spoken up a bit more she'd know exactly how to behave when it was her turn to face his mother.

Despite her red, swollen eyes Lady Smythe demonstrated that she had herself firmly back in control by spending less time dispensing with her servant than she had her son.

"You will leave this house forthwith, Miss Beagle, and receive no further wages. Neither will you have a reference from me." Lady Smythe's sentence was delivered without a glimmer of a smile.

Within five minutes Katy had lost her job and all prospects of future employment. She even had to give up the loathsome uniform and her only pair of boots.

By the time Charles was sullenly staring out of the train window, Katy was back at the lodge house confronting her

23

own mother. Her bare feet showing blatant evidence of her disgrace. If Lady Smythe's anger had frozen Katy in its austere severity, Agnes' tirade more than made up for it.

"Katy Beagle! I am ashamed of you. How could you lose your job? There's no chance of another around here or anywhere else for that matter if you've no reference! What was you thinking? And what's the reason for it? Hey, my girl? What *have* you been up to?"

By the time Bert came hurrying home early from the stables, Katy was in floods of tears in front of an unrepentant Agnes. Her mother stood before her with arms folded, lest she knocked her daughter from this week into next, she later told her troubled spouse.

Bert strode into his kitchen, white with shock. "Katy! Is it true? I know you've been out and about with Mr Charles, but I trusted you to know your place. To know when to stop! I thought you, with all your book-learning and cleverness, would at least have the sense to know where the boundaries lay."

Katy sobbed all the harder.

"Answer me, Kate!" her father's disappointment was evident in his distressed voice. "What on earth were you thinking, dressing up in Miss Cassandra's ball-dress?"

"What's this?" Agnes gripped the scrubbed pine table and leant forward to see Katy's tearstained face. "What dressing up is this? Have you stolen things as well as been dismissed, Katy?"

"No. *No!* Of course, I haven't. I just tried it on, that's all. It's a dress Miss Cassandra won't ever wear again. She's outgrown it. I just wanted to see what I'd look like in it."

"That's only part of it though, isn't it?" Bert looked grimmer than ever.

Katy nodded miserably.

"Go on, Katy. What else did you do?" Agnes said.

"I didn't do anything." Katy shut her mouth tight to stop it quivering.

"That's not what I heard," Bert said.

Agnes looked askance at her husband, usually so gentle – too gentle she'd often told him - with his eldest daughter. Katy couldn't speak but only cried louder.

Bert spoke for her. "Agnes, I'm ashamed to tell you, that Katy here was caught in Miss Cassandra's ball-gown, kissing Mr Charles. And that they were in Miss Cassandra's bedroom, of all places."

Agnes was speechless. She sat down hard on one of the kitchen chairs and stared at Katy, whose head was now laid across her arms to hide her scarlet face. It all sounded so sordid when her father described what had happened. How could she ever get them to understand?

Agnes caught her breath and said slowly, "And what else were you about to do in that bedroom, my girl, apart from kissing that is?"

"It wasn't like that! Charles had never touched me before. He said I was beautiful – as beautiful as any girl he'd ever seen – even at all the balls he'd been to."

Agnes and Bert exchanged the sort of look that only passes between husband and wife at times of family crises. Bert sat down at the head of the table with his wife and his daughter on either side. He shook his head, all the air gone out of him like a deflated balloon. The kettle started to whistle on the hob and Agnes wearily got up to answer its siren call. She lifted down her big brown teapot and spooned in the tea-leaves. She set the pot down on the kitchen table between them and put out some mugs and a jug of fresh milk.

"Come on, we all could do with a cup of tea." Agnes's voice sounded flat with resignation as she poured out. "Question is, what's to become of you now, Katy? I don't know what your prospects are going to be from here. Don't you see? No one will want you after this – not to employ you - and certainly not to marry."

"I will."

All three Beagles turned their heads to the door, left open by Bert's precipitous entry a few minutes earlier. Jem stood illuminated against the afternoon sunshine in the doorframe, as calm and as collected as ever. None of them knew how much he had overheard. Katy felt her heart could sink no lower.

"Jem, lad! Come in, come in. Er, I don't think you can have heard what's happened up at the manor." Bert got up awkwardly to greet him.

Jem walked into the warm kitchen, ducking his head under the door lintel as he did so. Silently, Agnes poured another mug of tea and handed it to Jem, while pulling up a chair for his long legs to tuck under the table. Jem sipped the tea and smiled his usual slow smile. The others watched and waited. Jem always took his time about things. Katy wiped her red eyes with the palm of her hand and sniffed. Jem held her other hand and pressed it firmly.

Putting down his mug with some deliberation, he looked into Katy's eyes, took a deep breath and said, "I have heard about it. There's no-one up at the manor who hasn't by now. It's all anyone's talking about. But it don't make no difference to me. I'll have you, Katy, whatever else has happened, if you will have me."

Jem took Katy's other hand in his and said, without his usual smile but with great solemnity, "Katy, will you marry me?"

Agnes clutched at her husband's tweed coat-sleeve and held her breath.

CHAPTER SIX

If Katy later regretted her decision to marry him, Jem couldn't tell. He watched her like a hawk in the few short weeks after her dismissal, proud of the way her chin would come up when the old women nodded in her direction as they gossiped about her. Secretly he wondered if she rather enjoyed being the centre of the scandal that rocked both villages. He knew some called him a sap for taking the flighty piece on.

She told her future husband that she was damned if she was going to give them the satisfaction of not seeing her wedding through. "It's going to be the best wedding day the village has seen in a hundred years, Jem. I'll make those old biddies eat their words or die in the attempt!"

Jem thought these were brave words, easily said, and worried about how Katy really felt about settling for him and the little estate cottage that would be conferred to them upon their marriage. Sometimes he wondered if she remembered why she'd been sacked at all and then she started kissing him back in earnest. Not that he was complaining.

With less than a week to go until the great day, Katy and Jem took a picnic up to the top of the hill above Lower Cheadle. It was Katy's favourite haunt. She would look across the whole county and pretend they were setting off on a long journey instead of submitting to married life in a tiny cottage. Jem indulged her fantasy as he did in most things.

Katy snuggled back into Jem's enfolding arms. Her ever present book lay in the grass, cast aside and apparently forgotten like the scandal of her dismissal.

Jem squeezed her tighter and looked over her head at the Wiltshire downs stretching out in a fertile patchwork before them. Katy's hair tickled his chin. For one so bright, he thought she had a conveniently short memory but was far too happy to say so.

Shadows of doubt had clouded his happiness at regular intervals ever since Katy had answered, "Yes, Jem. Yes, I will," on that fateful day in the lodge house kitchen. He would never forget the long pause that preceded her answer. He had waited years for that moment and knew it had been compromised by wretched, spoiled Charles Smythe coming home so unexpectedly to sign up for the war.

Would Katy have said yes otherwise? He had to know. He'd take bets that Agnes had harangued Katy into making a go of their forthcoming marriage once she'd committed to it. To be fair, Katy had turned to him wholeheartedly ever since. He still hadn't got used to it and didn't dare to believe she would really turn up next Saturday.

"Katy, I have to ask you something." Jem's heart thumped in his chest, but he couldn't let that stop him. He needed to settle this once and for all.

"What is it, Jem?" Katy seemed to sense the seriousness of his mood but stayed looking out across the downs. Her back went rigid against him.

"I need to know, before it's too late, whether you agreed to marry me because of losing your job over Charles Smythe or because you really want to – for me." Jem held his breath waiting for her reply.

There was another horrible pause before Katy said, still not looking at him, "I always intended to marry you, Jem. I can't say I wasn't flattered by Charles's attentions, but I knew deep down it didn't mean anything."

Jem would have felt more comforted by this if she'd looked into his eyes when she'd spoken but he supposed half a loaf was better than no bread.

"Shall I see you before the wedding, Katy?" he asked the top of her head.

"No! Certainly not – that would be bad luck. No, Jeremy Phipps, you shall have to wait until Saturday to do this again."

Katy turned around in his arms to face him and kissed him with enthusiasm. He tried to decide if her eyes were darkest blue, like the elderberries growing all around them or more brown, like the gills of the field mushrooms at their feet.

When he came up for air, Jem said, "It's going to be a long week."

"Ah, but then you have a day's holiday after the wedding. Two whole days to call our own."

"Hmm, not sure about that new curate though." Jem gathered up their things into Katy's basket. "I wish we had old Entwhistle to marry us, Katy."

"Oh, I don't know, he'll give a certain air of sophistication to the proceedings."

"Listen to you! I'll give you sophisticated proceedings."

Jem chased her down the hill back to the valley floor, his long stride easily outstripping hers. They stood awhile in Lower Cheadle's high street, hand in hand, looking longingly at the tiny terraced cottage that was to be their future home.

"His ears must have been burning," whispered Jem in Katy's ear. They turned and saw the new incumbent of their parish, Lionel White, bearing down on them. Jem smiled as Katy reached up and checked her dark brown hair was still tied up behind her head and not tumbling down her back. Jem knew she would never want the vicar to think she looked common. The vicar lifted his hat to the young couple. Jem wondered if Katy was admiring that blond mane. Old-fashioned his long hair might be, but it really was quite unusual, long enough to lay across those broad shoulders. As Jem looked at the energetic newcomer, he wished again that old Entwhistle hadn't popped his clogs so suddenly.

"How do you do? Miss Beagle, Mr Phipps?" Reverend White inclined his glossy head to them.

29

"Very well, thank you, sir," Jem answered for them both, letting his pride show in his voice.

"All ready for the forthcoming nuptials?" asked the Reverend.

"As ready as we can be." Jem kept his gaze steady. One muscular arm crept instinctively round Katy's slim waist.

"Good, excellent - and this is to be your future home?" Lionel White indicated the little cottage with a gracious nod.

Katy said proudly, "Yes sir, it is."

"I hope you will be very happy in it." Lionel replaced his hat.

Jem curled his lip at the way the curate was so careful not to disturb his neatly combed mane.

"Until Saturday then." Lionel walked briskly away.

CHAPTER SEVEN

The day of the wedding dawned bright and fine. The last shred of September sunshine shimmered on the lane that sloped down to Reverend White's church. The wedding party looked grateful for its leafy shade as the bride and groom walked past them into the cool of the small stone building.

The village postmistress, Mrs Threadwell, craned her neck to look round the corner of the lane. She'd been predicting to all and sundry that Mr Charles' gig would come roaring down the hill at the last minute and whisk Katy off in it.

"He ain't coming, Martha," said her husband, William. "That's tuppence you owe me."

Lionel felt certain he was making an impact officiating at his first wedding in the sleepy little village. He had become a clergyman due to his innate sense of right and wrong. He had been brought up by his father, also a Reverend, to believe in the duty of the educated man to instruct the unfortunate. He'd spent the last few years in India, tending the English aristocracy who ruled there. He had enjoyed the tea parties and elegant society but reports of the ill health of his mother had eventually drawn him home. She had rallied immediately upon his return and encouraged him to take up the curacy in Wiltshire and to continue his career in England where he might be noticed more readily by the local bishop.

Lionel aspired to be a great orator and his mother had always encouraged him in this. He was confident he could hold the attention of any female in his congregation in the palm of his hand. Men usually took a little longer to come around.

If Lionel's eyes rested rather more on the bride than the groom no-one, including himself, noticed. The scandal with Charles Smythe had obviously precipitated this hasty marriage. Katherine Beagle was certainly pretty enough to tempt anyone. It was a shame she was marrying this yokel. Lionel supposed she'd had little choice after losing her position at the manor. It must have left her with few other options. He speculated if she was carrying a child and if so, whose.

"I, I, do," stammered Jem. To Lionel's eyes, Jem looked as if his new starched collar was so tight, it might strangle his voice box and was glad his own rang out so clearly.

"And do you, Katherine Anne Beagle, take Jeremy Michael Phipps to be your lawful wedded husband? To have and to hold from this day forward until death do you part?"

It seemed to Lionel that every member of the parish held their breath before Katy's voice sang out, bright and true, "I do."

Lionel rested his eyes on the bride again. She looked genuinely beautiful in her smart dress and hat. He smiled encouragement at her, and she smiled back.

A beam of sunlight illuminated the young couple kneeling at the altar. Their two heads, both dark and newly washed, touched lightly together as they received their blessing. Lionel heard an audible sigh from his congregation as Katy Beagle finally gave Jem Phipps the commitment he'd longed for and they'd all said he deserved.

Even more audible whisperings reached his ears in the short pause that followed.

Martha Threadwell turned to the pew behind and said to Mrs Chubbs, the local farmer's wife, "And about time too. She's lucky to get that lad, if you ask me. All them airs and graces from working up at the manor. I reckon she thought she'd be the next Lady Smythe if she could have got away with it."

"Oh now, Mrs Threadwell, don't be uncharitable. Katy's a good girl underneath and don't she make a pretty bride," Mrs Chubbs said, as good humoured as ever.

"Hmm. Book-learning is all very well, but Jem will put bacon on the table and that's worth a deal of reading about things that don't concern you. And trying to be something you're not and never can be." The imitation cherries in Mrs Threadwell's large hat trembled as she spoke.

Mrs Chubbs said, "They'll make a good pair, Martha, you see if they don't."

Lionel watched the bride and groom sign the register. Jem flushed to the roots of his glossy chestnut hair with the unfamiliar task, but Katy wrote with greater confidence and applied her signature with a little, forgivable, flourish.

The bride and groom sat back in the front pew, holding hands, as if to fortify themselves through his sermon. He was gratified that it was so quiet you could hear a pin drop when he lifted the chalice high and the light from the oriel window caught the gold cup. His flock looked rapt as they gazed upon his fervently closed eyes and moving lips when he opened them again to look round. Of course, some feathers were bound to be ruffled. When Lionel's faith took him to previously unknown heights of passion, definite snorts could be heard amongst some of the bass voices in the gathering.

They all trooped out into the warmth of the late summer afternoon, blinking a little after the filtered light of the little village church. Sir Robert and Lady Smythe, as employers of most of the congregation, led the way to the George and Dragon at a frustratingly ponderous pace and, their new curate strolled at their side. Lionel cast a look back at the villagers, who followed with alacrity, no doubt encouraged by the prospect of the wedding breakfast paid for by their squire.

Inside the pub, Sir Robert raised his glass and said, "I give you Mr and Mrs Jeremy Phipps. Good health and happiness to you both in your new life together. Peace and prosperity to us all; especially peace."

"Hear, hear," Lionel, better informed than most about stirrings abroad, knew that Charles had now reached the British Expeditionary Force in France.

Somewhat belatedly, after meaningful looks from his spouse, Sir Robert added, "And I would also like to welcome Reverend White, who has come to live amongst us after the death of Reverend Entwhistle, God rest his soul."

Another toast to past and present churchmen was solemnly drunk.

Lionel stood up to address the wedding breakfast but was cut short by the father of the bride, Bert Beagle, seizing the moment, and saying hurriedly, "Ay, Reverend White!"

Bert drained his glass and, without drawing breath, said, "And now to my Katy. The most beautiful bride in Wiltshire! Here's to you, me darling."

Pride, tinged with considerable relief, had obviously made Bert very expansive, especially after two quick beers.

Thwarted, Lionel could only sit back down and watch Lady Smythe take her turn. She stood up and bestowed her most indulgent smile on her dependants. She didn't seem to be able to bring herself to extend the benefit of the gesture to the bride, he noticed.

He knew Katy had not seen Lady Smythe since her dismissal, but Lionel had heard from his housekeeper that Katy's old employer thought it impolitic not to attend the wedding. Mrs Hoskins had also reported that Lady Smythe wanted to witness the deed and "be done with the insolent girl". As if reading his thoughts, Lady Smythe smiled and nodded at Lionel.

Then she turned and muttered audibly in her husband's ear, "Now Charles is safe from the impudent chit, I think we may safely depart."

Sir Robert took the hint and, beaming goodwill on them all, led his wife away to their waiting carriage.

Lionel, believing that discretion was the better part of valour, followed.

CHAPTER EIGHT

Transparently relieved, the wedding party waved their betters off and settled down to attack the feast Sir Robert had provided. Free of all constraints, the mood descended into benign drunkenness and more toasts were made to Katy and Jem.

A few brought blushes to her cheeks, though Jem laughed heartily at the bawdy humour.

"'Tis only teasing, Katy my love," he said, squeezing her waist with relish.

"Well, I thought Sir Robert's toast far more elegant." The beer had loosened her tongue, perhaps too much.

"Drink up, Katy." Her Dad didn't seem to mind.

"Aye, top ups all round I reckon." George, her new father-in-law joined in, obviously eager not to be outdone by his perennial rival. "How's it going up at your windy ridge, then Bert?"

Her father replied, "Damn sight better than down here in this frost pocket."

Mary and Agnes smiled across at each other. Katy suspected that each potential grandmother was secretly wondering who the grandchildren would resemble. Suddenly the room felt too small. Claustrophobia threatened in the stuffy, smoke-filled air.

Katy gazed around at her wedding feast. Red-cheeked and flushed faces grinned back at her. Mugs of ale slopped onto the sawdust floor. A great haunch of ham was disappearing fast. Dear, familiar faces swam before her eyes but she had to admit that all were coarse and ruddy from their long days out in all weathers. It wasn't the same as those tasteful country weekends she'd witnessed working up at the manor, not by a long shot. She shivered, despite the roaring fire. Jem, sensing her mood, put his arm around her and kissed her soundly on the mouth. She smiled back at him and he beamed back looking utterly, blissfully happy.

At least Jem was content even if she wasn't. Katy swallowed hard; she felt trapped and breathless but there was no way out now. No, she'd just have to make the best of it. If she must be a village housewife – she'd be the best there was. That she'd had no other option was a thought she would just have to squash down every time it surfaced.

She made a private vow to love him back the best she could, and at last, she smiled at her new husband.

Once the whole village's repertoire had been sung from the rooftops and the only thing left of the ham was the bone, the young couple were escorted to their new home. The crocodile of weaving and singing villagers bounced them along the hundred yards to their love nest and, with plenty of ribald jokes, bundled them in through their new front door.

Their new next-door neighbours, Sally and Tom Fenwick, tried to muscle indoors with them. "Here, we'll come in and show you the ropes", Sally said, eyes agog to see inside.

"I don't think so, Mrs Fenwick, thanks all the same." Jem shut the door firmly. Old Tom rescuing Sally from spinsterhood had been seen as a kindness by the village but it was also acknowledged that Sally's housekeeping left much to be desired. Katy had been shocked at her neighbour's slovenly ways when she'd been scrubbing out her new home before the wedding and Sally had invited her in for a neighbourly chat. She was glad Jem didn't encourage them pushing in where they weren't wanted now.

Once inside their little cottage, the newly married couple fell suddenly silent. The quiet parlour stood waiting for them, its range still cold and the scullery off it not yet muddled with food. Mary and Agnes, as part of their truce, had put fresh flowers everywhere and made up the bed in the main bedroom upstairs, where they had also lit a fire. Jem swept Katy up into his muscular arms and carried her, tottering only twice, up the narrow winding staircase and laid her down on the bed as lightly as a feather. A slight burp marred the performance, but Katy was a bit tipsy too and let it pass.

Slowly, with trembling hands, Jem explored the intricacies of Katy's wedding dress buttons. Laughing softly, she helped him undo the puzzle. She slipped out of her new dark blue dress and stood in her underwear. Jem, ignited by a passion that transcended the beer, managed undoing her stays pretty well.

"How do you wear such stuff? I'm sure I couldn't breathe with that lot on!" Now he had to negotiate the delicate chemise and pantaloons. "God, this is complicated," he said, with some urgency.

"Here, let me help you, Jem." Now they were finally alone, now there was no going back, Katy couldn't wait to be naked before him; to expose her whole body and give him back some of the love she saw in his warm, brown eyes; to fulfil the vows she had made before the whole village. She felt no shame. No, instead she wanted to be generous, now she had committed to this marriage, not missish and mean. She'd made up her mind to it and she'd be a wife with her whole heart or not at all.

Katy unpinned her hair, letting it tumble down her bare back in a long, dark wave. Jem took up a tress of its silky length and kissed it. Katy laughed, as Jem tore off his clothes and his shirt and trousers flew off into the corners of the small bedroom. He picked her up again then, making her feel weightless, before he gently placed her back on the bed and lay down beside her.

As he stroked her slender body and full, firm breasts, he looked in awe of the licence she now gave him.

"Oh, Katy, I've loved you for so long! Even when we were little'uns in the playground and we fought and argued, I still loved you really. I can't believe I'm lying here right now, naked and alone with you, Kate. And that I'm allowed to touch you all over."

"Of course, you are, Jem, dear. Touch me anywhere you like, I love the feel of your hands."

Flickers of desire welled up through her body and when Jem hesitated for fear of hurting her, Katy pulled him impatiently down and wrapped herself around his taut, lean frame. She gasped with a transient pain and a deeper pleasure as he plunged into her with a joy so intense the sensation overwhelmed him all too soon. Wasn't it supposed to last longer? Puzzled and feeling short changed, aware of her ignorance, Katy looked at Jem quizzically.

He laughed and said "Don't worry, I shan't be long in coming back for more, my lovely wife. Mrs. Phipps, as you are! Who'd have thought it?"

Katy could barely believe the ecstasy Jem's strong body gave her when he kept his promise. He'd shaved his face for the wedding but kissed her so often her cheeks were rasped raw by his. She barely noticed the soreness, as nerve-endings in other, deeper parts of her body sprang into life in a way she could never have imagined. Jem's arms were as hard as wood and yet he held her with infinite tenderness. Hungry for more, she held him close, tasting his sweat and licking his young skin with wanton pleasure.

Finally, around the early pink dawn, Katy lay against Jem's naked body, coverless and exhausted, wrapped around him in happy abandon. Marriage had more compensations than she'd ever expected and might not be so bad after all.

She fell deeply asleep within Jem's embrace, sated and for once, completely at peace.

CHAPTER NINE

Young Mr and Mrs Phipps enjoyed their private holiday. Jem was particularly grateful no-one disturbed the love nest. So, it wasn't until the Tuesday morning after he'd returned to work at the manor gardens Jem learned the latest developments about the wider world. Albert, Katy's younger brother, bounced up to him, full of importance at being the first to break the news.

"Russia and Japan's joined the war! Not today, of course. It was about week before our Katy's wedding." He told the crowd of workers who had gathered in the stable yard.

"Don't be daft young Albert! Where do you hear that from?" Jem said.

"Sir Robert himself," Albert's nod was emphatic.

"What?"

"It can't be true?"

"I don't believe it!"

"The whole world is at it!" The other young men gathered round.

"Tis so. That new Reverend come up to the manor this morning and told the squire, personal-like." Albert was obviously enjoying the moment.

"Well I never!" Adam Fairweather said.

Albert crowed, "And I'm enlisting straight off, I am."

"What do you want to do that for, Albert?" asked Jem.

"See a bit of the world, won't I? Got to be better than stuck here forever the rest of me life."

Jem wasn't the only one to shake his head at Albert's youthful folly, though some of the younger ones' eyes lit up.

Albert's father, Bert senior, strolled up, wiping his muddy hands on a rag. "What's the commotion, lads?"

No-one wanted to tell him that Albert was all for war. To a man they stood back.

Albert told his father with glee, "Dad - the whole world's joining the war and so'm I. I'm going off to be a soldier."

"What are you talking about Albert Beagle?" His father looked weary all-of-a-sudden.

"Me too," piped up Adam Fairweather. He worked in the Estate Manager's office. "Mr Hayes had a telephone call from the steward on the Ponsonby Estate at Winterton. The whole county's abuzz with the latest retreat. We can't let them Germans march all over the place as if they owned it."

Mr Beagle went very pale – as pale as his son was flushed. "Come on, Albert, let's get you home to your mother and see what all this is about. We'll go and see Sir Robert on our way and find out the truth of the matter."

"It is true, Dad! Why don't you believe me?" Albert's voice trailed off as his father marched him swiftly towards the manor house.

Jem walked home that first working day of his married life with thoughts of war jarring against his new contentment. He resented every damn German who had disrupted his happy prospects. Still, maybe it wouldn't affect them much even if hotheads like Albert and Charles drove them all mad in their eagerness to join the fight. Good riddance to Charles Smythe. Perhaps the army might knock a conscience into him, but he doubted it.

He came round the last bend of the hill. Lower Cheadle nestled in the valley before him with his very own home snuggled in the middle. How good it felt to open his front door and find his wife standing there with open arms, supper simmering on the stove, its savoury aroma wafting out to greet him. A cloud of meadowsweet flowers graced the parlour table, their vanilla fragrance scenting the whole room. Katy had obviously worked as hard as he that day. He kissed her soundly and admired the flowers before breaking the spell with talk of war. He could see that Katy was put out that she had to hear the news from him second-hand. Before she'd lost her position, she would have been the first to hear anything important up at the manor

"Well, it don't make sense to me at all, Jem. Why are we at war with the Germans?" Katy carried the casserole to their table in the parlour.

"As I understand it," Jem said, washing his hands in the lean-to scullery, "it all started when some royal bloke got shot in, where was it? Some odd name, do you remember? Back in June it was. Mr Hayes explained it to me this afternoon. He says all the countries around there got all upset about it and started rattling sabres at each other."

"Yes, I remember that bit from when I was still working up at the manor. But what's that to us?"

"No-one thought it would be anything to us, Katy my love." Jem snatched a quick kiss as he walked through to join her in the parlour. "But, as far as I can make out, Russia got involved back in July when Germany declared war on it. Germany has already invaded Luxembourg and marched through Belgium. They gave up without a fight there."

"Shame on them. Does it smell alright?"

This was the first workaday supper she had served for her husband. Jem could see the news was taking the shine off the occasion.

"Lovely stew, Katy love," he said, through his first mouthful.

She beamed at him. "I've had it cooking this long while so it should be nice and tender."

"Hmm, really tasty." Jem ate silently, determined to show her how much he appreciated coming home to a good hot meal.

He knew he could rely on Katy's lively and curious mind, so he waited and smiled when she asked, "So why is Britain involved because some stupid Germans invaded, where was it? Oh, yes, Luxembourg and Belgium?"

"Well, we have an agreement to protect Belgium, so we have to declare war on any country that decides to march in and take over."

"Oh, I see." Katy looked doubtful, as if she didn't see, not really. "And our Albert's all for going off to fight, is he? We'll see what Mum says about that."

Jem laughed, "Ay, he won't get far with Agnes Beagle."

"Hmm, he's been proper wild lately though. She might have met her match on this one."

"I doubt it, Katy, I wouldn't argue with her."

Katy laughed, "You could be right Jem," and then declared with pride, "I made a pudding too."

"Ooh, lovely. What is it Kate?"

"Jam roly-poly with Mum's raspberry jam."

"My favourite – any custard?"

" I did try to make custard but it don't seem to have set right."

Jem declared the runny, lumpy liquid delicious but didn't tell her that sugar might have helped the flavour.

"Charles Smythe has got to the battlefield now." He thought it only fair to tell her and studied her face as he did so. There was still a little worm of jealousy in that department.

"Has he?" Katy looked fully aware of Jem's interested gaze. "And good riddance to him!"

***

As Katy went about her chores the next day, she had time to reflect on her newly married state. She'd always known she would marry Jem in the long run, and it seemed that her little skirmish with Charles Smythe would remain the only chance she was going to get in this lifetime to change her destiny. Her options might have closed around her, but she had decided, and Agnes had encouraged this, to look upon her home, not as a cage but as a different sort of an adventure.

"Don't you think I didn't want adventure when I was your age, Katy?" Agnes had said on the eve of the wedding.

"Did you?" Katy had never thought of her mother that way, as a young woman with no children clutching at her skirts.

"Oh yes, Katy, I wanted to travel too – just like you. Remember, I wasn't born here in Upper Cheadle. I came here because I went into service with the Smythes. Why, I was only sixteen when I took the coach and horses to the manor house. That was an adventure alright! I didn't know a soul on the road. Then your father met me for the last stage and that was it for me. He drove me here, see and I sat up on the box with him." Agnes smiled. "We chatted all the way. Two years later we was married and I never looked back. You'll see, it'll be the same with you and Jem, once you're living as man and wife. All that restlessness will just disappear."

Katy often recalled that conversation as she settled into her first week as Jem's wife. There was so much to do to get the place how she wanted it and, after Agnes had boxed Albert's ears (though she had to stand on tiptoe to do it) and put paid to his soldiering ideas, the war took second place to setting up their new home.

Katy and Jem's tied cottage lay in the middle of a row of six identical ones, set deep in the valley with the lane in front and the gardens rising sharply behind. The strips of garden ended in some woods that belonged, like everything else, to Sir Robert's estate. Although narrow the garden was long and no fence separated it from the trees behind the cabbages. The other five tenants in the row all grew vegetables with varying degrees of success and energy, making the whole plot look like allotments, some weedy, some neat.

Jem had great plans for theirs. On his wages home-grown supplements to their larder would certainly be welcome.

Agnes gave her eldest daughter half a dozen hens for her wedding present and Jem knocked up a chicken ark at the top of the garden, near the woods. On their first married Saturday, after his morning's work up at the manor, the chickens were installed amidst much cackling and fluffing of feathers and both their fathers came to supervise.

"You'll 'ave to watch for foxes like a hawk, Katy my girl," said her father flushed and puffing with the effort of toiling up the slope, a chicken under each arm. "That there copse'll hide a few, I reckon. You gotta get 'em in at night, every night, mind – no slacking - or they'll be nothing but feathers come morning"."

"I'll do it right, Dad", she replied, shiny-eyed.

"Well, you won't always feel like it when it's cold and raining but you mustn't forget."

"Alright, Dad, I promise I'll be careful."

"You're a good girl and them eggs'll come in handy, especially when you've little'uns to feed," Bert said, winking at Jem. Katy blushed and ran her hand through the golden kernels of corn feed. The corn slipped between her fingers like dry water. She threw a handful down for her birds who instantly forgot their outraged indignation and fell on the corn, shaking the nuggets down into their crops in the most comical way.

"They'll settle now," George said. "Now then, Bert, what about that pig we was discussing."

Katy's Dad grinned back at George. "Ah, yes, I were waiting for the right moment, see."

"Oh was you, hmm. Now then, you young'uns – me and Bert here, we thought to give you a share of our latest litter of pigs and Bert have given me one half of what a piglet's worth in hens from your Ma, see."

Jem said, "Ta, Dad, but we ain't got room here for a pig as well. Mind you, if Sir Robert would let us have a bit of that woodland here - that would suit nicely."

"No chance of that, young Jem," Bert said. "He'll never let a pig wander there 'cos his precious walled garden is t'other side."

"Ay, and it would be more'n my job's worth to have the veg ruined." Jem's father looked genuinely alarmed at the prospect.

"But if we fenced it?"

"Lord love you boy, how you going to pay for that much fence?"

"I could use some wood if I cut down a couple of those trees."

"Well, that's as may be, young Jem." George looked discomforted at so much youthful enterprise and free thinking. "But it wouldn't do. Everyone'd want to do the same and there'd be a bloody piggery up 'ere, stinking the place out. Sir Robert wouldn't like that, I can tell you."

" No, what we propose, lad, is for your father to keep the pig on in his cottage garden at East Lodge. He can raise it to butchering for you there. That way you won't have the bother of it – just the bacon." Bert laughed at his own joke.

"You can give me a hand at killing time, Jem, and we'll cure it and you should have it at Christmas. How do you fancy a nice flitch of ham hanging in the chimney, eh Katy?" asked George, beaming at his own benevolence.

Katy said, "I think that's a very good offer, Jem, especially as I'm not sure I want to look after a pig as well as hens just yet."

Katy was secretly horrified at the prospect of a smelly old pig at the end of her garden. Hens were attractive and relatively clean. Her garden was going to have roses and lavender. What if the pig got out and trampled the lot? No, this was a much better idea. To seal the deal, she kissed both fathers on their roughened cheeks and shyly asked them back for tea and a slice of the pound cake she had made. Her first visitors!

"Thank you, Katy, thank you kindly but a sup of ale would be more to my liking, I'm thinking. What d'you say to the pub, lads?" Bert said.

"Now you're talking, Bert," replied George, looking relieved.

Katy walked back to her cottage, annoyed the men had sloped off to the pub at the end of the terrace without her.

She made a pot of tea and cut into the pound cake with an unnecessarily sharp incision. She'd flavoured it with candied peel from a recipe she'd found in the cookbook her mother had given her on her wedding day. Now no-one would know if it improved it or not. She plonked down on the cottage chair next to the fire in the range, resolving to make a patchwork cushion for it before too long.

She surveyed her little parlour. In the corner, under the deep-set window, stood the table and chairs. A green chenille cloth gave colour to the scene and she had placed a vase of hedgerow flowers in the centre. Two larger wooden chairs hugged either side of the range and her pride and joy, a dresser displaying her treasured china - a wedding gift from Miss Cassandra - adorned the wall opposite. Handy Jem had made it from some oak going spare at his parents and she was very pleased with the result but, even so, Katy couldn't quite forgive him truanting off to the pub on their first Saturday as man and wife.

Katy poured herself a second cup of tea into her fine bone china cup. She sipped it delicately, unconsciously copying Lady Smythe by extending her little finger as she held it by the dainty handle.

She almost dropped her cup when there was a knock on the front door. She had visitors after all! She patted her hair and smoothed her dress before opening the door.

"Reverend White. How nice to see you. Please come in." Katy smiled her welcome.

"Thank you, Mrs Phipps." Lionel White took off his hat and crossed the threshold.

Katy's heart swelled at being addressed as Mrs Phipps. She hadn't got used to the title yet.

"Would you like a cup of tea, Reverend? I've just made a pot."

"Well, if it's already made, thank you." The vicar sat himself down by the fire and stretched out his long, booted legs to the blaze. He ran his hands through his blonde hair, smoothing it down in long, careful sweeps.

"I've made a pound cake as well, if you'd like some?" Katy felt proud to show off her baking efforts to somebody, anybody.

"That looks quite splendid, Mrs Phipps. I'd love a piece."

Katy cut the cake and carefully laid it on one of her blue and white china plates.

"Such pretty china. You've set your home up very well, considering you've only been married a week." The Reverend bit into the yellow sponge with enthusiasm.

"Thank you, sir. There's more to do, of course. I'm going to make some cushions for these chairs next. I hope you are not too uncomfortable?" Katy was anxious that her very first guest should feel at ease.

"I'm very comfortable, Mrs Phipps. This citrus flavour in your cake is an unusual touch. Very tasty. Excellent tea too." The Reverend was looking as relaxed as she could have wished.

The range gave a sudden belch of smoke, filling the room with a black cloud and making them both cough. There were times when Katy despaired of keeping the beast alight. She'd always been good at mending mechanical things and was determined it wouldn't get the better of her. She opened the draught and riddled the fire until it burnt cleanly again.

"I must say, Mrs Phipps, you're a dab hand with that range." The vicar was obviously impressed.

"I'm the only one that can make it draw." A bustle at the back of the house interrupted her moment of triumph as Jem came in from the pub.

Jem's face fell when he saw the vicar sitting in his chair, but he extended his hand courteously.

"Congratulations on your cosy home, Mr Phipps." Lionel stood up to return the handshake. "It looks as though you and Mrs Phipps have always lived here."

"Thank you, vicar. I see Katy's made you welcome," and Jem nodded at the cut cake and empty cup and saucer.

"Indeed, she has but I must be off on my rounds. Always plenty to do in the parish, you know! Plenty to do."

Katy felt cross that her tea party had been interrupted and felt Jem should persuade the vicar to have more tea but instead he showed him the door.

He turned back after shutting it. "I wouldn't mind a piece of your cake myself Katy, love."

"Here you are then, better late than never, I suppose."

The stove belched smoke again and Jem loaded some logs on.

"Not like that Jem! Here, let me," Katy elbowed him out of the way and took over.

Jem mumbled something and went back out into the garden. Once she had got the range settled Katy looked out of the scullery window. Jem was digging away at the new vegetable patch like a steam train.

Married life took some getting used to.

Gradually they settled into a routine. Jem took charge of the garden while Katy remained queen of the house. She came to love the old iron range; it breathed life and warmth into the centre of her little world. She continued to be the only one who could make it work and soon had the running of it off to a tee. It obviously annoyed Jem that he couldn't get the hang of it himself. If he loaded the logs on smoke would again billow out where it wasn't wanted.

Katy polished the stove till it shone and took pride in keeping the big range chugging away day in, day out.

However, she couldn't think of a solution to their water supply which was quite a different matter to keeping the fire alight. Sir Robert might be an indulgent squire, but he was no innovator and couldn't see the point in investing in new-fangled technology when old ways had served well enough in the past. So, although their cottage, like the others in their row, boasted ironwork ranges in every chimney they had no running water. They had a rain barrel by the back door, but all the other water had to fetched and carried back in pails from the village pump across the green. It had always been that way and looked likely to remain so, whilst Sir Robert was in charge. Any mutterings about it from the villagers fell on deaf ears up at the manor.

It was the worst chore of Katy's day especially on wash days. Still, at least she had a short distance to carry the heavy buckets - some had to go much further. One bucket served the range, the other filled the pitcher in the lean-to scullery at the back of the house and the rest filled the jug for washing upstairs in the bedroom. Slops from the china washbasin were simply slung out of the window or tipped onto the garden. No water was ever wasted or used only once. Washing up water served well enough a second time to scrub the floor before being thrown away. Katy learned very quickly how to economise on the use of this essential commodity once she had lugged it over the road once or twice.

CHAPTER TEN

September drew to its close and took the last of the summer heat with it, but the weather remained mild. A new Defence of the Realm Act enabled the railways to be taken under state control but as it was five miles to the nearest one the village barely registered the change. The war in France still felt very distant and there was more notice taken of the new tarmac road being laid in Woodbury for the new automobiles that made such a racket, like the one Dr Benson now drove on his rounds. Every time he parked his gleaming car outside one of the cottages, children would gather round and stroke its chrome curves, until Dr Benson would emerge and wave his doctor's bag to disperse them.

As Agnes told a very sulky Albert, "They still say this war will be over by Christmas so what's the point of you signing up? You'd be back before you got there." Her view was shared by most people in the two villages and the rhythm of the harvest beat on unchecked.

One evening Jem walked in through the back door laden with bruised apples and squashed raspberries from the manor garden. They often benefited from Mrs Biggs' rejections. It was so warm and balmy, they sat outside in their burgeoning backyard to eat them. Katy and Jem strolled up the garden into the woods behind after supper, past the little river and on up to the hill behind.

"I love coming up here, Jem." Katy stood on the very pinnacle of the hill and reached out to him.

He enfolded her in his arms while she talked.

"Sometimes I think I shall suffocate in that valley. I know you've always lived down in the dip so it feels like home to you, but I can hardly see the sky from our house, just the gardens opposite. That Mrs Hoskins is always looking over to see what I'm up to, the old bat. Just because she's the new Reverend's housekeeper she thinks she owns the whole village."

"Well, it don't bother me as much, Kate, but I do love to come up here and see the sun set, especially with you."

They settled down on the warm grass, he with his head in her lap, as they gazed at the sun sinking low in the west. Only when it was truly dark did they walk slowly back, hand in hand, stealing kisses in the secrecy of the velvet night.

Once back in the private haven of their home they revelled in the refuge of their double bed and made love with such tenderness that Katy cried out with joy. The war and all its many cares receded; for Katy and Jem only their private, tiny world existed.

Other villagers were made more aware of the general state of things when Mrs Threadwell displayed a poster in Lower Cheadle's post office calling men to fight at the front. Albert was incensed when he saw Lord Kitchener, now Secretary of State for War, wanted 100,000 men to volunteer and his mother still kept him to his promise of waiting until the new year. He took up smoking as his only means of rebellion, smartly stubbing out the cigarette if his mother came into view.

Jem privately sympathised with his new brother-in-law. There was plenty of talk amongst his fellow gardeners about the war. He was as fascinated as any of them to learn how trenches were being dug in northern France as troops fought to reach the sea borders but only managed to fight over the thin line of country between them.

Then everything foreign was forgotten as some very personal news took precedent. Nature will have her way, no matter what plans may have been laid by mice or even men and, by the time the last autumn leaves were flurrying down from the copse on to their chicken run, Katy shyly told Jem he was to become a father.

Jem felt a mixture of emotions that this had happened so soon into their marriage. His precious darling wife would swell and suffer pain and he would have to witness it, knowing he was the cause of her discomfort. And yet he would have a child born of this wonderful woman for whom he had waited so long. He held her in his arms as gingerly as if she was made of her precious wedding china. Katy laughed and hugged him as hard as ever.

"Aren't you pleased, Jem?"

"Ay, I'm pleased right enough but I shall worry about you too. Are you feeling alright at the moment?"

"Jem, my love, I've never felt better in my life. Now I can carry a bit of you around with me wherever I go whether you are with me or not. This little one," Katy patted her still smooth stomach, "he's made from me and you, from our love, and that love will give me strength for anything that comes."

"Oh, Katy, how I do love you." Jem's throat choked with the words he couldn't say.

"Dear Jem, come here." To his delight, Katy took him by the hand and led him up to their bedroom.

"See Jem, you can still make love to me. I won't shatter into a thousand pieces you know."

He still hesitated but she teased him so delightfully he could not resist. He looked into her eyes, the pupils dilated with pleasure, and kissed her. He knew every curve of her body and loved their easy familiarity and the way Katy had learned how to please him.

Afterwards Jem lay in her arms like a baby himself. Content to be quiet, one hand on her flat belly, disbelieving the taut skin could hide a new life and one he had helped to create. When he married Katy, he had never dreamt he could be more in love than he was then. Now he was like a man drunk on nectar.

He inhaled her sweet smell and fell asleep in the crook of her arm; deeply, profoundly complete.

CHAPTER ELEVEN

The news of Katy's pregnancy swept swiftly around the village grapevine. Mrs Hoskins, shopping at the post office and general stores, nodded at Katy's house across the street and said, "Well, I hope this will settle her down now and keep her busy."

Mrs Threadwell, busily counting out stamps, replied, "Can't say she hasn't made our Jem happy, though, Margaret."

"And doesn't he deserve it? Fine, upstanding and honest as the day as he is," Mrs Hoskins said, who had been born in Lower Cheadle and always maintained she'd never felt the need to go anywhere else.

"Yes, Jem does Lower Cheadle credit, I'll say that for him. He'll make a good father, I'm sure of it." Mrs Threadwell carefully laid the stamps into her desk drawer and shut it with a crisp click of the lock.

"And we'll see how Miss Hoity Toity takes to mothering in the meantime." Margaret Hoskins swept up her change and snapped her purse shut.

***

Margaret Hoskins went back to the rectory and told her employer the news.

"I don't agree with listening to tittle-tattle, Mrs Hoskins," Lionel White said and added, against his better judgement, "I think it would be a great pity if Mrs Phipps' lost her good looks with motherhood. I was struck by her pretty ways when she was a bride. If you ask me, she is wasted on Jeremy Phipps however good a gardener he might be. Katherine showed great potential at her wedding; a rushed affair as I recall. Now I suppose she'll fade like a summer rose, as is the way of these things."

Mrs Hoskins's eyes narrowed, and Lionel wished he'd bitten his tongue.

***

Only to her mother did Katy confess her fears about the birth and how on earth they would manage to feed another mouth.

"You'll do, Katy love," Agnes assured her. "And you know why? 'Cos you'll have to! We all gets by as best we can and are better off than most as far as I can see. I heard tell that them folks what's gone off to work in the cities are having a real hard time of it. Long hours in factories, living in miserable conditions, one house on top of the other and I don't know what else and for not much better pay than what Jem or your father gets in the gardens. At least we can have a rabbit for the pot off the land and we've got our hens and I daresay Mary and George can set aside another piglet for you when Betsy farrows again."

Katy nodded, "Yes, I have heard about the new factory jobs, Mum. I wouldn't like to be there, but more money would be handy. I've heard there are some women doing those jobs now and I do miss earning a wage. We shall have to make sure we get more planted in the vegetable patch this year. I love a new potato, fresh out of the ground with lots of mint."

"Yes, you done well to plant them herbs right close to the kitchen like that. They makes a lot of difference to how tasty a meal is, I reckon. I'm always asking your father to bring some from the manor gardens, but he always forgets. Got more time for his horses than us sometimes! Yes, I wouldn't mind a few cuttings or roots off of that, when you got time, like."

"Of course, Mum, I should have thought of it before. I'll do it this week and bring them up to you. A soft wet day would be best, so the cuttings don't dry out. March or April would be the best time, but we can try now and if they don't take, I'll do it again come spring."

55

"That's if you'll have time then, what with the baby due in July. You'll be busy then my girl and no mistake," and Agnes chuckled, as all established mothers do when talking to young mothers-to-be, obviously relishing her hindsight and experience. Katy found it just as annoying as any other woman carrying her first child.

"Yes, that's as may be, but I must be off to get Jem's supper on or the range will be gone out," she said briskly, and she picked up her skirts ready for the mile-long walk down the hill to the increasingly detested valley.

The contrast to her house became more and more apparent to Katy as the days shortened towards winter. The cooler nights had shown up how much condensation lurked in the valley depths. Her first task every day was to wipe the windows free of water every morning. She was convinced it was unhealthy to have so much moisture in the house. Her parents' house was set south west where the afternoon sun streamed in, unfettered by banks of brown earth. It occupied a windy spot, but Katy had never minded that; in fact, she had always found the stiff breezes and storms exhilarating.

As a child she had loved to sit and watch the sunset from the parlour window of the lodge house as it slipped slowly down over the Wiltshire downs away to the west, staining the sky with streams of gold, red and ochre. And she'd loved to watch wilder weather come racing in towards their stout little house and calculate how long it would take before the rain spattered across the latticed window.

You always knew when to get the washing in from that garden, she thought ruefully, as she picked up her pace back to her own new home, with a wary eye on some looming clouds billowing towards her on a brisk, gathering wind. She'd taken a chance and left the sheets out on the line and she'd be lucky to win the race back to rescue them before the clouds overtook her.

As she hastened her step, a wave of the now familiar nausea threatened to overwhelm her. That tea had been a mistake. Once her favourite beverage, it now turned her stomach. Swallowing hard she kept up her speed and got home just as the first drops painted her white cotton sheets with wet streaks, as they blew almost horizontally in the normally sheltered garden. Swiftly, she gathered in the fragrant linen and clutched it to her. She dumped the damp bundle on the table in the nick of time before heaving the curdled tea into the slop basin. Exhausted, she fumbled her way to her favourite fireside chair, only to realise that the fire had indeed gone out. Married life was beginning to lose its novelty.

Jem fussed and worried over her when he came in after dusk, looking tired and muddy. Having no warm food to greet him, Katy's stricken conscience only made her tetchier, as she watched him rekindle the fire.

"It'll have to be cold ham and eggs for tea and lump it," she said grumpily.

"Ham and eggs is my favourite anyway, love."

When she was queasy like this, Jem's constant optimism just grated on Katy.

"Just as well then." She stomped off to the scullery for the eggs. While she was slamming the frying pan on the stove another wave of nausea made her grimace and Jem caught her round the waist. "Don't squeeze me, Jem!" she said, hand over mouth, as she retched again.

"Can't you take nothing for it, Katy dear?"

"Too late for that." She threw herself into his open arms, crumbling into the comfort of his embrace.

"There, there, my love, don't cry."

"I'm sorry Jem. I don't mean to be so cranky. It's just this feeling sick all the time. It's so wearing. I thought this would be such a happy time, but I just want to dig a big hole, climb in and be left alone to be miserable."

Jem ventured a chuckle and got away with it. Holding her gently, he drew her to her chair and set her down.

Holding her face in his roughened, tender hands, he said, "It won't last much longer. My mum says, once you get to four months or so, you'll start to feel on top of the world, and you'll be hungry enough for two. I'll cook the tea so's you won't have to smell the eggs. You get the bread and set the table. We'll both feel better after a bite to eat."

Katy nodded, too miserable to talk. Four months! That seemed like a prison stretch from here. Dully, she set the table and managed some food. After eating, her stomach did settle a little and she smiled at Jem again, reaching for his hand and giving it a squeeze. Jem went pink with pleasure.

One day, as Katy re-read Jane Eyre for the third time, glad of the distraction and lost in that other world, Sally Fenwick popped her head around the back door and marched into the scullery before Katy could stop her. Living in a terraced house was trying at times, especially when you wanted a bit of peace. She laid her book down, carefully marking her place with the bookmark she'd plaited from old rags and summoned up a smile for her neighbour. As ever, Sally's eyes roamed around the room, spying out new things.

"Hello, Sally."

"Hello, young Katy. Just wondered how you was faring, like," Sally said, studying Katy's china.

"Still feeling a bit sick, actually, Sally. I find reading takes my mind off it," Katy said, pointedly holding up her book. Sally, as usual, didn't pick up the hint.

"Can't see the point of reading about other people." Sally fingered a teacup on the dresser. "Got any tea on the go? Thought you might like a bit of company, see, or need some water fetched?"

As this was the second time this week Sally had offered to do this, Katy felt irritated. "I told you on Wednesday, Sally, I can't drink tea at the moment. It turns my stomach so."

"You don't need nothing then? Anything from the shop? If you gives me the money, I'll fetch the shopping for you." Sally hopped from one arthritic foot to the other, her eyes just as busy as her feet.

"No thanks, Sally. I've got all I need in the larder."

Last time Sally had offered her shopping services, Katy had felt so nauseous, she'd given her some loose change just to get rid of her and asked her to get a half a pound of butter and some sausages. She'd given Sally plenty of cash for the purchases but had been horrified at how little change came back with the goods. She wasn't going to chance that again, and eventually Sally shuffled back to her own house next door, wearing a long face.

It didn't help that Sally wasn't too keen on personal hygiene. The tang of her old unwashed body always took at least half an hour to follow her out of the door. Katy retched, and got up, holding her hand over her mouth and flinging the windows wide open. She clutched the windowsill, narrowly avoiding being sick by gulping down the fresh air that flooded in.

Gradually the weeks passed, and Katy began to feel better sooner than she expected. By the time Christmas came she could join in with the muted festivities of a country at war with a willing heart and a swelling belly.

While the winter months proved to be a time of contentment for Katy, Agnes lost the battle with Albert. The warmth from Katy's baby guarded her against the cold biting winds and frost but the new year broke the pact between her mother and brother.

Katy was helping her mother to sort some baby clothes from the linen chest at her parents' lodge house one Saturday morning when Albert bounced into the house crowing in triumph. "Well, Mum, it's January and you said the war would be over by Christmas."

Agnes' lips pursed tighter. "Maybe I did."

"You know you did, Mum. Christmas has come and gone, and more and more men are signing up for it. You can't stop me being one of them now." Albert stood, hands on hips, his dark hair and eyes a contrast to the winter sun streaming through the window behind him.

Katy watched her mother school her face into a calm veneer. Agnes smoothed down her apron and stood up, one hand on her back to ease the effort.

She turned to face her eldest son. "Yes, Albert, I made a promise to you and I must keep it. I can't stop you going to war now. If you've still a mind to, you can sign up with my blessing, but I must tell you, son, my heart is heavy."

Albert crushed his mother to him in a bear hug.

"I'll be alright, Ma, you'll see. It can't last much longer, and I'll be a well-travelled man of experience when I come back. There'll be such tales to tell. I'll be the first one of our family to set sail abroad. It'll be a real adventure. Why, we ain't none of us ever even seen the sea before," he said, grinning from ear to ear.

Agnes struggled to reply, and Katy swiftly stepped in, sounding more like her mother than she would have thought possible a few months ago. A babe in your belly brought things home, right enough.

"You mind you do come home, Albert Beagle, and don't give your mother any cause for worry."

Albert kissed them both and snatched a fresh scone from the table, whistling his way out of the door.

"This damn war," muttered Agnes, bending once more over the lavender-strewn sheets. "I don't like it one bit. No good shall come of it, you mark my words, Katy. We'll rue this day."

"Oh, Albert will be back to pester us all, Mum. He only lives to be annoying. He'll come back and you never know, he might be all the better for a little soldiering and seeing the world." She couldn't quite keep the wistfulness out of her voice.

"Humph. I'm not so sure about that but you may be right. Whatever happens to Albert, at least we'll have your little one to welcome into the world. I'm looking forward to being a grandmother, whatever else happens."

Agnes gave Katy an uncustomary kiss and turned sharp about to fuss with the kettle, dashing the back of her hand across her eyes as she did so.

Katy stroked her swelling stomach. She understood her mother a lot better these days.

Katy's love of reading extended to the newspaper and she read the daily news to Jem as they sat round the fire each evening. Jem had said at first that it was a man's job. His father had always read aloud to his mother and considered it to be the part of the role of the head of the household. Katy had no truck with that. She enjoyed working out the long words and gobbling up news from further afield too much to yield to family convention.

"Listen to this Jem, 'tis awful – the worst yet."

"What is it, Kate?" Jem flopped wearily down opposite her and stretched his darned socks out to the blaze.

"It says, 'German airplanes called Zeppelins have dropped bombs on London.'"

"My God!" Jem stood up and paced around the room, shocked into forgetting his fatigue. "They attacked British soil? Women and children might have been killed!"

"Yes, Jem," answered Katy.

They looked at each other, both horrified.

War seemed a lot closer, all of a sudden.

CHAPTER TWELVE

By April his newly planted daffodils swayed in the breeze and Jem was kept busy planting up the garden ready for the summer. By harvest time when his crops were ready, Katy said she felt too heavy to lift much and Jem had to make sure the water and fuel were brought in for her before he trudged up the long hill to the manor gardens. He found it hard to concentrate on his work now Katy was so near her time.

Suddenly the new housemaid came running across from the big house. "'Scuse me, Mr Phipps sir, but could I have a word with young Jem? 'Tis his wife, sir - her time's come. Mr Andrews had words on that telly phone thing with Mrs Threadwell at the post office. She rung up, see, and spoke to Lady Smythe as well. Her ladyship said to tell 'ee."

"Oh, right, I see, thank you, Maisie. You get back to the house and I'll thank her ladyship later once I've finished here."

Maisie nodded and trotted back to the kitchens. Jem could see she was agog to let everyone know the exciting news and wonder at the modern speed of communication.

Katy was managing well, with her pains coming every hour or so, by the time Jem came thundering down the hill faster than he'd ever run before.

Luckily for Katy her mother had been calling frequently of late and was at their cottage when her labour started.

"I thought you'd want to know straight away so I popped across to the post office and got Margaret Threadwell to use that ugly new black telephone to get the message up to the big house. I didn't want to hold it close to my own ear. Who knows what that Bakelite stuff might do to you? Mind you, Mrs Threadwell don't need no new-fangled instrument to communicate the news! She's always managed spreading gossip well enough without such complicated things." Agnes didn't stop talking as she busied about.

Jem's fears and excitement fell flat once he got through the door and saw how quiet and surprisingly relaxed Katy seemed, sitting by the fire in her favourite chair with Agnes fully in charge of the situation.

"What about the midwife, Agnes? Does she know Katy's started?"

She informed him crisply that Mrs Armstrong would come in her own good time, just like the baby.

"Do you want a cup of tea or something, Katy, my love?" he said.

Katy shook her head, "No thanks, Jem."

"Best leave us in peace, lad," said his mother-in-law, hands on her hips.

Jem had been granted leave of absence for the grand event and felt he had been waiting for this day so long, he would burst with inactivity. Seeing he wasn't wanted, even by his own becalmed wife, he went out to the back yard and vented his pent-up frustration on splitting logs with such vigour that they fell apart like melted butter. He checked on the hens, weeded out the sprouting vegetables and then, unable to contain his curiosity a minute longer, strode into the scullery on the pretext of washing his soiled hands.

Peeping round the cottage door into the parlour, he saw Katy bent over her wooden chair, breathing as if to get a reluctant ember to burst into flame.

"What's happening, Agnes?" he ventured.

"Not much, Jem lad. Don't you fret now. First babies ain't in a hurry to join the world and Katy's doing right well. We'll be getting her up to bed in a little while." Agnes's smile ought to have been reassuring but he felt as worried and keyed up as before.

There was a knock at the door and Jem answered it. Mrs Armstrong, whose tiny, birdlike frame belied her toughness, had arrived at last. She came in and

63

immediately rolled up her sleeves and unpacked her big bag. She gave a little laugh when she saw him casting about for things to do. "You could bring in a pail of water to stand on the stove, if you've a mind."

Quicker than lightening, he brought in the bucket, brimful of water, and on to the stove it went, splashing onto the hot surface with a sizzle. Jem looked at Katy enquiringly but only got a thin smile in return.

"That'll do Jem, now get yourself off. We've work to do here." His mother-in-law's voice brooked no argument.

Jem was saved by Bert who turned up at the end of the working day and carted him off to the pub. It was so nearby, he told Jem, they'd still be the first to know if anything happened and could have a jar in the meantime.

It was a long night. The longest Jem had ever known. He paced the flagstone floor of the pub, his beer untouched. All the locals found it highly entertaining, but Jem was oblivious to their guffaws and jokes at his expense. Bert, father of five, helped himself to Jem's unwanted brew and, mellowing out, regaled him with stories of his own children's arrival into the world until Jem thought he might have to throttle him, father-in-law, or not.

Come midnight, the landlord chucked everybody out and the two men decamped to the parlour of Jem's little cottage.

Bert took the precaution of taking a jug of ale back with them, "Just in case our throats get dry, waiting like."

Back home, Jem could pace in peace but by now groans were emanating from upstairs and he could feel the sweat on his own skin pricking under his rough cotton shirt. He banked up the fire, brought in firewood and once attempted a foray to the hallowed first floor only to be flurried away by Agnes.

"We'll tell you if it comes, Jem. And I'll need that hot water then too, so keep it going. It always takes a while. Everything's fine."

Jem hesitated in the doorway as another long moan, strangely familiar from their lovemaking, issued forth. It took all his willpower to turn around when he again met his mother-in-law at the top of the stairs.

Agnes said, with some asperity, "Jem, get on with you, she's coping well. You're just keeping me from her."

Jem had one foot on the second step down when he heard Katy say through gritted teeth, "Oh, Mum, it's like a wave of pain that sweeps over you! I never knew it could hurt so much, oh!"

Agnes turned back to her daughter leaving the bedroom door ajar. Jem peeked through the open crack. He could see sweat trickling down Katy's face as another avalanche of pain surged through her straining body. Her long dark hair was clamped to her forehead and deep shadows left bruises under her eyes. Mrs Armstrong and Agnes exchanged looks and covered the bed in old sheets and an oilskin.

"Not long now my dear," said Mrs Armstrong, in her soothing voice.

"Really? Really not long?" gasped Katy.

"Let's have a little look-see. Agnes, she's crowning. Get that young father-to-be downstairs to bring up the hot water."

Jem quickly bolted into the little parlour below before Agnes scurried in to tell him the glad tidings. Seconds later, Jem ran back up the stairs, slopping hot water incontinently in his haste.

"Alright, Jem, that's all we need for now."

Disconsolate but encouraged things were happening at last, Jem clomped back down the narrow stairs yet again. Bert was snoring next to the hearth and even slept through the noise of Jem banking up the fire for the umpteenth time despite the warm weather outside. Both jumped though when the perennial sound of another soul entering this earthly sphere pierced the dawn silence.

The new father raced upstairs and undeterred by anybody's say-so, Jem brushed past both the middle-aged worthies and gazed at his daughter, hastily averting his eyes from the bloodstains at the other end of the cluttered bed.

Katy met his gaze full square, her eyes shining through her fatigue with pride and joy and her arms full of baby. "It's a little girl, Jem. You have a daughter."

Jem looked at his child. She was just like Katy with her pretty face and big eyes. Little tendrils of brown hair wisped around her head and her pink body looked too tiny to be real.

Mrs Armstrong gently peeled the baby away from Katy in order to give her a wash. "She's perfectly healthy," declared the experienced midwife.

As Jem stared, speechless, she gave the baby back to its young mother and watched with a satisfied smile as Katy instinctively put her new-born child straight to her breast. Jem, flushing with embarrassment, stood back feeling he was in the way both of the bustling pair of older women but also of the intimate embrace of his two dearest girls.

Katy seemed to sense his discomfort and looked up from her reverential gaze of their daughter's face.

"Come, Jem, see your little girl."

Jem knelt down in adoration and watched in awe as baby Florence guzzled down her first life-giving meal.

Agnes said, "Right then, I'll go and tell my Bert his first grandchild's arrived. Come on, Mrs Armstrong. I think we've earned ourselves a cup of tea. Let's leave 'em to it."

CHAPTER THIRTEEN

Florence proved to be a good baby. The village wives told Katy with relentless repetition how lucky she was to have such an easy child. Katy had never felt more exhausted in all her life. None of her domestic service, getting up at dawn and lighting fires, lugging pails of water along endless corridors and scrubbing floors until she thought her hands would dissolve in the cold, dirty water had prepared her for the all-consuming attention that Florence appeared to need.

Not that she begrudged a moment. Secretly she enjoyed nursing her little daughter in the wee, nadir hours of the night. All was still and soft in the darkened cottage and they two were alone in the world in their intimate, nourishing embrace. Katy studied Florence's face hungrily, drinking in every line, every downy curve of her sucking cheeks and curl of baby hair on her head. She knew Florence's whole being as intimately as an explorer knew his map of virgin territory.

Florence cried little, partly because of the sunny nature she'd inherited from her father and partly because she didn't have to. Katy would be there, anticipating Florence's every need before it could barely be realised. No wonder she was easy and good natured.

Agnes told her husband, "I'm that pleased with our Katy. She's turned into a lovely little mother, Bert. She always had her nose in a book and her mind set on dreams and adventures. 'Tis little wonder she was so restless, but you'd never think it to look at her now. I never thought she'd settle to married life with Jem, especially after that to-do with Mr Charles."

"Hmm and I wonder where he is now," Bert said, from behind the paper.

"It don't bear thinking about, that's what," Agnes said. "And with Albert over there in France and all. It's just as well I have got little Florence to visit. Little cherub she is too."

***

Jem, strangely enough, found adjusting to his new role as a parent a more difficult shift than he'd expected, and Katy appeared to manage despite her obvious tiredness. He loved his two girls with his whole heart but wasn't quite sure how he fitted in. Stunned by Katy's generous and sensuous loving before Florence was conceived and deliriously happy in that sexual embrace, he now felt the draught at its loss. Katy was now too tired for marital intimacy. She didn't seem to need it or want it, so wrapped up was she in the milky cocoon of nursing her little one. Jem was left to pick up the mundane chores of fetching water and wood before leaving his little family to gaze lovingly into each other's eyes, barely noticing his departure, as he slogged up the hill to work.

George reassured him that it was always this way with first babies and once more came along Katy would be damn glad of his assistance and they'd become more of a team. Jem took comfort from his experienced advice but wondered how they could make more children when he couldn't get near his lovely wife or even hold her attention when the baby was asleep.

He took to reading the paper to himself silently every night as Katy had given up reading it aloud. He spared her the worst of the news. There was plenty of it. The bulletin about the August offensives, particularly the huge casualties in Gallipoli, shocked him to his core. The whole village talked of nothing else.

Mrs Friedenburg's impeccable reputation as the local milliner counted for nothing against her German heritage. The revulsion everyone felt for the continuing slaughter vented itself on her. When children lobbed bricks through her shop window in Woodbury her hats were a sorry state, shredded and torn, the next morning but none of them got into trouble for it.

When she was helping Katy fold linen one bright morning later that week, Agnes said, "'Tisn't right, really. Mrs Friedenburg never did no-one no harm. Still you can understand folks being angry especially now there's this wicked poison gas they're using against our boys."

"Poison gas?" asked Katy, clutching the snowy pile of sheets to her mouth as if to protect herself against the imagined horror.

"Yes, there's no excusing it. They's using some sort of chlorine gas and it makes our boys eyes stream and wrecks their lungs. Started back in April in Ypres, so your Dad says." Agnes pronounced it 'Why-prez'. "Ain't you heard 'bout it then? Thought you read the paper from cover to cover?" Agnes said, as they folded a double sheet between them.

"Um, not so much lately. There's not much time with the baby to care for and I can't bear to read some of it. Jem does more'n me now."

Agnes looked sharply at her daughter. "It don't do to cut yourself off from the world entirely you know, my girl. You can't wrap yourself up in your child all the time – you've a husband to talk to – aye and listen to as well."

Katy pouted a little at this and was thankful Florence woke for her feed just then. Agnes stalked off to put the fragrant piles of sheets away upstairs. By the time Florence had devoured her milk and Agnes had brewed some tea, all was smoothed over and Agnes's visit ended on a more harmonious note.

One warm summer evening, when the little mite was tucked up in her cot happily dreaming in the world of nod, the new parents stood over their daughter together.

Jem seized the opportunity to tell Katy about his day.

"Little Bobbie Bedford nicked a load of strawberries today. He took 'em from the gardens and by the time he had carried them up the hill to the big house, there were barely three left! Old Mrs Biggs saw the tell-tale red juice round Bobbie's mouth. She said he looked like he was wearing rouge on his lips, he'd eaten so many. He felt the back of her hand then. She laughed with Dad about it after but said it wouldn't do."

Jem looked at Katy, but she was still gazing at their daughter. He ploughed on, "So Dad's put a set of scales in his office in the walled garden and he's weighing each basket of fruit after picking and told Mrs Biggs to do the same once they got to her kitchens. Woe betide the messenger if the weight's different from one to t'other!"

But Katy failed to see the joke. Her dreamy eyes rested on the infant dozing contentedly. Jem thought she was nothing less than besotted. He took himself off to into the garden where he pulled up the weeds with unnecessary force. It wasn't in Jem's nature to criticise Katy, but it was impossible not to feel left out of the love affair.

CHAPTER FOURTEEN

Launched successfully into village life by Katy and Jem's well attended wedding, Lionel White threw himself into local affairs in his first year of office with all the enthusiasm he'd previously given to his clerical work in India. The female variety of villagers appeared to accept him without reservation while Lionel felt that the men held back their judgement a little longer. By and large, he liked to think that they approved of their new cleric and appreciated his zestful energy when he launched a campaign to install proper plumbing in the workers cottages.

One wet Saturday morning Lionel knocked on the manor door. As Maisie let him into the marbled hall, he could hear Sir Robert saying to his wife, "I've begun to dread that new curate's damned rat-a-tat and Maisie's soppy smile every time she announces him. I'll be glad when Andrews returns from his annual holiday in Scotland. It'll be yet more earnest pleas for new sanitation in both villages, you mark my words, Amelia."

Lionel coughed loudly, to save Maisie's blushes and entered the dining room. Lady Smythe immediately got up, gave him a condescending nod and left, saying she needed to consult Mrs Biggs about something.

Sir Robert laid down his linen napkin with a thinly disguised sigh and pushed his breakfast aside with an exaggerated gesture. "Good day to you, Reverend White. What brings you up the hill on such an inclement morning?"

Lionel swept his fingers through his long, damp hair, and gave the squire the benefit of his brightest smile. "Good morning Sir Robert. I trust I find you well?"

"Indeed, Reverend, always in the best of health, thank you. Won't you sit down by the fire here and warm yourself? Autumn's coming in with a vengeance now

71

though it's still very mild for the time of year. Glad we got the harvest in safely. Bodes well for the winter, don't you know," and Sir Robert sat in the opposite armchair, stretching out his hairy-backed, veined old hands to the flames.

"Yes, indeed, sir. In fact, it is the health of our parishioners that I have come about. You may remember my speaking of the great works of sanitation promoted by Prince Albert in London in the last century and how this has improved infant mortality rates," Lionel said, deciding to ignore Sir Robert's attempt to disguise his second heavy sigh with some loud throat clearing.

Sir Robert had heard of it, "Humph, yes well. Big place, London, lot of people there. Different set up, you know."

"Larger, certainly, Sir Robert, but the smaller scale of things here would mean that installing proper plumbing would be a much easier thing to achieve."

"Don't hear of many infants dying in this parish, as far as I can see. Well, at least no more than average."

Lionel shifted forward on his embroidered chair to enthuse further. "There needn't be any, sir. I read a paper the other day by the British Medical Association definitely linking outbreaks of typhoid and cholera to poor sanitation in the slums."

"Slums. Slums! I beg your pardon, young man, but you'll find no damn slums on my land. I've always kept this estate in very good heart and my forefathers before me. I don't need a young upstart like you to tell how to run things. They have been well managed for generations." Sir Robert looked really cross.

Lionel sat back on the chair, studied his immaculately manicured nails and took a different tack. "Sir, I have never seen a parish run better. All the people under your benefaction are indeed content, but, Sir Robert, I put it to you this way. We are entering a modern age. The motor car is a wonderful piece of engineering that will soon replace the horse. We can travel miles on the railways in no time at all. Why, your own butler and housekeeper are even now up in their native country by virtue of the railway network. Do you really feel you want your estate to be left behind in all this progress? To be seen as old-fashioned and backward looking?"

Sir Robert's hackles did not appear to lower. He blew out his moustache with no attempt at disguise. "Well, well. I'll think about it. That's all I'm saying for now. There will be a great deal of expense, no doubt. This damn land tax of that ruddy Welshman, Lloyd George, has fairly scuppered me finances, what? I'm being squeezed left, right and centre, you know." He looked pointedly at his fast-cooling kedgeree.

"I'll see what Lady Smythe has to say on it but until then you'll have to wait. Now, if you'll excuse me, I have other pressing matters to attend to."

It was obvious to Lionel that finishing breakfast was top of the list.

Lionel made a tactical withdrawal not a whit abashed or downcast. Lady Smythe was a tougher nut to crack but her competitive streak in local society was a trump card. He would get his taps and drains before a twelvemonth was out and was confident all his parishioners would be grateful for his initiative.

CHAPTER FIFTEEN

Jem groaned. It was the third time that night that Florence had woken him up with her crying. Katy got up at once and cradled her in her arms.

"What do you think is bothering her, Katy?"

"I wish I knew." Katy had to shout over Florence's wails. "Mum says it's only teething and not to worry."

"I thought she'd sleep through now you've got her on real food at last." Jem was unable to keep the disappointment from his voice.

"I know, so did I, but she's that fretful." Florence confirmed her distress by crying louder than ever. Katy sat down on the bed and tried to breastfeed her baby. Soon Katy was crying too because Florence refused to suck. Katy buttoned her nightdress back up with one hand while trying to hold the wriggling infant with the other.

Wearily, Jem got up and took over. "You go back to bed, Katy. I'll take her downstairs for a bit so you can sleep. You've not slept a wink all night."

"Are you sure, Jem?" Katy yawned and tried to hide it with the back of her hand. It was still only three o'clock in the morning.

"Yes, if she's not settled by five o'clock, I'll come and get you to take over." Jem knew Katy wouldn't accept his offer otherwise. She always tried to spare him being awake in the night when he had to work in the morning. Katy was asleep before he reached the bottom of the little winding staircase.

He told his daughter, "You're causing a great deal of trouble, young lady. Your mother's smile came back last week and now it's been wiped away again with you crying at night." He paced up and down the parlour, glad of the night fire, burning low in the grate. He tried everything to soothe his child: patting her back, holding her on his shoulder, rubbing her tummy and crooning soft lullabies. Eventually Florence dozed off, exhausted with her own tears. Jem slumped down on his favourite fireside chair to grab forty winks before the dawn crept in and woke them both.

When Katy came downstairs, fresh from her sleep, she made his breakfast with an extra egg as a thank you, while Jem read the newspaper with gritty eyes.

There was enough drama in the papers to wrest anyone from their immediate concerns, thought Jem, as he read silently. The editor's column wrote how the disaster of the Gallipolli campaign had shocked everyone, merely to be eclipsed by the United Kingdom now declaring war against Bulgaria with France following suit the next day. Conflict was spreading throughout Europe like an ugly rash.

Jem read the article about the execution of Nurse Cavell out loud.

"She was executed by firing squad at seven o'clock in the morning of the 12th of October 1915," he read in a hushed voice. "She'd been caught helping allied servicemen to escape from Belgium to the Netherlands, it says. Think of that, Kate - a woman and a nurse - you know - someone who only wants to help others, shot down by a whole gang of German bastards."

Shocked, Katy turned to stare at him as she listened to the story, her wooden spoon held aloft as if frozen in mid-air. "Jem that's awful! The poor woman. Is there nothing the bloody Germans won't stoop to in this stupid war? It's barbaric, that's what it is." And the wooden spoon came down on his scrambled eggs with a vengeance.

Jem walked up the hill to work and chewed over the latest news reflecting on how the war was affecting them all. Bert senior often fretted to Jem about Albert, now fully engaged on the battlefield but Jem kept it from Katy. He didn't see the point in worrying her unnecessarily. Not when things had been looking up at last with Florence apart from these last couple of nights' tears.

Often, he would remember their first year alone together with heartfelt longing but then, when he looked at his little girl, his own heart swelled with a different sort of love.

As Florence had grown and started to recognise her parents' faces, rewarding them with winning smiles and gurgles, it became impossible to resent her gentle presence and bonny face. Florence was a happy baby, pink and rounded, and her sweetness of disposition promised well. Jem had suggested they had a little picnic the previous Sunday. He decided he'd make a real effort to get involved. The day had dawned bright and quickly became warm. They'd been enjoying an Indian summer and Jem wanted to make the most of it. Katy had packed up some salty ham and fresh cottage cheese she'd made. Into the basket went some of her home-made chutney, a fresh loaf of bread and a few rosy apples. Jem had contributed a jug of ale and a couple of mugs.

Katy had gone to give him the basket to carry but he had said, "No, Katy, it's not that heavy. I'll carry Florence." Katy had hesitated but Florence had put out her chubby arms to her father and decided for herself who would have the honour. Jem had felt ridiculously pleased as he took his baby in his arms and she chuckled when he tickled her rounded belly.

Jem remembered how he and Katy had held their spare hands together as they strolled up to the woods. At the riverside Katy had laid out a blanket and Jem had sighed in deep satisfaction as his little family tucked into the feast. They all three had dozed off after their picnic lunch and when they woke up, they were hot from the warm afternoon sun, so unusual for the time of year. Jem had peeled off Florence's booties and his own bigger ones and waded into the river. He'd dangled Florence's little feet in the cool, rippling water and she gurgled in delight. Katy had laughed and looked happier and more carefree than she had for ages, as she sat on the bank watching them.

Jem had felt more involved after that happy afternoon and looked forward to more family expeditions as Florence grew to know him more. How could he fail to be proud when he saw Katy standing in their cottage window, Florence on her hip, waving him off to work each morning with smiles and nods? What a tender, pretty pair they were, to be sure, he'd thought only a few days ago. It made this new, grizzling phase and sleepless nights even more irritating. One step forward, and two back, it seemed to Jem.

"It'll pass, lad," said his Dad, noticing the newly returned cheerfulness of his son beginning to fade as quickly as it had come. Working together on the gardens, George and Jem shared a special bond, beyond that of father and son. Jem saw how well his father managed all of his staff and guarded against giving Jem favouritism. Jem liked to think he had earned the respect of his fellow workers because, if anything, George made sure his son worked harder than the others.

George might not praise him, but Jem knew that he hoped he would fill his boots as head gardener when the time came. They were setting daffodil bulbs to dry for spring one afternoon when George shared his confidences with his eldest, and favourite, son.

"Our John's hankering to leave for the front like Katy's Albert. I tell you Jem, I'm glad you got married when you did, if it'll keep you home. I seen how restless you are now and how happy you was before Florence was born. Them heady early days can't last, lad. But I like your Katy, though your mother isn't so sure. She's got spirit but she's settled down to mothering for your sake. Marriage takes a while to build strength. Oak trees don't grow overnight. You'll find each other again, given time, just as me and my Mary done before you."

Reassured, Jem tried to have the same calming effect on his wife when he returned home that night.

His mood quickly returned to an anxious one, when Katy greeted him with, "I don't know, Jem. Mum said she's alright, but I can't relax about Florence. Seems to me she's lost her bloom. Look, her little cheeks aren't pink and round no more. She's cranky all the time and see how she clings to me. I can't get her to settle, no matter what I do."

***

Lionel White called round on one of his regular visits the next day, confident that Katy would welcome him in with her usual charming hospitality. Lionel's eyes widened in appreciation of her youthful beauty and regained figure.

Her slender neck arched like a swan's as she bent over Florence's cot by the range. The baby, he was relieved to see, was sleeping quietly on her own for once.

Even to Lionel's blinkered eyes Katy was looking tired. He noticed black shadows under the big violet blue eyes, themselves dark with anxiety.

"How's the little one, Mrs Phipps?" he asked, without a great deal of interest in the answer.

"Fine, thank you, vicar."

Lionel sipped his tea. It was really very good, especially compared to some of the disgusting offerings he got from his other parishioners in none too hygienic vessels.

He looked around the tidy parlour. The fire danced merrily in the grate, and the kettle steamed lightly above, ready to top up the elegant blue and white china teapot. Not only was the china attractive, it sat resplendent on the green chenille cloth on the table and the vase of fresh montbretia and hydrangeas, the last of the season's flowers, scented the room. Tasteful curtains framed the window and new patchwork cushions softened his seat. Katy might look a trifle strained but she obviously knew how to manage her little house. The homely smell of chopped onions wafted in from the lean-to scullery, promising supper.

Lionel congratulated Katy on her home, "You have made your house very welcoming, Mrs Phipps, and this tea is delicious."

"Thank you, Reverend," was the modest reply, eyes downcast, lips teetering on a smile.

"And how are you keeping?"

"I am well, but my daughter is a bit worrisome." Katy glanced over at the quiet cot.

"I'm sorry to hear that but infants are often so, are they not?" Lionel sipped his hot tea.

"That's what my mother says but it's no comfort in the middle of the night when she won't settle."

"No, indeed," Lionel said sagely, considering how blissfully ignorant he was of the desperate pangs of anxiety known only to parents in the long hours of sleepless nights. Katy tucked an escaped curl of her wavy dark hair behind her ear. Lionel found the unconscious little gesture disconcertingly alluring. She intrigued him more than he cared to admit, even to himself. Here was not your average village girl. She had something more. There was intelligence behind those eyes. Normally he would be leaving at this point of his visit, considering his duties fulfilled and eager for an excuse to relieve the boredom with something more interesting.

"Could I trouble you for another cup of this excellent beverage?" he asked.

Flushing, Katy took his cup and refilled it, "I'm sorry I've no cake to offer you to go with it, Reverend. I've been up all night with Florence, you see."

Lionel accepted the cup with a gracious nod, as she handed it to him. In the moment they both held the saucer, he delayed taking the tea from her just long enough to look at her face at close quarters, and their fingers touched. He settled back in his comfy chair and stretched his long legs out to toast near the cheerful fire.

"How do you pass your free time, Mrs Phipps? Do you miss working up at the manor where there was always so much going on? Do you find time hangs heavy, now you're a housewife?"

"Oh no, sir," Katy quickly replied, looking surprised at the question. "There's plenty to do and, if I do have a spare moment, I can always read. I dearly love a good story."

"And what sort of books do you prefer?"

"Oh, anything really. Sir Robert was always most kind and let me have free run of his library when I was working there."

Lionel smothered a smile. "And how do you get books now?"

"It's not so easy now but I have a few of my own and I re-read them. Sometimes, I find you enjoy it even more second time around, if it's a good tale and well written. You discover bits you missed the first time when you was," Katy paused and corrected herself, "*were* rushing through to find out what happens in the end."

"Quite so, quite so," nodded Lionel, his curiosity completely aroused now. A well-read parishioner - here in this tiny cottage. Astonishing. "Any favourite authors?"

The answer was swift and decisive. "Oh, I love Jane Austen best of all. Her characters are so life-like and funny. I like the works of the Brontë sisters too, especially Jane Eyre. Now that's a rattling good story."

"Yes, indeed, a very exciting tale. Have you read all of Jane Austen's works?"

"Well, I don't know how many there are. I've read Emma and Mansfield Park, I think."

"Not Pride and Prejudice?" Lionel looked surprised.

"No, I've not heard of that one." Katy shook her head.

"Oh, it's the best, I assure you. I'll lend you my copy. I shall be very interested to know what you think of it. I must not colour your opinion, but I believe it to be her finest work." Lionel drained his cup and returned it to its saucer.

"Oh, thank you, sir. That would be a kindness. And a rare treat too." Katy took the china from him.

"It's no trouble at all," Lionel said truthfully. "I'll pop in with it tomorrow and, er, ask after your child of course."

They smiled at each other.

"My mother would laugh at me, sir, she always told me off for neglecting my chores because my 'nose was stuck in a book again.'"

The moment was truncated, perhaps fortunately, by Florence waking and crying for her mother's instant attention. Lionel took himself off hastily. Mewing infants were part of his job that was less to his masculine tastes than chatting to pretty young housewives.

CHAPTER SIXTEEN

When Lionel knocked on Katy's front door the next day and received no answer, he took the liberty of trying the door-handle and, finding it unlocked, entered the cottage. If Katy was out, he would place the promised book on the table by the window and leave as quietly as he came.

Before he could put the slim volume down, a baby's frantic crying reached his unwilling ears. Thinking to beat a hasty retreat, Lionel turned back to the door. Against his better judgement and horror of domestic dramas, he could not fail to be moved by the rending sobs issuing from the first floor.

Leaving the novel on the table, he ventured tentatively to the stairs and called up, "Mrs Phipps? Is everything alright? Can I assist you?"

Confident the reply would come in the negative, he turned to go once more but before he could get clean away Katy's distraught face appeared over the banisters.

"Reverend White! Oh, thank God someone's here."

Gathering Florence in her arms, she stumbled down the staircase. She presented quite a contrast to the composed young housewife of yesterday's tranquil tea party. Her hair had tumbled down her back, her buttons were fastened all wrong and her eyes, black with dilated pupils, had puffy, reddened lids.

Lionel started forward. "Mrs Phipps! Whatever is the matter? Are you unwell?"

"Not me, sir, no, not I. 'Tis my child, my Florence. She's that ill, I don't know what to do. I wish my mother was here!" Katy said, looking distracted.

"Have you called the doctor?" asked Lionel, his worst fears confirmed.

"Nay, I have not been able to leave her."

"Where's your husband?"

"He's up at the gardens working though he's been up all night too."

"I'll get Dr Benson straight away." Lionel could see this situation was completely beyond his skills.

"Would you sir? I'd be that grateful. And, and could you, would it be too much trouble, to get a message to my mother, Mrs Beagle, up at the West Lodge?"

"Yes, of course I will!" Lionel said, glad of an excuse to run the errand and get away from the howling infant.

He walked as fast as he could back to the vicarage and saddled up his horse, Kashmir, named and bought in the first flush of his return from the east. The big bay mare looked delighted to be going out and swished her tail in his face as he mounted her. He rode up the hill to Upper Cheadle at a brisk trot. At the lodge house, he found Agnes in her garden, pegging out bleach-white sheets in the morning sunshine.

"Good morning, Mrs Beagle," he called across, without dismounting.

"Morning, vicar," replied Agnes, through the pegs in her mouth.

Lionel wondered how one woman could manage to wash so many sheets by herself, then recollecting his errand, said, "I've just come from your daughter's house in Lower Cheadle, Mrs Beagle. Her baby's not at all well. She's asked for you."

Agnes looked quite cross. "I've told her, she's just teething. She'll have to learn to manage. I'm knee-deep in laundry. I want to catch this sunshine while I can."

"I know nothing of infants, Mrs Beagle, but they both looked quite distressed and Mrs Phipps has also asked me to fetch the doctor. Have you seen him about this morning?"

"The doctor? Katy's asked for him?" Agnes' busy hands stopped still, a rare sight.

Lionel was relieved he had got through. "Yes, the baby did look really ill and Mrs Phipps was at the end of her tether, I'd say."

Agnes threw the last sheet over the washing line and pegged it quickly. "I'd better get down there in that case. Dr Benson is up at the big house. Sir Robert's gout's been playing him up again, he told me when he passed by earlier."

"Good, I'll be able to catch him. Shall I ask him to give you a lift in his car?"

"I'm not sure I wants to get in that contraption!" Agnes looked quite shocked.

"It would be a great deal quicker than walking." Lionel gathered up the reins of his big horse.

"We'll see about that," Agnes said. "I'll start walking anyway. Daisy will have to mind Jack and Emily for me."

Lionel chucked Kashmir back to a trot and left Katy's mother to organise her household. If he was a betting man, which he never would be, he'd bet that she'd get there before the good doctor and smiled, despite his concerns over her daughter.

Doctor Benson, once found at the manor house, immediately understood the urgency of the situation. "Katy Phipps hasn't a brass farthing to waste. She must be really worried," he said, as he cranked the engine of his motor car into roaring life. Kashmir reared up in fear at the modern, ugly sound of it. Lionel kept his seat and smoothed her mane. He sympathised with his horse, hating the sound of the raucous engine as much as she did. Doctor Benson must have private means to afford such an extravagant luxury, thought Lionel. He must love his work if he didn't need the income.

***

After Lionel left to round up her support team, Katy tried to shout her thanks above the racket of Florence's tears, but he had already turned and fled.

She sank back on her dishevelled bed and rocked Florence back and forth, clutching her to her breast. Florence would not or could not feed from her, however much she coaxed her. She changed her filthy nappy for the tenth time, distressed at the smell and colour of its contents. Florence's skin was red and very sore. Even when she soothed it with some cream her mother swore by, Florence didn't stop crying and now she seemed both exhausted and inconsolable.

Katy was fast becoming the same, "Hush, now little one, hush there. It'll be alright, don't you fret so. Florence, my lovely Florence, my little love." Katy stroked her daughter's dark hair away from her little flushed face in rhythmic, soothing strokes. Then she walked up and down her bedroom, rocking her to and fro and singing her favourite lullaby.

Florence did seem to calm slightly, and they lay back on the double bed together. Florence curled up safe in the cleft of her tired mother's arms. Katy gazed at her daughter, whose eyelashes lay dusky black against her flushed cheek. Katy smoothed Florence's baby curls and inhaled her sweet scent. Exhausted she might be but when she looked at her child's sleeping face, she could not begrudge a second of her broken night. The hectic blush on her baby's cheeks might even be healthy, she tried to persuade herself.

Katy dozed in the respite, drifting in and out of consciousness. They both jumped when another peremptory knock sounded on their front door, which she'd left unlatched. Katy scooped up her baby and went to the window to look down at the street below.

As usual, Dr Benson's automobile gave his identity away. Katy felt relief at seeing the shiny metal car but held Florence's body closer to her chest, feeling instinctively protective about any medical intrusion. The doctor didn't waste a minute, mounting the stairs at a brisk trot, two at a time. Before she had collected herself, he stood before her with his bag of instruments at the ready.

The doctor's face was serious under his mop of white hair as he looked at Katy and then at Florence, before saying, "Uncover your child, Katy, so I can examine her."

Katy hesitated to disturb poor Florence. She had so recently relaxed and begun to rest from her distress.

"She's only just fallen asleep, Doctor," she said, whispering so as not to wake her daughter.

Dr Benson shook his head. Obedient to his authority, Katy slipped off her baby's nightgown, exposing her body. Florence's immediately started up crying again but her complaints, though loud and insistent, fell on deaf ears.

Dr Benson explained, "Babies always object to being examined, Katy, but I'm used to them. I'll be as quick as I can, my dear."

Katy watched impatiently as his competent hands ran over her daughter's hot little body. Katy looked from the doctor to her daughter and back again. His set face and solemn looks sent a chill down her spine. She looked back at Florence and saw the reason. Her abdomen looked swollen and as angry as Florence herself. Dr Benson removed her napkin and shook his head again. Katy looked at the cotton cloth shocked to see streaks of blood on it. When the doctor's eyes met Katy's, they were grave. Katy dreaded knowing what he had to say; she was terrified of that look in his sad eyes.

Dr Benson stood up, covering Florence lightly with the cotton sheet as he did so. He cleared his throat as he put his stethoscope back in his leather bag.

"Katy, sit back down on the bed there with your child. You can dress her again now, but only cover her lightly. She has a temperature and doesn't need warm covers."

Katy dutifully sat back on the bed and made Florence as comfortable as she could. Florence's outraged cries subsided into quieter murmurings and her eyelids fluttered shut. Katy turned back to the doctor who stood patiently waiting until Florence was settled.

In the quiet moment that followed, Dr Benson drew himself up to his full height and looked her straight in the eyes. "I'm sorry, Katy, there is no easy way to tell you this, but your little girl is suffering from typhoid. There's no hope, I'm afraid."

Katy clutched at the bedclothes. She felt she would fall away, away into an abyss, back into the long endless night she had just endured. Last night she had hoped that, ill though Florence might be, she would be better come morning. And now, and now - she never would be again.

"No! This cannot be true," she cried. "See, doctor! She's sleeping again. She looks much better than she did last night. Surely she's on the mend?"

She reached out her hand and grabbed the doctor's arm. He put his other hand on Katy's shoulder and held it there firmly. He shook his head and said, "No, Katy, the bloody diarrhoea, the agitation, the tender abdomen: they all confirm the diagnosis, my dear."

Katy looked back at her daughter. Her heart seemed to have risen to her throat. It threatened to choke her. A strangled sob escaped her.

Dr Benson said, as he patted her shoulder, "Katy, you must be strong so that you can nurse her. I'll drive up to the manor and get Jem to come home. Your mother's already on her way. Do you need her here, do you think?"

"Oh, more than anything, Doctor!"

"She won't be long. I offered her a lift, but she didn't fancy my automobile." The doctor gave a grim smile and continued, "You must boil all your water. Don't drink any milk. Strict hygiene in the kitchen. Your mother will know what to do. I'll come back this afternoon to see how it's going."

Katy could not speak. She nodded dumbly. All she could do was stare at her little girl. To try and imprint her face on to her memory before it was snatched away forever. Lionel returned and came upstairs to tell Katy that he'd given the message to her mother about the problem and she was even now walking down the hill. Katy barely heard him. He and the doctor turned and came downstairs together.

Lionel spoke first when they reached the street outside, away from Katy's hearing. "I am more moved than I can say. Those damned manual water pumps. If only Sir Robert had listened to me. Things move so slowly when money is involved and now this young life will be wasted."

Doctor Benson nodded, "Her reaction is all too familiar, Reverend White. I've seen this before but not for a while. Things are supposed to be getting better. The sanitation in this village is completely anachronistic. This is the twentieth century! Typhoid is supposed to be on the run. Sometimes I hate my job."

Agnes arrived five minutes later, having declined the ride in the good doctor's noisy car and walked the whole way down the hill to Lower Cheadle. Much to Katy's relief, she swiftly took charge with quiet competence and a grimly set mouth, leaving Katy to focus on her child. Jem came home half an hour later, having readily accepted a lift in the doctor's car when Dr Benson had returned to the manor to fetch him. He sat by the fire with Agnes in stunned silence while Katy and Florence slept fitfully together upstairs.

This brief calm preceded a storm of anguish. Florence's cries pierced it with unearthly wailing. As they strived to ease her pain, the two mothers were busy enough, bathing her with lavender water and crooning every lullaby they knew. Worse, much worse, was to come when Florence lay quiet and lethargic; too ill to cry. Then all they could do was watch as her life drained swiftly away. By dawn, she was out of all discomfort and would never make a sound again.

The house hushed into an eerie silence. Even their exhaustion could not allow any of the adults to sleep. Huddled round the range, with the babe still and lifeless upstairs, they sat as quietly as Florence herself. The fire leapt and danced in defiance of death. It was the only thing in that silent room that seemed alive. Each of them stared at the flames, numb with fatigue and grief. None of them stirred. Soon the dawn arrived, punctual as ever and the morning sun filtered cheerfully into the room. Even in the bright sunlight, their blank faces avoided each other's eyes. They gazed only at the fire with fixed and immovable masks. So they remained, until the doctor's sharp knock broke the mood. All three started in surprise that life still existed outside of their nexus of gloom.

Agnes recovered first. Katy watched, as her mother prised herself from her chair as if glue restrained her. Agnes opened the door. Katy could see from the doctor's face that he knew the answer to his unspoken question immediately. He nodded at her with his compassionate understanding writ large across his lined face. He patted her shoulder before Agnes turned and led him upstairs, wiping her eyes with the corner of her apron. Katy glanced at Jem as the doctor passed them, but Jem's white face just stared into the fire, still transfixed by the flames.

Dr Benson followed Agnes down the stairs again. He'd only needed five minutes to confirm Florence's death and sign the certificate. "She must be buried immediately to prevent further contamination. We must consult Reverend White and expedite the arrangements. I'm so sorry."

Agnes's good kind face crumpled at last. She used her clean white apron to wipe her face again.

Dr Benson said, "The place must be thoroughly scrubbed down and all the clothes washed. The bed will have to be stripped and the linen washed too. Can you manage this Agnes? You must be very tired." He looked at the two mute parents and back at Agnes.

"I can do it, Doctor, if it must be done. She was such a pretty, good-natured little thing. God is cruel sometimes," Agnes said.

"It's not God, Agnes, but plumbing that's to blame for this. We must test the water that Katy's using and see what's caused it. This Indian summer is too dry. The water levels are very low, and contamination has occurred somewhere."

Agnes stared at the doctor. "I've never had to face this problem with my own children. I blame this deep valley. Hills are healthier, don't you think so, Doctor Benson?"

"Possibly, Agnes, but now's not the time to dwell on that."

Doctor Benson gave Katy a bottle of tonic to help her recover. She took it from him like an automaton. Then he turned to her husband.

"Look after her, Jem. She's going to need all your support in the next few weeks. And help your mother-in-law to clean the place up and get rid of the infection."

Jem nodded at the doctor.

Katy thought his words seemed to be coming from the next county, so distant did they sound.

Dr Benson clapped Jem on the shoulder. "They need you now, lad. You must help them all you can."

"Ay, doctor. I understand," Jem said.

"Good man. I'll call in tomorrow to see how things are."

Agnes let the doctor out and shut the door behind him. She filled the kettle and put it to boil.

"Jem lad, bring in some more firewood, would you? Let's get things put to rights."

CHAPTER SEVENTEEN

Lionel watched his flock proceed into his small church, following the tiny coffin with sad, heavy steps. The day was unseasonably mild again, like a jug of freshly harvested cow's milk, still tepid from the udders. Too rich and creamy but not chilled enough to be delicious. It remained slightly sickly in its fetid humidity and the air lay heavily stagnant - not quite letting go of summer's heat and hinting nothing yet of winter's bite. It lay in between, limp with lassitude, unable to work itself up into a cleansing gale or shine through with the energy of the sun.

The enervating gloom had pervaded all afternoon with mists that stole in from the surrounding woodland. Leaves dripped noiselessly from the trees with no wind to swirl them into eddying flight. Silently their autumn colours drooped towards the hungry ground in a vertical, suicidal suck of gravity and lay there, curling up in their death throes, submitting to the crush of oblivious feet.

Lionel dragged his gaze away from the careless landscape and willed his legs towards his own church, for once dreading the service he must deliver. Reluctantly, his limbs obeyed and conveyed him to the porch. Even then he could not continue until he took a deep breath from the dank, unfeeling air with which to power his walk up the aisle, cutting through the cobweb of grief that connected every parishioner from pew to pew.

His voice, usually so strong and reliable, trembled. His eyes locked on to the minute coffin with its single posy of autumn cyclamen and crocus. He pulled them away and gazed at his congregation. Gradually his sight focussed once more. The mute faces gazing up at him implored him to regain his composure so that they might rediscover their own. Lionel cleared his throat and began.

"Brethren, we are gathered together this afternoon to witness the passing of a life so short, it bore no sin. A life so innocent we must all consider ourselves blessed for having been a part of it."

He paused when Katy slid wordlessly on to her seat and Jem clutched at her. Alone they sat when everyone else stood and no-one minded. Katy lay her head on her husband's shoulder and her own shook with silent, exhausted tears. Flutters of handkerchiefs rippled through the assembly. Lionel kept the service short as befitting a child and his own forbearance.

Out they all shuffled into the misty, soft afternoon. The sun put in a belated appearance; too weak to be useful, it slipped furtively towards the horizon. Evening shadows crept across the graveyard, as little Florence was lowered into the moist, dark earth. Lionel looked at the bereaved young parents. Katy could barely stand, and he could see it was only Jem's strength that kept her upright. Everyone looked patently relieved when they shook Jem's hand and their own heads and turned tail for their firesides.

***

Agnes, Bert, George and Mary all accompanied Jem and Katy back to their cottage.

Jem had told everyone at the church porch, "There's no wake at ours. Have a drink at the pub if you want to."

He added to his parents, "How can we celebrate a life that's not had time to be lived? Florence didn't even live long enough to enjoy one birthday. Four months. Four short wasted months."

Agnes gave Katy some camomile tea and packed her off to bed. Katy went without a word, not even to Jem. Bert and George dragged him off to the pub after a while of patting hands and rattling of teacups in the cottage. Jem looked back in disbelief as Agnes and Mary clucked together almost contentedly, despite their sadness. They were still at it when the menfolk wove their way back much later.

George told Jem's unwilling ears, "They've had the length of years to trust all will come right again and don't forget, Jem, both these women have other children whose lives are equally forfeit on foreign soil."

Jem couldn't take it in. To bring children into the world only to lose them before your own time was up went against every natural law he'd ever learnt.

The bereaved grandparents left in a clutch, taking hope with them.

Jem, left alone in the privacy of his own home, the crackling fire his only witness, wept.

CHAPTER EIGHTEEN

Lionel charged up to the manor the next day, his zeal for new pipework re-energised by the tragedy. The butler, Andrews, directed him to the morning room where he found Sir Robert sitting with his wife and the papers.

"Good morning, Sir Robert; Lady Smythe," Lionel said, declining a seat.

He paced about the elegant room despite Lady Smythe's tutting disapproval.

"Good morning, Reverend." Sir Robert remained seated.

"Sir, I conducted a funeral in Lower Cheadle yesterday," began Lionel, pausing in his perambulations to stand directly in front of Sir Robert.

"I'm sorry to hear that, Lionel," was all the response he elicited.

"It was quite tragic, really," continued Lionel. "The deceased was an infant of only a few months. Typhoid was the cause."

"Typhoid, you say?" piped up Lady Smythe. Lionel, belatedly remembering his manners, whirled round to include her in the discussion.

"Yes, Lady Smythe. Typhoid, as you may know, is caused by a poor water supply. The bacteria are carried in unhygienic systems. Sir Robert, if we replaced the communal standpipe with properly installed plumbing to each cottage, this would never happen again! We need proper drains, sir."

Sir Robert looked unmoved in the face of Lionel's vociferous protests. "I've seen many children come and go over the years, it's all part of the natural cycle of life." For all his affable exterior, Lionel was shocked to see his squire was made of granite, when his wallet was involved.

Lady Smythe, when appealed to, was stonier still. She read the latest article in the paper about infant mortality out loud to them and added, "My dear Lionel, calm yourself. It's far more likely to be the slovenly habits of the mother. The probable cause was milk left too long in this unseasonal warm autumn weather."

Lionel felt an unfamiliar rage unfurl through his taut body as the lofty matron intoned her complacent opinions. With both a daughter and a son full grown in security and luxury, how could she identify with the agony through which Katy was now going? For that matter, why did he?

Lionel listened to their hot air whistling through his rebellious ears and ground his teeth. Staying barely long enough to be civil, he rose from his chintz chair, nodded curtly and turned on his polished heels smartly enough to be sure of chewing up the expensive carpet.

Before the door was fully shut behind him, he heard Lady Smythe remark to her husband, "That young man is a hothead, Robert. He is not the mature man his predecessor was."

"Quite so, Amelia. You are right, as always. What's for dinner tonight?"

Lionel sent the gravel in the manorial drive flying into the clipped grass edges as he rode along it, fuelled by frustrated anger. He would write to the local authorities and various charities today. Get them to impress upon Sir Robert and his steely lady the necessary changes to be made to the antediluvian water supply in the village. The doctor had already convinced him that that was the cause of this outbreak and had instructed everyone in the village to boil their water while the warm autumnal weather lasted.

As soon as Lionel got home to the vicarage he went straight to his study, dashed off half a dozen letters and felt a lot better for it.

Mrs Hoskins, his housekeeper, gave him his parishioners' viewpoint, along with his lunch. "Everyone is sad about little Florence Phipps, sir. She drew the two villages together, see. And that Katy might be toffee-nosed but she's made Jem very happy, though *some* people,"

Lionel noticed she neglected to include herself despite previously being Katy's loudest critic, "didn't approve of the match. And she gave him his pretty daughter, as sweet natured as her father has always been, at just the right time after the wedding. She's been a good mother too, as good as any from Lower Cheadle," said Mrs Hoskins, with only the slightest hint of a grudge. She tutted. "It's a shame and no mistake."

Lionel's silent chewing eventually arrested the flow and he was left in peace to pick at his over-boiled cabbage.

***

Meanwhile Katy and Jem struggled to comfort each other. Both silent in the face of their loss because no words could express the depth of their bottomless well of despair.

Jem toiled in the gardens mindlessly by day. It afforded some solace, and Jem found it easier to be at work than to come home to a white-faced and silent wife in an ominously quiet cottage. He found himself working longer hours than necessary and slipping into the pub on the way home for a 'swift half' that sometimes grew to a few pints. Then, appetite falsely satisfied, he would toy with the dried-up food that had waited too long for him. He could see it didn't help Katy one bit but didn't seem to be able to do anything about it.

At night they lay together not touching but avoiding each other's young bodies. No child could disturb their intimacy now but ironically there was none to interrupt. It was as if Florence still lay between them like an intangible barrier. The flimsy gauze membrane of her memory kept them apart. Neither could sleep well and Jem's appetite diminished further. He came home later and later from the pub, sometimes the worse for wear.

***

Katy found the smell of beer totally repulsive. The tentative attempts Jem made to reach out for her she nipped in the bud, revolted by the stale waft of sweat, beer and tobacco.

A huge cavern of loneliness overwhelmed her. She had little to do by day and the evenings stretched out as she waited for Jem to come home, tired, listless and monosyllabic. She drifted through the days, weary to her bones. She fed the hens, swept the cottage, prepared the unwanted meals and fetched the tainted water with mindless repetition.

Agnes said to Bert, "I hope Katy's moping will pass. She's that low, I can't bear to see her. I'm keeping my eye on our other children too. We don't want them catching that awful disease. And there's Albert fighting on the Front. With one thing and another I don't know if I'm coming or going with the worry of it all."

Bert lit his pipe and nodded through the fragrant smoke in sympathy.

Agnes slapped the bread dough she was kneading and added, "We'll just have to hope that time will heal that new marriage and they'll make another baby in the normal, natural way of things when they're good and ready."

***

Lionel's letter writing to the charitable and upper-class women who had little to do but advise those younger and poorer than themselves, was met by these ladies with alarming and enthusiastic alacrity. Faced with a barrage of forceful matrons, he quickly seized the opportunity to turn their energies to his advantage in his schemes for the village sewage system.

Through them he also learnt about the newly established Health Visitor scheme. In due course, a triumphant Lionel turned up at Katy's dusty doorstep with an aged spinster armed with a strict agenda. Lionel anticipated that Miss Bradbury would offer solace and kindness to Katy but when Katy's step could be heard shuffling towards the door and when she took her time in opening it, Lionel could see it did nothing to warm the Health Visitor's heart.

"Oh, hello, vicar. What brings you here?" Katy looked sleepy and held an open book in her hand.

"Good morning, Mrs Phipps. This is Miss Bradbury. She's a Health Visitor and has come to give you some advice. May we come in?"

Lionel was shocked to see the layer of dust that covered the homely furniture in Katy's cottage and embarrassed when Miss Bradbury drew her bony finger in it. Miss Bradbury sat down, after ostentatiously brushing the chair free of dirt. She sat on its very edge, bristling with importance and cleared her throat which Lionel thought closely resembled a turkey's.

"Mrs Phipps," began the spinster, "Allow me to extend my condolences on your recent loss."

Katy looked blankly back at her and then, longingly, at her book. Lionel noticed it was the one he had lent her before Florence died and began to doubt the wisdom of Miss Bradbury's visit so soon after the event.

"It may well be that someone in your, um, circumstances will have more children in the future and I'm here to instruct you on methods of hygiene in the care of infants."

"Have you got children of your own, Miss, er?" Katy looked directly at her visitor.

"No, but that is beside the point. I have a great deal of knowledge of the care of children."

"Do you?" Katy said in a quiet, passive voice, quite unlike her usual animated self.

It gave Lionel further disquiet. Katy listened to the lecture with bowed head and silence. When a quiet tear fell unchecked onto her lap, Lionel could stand it no longer. He had listened with interest to the Health Visitor's monologue on water-borne infections and had learnt much.

It was obviously lost on Katy though, whose shame was palpable to him, if not to her austere teacher. He felt it time to call a halt before Katy suffocated under the weight of her guilt. She did not deserve this criticism. The problem had not been her care of Florence but ignorance of the contaminated water, for which they must all carry the burden of blame.

CHAPTER NINETEEN

Jem had the routine of work to fall back upon. He didn't say much but found comfort in the mundane familiarity of the seasonal tasks. He exhausted his young body with physical hard labour and sweated out the beer of the night before, for despite every attempt to reach for Katy, still she kept him at arm's length.

She would go to bed early, pleading fatigue and pretending to be asleep if he tiptoed in and gazed at her closed eyes and shallow breathing. He knew she wasn't asleep. He looked at the dark lashes against their paler shadows. The smoky smudges beneath Katy's dull eyes never lifted, no matter how many early nights she indulged in. He would stand there for ages, longing to touch her but holding back, scared she might reject him again.

The frustration would build in him like an overfull kettle coming to the boil with a lid so tight the steam couldn't escape until he felt he would explode. Then he'd wrench himself away and clatter down the stairs, not caring if he woke her, hoping he woke her, anything to get a response; even anger would be better than those delicate shoulders turned forever away. Why wouldn't she let him comfort her? It wasn't his fault. It wasn't, it wasn't. He'd slam out of the house, banging the front door so hard each night the plaster started to break away above the lintel, and strode the few short yards to the ever-beckoning pub.

"Got yer pint ready, Jem." The landlord, Fred, had it poured out and standing to foaming attention at the bar every night.

Jem nodded as Fred notched it up on the tab that grew longer week by week. Jem made the darkest corner of the pub his own and Fred got into the habit of bringing another pint once his glass was empty. Fellow drinkers slapped him on the back in sympathy, having given up all attempts at conversation.

Chat from the men by the bar floated over Jem. Always it was of the war. Everyone's confidence in the hostilities being over by last Christmas had been eroded by the atrocities and casualty lists but the war still felt surreal to him despite Lord Kitchener wagging his finger from the Post Office door.

"Another poison gas attack on our lads, I see from the paper."

"Wicked stuff that."

"Cowardly too, if you ask me."

"How can you fight it? Must steal over them like a mist. Can't stick a mist with a bayonet."

"Have you heard about this new war committee we've got now?"

"Well, maybe they'll pull it our way."

"Something's got to give, that's for sure."

The politics of the day wove themselves into the back of his brain like a fisherman's net, ready for its catch.

***

Katy took to spending time at the graveside. She took fresh flowers to Florence every day and, when they were not in season, took another little gift to her daughter. Just country trifles she thought she would have liked - pine cones, pebbles, grass dollies and white feathers. She even sang lullabies and read stories to Florence. All the things she would have done had she lived. The villagers gossiped and whispered of grief turned to madness, but Katy never heard them.

Agnes did and was frank with her on one of her regular visits. "You got folks talking about you flitting about little Florence's grave, talking and singing like a madwoman. What are you about, my girl, giving cause for tongues to wag? You wants to think about me and your father, yes and your brothers and sisters too, and what people do think. Let alone that poor husband of yours. You ain't the only one grieving, neither, God help us all."

"But how is life supposed to carry on regardless? Must we go on sleeping and eating and cleaning and talking as if our hearts are not ripped out?" Katy dashed away tears with an angry fist.

"Katy dear, life is callous and it's cruel but don't forget other parents of older, grown children are also bereaved," she added under her breath, "God keep our Albert safe." This had become Agnes' private prayer and she repeated it often every day.

"That don't help one bit. I don't care what the old biddies say," Katy said.

"You might not, young lady, but plenty others do. What does young Jem say about your goings on? Hey?" Agnes meant business, Katy could tell; she knew that look from her childhood days and it always spelled trouble. Katy's pale face showed an unhealthy glow, but she offered no answer.

"Be you sleeping together again yet?" persisted Agnes.

Katy's eyes flew to her mother's in a silent plea.

"Don't you look at me like that. We's both grown women and you've had one babe, so you know what's what, after all. If you miss Florence so much..." Katy winced and squirmed, but Agnes kept on. In softer tones she added, "If you miss her so much, why don't you make another child together? People is also saying as how Jem's down the pub every night drinking away his wages. You won't get a family started over like that. And what you doing for vittles with pennies going down the drain?"

Katy mumbled something about making do.

"Making do ain't good enough, Katy. I'm worried about you both. Neither of you looks well. I swear you've both lost weight. I want to see your cheeks rosy again. Oh well, I can see I'm getting nowhere so I'll get off home." Agnes heaved herself up from the chair crossly, wrapping her shawl around her ample waist as she did so and complaining about the wintry wind whipping through the new gaps above the door.

She took herself off, "Sharpish," she told her husband later, "or I'd have boxed her ears if I'd stayed a minute longer. Such nonsense. Oh, I know it's sad, Bert dear, but life must go on."

***

The village women were not the only ones to witness Katy's graveside vigils. Lionel White could not help but see her as he attended to his church duties. Unlike them, however, he found her continuing grief and devotion immensely touching, seeing in Katy the sensitivity and delicacy he had always suspected, compounded by her bereavement.

At first, he left her alone. He didn't like to disturb this homage to motherhood despite the calling of his cloth. One December day in the bleak time between Christmas and New Year, an ugly sleet had begun to fall and by two o'clock of the short winter afternoon, icy water slashed the sky in sheets. Worried about the church roof, still not mended by Sir Robert's men even though he had pursued his campaign for its repair relentlessly, he braved the freezing torrent. With an umbrella for a shield, he went to investigate.

Lionel ran towards the church from his rectory through the sodden churchyard, gritting his teeth as the puddles splashed up his gaitered legs. His embattled umbrella could only protect his ecclesiastical torso and his earthen feet had to face the elements just like those of any other man. Heroically avoiding the temptation of a thoroughly rounded curse, he pursed his lips and hurried on only to be brought up short by the pathetic sight of a soaked Katy, flung across Florence's tiny grave as if to protect her from the deluge. This would not do. This was not normal.

Lionel resolutely laid his brolly down and, grimacing against the cold shards of water which quickly found their way inside his dog collar, he touched Katy on her shoulder. Raising his voice above the din of the rain, he said, "Mrs Phipps? Mrs Phipps! Come in from the rain. It's going to snow soon, and you are soaked through."

Katy looked up at him, her face white and glistening like alabaster. She shook her head and turned away again to the mound of earth as if the umbilical cord had never been severed.

"Katherine," Lionel forgot his usual punctilious manners. "Katherine, this won't do. You can't help Florence now. The sleet can't hurt her."

"Leave me alone. She's cold and I must protect her."

"Katherine, she can't feel the cold; come, come inside the church and get dry."

"No! No, she needs me."

"No, Katherine, she does not need you anymore but there are those living who do."

Lionel bent his knee into the icy pool on the gravel path and pulled Katy away. She screamed and struggled. Lionel was a powerful man, a man in his prime. It was no contest. He lifted her up and carried her into the church as if she weighed no more than an infant herself. He tried to lay her down on the nearest pew but then Katy became an avenging fury, pummelling her fists against his soaking coat.

Lionel had never seen anything like it. This raw emotion was a foreign land to him. Katy had always represented such a porcelain example of modest womanhood. This raging hysteric mesmerised him and cut through his veneer.

He caught hold of her wrists. He could have snapped them had he chosen.

"Katherine, stop this! Stop it right now."

Katy opened her eyes wide as if seeing him for the first time. She crumpled against him and Lionel found himself in an intimate embrace with a woman so desirable, so emotionally vulnerable, he felt his senses quicken in spite of his vocation.

CHAPTER TWENTY

Lionel could never understand how he managed to get Katy back home that day without giving way to the immense wave of desire that threatened to bring his ordered world tumbling around his ears. It was only with a supreme effort of will, his faith serving as a scaffold for his resolve, that he pushed Katy gently away and sedately walked her home.

He sat Katy at her hearth and gave her a rug to wrap around her. Still her teeth chattered in her white face. She sat silent, staring at his clumsy attempts to make her comfortable and unresponsive to his attentions. Lionel feared for her health and his own lack of skills. The fire had gone out and he tried to re-light it with single-minded concentration but struggled to make it catch. He called out to Sally Fenwick next door who came in with thinly veiled curiosity and offered willing hands with enthusiasm. Lionel felt glad of a chaperone.

Lionel took a deep breath. "Mrs Fenwick, Mrs Phipps is soaked through - could you find some dry clothes and help her to change? I will fetch her mother from Upper Cheadle and be back within the hour."

"Don't ee worry 'bout it, sir. I'll see to the chit," said Sally and shepherded a meek Katy up to her bedroom.

Lionel soon returned with Agnes who'd looked none too pleased to be from home in such filthy weather when pressed to come with him in his gig. Agnes immediately bustled upstairs. Shouts between the two older women confirmed that Agnes had found Sally rummaging gleefully in Katy's bedroom drawers.

Sally came swiftly downstairs and began fussing over the kettle. To Lionel's eyes she seemed to be thoroughly enjoying the situation.

"Thank you, Mrs Fenwick, you've been a tower of strength," Lionel said, grateful that Katy had not been left alone while he fetched her mother, who now came back down into the parlour with a face like thunder.

"Right, I'll manage fine now, Sally. Thanks for your help," was the most gratitude Agnes could apparently muster.

Sally sloped off, muttering, "There's thanks for you. Only trying to help the poor mite."

Agnes banged the back door shut on Sally and turned to Lionel. "She's always been light-fingered, that one. We was in service together and we never got on then. That Sally Fenwick, she's no children to feed being as she was past it when she got married so late in life. She just fritters Tom's money away on tinned food and bought cakes. I have plenty of hungry mouths at home, but I never resort to buying in stuff. I bake a stone of bread every week for my lot. Sally's got no right to come in and take over in my Katy's house."

"Blame me, Mrs Beagle. I couldn't get the fire going and called Mrs Fenwick in to help me. And, you must admit, there's a good blaze now to warm the place up. You know where I am, should you need me further," Lionel said, deciding to ignore Agnes' hostility.

"Thank you, Reverend. I'm obliged to you I'm sure. I'll knock some sense into her, you see if I don't." Agnes stood at the door, arms folded and lips thin.

Lionel beat a hasty retreat, speculating how even gentle looking women could be so damn fierce when they chose and how bewildering the entire species of the female sex could be. His own reaction to the feel of Katy against him was swiftly pushed to the farthest reaches of his mind and summarily dismissed. Only a residual feeling of bafflement lurked in the recesses.

To quell it, he spent a considerable time on his knees before the church altar in intense contemplation of his God.

***

Agnes had to walk home with only her umbrella for comfort. She met up with Jem strolling slowly downhill in the opposite direction despite the cold rain. Jem winced before the staccato questions that Agnes peppered at him.

"I've just come from our Katy, Jem. She got a soaking moping over young Florence's grave. She's looking that thin and look at you! You're just as bad. It's time you both got over young Florence's death."

Jem felt his heart contract as his mother-in-law's bluntness found its mark.

"Don't just stand there, Jem my lad. What do you propose to do about it, hmm?" Agnes' hands were now clenched fists, one on the handle of her brolly, the other on her broad hips.

"I don't know, Agnes, I'm trying my best, but nothing seems to work."

"And how are you doing that when I've heard you're down the pub every night? Katy's got no company of an evening. No wonder she's feeling low. It's got to stop, Jem. Do you hear me? Or Lord knows what's to become of her – and you for that matter!"

Jem knew she was right but that just made him feel angrier. She must have seen it on his face because Agnes softened her gaze and reached out to him.

She patted his hand. "I know how you feel, Jem dear, but Katy needs you now more than ever. She's not going to get over this without you. Go to her now. I've put a pie in the oven. Share it together this time and give her the love she needs."

She gave his arm a squeeze and then a brisk pat on his wet shoulder. "Go! Off with you then and next time I sees you I wants to see a smile on that handsome face of yours!"

Jem stood and watched Agnes climb the steep hill with determined strides. He scratched his damp forehead as if to make his brain work. As Agnes's stout figure got smaller and smaller, so did the anger he'd been carting about like a sack of potatoes for weeks. Jem squared his shoulders and turned for home.

Katy looked flushed that night and, despite her new thinness, very pretty. Having both had their ears burned by Agnes' sharp tongue, they each made an effort and sat to a meal together like old times. Agnes had baked them one of her home-made homity pies knowing it to be a favourite and the melting cheese, onion and potato dish, simple though it was, did much to comfort them.

"I'll be off to the pub," Jem said, before they had even broached it.

"Oh, Jem, must you go?"

Jem grinned at his wife. "Only going so's I can bring a jug back here to share with you, Kate."

The foaming ale relaxed them both.

Katy brought out two baked apples for afters and they poured cream on top extravagantly, each feeling expansive for the first time in months.

"I'll help you wash up, Jem."

Over the dishes in the scullery, Jem told her of his day and this time, she listened.

"You should have seen Dad's face when Mrs Biggs gave him a scolding over the muddiness of the first winter leeks he'd brought to her kitchen. He'd been that proud of them. But you know what she's like about dirt in her spotless domain."

Katy gave a little laugh, a sound Jem thought he'd never hear again. "I remember the time I dropped the dustpan after cleaning the fires. She almost roasted me alive on the kitchen one."

"She's a tartar alright! It's a good job she didn't hear what Dad said about her once he was out of earshot."

When they had finished tidying up together, Jem pulled Katy to the fireside and they both stretched their toes out towards its warmth. They had not done so, side by side like this, since the night of Florence's death when they had stared unseeing into its incongruous, merry dance. The crackle of the fire provided a cosy background to their muted confessions.

"I'm sorry I've been down the pub every night, Kate. You didn't seem to want me, and I didn't know what else to do," began Jem.

"I'm sorry too, Jem. I don't know what come over me. I felt it was my fault she died. If only I'd cared for her better. I should of seen it coming, like."

"How could you? One minute she was alright and the next – well…"

"Oh, Jem. I do miss her so. She was so beautiful. Just like you! And her ways – they were so loving - even though she was full young yet. You could see her nature already – sweet and true."

Jem nodded. The lump in his throat blocked the words he would have said, could he have found them.

He looked across at his wife, looking so slender and delicate now but her cheeks were rosier than he'd seen them in a long while. Maybe it was the fire or – could it be love rekindling again? A solitary tear rolled down the downy peach of her face like a clear raindrop and dropped as had countless others these last weeks, unnoticed, onto her empty lap. More moved than he could ever say out loud, Jem reached for her at last and, on his knees, drew her gently to him and enfolded her like a bear.

Katy melted into his strong arms and sank onto the floor with him. When she lifted up her face to be kissed Jem felt his bruised heart soar to heaven and brought his mouth to hers with infinite tenderness. Handling her as gently as he would her beloved china, he peeled off each layer of clothing with meticulous care. Afraid she might be feeling cold, he banked up the fire and with slow deliberation, feasting his eyes on her vulnerable nudity, took off his own garments and laid them aside. Taking the cushions off the chairs onto the floor for comfort, they

110

stretched out and explored each other's bodies, as if for the first time.

Slowly, Jem stroked his wife. The wonder he felt at returning to this blissful intimacy was - unbelievably - more intense than on his wedding night which, if you'd asked him then, he would have declared impossible. How could that feeling be bettered? He would think about that later. For now, it was as if time had slowed. Each second flowed golden and flickering, the fire the only witness to their reunion.

Katy glowed and glistened. Tiny beads of perspiration pearled her skin. When they fused together Jem revelled in their glorious rhythm, as they rose and fell to the ancient dance of life. All the pent up and repressed emotions of the past months welled up in him and when they had finished, he clasped her tight and they each tasted the other's grateful tears.

Jem covered them in Katy's shawl as a makeshift blanket and they dozed the night away in gentle amazement, waking occasionally to kiss and cuddle again.

It was hard to go to work the next morning in the bleak winter half-light, but Jem could hardly tell his father why he'd like to stay home. They clung together as if the parting was to the distant war, instead of a mile up the road and Katy stood a long time at the window after Jem had disappeared from view with one last wave and shameless blown kisses.

***

All that day Katy felt strange as she went about her chores. She shook her head to free it of the cobwebs and dizziness that troubled her. Smiling, she remembered how little sleep she'd had and why. She hugged the memory to her and sang as she worked. Her flesh had felt alive last night, like a separate entity in its own right and every touch from Jem had been a thrilling shock of present and remembered pleasure. She had never thought she would enjoy anything again. Momentarily she had felt a traitor to Florence and then she remembered how just at that point, Jem had claimed her for his own and her body had drowned in the sensation. The short daylight hours flew by in haze of afterglow and soon it was time for Jem to return. She lit the oil lamp and stood in its halo at the window, willing him to appear around the corner.

Down the hill he came at a smart pace. His eager eyes looked for her and a huge grin spread across his happy face when he saw her waiting.

He marched swiftly on and soon was through the battered door and in her arms. "I'd have run all the way except I could see Martha Threadwell's beaky nose pointing at me!"

He covered her in kisses and whisked her up to their bed.

"Don't you think you should have a wash first, Jem?" Katy said with a smile and a kiss.

"I don't give a damn about washing. This is urgent!" and made love to her with joyous abandon.

Katy laughed, feeling more lightheaded than ever and hugged him to her, loving his warm flesh and the earthy smell of him like a woman starved.

Giggling, they came back downstairs and attacked the beef casserole she had sung into spicy temptation. Jem opened the elderberry wine Agnes had given them for Christmas, but they'd not had the heart to drink.

"To us!" he said, and they chinked their glasses in a toast to the future.

Whilst clearing up in the cold scullery, Katy felt very shivery and dismissed it immediately. The sleet of the previous day had finally squeezed out a snowstorm and, as they wiped the dishes, the white flakes stung the cottage window.

"Let's shut up shop in here and get to the fireside double quick," Jem said, taking her by the hand and tugging her away from the steamed-up lean-to.

She came away readily. "Oh Jem, I'm freezing. I've got goose-pimples all over!"

"Then we must warm you up somehow," he chuckled, feeling safe in her love at last.

However much he banked up the fire, until he was sweating, Katy couldn't get warm. Instead of relaxing and cosying up to him, she started to shiver and complained of a headache.

"Let's have an early night then," Jem said. "It'll be a white world in the morning and with any luck I'll have a day off. Let's sleep now and then we can canoodle all day if we wants."

Katy gave a rather wan smile and willingly succumbed to the feathery mattress, sinking into a deep sleep within seconds. Jem let her rest. Her breath rose and fell in quick, shallow breaths; the hectic flush of her cheeks hidden by the blackness of the winter's night.

CHAPTER TWENTY ONE

The next morning broke as white as Jem had predicted. A blanket of snow shrouded the little village in a deep crystalline hush. Only hungry robins disturbed the pristine silence.

Jem got up and put the kettle on the stove-top.

There was a knock at the door. When Jem opened it, he found young Billy Threadwell from the Post Office standing on his doorstep. "Hello, Billy, you're up early."

"Mum says to tell you that she's had a message from the manor saying there's no work today."

"Righto, Billy. Thanks for letting me know. Are you going to the East Lodge to tell my dad?"

"Yes, Mr Phipps, I'm off there directly."

"You take care on the ice then, Billy. Here, have a bit of bread and jam to eat on the way."

"Thanks!"

Jem watched Billy speed off across the icy pavement. At the corner he managed a long skid without dropping his snack. Jem laughed enviously and shut the front door.

He was glad not to be working in the gardens today, not because they were going to spend the day in bed cuddling up together as he'd sincerely hoped but because Katy lay in it, restless with fever.

His heart, so recently brimming over with joy, had lowered again when he'd woken that morning and felt her overheated body radiating towards his despite the arctic conditions outside.

The snow lit up the morning with a bright, harsh sun, illuminating dark corners with an unforgiving torch. Katy's crazy devotion to her dead daughter had chilled her to the bone. Lying all night on the flagstone floor, with or without Jem's arms around her, had not been the best way to overcome it.

The snow lay too deep for help to come from Upper Cheadle and Jem decided not to get Mrs Threadwell to send a message via the post office telephone and worry Katy's mother. It was hardly surprising if Katy had a bit of a cold after her soaking.

He stoked up the fire and went to the garden to sort the hens out. When they peeked out from the hen house, the chickens were outraged at the obliteration of their grassy run and fluffed their feathers out in protest. Jem laughed as he cast corn for them and cut some winter cabbage to throw to them. Giving them greens made all the difference to the flavour of the eggs and brought out the yellow of the yolks. He brought the heart of the cabbage back down to the cottage for dinner, relishing the prospect of a day spent in the enjoyment of his own backyard and with the added deliciousness of it being one stolen from the workaday routine.

The winter sun poured in through the cottage front window. Jem stood there while the kettle came to the boil, smiling at the children, school day cancelled, throwing snowballs at each other. There was no doubt about it – snow and sunshine were a beautiful combination. With a lighter heart and step he took a cup of steaming hot tea and a slab of toast, smothered in jam and butter, up to Katy.

Jem was a little dismayed to find her still shivering despite the covers piled up on the bed. He put the tea and toast down beside her and felt her forehead.

"Katy dearest, I could have boiled the kettle on your head, you're that hot. Ain't you well?"

Katy shook her head and tried to sit up.

Jem gave her a helping heave. "Look, love. I've brought your breakfast up as a treat."

Katy smiled wanly. Jem hopped back in beside her, aware that he smelled of frost and fresh air in contrast to the stuffy room.

"You've gone and got yourself a nasty chill, getting soaked the other day. But look out of the window at the snow, Katy. It's so beautiful."

He drew the curtains and smiled once more at the snowball fight below them. The children now monopolised the High Street, confident no wagons or horses could stop the fun today. Jem felt tempted to join them and turned back to Katy, grinning.

"Come on, Katy, drink your tea."

He felt frustrated at her lack of enthusiasm. A day off was a rare treat and the snow a seasonal and free excitement. It didn't seem five minutes since they used to sledge together as tiddlers themselves.

Katy had a brief look out of the window and shuddered with the cold. "All I can see is ice creeping up the windowpanes."

She crept back down under the covers like a tortoise into its shell. "Oh, Jem, my head is banging like a drum. I just can't get warm even with this scalding cup of tea."

Jem said, "I suppose you'd better stay in bed then?" rather wistfully.

Days off weren't much fun without a playmate. Lord alone knew Katy hadn't been one of those for many a long month and he, collecting himself, remembered why.

More tenderly he added, "I'll light the little fire in here and then I'll go and get the chores seen to. I'll come back and see how you're doing after that, alright?"

Katy nodded, "Yes, Jem, I could do with some peace and quiet, if it's all the same to you."

He lit the bedroom fire and stacked up some precious coal in it before leaving her. When Jem came back, she was sleeping and regretfully he left her to it, feeling lost in his own small domestic world and altogether too big for the tiny cottage. Pulling on his overcoat, he went out and was disappointed to see the children had gone off to fresh hunting grounds.

116

He crunched through the snow, surprised and delighted at its depth. Wandering at will, he found himself drawn to the churchyard even as Katy had two days before. Jem stared down at his daughter's grave. His disbelief that this enormous thing had happened to them had never really gone away. Florence's sunny little face burned into his memory and he was unusually glad when he saw the young Reverend coming his way.

"Good morning!" Lionel greeted him with just enough superiority to irritate Jem. "Rather a chilly one."

"I like a bit of snow myself." Jem stood squarely before Florence's little cross. "Sunshine's nice, too."

"Yes, indeed it is, indeed it is. And, um, how is your wife, Mr Phipps?" asked Reverend White, all solicitude.

"Think she caught a bit of chill. She's staying in bed, with it so cold and that."

"Best place to be in the circumstances, wouldn't you say? Quite, quite."

Pompous ass, thought Jem. Rather unnecessarily he added, "I'll look after her. I got the day off, see? Soon have her back on her feet and mended."

"I'm sure you will, Jem, I'm sure you will. Give her my regards, will you?" Lionel looked very concerned and gave a little shiver. "Well, must be off on my rounds you know. Never a dull moment."

And with an unconvincing cheery wave he took himself off, looking full of busy purpose and determination.

"Dull's the word," Jem said to the departing clerical back. "Well, no use crying over spilt milk, Florence, my love. I wish you was here with us still and no mistake, but I can't put the clock back, no matter how hard I try, so I'd better get back and check on your mother. We wouldn't want the Reverend worriting about her, now would we?"

Jem turned sharply about and headed back for home across the icy street. Not so quiet now, as villagers came out to exclaim at the deep fall of snow and clatter into the shop for a satisfactory gossip about it.

Katy didn't improve during the snowbound day and by the time the short daylight hours had plummeted into velvet blackness, Jem was really worried. Donning his coat once more, he sought out Mrs Threadwell at the Post Office and got her to telephone the doctor and hang the expense.

Dr Benson came on his old mare, complaining that his new beloved car was useless in the wintry conditions.

Climbing the stairs, he said to Jem, "Sorry to be returning to your home again so soon after you lost the baby, Jem."

He felt Katy's hot forehead and gave her a quick inspection.

The two men clomped back down the wooden stairs and Dr Benson said, "Katy's got a high fever and I am concerned about her. You'll need some help."

His intelligent face showed grave alarm under his shock of white hair. He gave Jem instructions on how to nurse her and promised to get Mrs Armstrong, the midwife, to come over in the morning.

"She lives in Lower Cheadle and can easily walk here through the snow. She'll be a safe pair of hands to get you through this, Jem."

And he patted Jem on the back before mounting his horse who padded silently away on the white blanket of snow.

A long drawn out winter's night Jem had of it. Katy tossed and turned and cried out for Florence pitifully. More accustomed to gardening than to nursing, Jem felt clumsy and powerless as he sponged her down and tried, unsuccessfully, to ease her discomfort.

Eventually the dawn shone pink and pretty as if to mock his anxiety but never had he been more desperate to see it. He stared out of the window watching the tiny glow begin on the horizon, spread out over the rooftops and inexorably, wonderfully, filter out across the sky; banishing night for a few short hours.

Jem was haggard and grey when Mrs Armstrong rapped on his battered front door and he almost kissed her worn old face when she stepped over the threshold.

"Lead me to her, young man, and let's get on with it."

A fresh lease of life flooded into Jem's veins at the sight of the tough old bird and relief lifted his lonely spirits.

Mrs Armstrong shook her head as she felt Katy's hot body but nodded approval at the evidence of sponging her down.

"We must try and control the fever, lad. You done right well to sponge her down. Change the water and add a little of this lavender water to it to soothe the poor lamb. Here's a packet of herb tea. I want you to make a big pot of it, and bring a spoon up too, and we'll try and break this fever. If she sweats, she'll live. 'Tis pneumonia, I fear. Did Dr Benson say as much?"

Jem shook his head. Fear stopped his tongue. His heart hammered in his chest. "Not Katy, too," he thought, and sat down abruptly on the one rickety bedroom chair.

"Now don't take on so, young Jem. Katy's young and has everything to live for. We need to get her through the crisis and these herbs will ease her pain and help her to sweat, see? There's yarrow, meadowsweet and boneset in that mixture and they'll do the trick, you see if they won't."

Still dumb, Jem nodded and went to his tasks. Gently, they spooned the warm tea into Katy and kept sponging her down. The doctor called again, and he and Mrs Armstrong closeted themselves together downstairs. Jem strained his ears to listen while he kept watch at Katy's bedside, but he couldn't make out the meaning of their low, urgent whispers.

Dr Benson slipped out to the Post Office to send a telephone message to the manor asking Agnes to come down once more from Upper Cheadle.

On his return he told Emily Armstrong, "I wish this little family wasn't such a frequent target. Agnes's flock has always been such a healthy bunch. Two blows in such swift succession strikes me as unfair but young Katy never got over her baby dying, that's the trouble."

Bert brought his wife down in the gig but had to go straight back to work at the manor.

Agnes and Emily left Jem with little to do but bring in firewood and coal and fetch water. The ground was too frozen to dig so he set about making the log store he'd been meaning to get around to for a while. As ever, the physical outlet was a blessing for his frayed nerves.

As he savagely sawed the lengths of wood and hammered in the nails he wondered if their bad luck would never end, knowing all the while Katy was fighting for her life upstairs.

Emily and Agnes took turns to nurse her and dozed between. They told Jem another long night lay ahead, and its outcome would decide Katy's fate.

Jem took another chair up to the bedroom before nightfall, hardly daring to look at his wife. It seemed a bare five minutes before when these two ladies had cared for her during her birthing pains, smiling the while. Now they were stony faced and determined and he took his hat off to their skill and dedication. The three of them took turns in the long vigil, two in the room and one downstairs resting by the range.

In the dark deep of the night Katy stopped tossing and turning and lay still, scarily still, and eerily pale.

Then, just before dawn, her breathing changed. Agnes was on watch. Sensitive to any slight alteration in her child, she leapt up from her chair, her fatigue forgotten. The noise woke Emily and they stood over their patient together.

Emily laid the back of her hand onto Katy's forehead and felt the glimmerings of perspiration on her white skin.

Triumphantly, she grabbed Agnes across the bed and smiled. "She'll do, Agnes, she'll do!"

Grateful tears pricked Agnes's eyes and she sank back on to the chair clutching her blanket to her.

"Thank the Lord," whispered Agnes and whisked downstairs to tell Jem, who was taking his turn by the range. Befuddled with lack of sleep, he hugged his mother-in-law to him in a thankful crush.

Jem went to go upstairs but Agnes held him back. "No, Jem, I know you long to see her, but she must sleep now the fever's broke. It'll take a might of getting over this, mind. A slow old job, right enough."

"I don't care for that. As long as she'll live!" cried Jem, unashamed of his manly tears.

Agnes hugged him back and kissed his forehead as if he were her own son.

Her red-rimmed eyes looked full of love. "Ay, lad. She'll live."

CHAPTER TWENTY TWO

Katy recovered at a snail's pace. Jem found her frail and listless condition more of a trial than her previous withdrawn grief. She clung to him now when he had to go to work and looked bereft when he took his leave. Married life was proving challenging in ways he could never have foreseen. He was beginning to suspect it was over-rated.

He didn't return to visiting the pub every night but just went on a Friday evening, along with the few working men still left in the village.

"Evening, Jem." Fred poured his pint as soon as he came through the door.

"How do." Jem rubbed his hands together for warmth. "That wind is bitter out there. I think I'll sit by the fire tonight."

"It's a tough old winter alright. Reckon we'll have another dose of snow even though it's nearly February." Fred gave him his change.

"Over here, Jem!" His neighbour, Tom Fenwick, whose glass was already half empty, sat hogging the fireside.

Jem sat down on the settle next to Tom within the warm embrace of the inglenook fireplace. He took a glug of beer and wiped the froth with the back of his hand.

"That's better."

"That's it, lad, get it down you, while you can!" Tom shook his bald head.

"What do you mean, Tom?"

"Ain't you heard? There's a new Military Service Act coming into force. They's going to start conscripting men."

"Conscripting?"

"Yes, you know, making 'em join up whether they likes it or no. Still, you're married, so you'll be alright."

"It's only for single men?" Jem frowned before taking another sip.

"That's what I heard. Luckily for me, I'm past it. It's many a long year since I was forty-one!" Tom finished his glass in one gulp and belched. He set it down pointedly in front of Jem who took the hint and went to bar to refresh Tom's glass.

"Do you know about this conscription thing, Fred?"

"No need to for you to worry yet, young Jem. You're exempt because of Katy. Want another half in yours?"

"Yes, um, yes please." Jem held his tankard out, deep in thought.

After that Jem took to reading the paper every day and followed events in France with an obsessive curiosity.

Another poster went up in the Post Office. "What did YOU do in the Great War, Daddy?" The little girl asked accusingly, as she sat on her father's knee. If Florence had lived, would she now be asking *him* that question?

Katy gradually grew stronger but remained a wraith compared to her former curvaceous self. He'd never found thin women that attractive. She kept making tentative advances for his affection in an unconscious imitation of his own one-sided desires before her illness, but he found himself uninterested. He still loved her – he always would – but she looked like a fragile doll who would snap in two if he squeezed her tight and if they made another child – what the hell would happen then?

He kept making excuses and held her at arm's length. He felt imprisoned in this domestic life that had promised so much and for which he had waited so long. His heart felt torn in two. For the first time in his life he felt the need to break free – to be with other men – to see a bit of the world.

A decision began to curl around his mind like a coiled snake.

***

Katy also steered clear of sexual intimacy. She just wanted to rest her weary bones, be enfolded in Jem's strong ones now and then and watch the tender shoots of spring slowly emerge from the frozen ground. She spent hours staring out of the window at their back garden watching her neighbours coax the rich Wiltshire soil back to life, hearing the birds trumpet spring and willing the primroses into flower. And yet she longed for Jem's embrace. When it didn't come, she felt too feeble to pursue it and, after a while, gave up the unequal struggle.

Spring broke through at last in March and brought Katy's health with it. One bright morning, as the first fingers of warm sun lifted the breeze, she made her first return to Florence's graveside. As she placed daffodils on the little mound, she said goodbye to her tiny daughter and turned her face to her future – to the possibility of other children - and returned to Jem with a lighter, freer heart.

She tried to tell him how she felt; that it was all behind her, and reached for him, as he dug the ground for potatoes.

"Jem?"

"Hmm?"

"I've been to say goodbye to dear Florence, Jem. I want to put it behind me. Begin again. After all, we have the rest of our lives to live together, haven't we?"

She let her eyes dwell on the muscles in his arms, marvelling how they bulged with the effort of lifting the heavy soil. She was disappointed that Jem kept his eyes firmly on his trench.

"That's good then," was all he said.

She lingered for more. None came. Folding it into her, she held his rejection within her like her dead child. Dutifully she went inside and set about making their lunch, looking up through the scullery window now and then at Jem. She gazed at his strong back as he worked away with his spade as if it could explain his new coldness to her.

Her intuition was not wrong. She could see Jem was thinking hard as he dug. She felt she must credit him with feeling grief for Florence too but knew men wouldn't let their emotions show. She shook her head and threw the black thoughts away. By the time Jem came in for his Sunday dinner with a set look on his face, she was humming contentedly as she served the hot soup and cut the new baked bread. Just to return to being useful was a balm, and she'd enjoyed her morning's baking with Jem's distant companionship in the garden. She was determined to start afresh and hold no grudges.

Tonight, she meant to hold him in her arms and embrace whatever the future might send them. They had got through this last ghastly winter, hadn't they? Things had got to start looking up. She had not forgotten that wonderful night in front of the fire – before her illness. She plotted as she ate.

When Jem cut through her racy reverie, Katy was startled. She had become used to silent meals and quiet platonic companionship. It was as if they had been living parallel lives, together in the house but apart in essence.

Her eyes flew to his face, as he began, "Katy, my dear."

"Yes, Jem, love?"

Jem laid down his spoon, her lovely vegetable soup half drunk and his fragrant bread untouched. He met her gaze steadily. She remembered how Jem never flinched from anything once he had made up his mind to do it. He cleared his throat as if it had suddenly become constricted.

The look on his set face made her heart skip a beat, as he continued, "Katy, I've been thinking."

"Yes, Jem?" Katy laid her own spoon down and smiled at him sweetly, hopefully.

"Well, see, it don't seem right to me that I'm stuck here, safe as houses, when there's others fighting for their country in France. Adam Fairweather has gone off and young Fred Malloy too, as well as your Albert. They're all younger than me but they've enlisted. I'm thinking to do the same. Do my bit, you know."

"No! Oh, Jem, no. Please don't! Adam and John aren't married. And Albert hasn't the sense he was born with. Besides they've no-one to leave behind. Oh, please, please, don't do this, Jem." The new healthy blush on her thin face drained completely away, leaving two huge eyes dilated in fear.

Jem's chin lifted in determination. He looked quite decided.

"It's no use Katy, my love." The longed-for tenderness softened his voice, if not his message. "I've made up my mind. I'll be conscripted soon anyway so I might as well bite the bullet."

Katy burst into tears. His flippant talk of bullets crystallised her fears. Jem got up and put his arm round her and this time he did not retreat as she clung to him.

After a while he lifted her head and looked into her swimming eyes. "I can't stand it, see. The way it's been. Florence gone and you ill. I'm afraid to touch you, Katy, for fear what might happen. Seems every time we've lain together something awful's happened. I need to get away and think it all through. Do something different 'til my head's straight. Tell me you understand."

Katy became very still. She wiped her eyes on her dress sleeves and looked at her husband clearly for the first time in a long while. Her breathing was still ragged, and she took a deep draught of air, as if she was drowning. Slowly she nodded and released him.

Katy had not expected this. She felt his decision like a blow in the pit of her stomach. She felt as if he had beaten her into submission with his hands rather than his words. Sitting back at the table she tried to fill the hollow in her stomach with more food. Delicious though it was, it tasted like dust.

"When will you go?"

"Soon as I can. I'll go to the barracks in town next Saturday and sign up. Like I said, if I don't do it soon, I'll get conscripted anyway – or worse - a white feather from the likes of Mrs Hoskins and her lot. They'll be lifting the ban on conscripting married men shortly, I reckon. As soon as I get my papers sorted out, I'll tell Dad - this week hopefully. I think I'll get through the medical inspection alright." Jem glanced at her and added quickly, "I'll make sure you don't go short, Katy."

Katy gave up the pretence of eating then.

***

The following week shrank in a flurry of activity. Jem went off to the barracks and filled in countless forms which the acting officer called his attestation process.

"Right, go into that next room, please, and the doctor will see you in there." The officer pointed to the door.

Jem was shocked when the army doctor told him to strip down to his underpants and stand in line. It was his first lesson in leaving his dignity at the door.

"Good height and weight." The doctor's stethoscope felt like ice against Jem's goose-pimples. Jem was reminded of the cattle markets he'd attended. He wondered if he might moo like a cow but doubted the army would appreciate the joke.

The doctor peered into his eyes and ears. "Yes, you'll do. Put your clothes back on and go back into the recruitment room."

Jem hurried his clothes on, went back to the desk and handed the paper he'd received from the doctor. The officer in charge didn't even look up as he stamped the document. A sheaf of others was produced and slapped down in front of him, next to a fountain pen in an inkwell. Jem worked out that meant he'd enlisted and scribbled his name at the foot of each paper without bothering to read them.

He was given the King's shilling and told to report back tomorrow for his departure details.

As it took him nearly two hours to walk the five miles home, Jem had plenty of time to think about signing his life away for the duration of the war. He went into the manor gardens on his way back and broke the news to his father.

"You've done what?" George dropped his trowel with a clatter on to the greenhouse floor.

"Dad, would you rather I had a white feather?" Jem picked up the trowel and handed it back to his father.

"I don't think I'd better answer that, Jem. I suppose you've no choice, but your mother will be very upset."

"I can't help that, Dad. They're conscripting single men at the moment but I've a feeling married men won't be long for the chop either."

"Come and see your mother before you go. Do you know when you'll be off?" George scraped mud off his trowel with furious concentration.

"No, I've got to go back to the barracks tomorrow. Bloody long walk each time."

"I'll ask Bert to run you there in the gig."

"Don't trouble him, Dad," Jem said, hating the fuss.

"He usually goes in on a Thursday anyway, Jem. You can catch a lift. Now mind you pop in this evening. Come to supper. Katy's welcome too, of course."

Supper at his parents was an ordeal Jem could have done without. Neither Katy nor Mary spoke much, and it was left to Jem and his father to cut the tension. He was glad of his younger brothers and sisters piping away with their usual banter to cover the silences.

"Well, we'll be off now, Mum," Jem said. He ruffled his siblings' hair as he passed each one at the table and shook his father's hand.

"Take care, lad. Write to us, won't you?" George's voice had gone unusually gruff.

"I'm not going yet, Dad!" Jem felt really irritated with all this sentiment.

"I'll see you to the door, Jem." His mother, Mary, clutched at his sleeve, pointedly ignoring Katy who stood outside waiting patiently for him regardless of the soft drizzle that had set in. Mary hugged him tight for a long while before releasing him with a kiss to his forehead and a muttered goodbye.

Katy held his hand tightly as they walked the short distance home. She didn't let go all night.

His usual routine was broken the next day by Bert driving him into town. He went into the barracks again feeling a lot less excited this time.

"Mr Phipps?" The recruitment officer still didn't look up from Jem's identity papers.

"Yes."

"Yes, *sir*!" said the officer, his solemn brown eyes finally connecting with Jem's.

"Yes, sir," Jem replied.

"Obedience is the first principle of war, young man."

"Yes, sir."

"Departure on Saturday. 1400 train to Aldershot. Make sure you catch it."

"Yes, sir. Do you mean *this* Saturday, the day after tomorrow?"

"I certainly do. You can collect your uniform now. Dismissed."

***

Before either of them could take it all in, Jem was standing in their cottage, grinning sheepishly in his regimental gear.

Katy looked at the stranger standing in front of her, all dressed in khaki and said, her voice barely a whisper, "I hardly know you, Jem. You look so different in your cap and uniform."

Jem laughed. It sounded forced and unnatural. Katy looked at him, but Jem wouldn't meet her eyes. "Come on, or we'll be late for the train. The omnibus will be here any minute! Are you sure you want to come with me to the station, Katy? I don't mind going on my own."

Lose another second of looking at his dear face? Katy said quickly, "No Jem, I'll come with you. I'll stay with you until the end. I'll wave you off."

"Right then." Jem looked every inch the soldier. He picked up his haversack and stood to attention. "Wagons roll!"

Katy went to him then and stood on tiptoe to straighten his cap. She kissed him on the lips, lingering as long as she dared, feeling how closely he had shaved his face that day. It was as smooth as on their wedding day. She let her hands drop down on to the new rough cloth of his green jacket, tucked her fingers under the beige webbing, longing to restrain him and hang on to its tough ribbed bands, to make him stay. Jem fidgeted and shuffled his feet. He cleared his throat. Katy took the hint, dropped her hands after one last squeeze of his friendly chest; remembering it naked. She knew every inch, every freckle, every hair.

"Better go, Kate." Jem's voice was softer now, more gentle than it had been for weeks.

Kate's throat constricted. She could not answer but nodded and turned for the door.

They were silent on the omnibus. Jem looked out of the window as if memorising his beloved countryside. Katy was content to study his face, no less loved.

She stood with the other wives at the station in the local town. They looked as numb as she felt as they waved in unison to the departing train. Katy was the last to leave, long after the train was a distant speck on the horizon and its steam had evaporated into the spring sunshine.

Last night she had reached for Jem in their marital bed, wanting the intimate reassurance of making love but still he had held off as if he didn't trust himself to get any nearer. Jem had said, when she pressed him for the reason, "See, Katy, if you got pregnant again, I, well, I might not be here to provide for you. I couldn't leave for war if there was another child on the way."

He'd kissed her tenderly, his eyes brim-full with unshed tears, but then he had turned over and seemed to go to sleep. Katy had feigned sleep often enough to know he was faking it.

And now, on this morning of his departure, he'd looked like he couldn't wait to get away. His eyes had shone with excitement. Katy could see that a sense of adventure had tempted him at last. Yes, this dreadful war had called out to her steady Jem whom she had called a stick-in-the-mud so many times before they were married. Now he'd gone, looking ready to leap forward into unknown territory – to test himself as a man - while she still stayed at home.

Once or twice he'd tried to explain his leaving of her, saying that only when he could return to her with a clean slate and a clear conscience, could he start again. "I have to believe you understand, Katy, or I'll never be able to place my boot on that train step and climb in."

She'd had no answer to that.

CHAPTER TWENTY THREE

Army life afforded a welcome change for Jem. He didn't even mind the square-bashing, boring and pointless though it was. His gardening work and long walks to and fro between the Cheadle villages had kept him fit and strong. He found the break from beer refreshing too and mornings, though as early as ever, had a new, welcome clarity. And it was good to be somewhere different and on neutral territory; one that was exclusively male. He even welcomed the routine though he suspected he was alone in that.

Davey Pringle, in the next bed, turned out to be a right wag, constantly imitating the Sergeant Major's frequent harangues at their civilian sloppiness.

"Look lively, lads," he would mimic in their rare moments off. "No slacking – pull on that cigarette for all you're worth – the outcome of the whole bloody war depends on you."

The grub was regular, if monotonous, and the uniform scratchy but getting into the bed in his dormitory every night, blissfully free of female resentment and moody withdrawals, was a relief. And no-one cried. Instead it was rough banter with plenty of swearing and bragging. Jem relaxed for the first time in ages.

"Alright, mate?" asked Davey, one evening. "Want a fag?"

Jem took one, enjoying the novelty of the fragrant smoke curling up to the wooden hut ceiling.

"Heard from yer missus yet?" Davey was unmarried but had hopes of his Edith after the war.

"Yes, got a letter today. Says she's alright. Not much happening at home. She's planted me leeks up though I suppose I shan't be home in time to see 'em." Jem coughed a little at the unfamiliar tar from his cigarette.

"Nah, we'll be giving Gerry what for by then. Show the bastards what we're made of, instead of this ruddy trundling up and down the parade ground."

Jem watched, fascinated, as Davey blew his smoke through his nostrils without opening his mouth.

"Dunno what it's supposed to achieve," nodded Jem. "Seems pointless to me."

Davey took another drag on his cigarette. "It's discipline, ain't it? When we're up against it in the trenches it'll all pay off, least that's what I overheard young Captain Harry Mountford saying in the mess at lunchtime."

"He's scarcely out of nappies that one, what's he know?" Jem said, experimenting with tapping the ash from the end of his cigarette.

Davey laughed. "Aye, true enough, but he's a savvy lad just the same."

"You reckon?"

"Mark my words, Jem, you wait and see if I ain't right about him."

They blew smoke clouds towards the ceiling. Jem almost managed a smoke ring.

He even smiled during his medical examination when the distracted doctor muttered incoherently all through it.

"Hmm, fine specimen. Good height. Chest clear. Scales over there. Silly business, war. Mouth open – wider – now. Excellent teeth. Total waste. Never liked Germans anyway. Say 'aaah'. Say ninety-nine. Passed – next!"

Jem did miss his garden and fresh vegetables even more. The soup the British Army served up wasn't a patch on Katy's fragrant offerings. She'd become a really good cook since they had wed. Katy had the ability to turn her quick mind to most things even mechanical things like the range, he reflected, lying on his bunk in the quiet time before sleep, trying to ignore the grunts and snores of the other men. She was never far from his thoughts, but the geographical distance lent some much-needed perspective.

Jem made new friends too. The new recruits in his hut bonded together in a camaraderie that formed incredibly quickly despite the wide variety of men billeted in it. There were farmhands next to men who drove in chauffeured limousines and lunched at the Savoy; miners next to bank clerks; photographers who were all for progress sleeping next to pig farmers who'd never left home. Davey Pringle, his talkative neighbour, was proud to inform anyone prepared to listen that he was a true cockney having been born within sound of the Bow Bells of London.

Their next in command was Lance Corporal Tom Anderson. Tom was tall, with a long face and a high, intellectual brow. He spoke little but smiled a lot whenever he was with the other men. Most of the time when he was off duty he could be found lounging on his bed, deeply engrossed in reading a book or scratching poems in his tatty notebook. His fingers were always stained with ink and the pencil he kept for emergencies was chewed right down to the lead at the end. He struggled to shout at them, as demanded by their sergeant, but his benign and gentle attitude and sense of fair play invited respect. The men would shuffle into line for him with good humour and a willingness that the sergeant never managed.

They all acknowledged they were fortunate in their senior officer too. Captain Harry Mountford had a grin as wide as his cap and withstood the ribbing about his young age with remarkable good humour, not that they had much to do with him.

In fact, his own senior officers frowned at the familiarity he allowed in the troops below him but as Jem overheard one Major say to another on their passing out parade, "Got to take little boys as officers these days, because we're running out of more mature men."

His colleague had replied grimly, "And I wonder how long this lot will last."

Jem had the coveted corner bed in the narrow dormitory with a fine view of yet another Nissen hut to gaze on at his leisure. They were housed in one of the thousands of similar huts spread out across the heath-land of southern England. The beds were hard and narrow, and Jem struggled to sleep in them. Farts and belches from the other men didn't help. Quite of few of them snored too. He'd not reckoned on missing privacy so much and the novelty of entirely male company soon wore off.

The local countryside was markedly different here underpinned by a sandy soil and covered in heather and gorse. When he got the chance, which wasn't very often, Jem walked amongst the pretty hills and enjoyed watching the spring unfold somewhere new. He marvelled at the silver birches with their delicate white trunks and slender branches that tickled him when he brushed past them. He soon learned that the sharp thorns of the ever-flowering gorse would provide quite the opposite sensation, but he loved its lemon-yellow florets and its odd exotic coconut aroma, reminding him of the coconut shy when the fair visited Woodbury. It was all such an interesting contrast to the tall elms and sturdy oaks of his native county. After one alarming encounter with an adder, he realised they were fond of this habitat too and stood to lean against a tree for a rest rather than seating himself on the ground, however sunny and warm the day might be.

Davey never joined him on these rare forays into the local flora and fauna.

"You must be bloody joking!" was his response the first time Jem asked him to venture out beyond the confines of the parade ground. "What do you want to wander about the heath for? It'll be full of flies and spiders and worse I dare say. No, mate, you can count me out on that one. I got me packet of Woodbines and the newspaper and I'm going to put me feet up and give 'em a well-earned rest - not more leather-bashing."

Jem laughed at his friend and went on alone. These solitary walks did much to soften his grief for Florence though he suffered pangs of guilt at leaving Katy to cope with hers alone. He knew in his heart of hearts that he could no more have helped her by staying than he could have helped himself. He came to the conclusion that he'd been right to leave, to test his courage in the world of men; right to find out if he could withstand the privations and challenges that lay ahead.

Jem was also curious about the other men. In Davey, he found a willing raconteur, always eager to describe the slums he'd left behind. Davey had signed up the minute he was eighteen. No need for him to suffer pangs of guilt in leaving his home behind, he told Jem.

"Bloody glad to leave home, mate. My old man - when we did see him which weren't often - all he'd give you was a clout. I couldn't stand it when he'd take the back of his hand to me Mum. What she puts up with, you wouldn't credit."

"Have you got brothers and sisters, Davey?"

"Have I got...? Where have you been all your life? The one thing my dad knows how to do is to make babies, no – tell a lie - the other is how to drink beer. What he can't seem to do, is look after 'em. Mum takes in washing and does charring – you should see her hands. I worked in Covent Garden – with the veg you know – selling spuds and carrots and suchlike but the wages were rubbish. I can send her more now I'm in the army. She was well pleased to see me join up, I can tell you."

Oh, Davey could tell a yarn alright but how he struggled to obey orders. For a start, he didn't know his left side from his right which was something of a disadvantage on the parade ground. Their sergeant despaired of Davey keeping in line and he was often in detention.

"How am I supposed to know which way he means?" he grumbled to Jem one evening over their grey supper.

"Think of it this way." Jem spooned some gloopy stew into his mouth and tried not to shudder. "Which hand do you write with?"

Davey's pinched young face showed a tint of unlovely pink. He stared at his congealing food and muttered, "Can't write, can I?"

Jem thought for a minute. He wasn't too brilliant at writing himself and sympathised. "Ah, I see, but you smoke, don't you?"

"Suppose I do?" Davey said into his dinner.

"Well then, do you always use the same hand? Let me see your hands, Davey." Jem held out his own open palms.

Davey spread out his calloused fists. The fingernails were rimed with dirt, their black edges frayed.

"There – look at that index finger – brown as a tea leaf. You must always use that hand to hold your cigarette, see? Now, when the Sergeant says right turn – just picture having a fag, and Bob's your uncle – you'll know which is which!"

Davey grinned, displaying equally yellow and crooked teeth. "You are a right good geezer, Jem! That is nothing but a stroke of genius."

Davey marched in a straighter line after that but still insisted on questioning orders and never could quite get up quickly enough of a morning to avoid being late. Or shine his boots enough to satisfy the sharp eyes of their sergeant. He passed muster in the end though, and, after what seemed a very short month, Jem and Davey received their orders for their departure to France.

CHAPTER TWENTY FOUR

Jem's absence didn't fully hit Katy until she came home from the crowded train station, shut her front door behind her and found the range unlit. She sat before its cold, empty grate for a long time, contemplating the hours and minutes ahead, unpunctuated by Jem's smile.

Saturday afternoon was usually the highlight of the week. Jem would finish work early and they'd fallen into a companionable routine that made the most of it. Without Jem getting up on a work-day morning she couldn't see how she would get out of bed, let alone get through the long days stretching before her.

And yet pass they did, in a seamless, endless monotony of dreary chores. Katy fumed that it was home-loving Jem that was having the adventure now. Adventure he had never sought or looked for. *She* was the restless one. *She* had longed for travel all her life and here she was stuck at home while the careless March sun shone on ruthlessly, displaying its usual cheerful displays of colour and scent with no respect for her loneliness.

Katy found solace in her beloved books. She re-read all her favourite volumes and, casting about hungry for more, remembered the novel Reverend White had lent her and lost herself within its elegant pages. The curate – now promoted to vicar (though everyone had always called him that anyway) – had never neglected Katy after her illness and had called regularly to enquire after the patient. His visits were the one bright light in an otherwise dull existence of waiting for news from the Front. The futility of keeping her little house clean and herself fed and watered crushed Katy's spirit.

When Lionel White called, one perfect April morning, the cheery daffodils dancing in the warm breeze outside mocked her heavy heart as she opened the door. She noticed the Reverend clamped his hands to his clerical sides. Didn't he didn't trust his hands to be let free when he stepped out of the blinding sunshine into the darker confines of her house?

"Good morning, Mrs Phipps. I trust I find you well? Ah! Reading again I see? What have we here this time? Hmm, 'Wives and Daughters' by Mrs Gaskell! Now that's a book you can get your teeth into."

Katy smiled her agreement and offered tea. She had taken to baking cakes again in anticipation of his regular visits and took pleasure in bringing forth a particularly good ginger cake and slicing it before him into dainty, spicy fingers.

"Congratulations on being promoted to vicar, by the way, Reverend." Katy handed him the plate.

"Thank you, Mrs Phipps. News travels fast around here! Though I'm not convinced the other villagers understand the distinction. They've always addressed me as 'vicar' since I arrived in Cheadle." But he looked very pleased at the compliment all the same.

They talked of books they had both read and in turn of travel, necessarily one-sided as Katy, for all her yearnings, had never left her native Wiltshire. She was glad when the vicar settled himself more comfortably and embarked on a vivid description of India.

"The thing I remember most about India is the colours. Oh, I know we have splendid gardens – yours is looking particularly lovely with that forsythia in bloom by the front door but you should see the *size* of the flowers there, Mrs Phipps. The climate lends itself to growing the most exotic species. Fruits, too, are outsized and very delicious."

Katy listened rapt.

"The Indians are particularly fond of tea, you know. Partly due to our colonial influence, I like to think. They are very good at making it and you can buy it on street corners everywhere. I was especially fond of their sweet mint tea. Its fragrance was often welcome – the slum areas, you know, are less than salubrious." Lionel sipped his brew.

"Did you travel much in the country? Were you always in towns or did you see the countryside too?" asked Katy, drinking in every exotic word.

"Ah, now then, my favourite places were the tea plantations. You've never seen green until you have gazed upon those lush hills. You never know, Mrs Phipps – this beverage you have made might even have come from there!" Lionel placed his empty cup back on its saucer.

"And what do they eat in India, Reverend?"

"Everything is curried. The scent of spice is everywhere, carried on the breeze and..." Reverend White's aromatic reminiscences were rudely curtailed by the clatter of the post through the letter box.

It was a letter from Jem. Her first. All wonderings about India's fragrant continent were abandoned in an instant by the square brown envelope, marked with a green cross, that she held in trembling hands.

"It's from Jem. Real news at last!"

Her bright eyes dismissed Lionel and he withdrew abruptly. "I'll leave you to read it in peace, Mrs Phipps. Solitude will serve you best on this occasion. Good-day to you."

Katy didn't even hear the door slam shut. She raced to the window, not to watch the vicar leaving, but to get the best light with which to read Jem's news.

Jem's hand was clumsy and the letter grimy. Katy spread it out on her chenille cloth and sat down in front of it to concentrate. It was not a long letter and she felt dissatisfied with it, sensing much had been omitted. In that she was not wrong.

Jem wrote:

"Surrey base camp, 30th March 1916

Dearest Katy,

I've met some grate blokes at our training base. We're here for a few more weeks and then it's off to France for a crack at Gerry.

Good grub but lots of square-bashing.

All my Love
Jem xxx"

So long a wait for so little! It didn't tell her anything that she hadn't read in the paper. She read it through again more slowly but couldn't wring another word from the page. Katy looked across at the tea things, half eaten and drunk. Resentment swirled in the pit of her stomach and she felt cheated on all counts. She cleared away the china crossly, clattering the plates together, then pounded her ironing to relieve the frustration. Katy slammed the iron, hot from the top of the stove, over the white sheets. Then the injustice of Jem's departure welled up in her like the steam rising from her laundry.

Her face flushed with the warmth of the steam and the force of anger suppressed too long.

How could he go and risk his life when they were only just getting back on their feet? Hadn't they been through enough this year already what with Florence dying and her own illness?

Without realising it, she started talking to herself out loud, "And I've no other babe in my belly to keep me company - he made sure of that by never coming near me. What if he dies out there? What will become of me?"

Tears hit the cotton; they hissed under the searing hot iron.

"And I sent the vicar packing just for that miserable letter. It didn't say anything, and we were having such an interesting chat. How I would love to travel but here I am stuck in this trench of a valley. I can't even see sunrise and sunset properly. I might as well be buried alive. I'll have to do something, or I shall run mad."

Katy abandoned the ironing – after all who did she need to finish it for? No-one else would be slipping between fresh, smooth sheets with her. She set the iron back on the hearth, pulled on her bonnet and grabbed her shawl.

She marched straight over to the vicarage and rapped smartly on the door, deliberately averting her eyes from the nearby graveyard, scared her resolve might fail her.

The housekeeper, Mrs Hoskins, showed her to Lionel's study with thinly disguised disapproval and eyebrows raised just enough to make her opinion of the young woman's forwardness very apparent.

Katy had never seen Lionel in his own lair before. He was usually in church, preaching from the pulpit or dutifully visiting her on his parish rounds. Here, surrounded by his own things, she saw him in a completely different light. The morning sunshine shone on the polished mahogany desk and the blonde head bent over it. Through the graceful French windows, the neat lawn stretched out, the river winding quietly below it. Plush velvet curtains swept to the floor in ruby red folds framing the pleasant view and their warmth was matched by the books that lined every wall. Here and there exotic reminders of Lionel's work in India punctuated the scholarly scene. Fuchsia and turquoise ornaments mocked the heavy Victorian furniture.

The housekeeper sniffed. Lionel looked up at last, distracted from the letter he was so absorbed in writing.

"Mrs Phipps to see you, sir," intoned the housekeeper with evident distaste.

Lionel's face flushed pleasure and surprise. The pen was cast aside. He leapt up from his desk and, dismissing Mrs Hoskins with a brief nod, drew Katy to the inviting wing armchair set to catch all the daylight near the pretty windows. Katy thought she had never seen a room more to her own taste or sat in a chair so conducive to curling up with a good book. She sighed her satisfaction as she sank into its comforting arms and looked out across the valley floor at the distant view. How she yearned for a vista like that instead of being locked in between the cleft of the valley sides. She felt very at home.

Lionel slowly let go of her hand and went back to his desk which now stood between them.

"To what do I owe the pleasure, Mrs Phipps?" asked the vicar, hands clasped before him, forefinger over mouth.

It did not occur to Katy that this gesture was anything other than contemplative; that it might be one of restraint - or to taste her skin.

CHAPTER TWENTY FIVE

Lionel restrained himself by drawing a long breath and stifling his instinctive response to tell her exactly how useful she could be to him. He was startled at his own reaction to seeing this intelligent and comely young woman seated before the window in his very own study, his private sanctuary. This was the room where, only that morning, he had wrestled with his conscience but then accepted his feelings for her and the impossibility of its consummation. He had left her cottage seething with resentful frustration after Jem's letter had arrived and stomped home to throw himself into organising war efforts on the home front. And now here she was, as if drawn by the magnet of his feelings, into his solitary den.

He looked at her profile against the sunlight. How delicate she looked since her illness. Her youthful plumpness had refined into real beauty. Her hair was always swept up onto her head nowadays, as befitted a mature woman, instead of hanging loose and free and it allowed him to admire the length of her slender neck, the curve of her fine-boned cheek, the down above her full lips, the sweep of her long lashes. She turned from gazing at the lovely view and smiled at him. Lionel knew, in that moment, that he was lost.

He collected himself hurriedly. "There is much you could do, Mrs Phipps, to help the war effort. You don't have to go abroad to do it."

Lionel noticed how Katy's face fell at this and he smiled before carrying on.

"There are jumpers and socks to be knitted. I know of a group in Woodbury who are always looking for more contributors and there is another society of women who roll bandages and post them to the Front. I could put you in touch with the organisers, if you would like."

Katy did not reply.

144

Against his own wishes, Lionel continued, "Or, if you did want to travel, the Volunteer Aid Detachment need nurses, or you could contact the Red Cross. They have an office in Woodbury."

"I think I might be interested in that, Reverend," she said, a little breathless.

How had he kept his hands to himself, while his voice mumbled facts about well-meaning societies, when all the time his mind raced with pictures of Katy without her hat; with her hair down in a cascade through which he could run his fingers? He shook himself back into the mundane realm of parcels of brilliantine, toothpaste and socks being sent to the British Army by loyal wives and mothers.

"See, vicar, I want to be a part of it all too. Jem and Albert are away fighting. I can't be a soldier but there must be something I can do. The news in the papers is so alarming, I can't sit on my hands any longer."

"I see, well, I'll gather the addresses I have here and put them in a portfolio for you, shall I?"

It didn't help that Katy had continued to gaze upon him as if he was the fount of all knowledge and wisdom and had looked so wistful – excited even - at the prospect of serving her country in France.

In the end he had rung the bell for Mrs Hoskins, whose swift response confirmed his suspicions she was eavesdropping nearby.

Mrs Hoskins showed Katy out with even greater hauteur than had attended her frosty welcome. Lionel could not judge Katy as objectively as his upright housekeeper obviously did. He was far too preoccupied by his turmoil within. His stricken conscience argued vociferously with his self-confessed and illicit desire for another man's wife. A man who was, at this very moment, fighting for his country. That Jem might be killed in the conflict he could not allow himself to acknowledge. To do so would be to fall into a quagmire of immorality as slippery as the mud in Flanders.

He congratulated himself on somehow getting through the encounter unscathed. He would keep to his promise of gathering information and addresses for Katy and drop them by when next he was passing. He convinced himself that he would carry out this simple service just as he would for any other of his parishioners.

And yet he could not help but be aware that several of these options would take Katy away from the village. Lionel found himself torn between pushing temptation out of sight and remaining an upright man of the cloth, reputation intact, and the overwhelming urge to take Katy into his arms and never release her. After all, he was no longer a curate but a fully-fledged vicar of the parish and, as his mother constantly reminded him, destined for further promotion in the wider church.

Thoughts of his mother didn't hold his attention for long. His mind returned to the woman who occupied his every waking thought. Such an ordinary little woman too. She wasn't in his class or of his world. Why did he have these feelings at all? Were they simply biological urgings? Was he, too, subject to carnal wantonness like any miserable peasant – animal - even? Had all his teachings, his faith, his experience of life, not lifted him above such base cravings?

He turned away from the window. Paced again. Sat at the desk. Got up. Kneeled to pray and found himself remembering her instead.

With these opposing forces still not reconciled, he resolved to deliver the little portfolio to her cottage in the clear light of morning on the following day.

It turned out to be one of those days where nothing went according to plan. Old Joseph Buckle, an ancient but beloved farmhand, was "taken bad", according to his worried daughter, Bessie Buckle, now called Mrs Todd. Bessie had married the feckless Samuel Todd when too young to realise what she was letting herself in for. She was now mother to a clutch of young Todds, many of whom displayed an alarming tendency to follow in their father's footsteps. Lionel knew that for Bessie to take the trouble to walk a full mile to the vicarage to ask him to pray over her ailing father, Joseph must be very ill indeed.

As he had anticipated, Joseph did pass away during his visit, and poor Bessie, despite the demands of her large family, had enough spare energy to grieve for her departed Dad with loud, and to Lionel's mind, excessive, sobbing.

"Oh, Father, Father!" wailed Bessie, rocking to and fro in her chair, next to the still body of her aged father.

"There, there, Mrs Todd." Lionel felt wholly inadequate, as several pairs of young eyes stared at their mother. One little girl began to sob in sympathy and soon the whole pack was at it.

In all conscience he could not leave the distraught woman and wondered if he would ever get away. Relief came at last in the kindly form of Mrs Chubbs, the farmer's wife, who came to enquire what all the fuss was about, as Bessie's mournful wails could be heard in the cowshed some three hundred yards distant.

By the time Lionel had run his other errands, the soft spring evening was beginning to billow and hush the bright day into the stealth of night, and he was frustrated, tired and hungry. Lionel vowed this would be his last call. Frazzled by the way the day had slipped away with nothing to show for it, he looked forward to seeing Katy with an unacknowledged longing that this was his very own front door. And she was … he didn't dare to finish *that* thought.

He was saved by the door opening the tiniest crack and Katy's voice saying, "Who is it?" in an earnest undertone.

Lionel announced himself.

"Oh, vicar, it's you. 'Tis late for your visit."

"I have those papers you wanted, Katherine." He surprised himself by dropping her formal title. The night cloaked him in privacy. "Can I come in?"

"Um, I was washing my hair. I'm not sure."

147

"Oh, I see. I won't disturb you, but you'll have to open the door a little for me to give you this bundle. There are too many things to go through the letter box."

Katy hesitated for a fraction of a second and then, as if reminding herself that he was the vicar after all, she opened the door wide.

There she stood, in her long white nightgown, with her dark brown hair around her shoulders and little wet strands already curling as they dried around her face. She stood back a little to allow the vicar to pass his package to her, but he found he could not part with it and stepped over the threshold.

Katy gasped at the breach and retreated a step. Lionel came forward again, his eyes locked on to hers. He kicked the door shut behind him with his booted leg and stood before her.

His hand trembled as he extended it to her. "This is the packet of papers I promised you, Katherine." His voice sounded strange to his own ears, gruff and low. He cleared his throat.

"Thank you, sir." Katy sounded surprised, as well she might, at his use of her Christian name. She flushed as she held out her hand to take the bundle.

Lionel parted with the packet reluctantly. He glimpsed her naked body through her thin nightdress. It was as beautifully curved as he had fondly imagined.

As if sensing his gaze, Katy folded her arms, holding his packet across her chest. She said, "Well, good night then, vicar. It was good of you to bring this so late in the evening, but I must finish drying my hair. I don't want another chill."

Lionel pulled himself up to his full height. "Mrs Phipps, how rude of me! Of course, of course, please do not get cold on my account. I hope you find the information useful. Please let me know if there is more I can help you with."

He tore his eyes from her deep violet blue ones and wrenched himself away. He opened the door and clumsily tripped over the sill, muttering, "Good evening," touching his hat as he stumbled.

I feel like a young clod of about fifteen, he said to himself. He planted his hat firmly back on his head, glad of the chilly night air. He breathed in a great draught of it and marched swiftly back to the vicarage. He went straight to his study, fell on his knees and prayed fervently to God to give him the strength he so desperately needed.

"Please, our dear Lord, forgive my trespasses. Help me to bear the burden of my love for this woman. She belongs to another man but oh, dear Lord, how much I love her."

CHAPTER TWENTY SIX

The men looked at young Captain Harry with various degrees of shock when they docked at the miserable French quayside. Stretchers of wounded soldiers lay in serried ranks before them, effectively denying them the chance of any exhilaration on landing. The crossing had been bad enough as the crowded boat pitched and tossed across the channel. Not many of them had even seen the sea before, let alone been on a boat and seasickness was rife. Jem suffered more than most and the unfamiliar nausea plagued both his body and his mind especially when he remembered Katy's constant sickness when expecting Florence. He was so grateful when his feet first touched foreign French soil and found it as steady as the fine Wiltshire loam he had dug so often.

Moans from the wounded men on the dockside were unwelcome reminders of the price of maleness. He caught the eye of one stripling. Only one eye was left to catch. All the suffering in the world lay in that wide-pupiled stare. The boy couldn't have been more than eighteen. He'd probably lied about his age just to get there.

Jem heard him mutter, "Water."

He reached for his canteen only for Sergeant Baker to snap, "Keep in line there, Private Phipps. March on!"

That single eye haunted Jem through many a long night afterwards.

His spirits lifted a little after they had disembarked, and their sergeant barked his orders to file in and assemble on the quayside. They stood smartly to attention, showing that the sergeant's work had been well done and exchanged sheepish glances of self-conscious pride.

A few formalities, a bit of grub and they started marching towards the freight train that would take them to the "Bullring", otherwise known as Base Camp, at Étaples in northern France.

Any initial euphoria was soon whittled away by the nightmare journey. They lay in a cramped train truck that bore the legend 'Hommes 40 - Chevaux 8.' on its outside wall. And as Tom Anderson said in his mild way, "That ought to have given us a clue."

"What's it mean, sir?" asked Davey Pringle.

"Men – forty. Horses – eight. It says the numbers that can travel in each truck," Tom said, without his usual smile.

Fifty of them huddled together in the carriage by the light of a single guttering candle and felt more like cattle than noble fighters out to save their kith and kin. Some soldiers actually shared these miserable quarters with a few horses, who kicked and fretted at the ends of each truck, their hooves narrowly missing the fidgeting soldiers in the middle. They waited such a long time on the quay side it was the middle of the night before they trundled off at a snail's pace.

During a quick stop to relieve themselves in the woods while the train refuelled Captain Harry Mountford, ignoring the usual protocol in the informality of the occasion, told them about one of their neighbouring carriages on a previous journey. "Did you hear about the truck next door last night? One of the bloody horses panicked as they went around a bend, came crashing down to the floor and almost flattened a young lad! Then their candle snuffed out and they had to stand on the footboard outside the truck while the horse-handlers got him upright in the pitch dark."

Jem laughed. "So actually, being squeezed in with fifty 'hommes' isn't so bad after all." Ten extra men suddenly seemed a small price to pay for the absence of flying hooves.

"Quick, lads, look lively. The train's moving off again." Sergeant Baker chivvied them back to the track.

They ran back to the railway line and scrambled back on the truck and it lumbered slowly off again.

Sleep was impossible and the sight of the huge base camp at Étaples, with its sea of tents and the familiar Nissen huts, was a welcome one however drab and monotone. The relief was short-lived once the gruelling training began.

"Thought we'd done all that in Blighty," grumbled Davey, as yet more drilling punctuated the days. The parade ground was grassless from months of being stamped upon by thousands of army boots. Each company formed up and marched back and forth according to the instructions of their sergeant.

Jem could put up with marching but struggled with the bayonet training. The boast: "We're lion tamers here!" by their new drill sergeant had promised much but disillusion soon set in with his cries of: "Hurt him now. Get him in the belly. Tear his guts out."

And with permanent ghastly grins, "Use the butt in his privates. Ruin his chances for life! No more little Fritzes!"

They charged at straw dummies in German uniforms, one hanging from a gibbet and the other on the ground. As they plunged the steel into the manikins in quick succession, they tried not to imagine the real guts falling out, much as the drill sergeant would have liked them to.

"Alright, Jem?" asked Tom Anderson one night, as Jem lay on his bunk, smoking, and trying to forget the prospect of bayoneting for real.

"Evening, sir," Jem made to sit up and salute, but Tom waved his hand away.

"At ease, soldier. Got a light?" Tom sat on the edge of the adjacent bunk and puffed with him.

"Don't know about you, sir, but I can't say as I fancy sticking a bayonet in anyone even if he is a Hun."

"Hmm, I know what you mean."

"And them sergeants – the way they speak! Stick it in him – turf his guts out and all that? It's a bit much," Jem watched his superior's young face.

"Yes, I know, Jem, but they've got to get us in the spirit – get the old dander up and fighting. Can't go into battle like milkmaids." Tom's polite smile didn't reach his eyes.

"They'll turn us into murderers instead." Jem didn't insult him by returning the smile.

"Well – won't we be?"

They drew heavily on their cigarettes, their eyes blank and unseeing.

A couple of weeks later, when they thought they'd never get off base and would spend the entire war drilling the leather off their heavy boots, they were rudely awakened at an even more ungodly hour than the normal six o'clock.

"Come on now, look lively!" Dawn had not yet filtered through the mean windows of their hut as Sergeant Baker ran his baton along the metal bedposts.

"It's enough to wake the dead," moaned Davey.

Jem opened one bleary eye, "Feels like we've only just gone to bed." He raised his unwilling head from the lumpy, still beckoning, pillow.

"Up you get, my beauties. Rise and shine. Time to go on your travels. Let's see a bit more of la belle France, shall we? Up you get, I say!"

Sergeant Baker's burly frame strode into the next hut. They could hear the same hearty commands and the clatter of his baton against another set of bedrails clearly through the thin walls. He wasn't brooking any argument from their fellow soldiers either.

Lance Corporal Tom Anderson, not a natural soldier, followed up Sergeant Baker's strident tones with more muted encouragement and therefore met with far more resistance. "Right, boys, do as the good sergeant says now and dress quickly, will you?"

"Oh, Tom, it's not even bloody daylight," pleaded Davey.

"Are we going back on that damn cattle truck?" asked Jem.

"'Fraid so lads. Now come on. Look lively, please!" said Tom, with his usual politeness.

They scrambled into their scratchy wool uniforms. The feeble light of the single oil lamp, glowing faintly in the middle of the dormitory, made them clumsy and slow. Soft curses filled the corners of the wooden shadows.

By the time Sergeant Baker barked, "File in!" they were more or less fully clothed, and their kit thrown together in their knapsacks. "I've seen tidier school children, but you'll have to do. Off to the Mess for breakfast. You have fifteen minutes to eat, wash and assemble in the squad. Look sharp!"

Half an hour later they were rattling along in another crowded train, headed they knew not where. At least it was an open-air truck. It might be cold, in spite of the April sun, but it was free of thrashing horses and at least they could see where they were going. The countryside was remarkably flat and unlike Jem's native shires. Rumbles of artillery could be heard as they got nearer their destination – as yet still unknown to them. Vestiges of villages, their once pretty houses frayed at the edges, stood mute witness to man's ability to destroy.

"I don't know about you, Davey, but my breakfast egg isn't sitting too well in my stomach," Jem said ruefully.

"I'm bloody glad to be out of that bullring myself. Let's get on with it. See some real Gerries instead of all this blinking playacting and slitting dummies in half."

Jem nodded back without conviction.

Two more days of rumbling along train tracks brought them to a place none of them had ever heard of, called Albert.

"Blimey, it's got an English name, who'd have thought we'd end up in a place called Albert!" joked Davey, obviously relieved to be getting off the train, whatever the destination.

They were allowed an hour at ease before they had to march to the front line. Jem wandered with the gaggle of other men through the red brick archway of the station into the town square. Not one building remained unscarred by the fighting.

"Would you look at that?" Davey pointed to the church.

Jem looked up beyond his pointing finger. On top of the tower, also red-brick with white tiling, lay a golden statue of St Mary and her child, Jesus. No longer upright, they leant at an acute angle in a near horizontal position, as if clinging on to dear life despite every attempt to dislodge them. Jem felt a lump in his throat seeing how the Virgin Mary refused to let her child be dislodged however much men tried to kill each other around her. Katy, he knew, would have done the same for Florence.

The hour was soon up, and they fell into line, ready for the three-mile march ahead, ending up near to large meandering river called the Somme. Soft undulating hills rolled endlessly away on either side of it to apparent infinity.

Halfway along, they were allowed a ten-minute rest. They sat about on the edge of the dusty road, waiting for further instructions and glad to be stationary. A pretty little girl, of about six years old, came up to them offering a tempting tray of chocolate – for one franc each.

"How much?" Davey said, eagerly a tendering a French franc.

"Don't you speak the lingo then Davey?" laughed Jem.

"I'm working on it and a bit of choccy will ease me into it, Jem. See - she understands if I show her a bit of silver. How much is a bit of chocolate worth anyway?"

"Ooh, about tuppence, I should think, for a little piece of chocolate like that but a franc is worth more than three bob, isn't it? See if she's got change. She must have sold loads up and down the line. We're all hungry, that's for sure." Jem smiled at the heart-shaped face of the little girl.

The sweet-looking infant snatched the coin, tossed the small slab of chocolate at a surprised-looking Davey and sprinted off, grinning.

"Oi," shouted Jem and ran after the little mite. "Come back here, you! Give my mate some change, you little minx."

"G'arn you fuckin' long barstid," came the swift reply.

Jem stood stock still in the road and didn't even hear the roar of laughter from his comrades in arms. He just stared as the little chocolate seller sped off, pink ribbons flying, and disappeared from view.

"Well I'll be buggered," Jem said to Davey. "Did you hear what the little varmint said?"

Davey had been too busy guzzling his sweet to give chase and simply shook his head, his mouth too full to answer.

"Probably just as well." Jem scratched the back of his head. "I can't believe it myself. Just hope that chocolate doesn't give you indigestion. Or worse." He added, refusing the last precious square Davey offered him as a thank you for pursuing the petite seller.

"Expensive but bloody nice." Davey laughed out loud. "What's a few shillings to an empty stomach? Can't eat money."

"No, but it could buy you more grub later," Jem said, feeling old.

Davey shrugged.

Jem remembered Davey had no young family to support at home. He speculated how many pints at threepence each that would have bought him and how much further Katy could have stretched three shillings and eightpence. They trudged up the endless lane towards their new camp and Jem remained quietly pensive the rest of the morning.

"Another Nissen hut – bloody great," Davey said, as their interminable march ended in a woodland clearing in which stood about ten huts, obviously erected in haste, judging by the state of the workmanship. Already the grass was dissolving into mud.

"At ease men," shouted Sergeant Baker, as they formed up on the damp ground. "Go to your billets. Each platoon to one hut and make yourselves at home."

"Sounds like thunder again," Jem said, as the ever-present sound of artillery boomed out. "And it's a lot nearer now."

"Have you got butterflies too?" whispered Davey, as they emptied their few belongings on to their beds.

Jem nodded. The two men's eyes met for a brief, embarrassed moment.

CHAPTER TWENTY SEVEN

When the news broke about Charles Smythe's death, it ricocheted between the two villages like the bullet that killed him. As soon as Lionel heard that Sir Robert and Lady Smythe were not exempt from the bereavements peppering his parish, he paid them a visit. Knowing their only son, the music-loving, reckless Charles, who had signed up in such haste, was dead, had shocked his parents to their core and through them, the whole community.

Lionel was kept very busy visiting grieving families. The losses were completely random. He'd comforted weeping parents in cottages with earth floors and outside privies and now, as he approached the grand house of Cheadle Manor, he reflected how this global conflict respected no-one.

Cassandra had been partying at a frantic pace since Charles had signed up and had even bought a car which she'd taught herself to drive. Then, when the impact of losing some of her friends hit her, she had enlisted with the First Aid Nursing Yeomanry or FANY as it became popularly known. Shortly afterwards she too went to the battlefields of France, leaving her parents completely alone.

"See here, Lionel?" Sir Robert shoved a letter under his nose. "Cassandra's gone off now. Read it! I can't believe a word of it. Driving ambulances. Hair-raising conditions! She was always a tomboy; always putting her hunter to a gate and whatnot but really - driving ambulances - I ask you."

Lionel tried to console the elderly couple but knew he had failed. They looked lost and too small in their big, empty house.

After that, every time Lionel paid a visit to Cheadle Manor, he saw the squire drift around its large, empty rooms in bewildered confusion, as the twentieth century stuck its bloody claws into his insular world and stripped it of its protective armour. His wife marshalled various women into an organised party of workers with the ruthless efficiency of an army general. The new era had marched boldly into their cocoon, braying its mechanical noise and brutality so loudly, it could no longer be denied.

Sir Robert surprised Lionel enormously one breezy spring morning. The mocking sun caressed the oblivious singing birds as they built nests for their offspring and he rode up the hill to the manor on Kashmir. Lionel felt exhausted. He was glad of the big mare's homing instinct as she plodded placidly up the road to the manor and submitted to the admiration of the stable boy with her usual grace.

Lionel took a deep breath and entered the house, once so redolent of comfortable complacency and now full of echoes. Sir Robert offered him a whisky, saying he found it a useful anaesthetic these days. Lionel accepted it gratefully. Mrs Hoskins would have frowned on his change of habit, as well as the consumption of alcohol so early in the proceedings but Lionel too needed a little numbness.

There was a further departure from convention by Sir Robert who, drawing himself up to his considerable height from his recently acquired slumped stoop, opened the conversation with a proposal.

"Reverend White, I've been thinking lately of your ideas about the water supply to the village. With Charles gone," his voice broke and he took another hefty slug of whisky. "Well, life is short and all that and I've been remembering that young woman's child dying. What was her name?"

The comfort of the liquor evaporated. Lionel mumbled incoherently, "Katherine Phipps."

Sir Robert was barely listening anyway, focussed as he was on his new project, "What? Oh, Phipps. That's the one, yes. Ah yes, I remember now, wasn't she Katherine Beagle before she married? Had a thing with Charles.

Pretty girl. Can't say he didn't enjoy life, what? Much good it did him."

Sir Robert took another glug of whisky and stared out of the window at the unchanging Wiltshire downs. He coughed. "Anyway, I feel I was a little harsh in not putting my hand in my pocket to save a life."

He looked at Lionel, who recoiled from the pain in the older man's eyes. He noticed that Sir Robert's hair had gone quite white. He couldn't understand why he'd not noticed it before. He gave Sir Robert his full attention.

"Yes, you see, I think we should install that modern plumbing you were always harping on about. Lady Smythe still thinks it's a waste, what with all this estate duty and whatnot but I've overruled her." His chin came up and he looked at Lionel defiantly.

Lionel, breathing again now his guilty secret seemed safe, nodded encouragement, "Sir?"

"I've discussed it with my estate manager, Hayes, and we've set aside a sum for the improvements. I know you've got various schemes and designs, so I'd like you to meet up with him and get things in motion. We can't afford to lose any more young ones. Not on my account, we can't."

Lionel stood up and strode across the Aubusson carpet to shake the old gentleman's hand.

"Thank you, sir! I'll see to it right away. Is Mr Hayes in his office?"

"Yes, always is on a Wednesday - sorting the wages, you know. Above the stables," said Sir Robert, gruff with emotion.

"Yes, sir. I know. I'll go now. Thank you again, Sir Robert."

With a look of deep compassion that comforted the bereaved father more than he could ever know, Lionel left, galvanised. He could do some good at last and salve his weary, sore conscience.

CHAPTER TWENTY EIGHT

Jem's heart sank into his heavy, mud-encrusted boots when he finally arrived at the front line. His back was in knots from carrying his heavy battle kit. He heaved it to the ground but the relief of freeing himself from his burden was fleeting. He looked about him. Walking along the road had been fraught enough, as stray artillery fire killed men as they marched ever nearer the battlefield. They had left their camp after only one day of rest. Putting one foot in front of the other had taken greater willpower with every step.

Stones and debris littered the roadside. Platoons of soldiers stayed in that deadly zone simply clearing the road of dead horses, overturned carts and wounded men. As they filled craters with the remains of broken houses, they resembled zombies; their faces blank masks showing no emotion. Pieces of homes smashed to smithereens now became the uneven surface they reluctantly marched upon. Each time a member of their party fell, picked off by a random shell or stray bullet, the roadside workers dealt with him mechanically. Jem felt his own senses deaden as the deafening roar of full battle filled his ears. Without the momentum of his fellow marchers he could not have gone on.

They hit the trenches in full battle mode. There was some comfort in the sandbags piled high around them. Some refuge in the dugout. At least you couldn't see the bullets and the bodies from there. Newly arrived, they were sent to the second line trench, removed from the heat of the lethal exchange. Jem learnt they would be on the front line for two weeks and at the rear for another two weeks. Turn-and-turn-about. Like Russian roulette.

Stretcher bearers, caked in mud, eyes staring with fatigue, brought an endless supply of freshly wounded men, placed them down in a queue and, with a swift glug of tea, went back out into the maelstrom, only to return with yet more bloodstained victims.

Gentle Lance Corporal Tom Anderson paid for his dreaminess on the first day. As ever, he was scratching away with his pen and notebook completely unaware of everything around him. His men had mocked him unremittingly for his love of poetry during their training. When he was picked off by a random bullet, his book still in his hand, his life snuffed out so quickly and quietly, none of them could believe it. He'd been leaning absentmindedly against the line of sandbags, his deep forehead clearly visible to enemy lines and presenting them with the ideal target. The bullet hole was a perfect bulls-eye on that thoughtful brow.

Captain Mountford, charging up and down their line, stopped to talk to Jem. Maybe his youthful face was too transparent for an officer, but the young captain looked as shocked as Jem felt.

"I can't believe Anderson's gone," he said quietly, almost to himself, "I've not lost a friend before. We mustn't let it get in the way of duty."

Jem could only nod at the younger man; younger, yet so much senior but as green as any of them.

Captain Mountford turned and raised his voice to the other men. "Come on now, keep going, lads, and if you don't want it to happen to you, keep your damn heads down below the line of fire!"

Jem wondered if it was his public school experiences that enabled Captain Mountford to dig deep and find his stiff upper lip. Was it instinct or his upbringing driving this young aristocrat?

"Come on, men! Don't just stand there staring at me. There's plenty to do." And Captain Mountford set to checking along the line personally, making sure everyone kept their heads down, their hands busy and their sergeants and lieutenants kept a close eye on their men.

Jem quickly discovered there was no end to the long list of jobs behind the line. There was tea to be delivered in dixies, food to be carried to the front line, wounded to be tended to and ammunition ferried across. Two weeks of this and then it was their turn to face live bullets.

Jem and his fellow soldiers slept where they lay, counting themselves to be lucky to be asleep, rather than dead. Having been active all night, making the most of the darkness to observe the enemy's trenches, they had to rest how and where they could in daylight.

He smelt the gagging stench of death everywhere. Quite sweet, definitely sickly. Blood mixed with the ever-present mud formed a thick slime. Jem's boots stuck to it like glue and became heavier than ever, weighing him down, so that each step had to be sucked out of the gooey mess, pulling every muscle in his weary thighs. As Jem had anticipated back at camp, the ground was marshy and low. Lower still it sank under the weight of thousands of men trying to kill each other. Soft low hills undulated away to the distant horizons, with very little as landmarks between them. Jem got used to the sound of the crump of the shells and the whine of bullets but never the smell and feel of the mud. He felt he would never wash it out of the pores of his skin. Lice thrived in these wet conditions and soon Jem was itching along with the rest of his platoon.

He found the very worst thing of all was the rats. Great big fat slithery creatures that sneaked up on him while he dozed fitfully at night. They nudged their filthy noses at him, hoping he was dead so they might guzzle contentedly and get even fatter. Jem woke every time he felt one, shouting, "Get off you little bugger!" and kicking out at them viciously.

"Here, Jem, don't kick me – I ain't gonna eat yer!" Davey protested at little these days, but he did object to that. Davey and Jem became closer in this desperate bath of death. The other men relied on their jokey banter and they all clung to the friendships they'd built so fast but so strong.

They all loved Captain Harry Mountford too. He never asked his men to do anything he wouldn't do himself. In that he was virtually unique. Most staff officers kept themselves far removed from the messiness by billeting themselves at elegant chateaux, well supplied with food together with plenty of servants to keep them running smoothly. But Captain Harry was as involved as his sergeant and made sure every man in his command knew him personally.

"It's just the bloody same as at home," grumbled Davey, as a Brigadier General, attended by their Colonel and several other of the lower orders, graced them with his presence. The officers' uniforms were hardly dusty while the wool of their soldiers' could barely be seen for mud.

Davey was slouched against the sandbags as he said this, the usual fag dangling out of the corner of his mouth. His tunic was undone to the waist as a concession to the warm summer's morning and his cap had long been discarded. They were engaged in digging out another trench that had fallen in. Before they could even start moving the dirt about, they'd had to clear it of dead and decomposing bodies, kicking away the rats first. The sun shone down relentlessly and there was no tree left standing to shield them from its rays.

Their commanding officer, Colonel Harrison, obviously very aware of the Brigadier General's presence, stopped abruptly in his perambulations and pulled up short in front of Davey. Davey slouched on regardless but gave the two military veterans the benefit of his best smile.

"How do?" he said, displaying his skill in keeping his cigarette dangling securely to his bottom lip.

"Stand to attention, soldier!" shouted the Colonel. "Where's this man's captain?"

Captain Mountford rushed up and saluted smartly, "Sir!"

"Look at the state of this soldier," said the older officer.

"What rank are you, man?" barked the Colonel.

"Private, I think they call it," drawled Davey.

"Private, *sir!* And stand up straight when being addressed by a senior officer," said the Colonel.

Davey slowly brought himself vaguely upright.

"Smarten yourself up, man. Where's your cap? Do up those buttons!" said Colonel Harrison.

"But it's awful hot," Davey said, with more truth than wisdom. "Sir," he added belatedly.

"How dare you answer back!" The Colonel whipped Davey's cigarette from his mouth. He looked like he was having great difficulty restraining himself from slapping him round the face. His own was rapidly becoming purple and beads of sweat broke out on his outraged brow. Davey studied them with interest, as if calculating how long they would take to form droplets and drip down the red, stocky neck.

"Captain!" shouted Colonel Harrison.

"Sir!" Captain Mountford stood to attention.

"What's your name again?" said the commanding officer.

"Mountford, sir."

"Captain Mountford, this Private – what's he called?" Harrison glared at Davey.

"Private Pringle, sir," Harry said, staring straight ahead.

"This specimen, Pringle, is displaying a severe lack of discipline. Do you hear me?"

"Yes, sir," still Captain Mountford didn't look to left or right.

"If I had my way, he'd be shot," the Colonel's chin stuck out above his tight collar.

Jem noticed that beads of perspiration had begun to sprout on Davey's own forehead now.

The Brigadier-General intervened. This senior officer spoke in a soft, cultured voice. "It is a very warm day, Harrison." He laughed and added, "I've been longing to throw off my own cap and undo my tunic all morning. I think that would be excessive punishment for this offence, Major."

The Colonel chewed his impressive moustache. "Captain Mountford? Give Private Pringle here Field Punishment Number One for no less than three days. And smarten him up!"

"Yes sir, of course sir," said Captain Mountford, back still like a ramrod.

"Right, see that you do. Come on, sir, we must crack on," said Colonel Harrison, turning to his colleague who looked distinctly uncomfortable.

The two officers walked off further down the line, with the Colonel continuing to bark orders and his senior officer continuing to look unimpressed with his bullying.

Captain Mountford turned despairingly to Davey. "I've got to do it, Private Pringle. No choice I'm afraid. Present yourself – smartly turned out – at my dugout at 1300 hours today." He looked at Jem as if to say, "Help me out with this one."

Captain Mountford went back down the line and left Jem and Davey to mull over the likely consequences of the exchange.

Davey grumbled, "The toffs parade around, giving orders, and we get to do the dirty work. I wonder what I'm in for now. It's just the same as school. I never could do as I was told. And where's the sense in wearing all that uniform when you're doing a filthy job like this?"

Jem sympathised but made sure Davey presented himself at the dugout at the due time and then went back to work. He was as shocked as anyone half an hour later when he saw Davey strung up to the gun-wheel of their heavy Howitzer gun. His arms were clamped to the rim of the wheel by handcuffs and hung a foot above his head. Every sinew strained in his arms. He was sweating profusely in the exposed position. Flies feasted on his face and any part of his torso they could find uncovered.

Jem went to offer him water but the sergeant on guard blocked him with his rifle butt. "He's got to do two hours minimum and no fraternising during the punishment. Colonel's orders."

Davey craned his neck round to look at Jem and smiled his crooked smile. Jem tried to smile back and gave him the thumbs up sign. That didn't suit the sergeant.

"I said, no fraternising! Back to your duties, Private Phipps. About turn!"

Jem had no alternative but to return to bolstering the trench defences and wait for Davey to reappear.

Davey strolled up as nonchalantly as ever later that day. The sunburn on his face was obvious and Jem was sure there were other parts that stung too but he took his cue from Davey and didn't comment.

Davey endured this for two further days before Captain Mountford could say, with tangible relief, that he had served his punishment.

Davey's expletives on having his pay docked as well gave Jem a whole new education in cockney slang. "I'd like to see that fucking bastard of a Colonel heave sandbags in this heat with his sodding cap on."

Jem nodded. "You don't see many of them getting shot or going over the top."

This spectre now loomed large. Jem was called into the officers' dug-out one morning. A persistent drizzle had set in and the relatively dry dug-out, with its floor boards and lamplight, seemed positively civilised compared to the open wet trench.

"Private Phipps - good to see you." Captain Mountford shook his hand warmly, apparently not even noticing its muddiness. "I've seen how the men look to you and I'm making you a Lance Corporal, to, um, replace old Tom Anderson. You'll get a bit more money and when we go over the top – which we will soon – I'm waiting on orders on that – I want you to chivvy the chaps along. Do you think you could manage that? You'll get a stripe on your arm for the privilege."

"Yes, sir, thank you, sir," Jem said, genuinely surprised.

"Righto. You'll report to Corporal Smith as your next in command. He's under Sergeant Baker. I'll be going over with you of course but I can't be everywhere, and each section will need to be supervised."

"Yes, sir," Jem said. He could send Katy some more money.

"Also, there will be messages passed down the line from corporal to corporal in a chain of communication, via your sergeants, who'll receive instructions from me. It's important we all go at the same time towards the Germans. We aim to get through no man's land and to enemy lines with this big push. Savvy?" The young Captain looked at him. No smiling now.

"Yes, sir. When do you expect this assault to take place?"

"Don't know yet, Lance Corporal."

Jem flushed under the mud at his new title.

"Officers who are more senior than I decide these things." Captain Mountford looked at Jem. A world of sympathy lay between them.

"Very well, that's all. You can send in John Page next. He's in the platoon on the left of you." Captain Mountford turned away to his papers on the makeshift desk.

"Righto, sir. Thanks again." Jem gave him his best salute.

"You might not thank me in a few days," muttered Captain Mountford to Jem's departing back but he could still hear his depressing words and his elation at his promotion was instantly extinguished.

Davey had the hump for half an hour when Jem came back and told him of his promotion. "Alright for some," he said at first, and then, more charitably, "well, it'll be good for yer missus at least. A few more coppers never hurts."

"Yes, she'll be proud of me I reckon. I must write to her."

Jem got out his stubby pencil and some paper from the depths of his haversack. Leaning on a lumpy sandbag, making quite certain he was well below the sight line unlike his unfortunate predecessor, he wrote:

"The Somme battlefield, 20ᵗʰ July 1916

Dearest Katy,
Well, my dear, we're in the thick of it now and no mistake. I hope you are keeping well. Give my love to the family. I thought you might like to know that I've been made up to Lance Corporal. Our Captain, Harry Mountford, is a great chap and he wants me to help lead our little band of men when we go over the top in a few days. It'll mean a bit more money too, so I hope that'll be useful to you, Katy love.

I think about you often, my dearest. Out in the garden mostly, feeding the hens and doing a bit of weeding. Just thinking of that keeps me going, like.

Your ever-loving husband, Jem"

Jem's hand started to wobble. He finished quickly with a fond farewell. When the char carriers came around with the tea, he slipped one of them the note and made sure the address was legible so he could be confident that Katy would hear the good news.

All his letters from her were neatly folded in the very bottom of his knapsack. He read and re-read them constantly. At least he had until now. Now in this hell of mud and noise and above all, the dreadful stench, he couldn't let himself feel too tender. Better to swear along with the other men as he shot his rifle over the lip of the trench and took out some other woman's husband.

CHAPTER TWENTY NINE

Two days after Lionel left his packet of information about war work Katy walked up the steep hill, rather reluctantly, to the Manor house.

Agnes had given her a flea in her ear during her regular weekly visit to the little cottage in Lower Cheadle the previous morning. "What you going to do with yourself now? Jem's been gone this long while and you're just sitting around marking time and making yourself miserable. And you're so thin, Katy! Ain't you eating nothing at all?"

Katy's bottom lip protruded silently.

"Eh, my girl? Answer me! What are you going to do with yourself? Sit this stupid war out like an old woman by the fire or what?"

Still Katy could not answer. She'd barely looked through the papers the vicar had given her. His visit had unsettled her for some reason she couldn't fathom, and time had slipped away in a dream.

"Katherine Beagle!" Her mother seemed to be losing the battle of keeping her temper.

Katy looked up, eyes wide. Had Agnes forgotten she was married and had changed her name? Her mother's weary face wore the fierce look she remembered from the many times she'd been naughty as a child.

Agnes looked thoroughly exasperated, "Look, young lady, I've got Albert at the Front now soldiering his life away, God help us all. Your father's doing the work of ten men what with the others gone. And Miss Cassandra has signed up to something called FANY – driving ambulances, would you believe? The last thing I need is to be worriting about you an' all. Now, I'll say this one more time – what are you going to do with yourself? You can't bide here for months on end with nothing to do. Now then, Lady Smythe – her only son dead and gone, mind – but even so, she's got up a working party for making bandages, socks and other such stuff and sending it off to France in parcels and she's looking for helpers. I've put your name down, like it or not. Unless you've got a better idea?"

"Yes, I have, as it happens. I went to see the vicar about it, and he's given me a load of papers about volunteering. I was thinking to try for the VAD service."

"VAD? What's that when it's at home?"

"Voluntary Aid Detachment. It's the women nursing the soldiers at the Front. Why shouldn't I go to France, just like Jem and Albert?"

"There's plenty to do at home. You don't have go off abroad. I *need* you here, Katy."

Katy looked at her mother, whose voice had gone all scratchy. She was alarmed to see tears welling up in Agnes's eyes and ran to her mother's side. She put her arm around Agnes's plump waist and squeezed it. Agnes took out an immaculately ironed handkerchief and blew her nose loudly.

"Oh Mum, I'll stay, I promise. I'll give Lady Smythe's war effort a go," Katy said quickly before she had time to think about it.

Agnes shrugged off Katy's arm and sniffed. "Right then, that's settled. You can start tomorrow morning. She's got people there from nine in the morning till four in the afternoon every day except Sundays. Don't see why you can't do most days. You can have supper with us after too. That way you'll get some vittles inside of you. Lord knows you need feeding up. Have you heard from Jem lately?"

Katy nodded. Her fate had sealed itself over again and she resigned herself to doing her duty, however dull it might be. She got up to the cupboard in the corner and pulled out a box of letters. "He's written quite a few times lately. I still can't picture him there, in uniform, in another country."

"What's he say, then?"

172

Katy read aloud from the stained pages. "He says he's alright. Said it's a bit boring most of the time. Hanging about behind the lines, killing time. Said his captain is a good lad. He's only twenty but a right good'un."

"Well that's something, I suppose. Twenty years old. It don't seem right to me. How come he's captain at that age?"

"He comes from an army family, I think, and very well off. It seems the rich can do just as they like in wartime, same as they do always."

Agnes shrugged. "Some things never change, even when the world's topsy-turvy. Now, I've got to traipse up that hill to get dinner on the table for your Dad. I don't want to be coming to fetch you tomorrow and have to climb it back again neither so mind you turns up at the house in the morning, nine o'clock sharp. You're not too old to feel the back of my hand, married or not."

Katy smiled broadly at her mother. Agnes had never struck her in all her life nor any of her other four children, apart from the one time she'd boxed Albert's ears for signing his life away for King and country. The lashing from her tongue had always sufficed to keep the rest of them in line. They both knew Katy would be at Lady Smythe's tomorrow at the appointed time.

CHAPTER THIRTY

Even though he'd known his uncanny luck couldn't last, Jem was surprised when the bullet struck. He had dodged so many. He had lost count of the number of his comrades that had fallen before, by the side, in front, or behind him and had begun to feel immune.

The French mud came towards his face with such velocity, his mouth was still open from his shocked scream and he swallowed some of the filthy, slimy stuff. He knew he wasn't dead when he became aware of its disgusting taste and texture and attempted to spit it out.

He felt vaguely pleased when he succeeded in clearing most of his mouth out but less so when the searing pain in his left arm transcended all other sensations. Involuntarily, he screamed again from the pain of it. His cry was drowned in the moans of others and the thunder of cannon fire. Surrounded as he was by desperate humanity, he had never felt more alone.

Bullets still whistled overhead. He looked to the left of him and saw Captain Harry Mountford spread-eagled on the sludgy ground.

"Sir? Captain Mountford?" Jem's voice was a croak. He swallowed, gagging on the foul mud. "Harry!" he shouted, hoping the shock of using his first name might shift him. Nothing.

How could he not think of him just as another young lad caught up, just like him, in this ghastly mess? To hell with army protocol now.

Jem squirmed over, dragging his wounded arm along like a dead thing. It took him half an hour to reach the senior officer. He was only a yard away. Jem had to rest a minute before he lifted his good arm and shook Harry Mountford on the shoulder.

Harry's head was turned away from him, but he knew him from his uniform and the signet ring he always wore on his little finger. It bore a coat of arms that Jem suspected was from Harry's family. The other blokes had laughed at the poshness of it. Now it gleamed incongruously through the smoke of battle. Clamping his wounded arm to his side, Jem managed to lift himself up enough to throw his good arm right over Harry's body. He reached for his neck and turned his head. Harry's eyes remained shut. He was very pale. Jem wouldn't believe he was dead until he made sure. He remembered in training how they were taught to feel for the pulse at the neck and see if there was breath coming from the mouth of a wounded man.

"Captain! Sir, I'm going to check up on you, sir. Yes, I am. Hold still, Captain Harry, lad." Still Harry certainly was. Jem felt the neck and the mouth. A pulse throbbed uncertainly, and warmth issued from the slack lips. Jem's heart leapt.

He risked raising his head a bit higher and looked around the desolate place. Bodies were strewn everywhere. What a bloody waste. Twenty yards to his right was a huge crater caused by a shell falling some days ago. He'd heard the officers talking about some stretcher bearers who'd waited with some wounded men there for hours until things had quietened down. If he strapped his wounded arm up to stop the bleeding, maybe he could drag Harry there.

But what could he use? Then he had an idea. He cut off his one of the webbed straps from his haversack with his army knife and, with great difficulty, strapped it round his arm above the wound. Using his teeth, he pulled up the strap, and after fumbling for what seemed like hours, finally got a knot fastened. He cried out with the increased pain of the throbbing arm but the ever-reddening patch on his sleeve grew no more.

Despite the cold and persistent drizzle Jem was sweating now. He had to get his breath somehow and steady himself against the pain. He felt again for Harry's pulse. It was the same and Jem felt heartened it was no weaker. There was a massive dent in Harry's tin helmet. Maybe he was concussed? Jem couldn't see any other wound. He took another deep breath, put his good arm around the officer and rolled him over onto his back. Harry's face was very pale and slick with the rain. At least it was washing off some of the revolting slime. Jem crooked his arm under his captain's armpit and, using his legs like a frog, dragged Harry, and his own useless arm, a few feet towards the crater. Twenty yards in the other direction, another shell crumped the sticky clay apart.

"One of those near us and we're done for, Captain. Now come on, sir, let's have another go." Five more frog movements and he was a quarter of the way there. "Rest and go again. That's what we'll do, sir. Five breaths and five pushes; five breaths and five pushes."

He stopped for a rest as his good arm cramped up. "Four breaths will have to do and two pushes, Captain. Ah!" He screamed as a bullet whistled past his ear.

The measured breaths became gasps. He gripped Harry fiercely and hunched over his captain to stem his own panic. Jem waited until his breath settled again. He reckoned it was another quarter of an hour before his trembling stopped long enough to push his weary, heavy legs out and in again.

Five yards to go. Harry moaned.

"Captain? Captain? Can you hear me, sir? We're nearly there, mate, nearly bloody there!"

Encouraged by this sign of life and not feeling so desperately alone in the sea of death, Jem made a final heave and they rolled over together into the crater.

"Ah, God, my arm!" The searing pain cut into Jem like a knife, as Harry's body crushed into Jem's wound and they fell, pell-mell, into the watery pool at the bottom of the shell hole. The hole was deep – about fifteen feet - and the bottom two feet of that was filthy water. Another soldier lay face down in it, still as a block of wood.

Whether he had drowned or been shot was impossible to tell but he was certainly dead. Jem's feet went first, so he was alright with his head above the water-line but Harry was the other way around. Jem leaned over and hauled his captain upright to a sitting position. He clapped him on the back and the young man vomited out French soil and rainwater, mixed with other things he couldn't bear to think about.

The involuntary expulsion brought Harry round and, coughing and spluttering, he cried out, "What the hell is going on?" to no-one in particular.

The shelling had quietened down a little by this time. Jem laughed. His voice came out high and strange. Harry swivelled his head around to hear where the odd noise had come from and stared into the face of his newest Lance Corporal.

"Hello, sir." Jem grinned with relief.

"God, my bloody head." Harry pushed his helmet back and felt the lump on his head. "Blasted shrapnel or grenade or something's hit my damn helmet."

"You're lucky to be alive, sir. It must have struck the helmet but not gone through, whatever it was."

"How about you, Jem – are you hit? What happened to the rest of them?"

"I'm alright, sir. Got a bit of hit in the arm is all," Jem said, trying not to grimace as Harry touched his wound.

"Where? Let me see." Harry's voice gathered strength. The dim light revealed little. "Can't see much, Jem, but I can feel the sticky blood on your arm. It feels different to the rain-sodden bits of your uniform. You must have bled a fair bit, old chap. Who put that tourniquet on?"

"I did it myself, sir."

"Bloody good show. Impressive. How are you feeling?"

"Bit lightheaded but alright, sir. At least we're alive." They both ducked down as a shell whined over them. They waited for the explosion. The water in the crater rippled in a sympathetic wave.

"That was a close one. Now, I want to see what's happening out there. What about the rest of the men?"

"No, sir, begging your pardon, if you raise your head above the crater, you'll be killed instantly." Jem put out his good arm to restrain his senior officer.

"But I must look after my men."

"No, sir – it would be suicide!"

"I must, Jem, I must look after my men," repeated Harry.

"But sir, they're long gone." Jem clawed frantically at Harry, who was pulling away.

Harry tried to stand up. Jem punched him on the jaw. Harry went out cold for the second time that day. Jem lay back against the side of the crater. He had never felt more exhausted. His eyes slowly closed. Sleep overwhelmed him. No amount of noise could have kept him awake.

He drifted in and out of sleep, becoming increasingly numb with the cold. It was the absolute quiet that woke him when the guns ceased their deadly fusillade and dusk began to fall. He felt himself lifted on to a stretcher and, silently but swiftly, carried back to his line. Then he passed out.

He woke again to the smell of antiseptic and the sound of collective moaning. The field hospital was busy. The Big Push had claimed the lives of thousands of men and detached equal numbers from various parts of their bodies. Nurses busied about, seemingly tireless, and hollow-eyed doctors tried to do the work of ten.

A nurse bustled up on seeing him wake and gave a weary smile. "Hello, soldier," she said, her smile widening, as Jem cracked his own face in response.

"Hello, nurse," replied Jem dutifully, and experimentally, to see if his voice still worked.

He felt such relief when it croaked back into life. Instinctively the nurse gave him water. Never had anything

178

tasted so good and it lubricated his throat enough for him to ask, "What's the damage?"

"Not too bad at all. We can fix you up here at the Stationary Hospital and you'll be right as rain soon enough. It's just your arm that's taken a hit, but the bullet has only grazed and not lodged in it. I'll get Doctor to come and talk to you."

Jem sank back on the pillow – a pillow! And luxuriated in the support of the bed.

Just his arm then. So, he would have to go back.

CHAPTER THIRTY ONE

Katy replayed her conversation with Agnes many times over in her head during the next few weeks every time she questioned why she had allowed herself to be back under Lady Smythe's thumb. If her mother had not crumbled and shown the strain of Albert being away; if she did not love both her parents so much, would she now be driven crazy with Lady Smythe's boring monologues?

The loss of her only son had hardened rather than softened the formidable matron. Sir Robert, his hair white from shock and his cheeks red from whisky, wandered silently around in the background. His loud laugh had gone, along with his only son and his comfortable paunch. Sir Robert seemed to be grieving for both of them; only heavy sighs escaped him now. Lady Smythe never once mentioned Charles. Instead she threw herself into supporting the war from her obscure country fortress as if it were the general headquarters for the whole army.

"Katherine Phipps! How many times have I told you to fold the socks before they go into the parcel? We want our boys to see the care we have taken. It won't do for it to look shoddy. By packing their things neatly, we can demonstrate our concern. The last thing we want them to feel is that we couldn't care less. Now, start again and do it properly this time!" She tutted and raised her eyes to Mrs Ponsonby who was visiting from the next estate as if to say – the working classes – hopeless!

Katy ground her teeth, took every pair of socks out of the huge tea case and began again. She felt sixteen and stupid to boot. Agnes refused to listen to her complaints when she went around for supper at the end of the tedious, long day and kept plying her with second helpings for which Katy had no appetite.

"Lady Smythe was trying to outdo Mrs Ponsonby again, Mum." Now this was fertile ground for gossip. Katy had found this the best tactic for deflecting another heaped spoonful of mashed potato.

"Oh?" Agnes said, conceding defeat. She sat down to eat her own supper.

"They were both trying to say they'd each sent more parcels than the other. Mrs P. had come over to crow about her working group. They're doing bandages rather than socks and Lady Smythe said that was quite a different matter, as socks had to be knitted. She went on and on about how she went around all the houses on her estate to collect the socks people had made. She said you didn't have to do that with bandages. They just needed rolling up and pinning. You should have seen Mrs P.'s face."

New lines in Agnes's face cracked into a rare smile, "If it helps our boys, I don't care how much they race each other for the biggest prize. By the way, there's a letter for you on the dresser. Billy Threadwell brought it up earlier on his way to the manor."

"Why didn't you say before, Mum?" Katy abandoned her food at once, snatched it up from behind a beautiful bowl of red roses and ripped it open. She could see it was from Jem by his handwriting on the envelope; though it was a wonder it had reached her his writing was worse than ever. She sat back down at the table and held the letter to the lamplight, relieved that Agnes had given up the attempt to get Katy to eat her old favourite, chicken and leek stew with dumplings. Agnes busied herself clearing away the plates from their meal. Katy could see she was trying but failing to hide her curiosity as she fussed about.

Bert obviously had no such scruples. He'd wiped his own plate clean with fresh bread and now, looking well satisfied, went to put another log on the fire. "What's he say, Kate? Read it out for us. Maybe Jem's seen our Albert out there?"

Katy, having begun to read it to herself, stopped and cleared her throat. "Alright, Dad. Captain Harry – that's what the men call him now apparently – because he's so young – he got hit on the head by a shell fragment or a bullet - they're not sure which but his helmet saved him. It still knocked him out though."

Katy gasped and looked up at them, eyes wide, "My Jem got hit in the arm himself..." Katy went pale and read on silently, her knuckles white, as she gripped the letter.

Agnes snatched her hand away from her husband's enormous paw and put it in her mouth. She stared at Katy and seemed to brace herself. Katy's colour returned a little as her eyes scanned down the page quickly.

She looked up at them and smiled briefly, through brimming eyes, "S'alright Mum, he said it weren't too bad." Katy wiped her eyes on her sleeve, impatient to read on. She continued, "Anyway Captain Harry was knocked out cold, Jem says. He didn't know at first if he was dead but when he realised he wasn't, he managed to drag him to a crater."

"A crater? Are they fighting on the moon?" asked Bert, his eyes fixed on his daughter.

"The shells make craters. Look at the newspaper, there's a picture there."

Bert picked it up and looked at the grainy picture on the front page. "There's not a tree left."

"'Tis like the moon for all that," whispered Agnes. Katy guessed she was thinking all the time of young Albert.

"I know. There's little left on the battlefield because they're making no headway. Just yards to and fro – it's a stalemate right enough, Jem said in his last letter. Anyway, they went into one of them craters, like in the picture, and they stayed there for hours. He fell asleep because he was so cold – oh, poor Jem - and when he woke up, he was in the hospital. Oh, he must have been badly hit after all!"

"I don't understand. How have they got hospitals out there in the middle of nowhere?" piped up Daisy.

She, at eleven years old, always sat next to her father on a little stool by the fire. Katy ignored her little sister and read rapidly on.

"They're just tents, like the ones they sleep in behind the front line." Bert consulted his paper again. "But they've got doctors and nurses just like in a regular hospital."

"Never mind that!" Agnes said, "How is Jem now? Is he alright?"

Katy read on, "He says they fixed him up so he could go back and re-join his regiment."

"More's the pity." Agnes sniffed and blew her nose on her apron. "You must be that proud of Jem, Katy."

"Ay, I am. Rescuing Captain Mountford like that – why he's a proper hero and no mistake." Katy's conscience gripped her heart like a vice. If only she'd been more loving before he'd gone.

Bert tapped his pipe against the mantel. "I always said you had a good feller there, Katy. It's good to see the army have recognised it. Does he tell any more about what happened?"

"Oh, don't you wish you were part of the excitement, Albert Phipps? Well, let me tell you, I'm glad you're too old and you're biding home with me." Agnes' voice caught. "One's enough out there."

Bert took her roughened hand in his and squeezed it.

"No need to worry Agnes, soldiering's not for me." Bert let his hand fall and pulled gently on Daisy's pigtails. "Come on, young lady, time for bed. That's enough soldier stories for one night."

Daisy and her little brother, Jack, trooped up the wooden stairs.

Agnes bustled after them, muttering, "War. Upsetting everything. Wounding young men as should be home with their wives."

She lifted baby Emily from her fireside day cot and carried her, still sleeping, to their shared bedroom.

"I'll be off then, Dad." Katy was itching to go home to read and re-read Jem's letter in private and write back to him without delay.

"You sure you wouldn't rather stay here for now, Katy love, after that news and all?" Her father's brown eyes were full of concern.

"And where would you put me?" laughed Katy.

"You could have Albert's bed."

Katy shivered. "No, Dad, that would be inviting trouble, as if – you know - something might happen to him as well?"

Bert nodded quietly. "Ay, you may be right. Off you go now then, back to your own. And take care on that road. These new motor cars like Doctor Benson's got now, they go so fast down that hill. It's all bloody unnatural if you ask me."

Katy smiled, and kissed his weathered cheek affectionately. "Say goodnight to Mum for me. I'll be round again tomorrow."

Bert watched her from the front door. The oil lamp on the kitchen table behind him illuminated his burly figure. Katy felt a lump in her throat for both her parents. What a worry it all was for them at their time of life.

So much had happened this past year, it felt like a bad dream. Suddenly, hearing about Jem's injury, the danger he was in became real. Her denial of love to him smote her heart and she wished she could undo it. She ran down the hill as if demons chased her and pored over his letter by lamplight. By the time she had written back to him it was long past midnight, but her guilt had not been purged. She wished she'd recovered quicker from her illness and, for that matter, got over Florence sooner. If she had, maybe Jem would still be here by her side. Maybe she'd have another child swelling in her stomach.

Gradually the days and weeks crawled past. Katy felt increasingly confined as the autumn of 1916 drew on. When snow set in just before Christmas, she gave up the struggle to keep the range alight and stayed on at her parent's lodge-house each night. Lady Smythe needed her cottage for some temporary farm workers to move into anyway for the winter hedge-laying.

More and more, Katy felt like a child again without the status of a married woman whose man was fighting at the front. She felt small and diminished. The hens had been re-instated into Agnes' care, just like her.

It was as if she had never left home.

CHAPTER THIRTY TWO

Considering how tired he was, Jem healed surprisingly quickly. Within a few days he was up and playing one-handed at the popular, forbidden card game of 'Crown and Anchor' in the mess tent, next to the General Hospital. After he'd left the Casualty Clearing Centre, or field hospital as it was sometimes called, he been sent to the General Hospital to recover. It was out of artillery range, but the odd distant crump could still be heard.

Captain Mountford came up to him and extended his hand. Purple bruises ran up the side of his jaw as well as around both eyes.

"Hello, Jem. Seems I owe you one," Captain Mountford said, with a lop-sided grin.

Jem threw in his hand of cards and stood up to salute.

"At ease, man. For God's sake - no ceremony while we're on sick leave. And do me a favour and call me Harry!"

Jem laughed, "Do you mean you owe me a punch or a favour?"

Harry clapped him on the back and, still laughing, they sauntered outside. The rain had stopped for once and both men stood stock still to stare at the most beautiful rainbow left in its wake. It arced over the battlefields, from where yet more shelling could be heard.

"Will it ever stop, do you think?" asked Harry, as if Jem was his commanding officer not the other way around. There were only four years between them but right now it felt like forty to Jem.

"I always think a rainbow is a sign of hope, Harry," Jem said in tacit acknowledgement of the respect he saw in the younger man's eyes.

"Do you? Or is it just God laughing at how stupid men are?"

They gazed at the wondrous colours.

"I wonder if they can see it on the battlefield?" mused Harry. "And would it stop them if they did? I say, Jem, I owe you my life. Although I only had concussion, I probably would have been hit again if I'd stayed where I was. How you dragged me to that shell hole, I can't imagine."

"Wasn't anything much, sir. You'd have done the same and sorry about the punch on the jaw. Couldn't let you go out there. You didn't know which way was up!"

Harry laughed gingerly. "I'll have you for insubordination if you try that trick again."

Jem laughed back but then looked solemn. "I'd like to know how Davey Pringle is. Do you know if he made it?"

They walked over to the list of the thousands of men who had been killed in action. Jem was deeply saddened but not surprised to see Davey's name amongst them. Jem looked back up at the blue sky again. The view misted suddenly, and he brushed his eyes with his good arm, taking comfort in the abrasive scratch of the wool on his wet face, "Such a long list, sir."

"I know. It's a slaughterhouse. And Davey was a good lad, as brave as he was cheeky. He would have gone a long way in life." Harry shook his head and took a deep breath. "Come on. I've been given a weeks' leave. I'll take you into the village for a slap-up lunch."

Jem felt almost human as they sat outside the local estaminet in the sunshine. The rough and ready eating place was just an ordinary home, whose housewife had improvised a running cafe for the thousands of soldiers billeted nearby. She was doing a roaring trade, as was her daughter, except the younger woman wasn't selling food.

Geraniums were in full flower in the over-flowing window-box. Jem wondered how on earth plants managed to keep doing such ordinary things as grow and flower in due season? Along the side of the road Nature was burgeoning regardless. Nettles thrust up behind the dusty verges and little spears of blue verbena pointed skywards.

The herb of grace – what a joke. There was no grace in this war.

Madame brought out vegetable soup and chunks of French bread to dip in it, slathered in white creamy butter that melted into the savoury, hot liquid. They both scraped their bowls clean with the chunks of crusty loaf. Then came the ubiquitous egg and chips. Two eggs each.

"Egg and chips remind me of home," Jem said.

"Oh yes?" enquired Harry offhandedly, as he sprinkled salt over his chips.

Jem concentrated on dipping the points of the crispy chips into the golden egg yolk so that it punctured the membrane and the yellow goodness oozed out onto the other potatoes. Carefully, he placed the coated chip into his mouth and chewed, eyes shut in deep appreciation. "Hmm, that is so bloody good."

He took a sip of the unfamiliar white wine. "Didn't think we'd get wine with this." He pursed his mouth at the sourness of it.

"Got to have wine in France, Jem. Unthinkable to have lunch in Frogsville without a bit of plonk," Harry said, fork in mid-air.

"I have egg and chips at home, but I don't get vino with it! Can't beat a good old pint of ale, if you ask me." Jem put his tumbler down with distaste.

Harry used the last chip to wipe round any lingering trace of egg. "Now you're talking! What I wouldn't give for a pint of freshly drawn beer from my local pub."

"And a good hunk of cheese with it." Jem felt much restored and at ease with the world, upside down though it might be. They stretched out their legs and puffed on their Woodbines.

"It's good to be alive, isn't it?" Jem said, "no matter how daft the world's become."

"Yes, Jem. Yes, it is. I don't suppose Davey would think differently either if the tables were turned."

Jem nodded and lifted his glass in a silent toast to his Cockney friend. "You know, some men are putting mud in their wounds – to make them infected and get worse – just to get back to Blighty?"

"Well, can't say I blame them. Can't say it's right either but I wouldn't condemn a man who'd had enough of this Godforsaken place. I mean, what if he's got a family back home? They're all conscripted now – it's not volunteers anymore." Harry swirled his wine round in his glass. It glinted in the spring sunshine.

"No, lost too many. Suppose they have to make up the numbers somehow." Jem took another swig finding it more pleasant the more he drank.

"I had to wait until I was eighteen. Mater just wouldn't let me enlist before and she knows the Colonel in our town. In fact, she knows everyone. Couldn't get away with cheating about my age. Had to kick my heels until the birthday."

"I was old enough but what with one thing and another didn't get away before. Thought about it and all but it didn't seem right, what with Katy..."

"Who's Katy?"

"My wife, sir."

"Didn't know you were married, Lance Corporal?"

Jem wasn't sure he'd ever get used to that title. "No, well...I don't talk about it much over here. Best to just get on with the soldiering, not think about home too much."

"I can't imagine being married, Jem. What's it like – you know?" The wine had loosened Harry's tongue.

Jem looked at him. He was so young. "If you mean what I think you mean, it's very nice, is all I'll say, Harry, but you need the right woman."

"You wouldn't recommend going with Madame's daughter over there then?" Harry nodded in the direction of the buxom but none too clean daughter of the house, as she laughed with a group of French soldiers at the next table. One of them had a familiar hand on her ample rear.

"For myself, like, only dear Katy would do. I waited for her long enough."

"Was it worth it?" asked Harry, all ears now.

"Oh yes," smiled Jem, as the soft memories played on his face. His eyes gleamed, picturing his Kate in the first glorious months in their tiny house together. What a time they'd had.

"How could you leave her?"

"Good question," Jem said, the wine dissolving his restraint, "we had a daughter, see. Little Florence." His voice caught. He swallowed a big gulp of wine.

"Florence is a pretty name," encouraged Harry.

"She was a pretty baby right enough." Jem swallowed and looked across at the Frenchmen laughing raucously together. They took no notice. Jem sniffed and cleared his throat. "She, um, she died, see. Typhoid it was. Quick as anything. Vicar said it was the water – we only had a standpipe in the village - and we'd had no rain for weeks and it was that hot for October. She didn't stand a chance, doctor said."

"How old was she, Jem?" asked Harry softly.

"She'd not had one birthday. Then Katie got ill. I thought we was going to be alright – she sorrowed so after Florence went - and then she seemed to pick up only to go down with pneumonia herself. I couldn't stand it after that. She was so thin. Took forever for her to be well again, the whole dreary winter, in fact. By the time spring came, I'd had enough. I was scared to touch her. They was calling for more n' more men to join up so I thought - bugger it. I'll get away, take me chances and then see after."

"What did Katy say?" asked Harry, demonstrating that the inner workings of marriage remained a foreign country to him.

"Well, she didn't like it, course. But I'd made up me mind by then. She were brave at the train station, fair-play, when she waved me off. I don't think she'd really taken it in."

190

"Do you think of her much now?"

"Never a day passes when I don't. The letters are a comfort. She tells me all the village gossip. What's growing in the manor gardens. Just ordinary stuff, you know. Sometimes it don't bear to think about it, I just wants to run home. So, I sets to polishing buttons or something else to take me mind off it. I'm glad we've got no little'uns now. At least if I don't make it, Katy's young enough and pretty enough, God knows, to start again with someone else."

"If there's anyone left," Harry said, sober enough now.

CHAPTER THIRTY THREE

Every Sunday Lionel stood in the pulpit, with his congregation looking up at him, waiting for his guidance on their morals. He preached principle and text to uplift and inspire these simple people while their sons died, lemming-like, on the other side of the thin strip of sea to the east.

Were anyone to look closely at those intelligent blue eyes, they would notice the ghost haunting the back of them and the hollows underneath. To his profound relief, nobody did. Grief stalked the two neighbouring villages as young men were cut down in the French killing fields as regularly as daffodils in spring. The village women took to waiting in a huddle every morning for the post and many were inconsolable after it had arrived. Lionel was kept busy visiting the bereaved and organising memorial services.

So, people showed no surprise when even Lionel's immense vigour and health became undermined. But it wasn't the war that weakened him. He could not sleep for thinking about Katy. He lived for his short visits to her little cottage and acknowledged privately that his feelings were becoming an obsession.

He knew his fatigue was showing on his countenance when he overheard Mrs Threadwell praising him for it. "That vicar's looking a bit peaky. Fair-play mind, he do his bit for the war, can't say he don't. Don't see why he stops here though. You'd have thought he'd want to be over there too with our boys. Still there's plenty wants doing at home and he's not shy in coming forward and that's a fact."

Bereaved, gaunt parents told him they were glad of his stalwart comfort and grateful just for a young man to be still present amongst them, keeping the balance between the grave and the forceps, as it should be. They needed to witness a young man's life while it was still green and shooting up to the sun instead of sinking moribund under alien clay, but Lionel's conscience became a weight almost too heavy to drag around the parish.

As Lionel set to work on the new plumbing for the village, his doubts about staying home stole a sneaky march on him. The more he set things to rights and dragged the community into the twentieth century, the more his guilt nagged at him. Try as he might to assuage it by finally completing his pet project and to feel rightly proud to be guardian of his flock, the more insidiously did his lack of courage worm its coils around his mind. However much he persuaded sceptical villagers that the change would be healthy and beneficial; however many quotes from hard-pressed plumbing engineers he collated; however many matrons he charmed into sponsoring the pipe-work, nothing could salve the niggling censor hissing "hypocrite" incessantly into his reluctant ears.

One morning, in the sanctuary of his study, Lionel prayed on his knees for guidance about his role in the war and his love of another man's wife. He looked up and gazed mindlessly at the mist rising from the river valley. For a moment he just rested his eyes on the beauty of the scene. The white drifts curled serenely up from the water as they had since time immemorial. When he had gone, when this mad, ghastly war was a distant nightmare of a memory, this river would still provide a beautiful backdrop to someone's morning.

Lionel let himself fall back on his haunches and slumped to the floor, all resistance melting like the rising river mists. He pressed his open palms into his face and rubbed his tired, gritty eyes. How could he release this passion for Katherine? That he loved her, he did not doubt, but did he respect her? What sort of love was this? Did he want her for his *wife*?

He almost started out of his skin when Mrs Hoskins knocked briskly on the door and, as was her habit, marched straight in without waiting for permission. She stopped short on seeing the Lord's representative sprawled on the floor and his flustered excuse of searching for a dropped pencil would not have convinced the simplest of souls, never mind the curious eyes of the chief village gossip.

Lionel felt himself flushing like a schoolboy and stood up, smoothing his golden mane into some semblance of propriety.

"Thank you, Mrs Hoskins, leave the tea tray there on the desk please. I shall ride out to breakfast as I have pressing business in town. Oh, and I shan't be in for lunch either."

Giving orders to the arched eyebrows of his housekeeper's curious face acted like a sedative and he felt his racing heart calm a little.

With a regal posture to equal anything Lady Smythe could rustle up for the lower orders, Mrs Hoskins withdrew. The glance she gave her employer could have shrivelled a walnut. The heavy oak door shut with a crisp smack.

Lionel slumped into his leather desk chair and shakily poured himself a cup of tea. He knew he ought to enlist as an army chaplain and join his peers in France but in this private moment of truth he acknowledged that not seeing Katy every day, not having the chance of catching a glimpse of those fine cheekbones, not checking that she was well; all these privileges were now too important to be denied.

While she was here, he would stop home and watch over her, whatever anyone else thought about it.

CHAPTER THIRTY FOUR

In France, Jem, surviving still, witness to too many deaths of his new friends, steadied himself again. He had led a charmed life so far. His wounded arm had healed quickly and although it ached a bit in rainy weather it appeared to function as well as ever. The summer flowers had long gone now and rain, increasingly cold rain, was the norm. After Christmas they had frost and despite the cold it was easier than the mud that followed in the spring, when his unit was shifted to Arras.

He'd slipped into a kind of fatalism by then. Going over the top, weaving in and out of shells, stumbling over disgorged soldiers and getting splattered in their young, red blood, had hardened and sickened him. The futility of it congealed inside him to form a single core of determination to get out alive. He knew fear and felt it often. He saw it everywhere but within the depths of his being he found a way of battening his down. He would either die fighting in this pointless battle or he would live like he had never lived before. He would enjoy every moment, seize every opportunity, savour every sweet thing away from this hell of mud and slime.

The grey area between belly-dropping nerves and succumbing to nightmares he would not visit. Jem felt he'd be better off dead. He'd seen men quaking in their sodden boots, piss running down their khaki legs. He sympathised with them. He wanted to do it himself but some inherent bloody-mindedness, probably pride, kept him from that miserable state. He felt compassion but quickly realised he must shut it off like a tap or his own watery courage would also run away.

He visited memories of Wiltshire sparingly. They were his secret cache of reasons for staying alive but were too beautiful to be allowed to surface often. It would be so easy to spend his hours vicariously tending his garden, making love to his wife and joking with his gardening workmates as they tended young seedlings burgeoning into life. It would soon be daffodil time at home. The long drive of Cheadle Manor would be lined with the yellow trumpets of his favourite flower. Yes, that world was full of colour and scent. He could draw on it like a draught of ale to support him but too much made him weak and drunk. In this drab world of mud and khaki, he had to hunker down and endure, or die.

It was also dangerous to become too attached to his comrades - only to see them stopped in their tracks and their endearing mannerisms or infuriating habits stilled and silent - eyes staring, brains blown out, innards disembowelled, limbs elsewhere. Every part of the human anatomy was displayed from the inside out. He'd seen parts of bodies he'd never even guessed at; yards of intestines, the blancmange of the brain that had quipped over tea that morning, the muscles in the legs that had climbed the ladder of death into the killing fields of mud.

It couldn't be thought about. It must be registered and shoved down into the recesses of his being or it would truly overwhelm him. Jem took to cleaning his kit with great attention to detail. He was meticulous in keeping himself as tidy and well-ordered as possible and took care with his hygiene. He became expert at killing lice with the blade of his bayonet.

"The secret is to heat the bayonet, see," he told a new recruit called Sam who reminded him of Davey. They were sitting around with nothing to do one day away from the front line. "Hold it over the candle in the tin here. Get it nice and hot and then," there was a hiss, "slap it down on the critters along the seam." Most of the lice crawled away but Jem caught some and cracked them between his thumb and fingernails.

"That's got 'em!" A few others had joined Sam to watch Jem catch the beasts.

196

"Only thing is, there's eggs in the seams you can't bloody see and they'll hatch out soon as I put the jacket back on but at least these little buggers'll lay no more."

"Polishing those damned buttons again, Phipps?" Captain Harry Mountford appeared on one of his rounds. The faces of the private soldiers under him might have changed but his attention to them on a personal level had never wavered.

They were back in the front-line trenches. Once more bullets whizzed overhead. They didn't bother ducking anymore.

"Dunno who Jem Phipps thinks he's gonna meet in no mans's land – bloody Tzar of Russia or summat," grumbled Sam.

"You know, you'd make a damn good batman, Phipps," Harry said. "I'll see about it."

"No thanks, sir." Jem was alarmed at the thought of being sent behind enemy lines when his section would still be in the thick of it. "I prefer to stay where I am."

Later, in the officer's dugout, he asked permission to speak to his senior officer personally. The sergeant looked cross when his captain gave the affirmative.

Alone and out of earshot with Harry, Jem said, "I'll not be a bloody servant to no-one. Never have been and never will. Thanks all the same."

"Sorry, sorry, just trying to keep you safe so you can get back to that lovely wife of yours. Anyway, I thought that's what you had been in your work before the army."

"Gardening's different. You might be on the payroll of the estate but you're your own master when you're working with plants outside. It's just not the same somehow. So, thanks all the same, sir, but I'll stay as I am, if it's alright with you."

"I could order you to obey, I suppose. By the way, they're handing out those medals in two weeks when we go back to the support line, after the next push that the Generals keep going on about."

"There was no need of that medal, Captain."

"Don't tell me my job." Harry pulled himself up to his full six feet which made him look a lot more than his twenty-one years. "It's good for the morale of all of the men. I'm not doing it just for you, you know."

Jem saluted his superior officer, smiling, and catching his hand on the low-slung oil-lamp. It swayed precariously and he had to hold it steady. A shell broke overhead and dust cascaded down over the rickety makeshift table.

"If we live as long as a fortnight, I'll be honoured, sir."

Harry coughed out the dust. "Yes, well, it's only an 'MM' but it's yours. Now back to the boys and look sharp."

The following week they were back in the trenches near Arras. All the available troops had been gathered together and Harry told them they were to launch another major offensive.

Captain Harry called the platoon leaders together and explained that the next offensive would mean a massive assault on the German forces holding the nearest hill. Sam, shocked after hearing about Davey's experience on the gun-wheel, swore roundly. "Why the fuck should I go over that top for these bleeders?"

Nevertheless, when the whistle blew from Harry's shaking lips, Sam too crawled over the parapet with the others.

"Don't stand up when you go over," Harry had instructed them, "or you'll not last a second – just crawl your way to the hill and lob grenades when you get near the German pillbox."

Already, British soldiers who had gone before them littered the ground and all around, as a muted background to the sound of gunfire, was a continuous collective groaning from wounded men.

Jem wanted to stop and help Sam who lay in agony, his stomach outside of him, calling, "Mother, Mother!"

He saw Jem looking at him in horror and whispered, "Please shoot me."

Before he could get his gun ready, young Sam died. Jem swallowed and jogged on through the glistening cold mud, streaked with the red blood of his comrades.

The noise was deafening and there was so much mud flying about he couldn't see where he was going. He coughed and wiped his eyes which had teared up from the smoke that clutched at his throat. He hoped he was still running in the right direction: running blind into a cloud that rained bullets.

Suddenly Jem was lifted up off his feet, floating in mid-air as if he was flying. He hadn't heard the shell burst – many of them were submerging in the deep mud and detonating safely beneath it. For a few seconds he felt weightless and the battle below him unreal. The painful crunch, as his body returned to earth, brutally reminded him it wasn't. He landed spread-eagled in a shell-hole with his arms out to save himself. The shock of landing knocked all the air out of his lungs. He gasped for breath, snatching at the smoky air for a whiff of oxygen. His back felt like it had cracked in half. He opened his eyes and looked up, astonished to be alive; to see sky above him. The sounds of war receded and were muffled. Very carefully, he shook his head from side to side. Gradually the roar of shellfire seeped back into his unwilling ears.

A stretcher-bearer stood at the lip of the crater, peering over a prone soldier. He beckoned to a mate. "This one's alive – bring the stretcher over." The man's voice seemed more distant than he was.

Then the stretcher-bearer himself crumpled forwards, past Jem, who was pressed against its muddy wall and joined him in the pit.

"You always know they're dead when they fall like that," said someone, near enough for Jem to hear his words clearly. "They always fall forwards, don't they? They never put their hands out to save theirselves, like."

Jem nodded, still numb from his own fall. Gingerly, he extended his hands and feet and found them operational. A long moan beside him made him turn. Another young boy – surely, he'd lied about his age – he looked about fifteen - slowly slid into the deep water in the bottom of the shell-hole, leaving only his shoulders and head free. He was scrabbling at the soft mud in a futile attempt to gain purchase and heave himself back up from the clinging water.

Jem went to pull him up, but his neighbour said, "Leave it, mate. He wouldn't want to live with them injuries – lost half his body - see? Probably dead already."

Bubbles blew lazily up through the brown thick water as the severed body slid beneath it.

Jem took a swig of rum and his hearing cleared. The warmth spread throughout his belly and took the edge off his rising nausea. He climbed to the top of the shell-hole and crawled over its lip.

"What are you doing? Stay here, mate," called out his new companion.

Jem took no notice. Another wounded man to his left said, "Go on, boy – give 'em hell."

The warmth from the rum comforted his stomach. He pressed the man's hand as he crawled past him and was rewarded with a grin. The man's teeth were white in a mud-caked brown face, then his body rippled open as shrapnel tore through it. His face buried itself in the mud, still grinning. Another explosion behind him showed the shell-hole, into which Jem had just fallen, bursting into a fan of mud and limbs. If he had stayed there, he would have been killed.

If it was going to happen, it would happen anyway. Jem took another slug of alcohol. His blood expanded in his veins and he crawled on.

"Jem! Lance Corporal Phipps!" Only young Harry could remain formal in these circumstances.

"Captain! We meet again." Jem was relieved to see Harry alive, crawling along like a snake, towards him.

"Getting to be a habit in battle, Jem," laughed Harry, an edge of hysteria in his young voice. "See that pill-box?"

Jem nodded.

"That's our quarry. Reckon we could make a break for it?"

"Yes, sir," Jem said, his rum talking for him and his new sense of fatefulness making him reckless.

Harry seemed to be reckless without the booze and stood up but stayed bent double. "On a count of three then."

"Have a swig of this first, sir." Jem passed him his flask.

Harry hunkered back down to the ground and took a sip of rum, ducking his head as another shell whizzed over them to splat only yards away.

They crawled along, keeping as low as possible. They could see the pill-box clearly at last when snipers put a bullet in each of them.

Harry shouted, "Blast!" and rolled over, clutching his wounded leg.

Jem stared at him. He stopped crawling forward and turned to go to Harry's aid, thinking that Harry couldn't even swear when injured. Jem more than made up for it when the arm he had wounded before ripped open with shrapnel. They lay together, only yards away from the German line, stuck fast in the quagmire of churned up mud.

"It's your arm, Jem. Let me put a tourniquet around it. Same one as last time, isn't it?"

Jem nodded, as a stream of expletives poured out of his mouth in concert with the blood leaving his arm. Harry strapped his Sam Browne belt around Jem's arm, copying exactly what Jem himself had done before but it was easier with this leather, officer-quality, buckled one. The pain was ten times worse than last time. He had a job not to scream as the tourniquet applied pressure to his upper arm.

With his remaining hand Jem took his own fabric belt off and helped Harry to place it around his thigh. It helped to think about something other than his throbbing arm. His strength was almost gone when he finished and he lay back, too tired to talk. Harry too was silent, his bottom lip bleeding from where he had bitten it.

Dusk began to fall, and the shelling faded. Jem looked back across the ground they had crawled along and realised not a single member of their troop had made it as far as them. Groans from the wounded formed a chorus of agonised humanity but at some distance away. They were nearer the German pill-box than any of their own men. They could see the metal barrels of the guns that nestled there but neither had the strength to lob a grenade into it.

By the morning, as the chill grey dawn mist crept over the desecrated ground, they were shivering and blue with the cold after the moist spring night. The last drops of Jem's rum were shared with impeccable equality until first Harry, then Jem slipped into blissful oblivion.

A weak sun mocked them as it filtered through the white mist and rose gracefully from the killing field upon which they lay; their blood seeping gently into the frigid soil of German territory.

CHAPTER THIRTY FIVE

The long winter dragged by for Katy. 1916 slipped inexorably into the new year with Jem's letters the only highlights in her dreary routine. She regularly checked up on her old home once the hedge-layers departed. She needed to remind herself it was still there, waiting for Jem to come home. She didn't want to miss any stray post either. She planted up the window-boxes with flowers when spring came and kept the garden as free of weeds as she could. One Saturday in April, when daffodils bloomed all over both the villages, Katy took the opportunity to pop into the Post Office over the road from her cottage. She'd promised to buy some groceries for her mother.

Mrs Threadwell's beady eyes took in every detail of Katy's appearance. "Morning, Mrs Phipps. You're looking well. Agnes's cooking looks like it's doing you good?"

"Good morning, Mrs Threadwell." Katy decided to ignore the reference to her lack of status. She didn't need reminding she'd gone back to her parents' house to live. "Have you any letters from my husband?"

"Nothing this week, I'm afraid," said Mrs Threadwell, through pursed lips.

Katy turned away to look along the shelves for tins of sardines for her mother. Then, bracing herself, she scanned the Casualty Lists. She did that every time she went into the shop, not daring to breathe until she reached the end. A new poster caught her eye. It was pinned next to the old one that had been there for months for VAD volunteers. The image of the VAD nurse in the picture had been nagging at Katy for some time.

The newly formed Women's Auxiliary Army Corps also needed volunteers.

"Every fit woman can release a fit man!" It shouted. Katy's heart leapt at the freedom it promised.

"Join the WAAC today for work with the Forces..." the next bit really got her heart racing... "at home or abroad!"

At last! A chance of being with Jem at the battlefield! She peered at the small print underneath the headlines.

"Apply at your nearest Employment Exchange for more information."

Schooling herself not to reveal her excitement, she asked, "Could I have a quarter of tea, Mrs Threadwell?"

The postmistress busied herself with the groceries and said, "Have you seen the new poster? They'll have women fighting like men next! A Women's Army indeed!"

Katy squared her shoulders, "I dare say women can fight as well as any man."

"Oh well, they're making bombs in factories and ploughing fields, so they might as well get themselves killed too, I suppose." Mrs Threadwell put the packet of tea on the counter.

Katy placed her money down, carefully counted out to the right amount and took herself and her purchases out of the shop, deep in thought. The image of the poster remained with her throughout the weekend. She went for a long walk on Sunday. As she wandered through the Wiltshire lanes, so familiar and dear to her, those images of foreign war-torn places forced themselves in her minds-eye and displaced her immediate surroundings. Her mother might want her here, but didn't she also have a duty to her king and country, just like a man?

On the following Monday morning, after Lady Smythe had said, "Oh stupid girl!" once too often, Katy threw down the string she'd been tying and stood up to face her employer.

"Lady Smythe?" Katy looked her old enemy straight in the eye. "I'm afraid I can't do this anymore. I am going to volunteer as a nurse for the war."

For once, Lady Smythe was silenced although her mouth, as usual, was open.

Emboldened, Katy continued, "Yes, I'm going to leave; today actually. At once, in fact."

She turned to the other ladies who all stared at her as if she had two heads.

Lady Smythe said, "That's all very well, Katherine, but we need help here. Our work is very important, you know. You don't need to join an army to be useful."

"I'm sorry, Lady Smythe, but my mind is quite made up. Good day to you." With that parting shot, Katy picked up her hat, pinned it to her head without consulting the mirror, gathered up her coat and gloves and made a beeline for the door. With her hand on the doorknob, she turned to the startled-looking group.

"Goodbye, everyone. I don't know when I'll be seeing any of you again, so good luck and good health!"

Belatedly, the gathered women clucked, "Goodbye, Katy!" and "Good luck to you, dear!" in various voices of surprise. As one flock they rose and went to the large bay window to watch the young woman march determinedly down the drive and out of sight.

Lady Smythe alone kept her seat. "That girl always was flighty." Her darning needle never faltered in its little darts of silver through the army sock in her white, unlined hands.

Katy marched down the gravelled drive in high spirits. It was omnibus day so she knew her mother would be out shopping in Woodbury, which was just as well, as she couldn't avoid passing the lodge house on her way out through the massive estate gates. She popped into the empty house and left a note, saying that she would sleep at her own cottage that night but omitting to say she was unemployed again. Leaving the note on the table, she left as quickly as she could, unwilling to share her decision with Agnes, knowing she wouldn't approve. That confrontation could wait. For now, she would just enjoy this heady moment of freedom.

That told Lady Smythe, the old battle-axe, right and proper, she crowed as she skipped down the hill, admiring the blackthorn blossom scenting the hedges. Her heart lifted. She felt like a sack of potatoes had come off her shoulders.

The sun came out and joined in with her glee. Katy felt such a spurt of energy, she ran the last bit home. She steadied her pace only when she got to Lower Cheadle and resumed her normal steady walking speed. She walked sedately past the post office and tried to ignore the excitement bubbling away inside her.

It felt quite decadent to come home to her own house in the middle of the afternoon when she should have been packing boxes under Lady Smythe's critical eye and listening to the repetitive gossip of the good ladies gathered around her. Inside there was no Agnes to admonish her so she swept off her hat and flung it across the room, crying "I'm free!"

She danced round her sitting room - just because she could. Ah, it was such joy to have her little house all to herself again!

Katy slung her coat over the back of the fireside chair. Dust flew up in the air. It had been a long time empty, her house. She would set to and give it a really good clean before settling down to study the papers the vicar had given her all those weeks ago.

Then the edge of a letter on the floor, that had snagged under the doormat, caught her eye and she seized upon it.

Katy tore open the envelope expecting it to be news from Jem.

It wasn't.

It was a letter from his regiment instead.

Katy read the official form with feelings so mixed, she could make neither head nor tail of it. She took it to her front window and spread the single sheet out on her chenille cloth so she could read it carefully, over and over again. Most of it was typed and could be applied to anyone with only the personal details of Jem's name and rank filled in by hand.

82

No. 108,654

Dear Sir/Madam,

It is my painful duty to inform you that a report has this day been received by the War Office notifying the death of:

(the letter here gave his rank, regiment and serial number)

which occurred at:

the battle of Arras on the 9th of April 1917

and I am to express to you the sincere sympathy of the Army Council

at your loss. The cause of death was:

missing, presumed killed in action.

If any articles belonging to the deceased are found they will be forwarded to this office, but some time will probably elapse before their receipt, and when received, they cannot be disposed of until authority is received from the War Office. Application regarding the disposal of any such personal effects or of any amount found to be due to the late soldier's estate should be addressed to the 'Secretary of State, War Office, London S.W' and marked on the outside 'Effects'

I am your most obedient servant, Officer in Charge of Records

An indecipherable signature scrawled in pen scattered across the rest of the page next to an official stamp.

There was a round metal object on a ribbon enclosed. Stupidly, she turned the medal over and within the laurel wreath on the back, were inscribed the words,

"For bravery in the field."

Jem must have left it behind somewhere, how odd.

If her emotions had been in turmoil before, they now performed such loops and dives and twists and turns, she hardly knew what to do with herself. She got up, knocking her chair over without even noticing and paced around her little cottage as guilt, concern, loneliness and a myriad of other feelings grabbed at her all at once.

Katy sobbed out loud, "I don't know what to do. Someone tell me what to do. Oh, God, what must I do?" She went round and round her parlour, touching things Jem had touched, smelling her fingers to find a trace of him. She couldn't breathe. Who could she turn to?

***

She ran to the back door and flung it open for some fresh air.

Sally Fenwick was sitting in a pool of sunlight on her back-doorstep, shelling early broad beans into a chipped enamel basin. "Hello, Katy. Got me first beans for supper. My Tom loves his beans alright."

Katy muttered something incomprehensible and walked up the garden to avoid further contact. She had always accepted the garden as Jem's domain. She'd tried to keep it tidy while he was away but had never really had the knack of it. There was the log store he'd made. Here the cold frame he'd knocked up in a trice. He'd been so handy, so hardworking.

She tried to remember his voice. She had loved the sound of it. And his hands – so capable and strong but they could also be gentle and kind. She pictured his face, but it was all blurry. Could she have forgotten the smell and look of him so soon? How could it be possible she wouldn't look on him again? Why on earth had she put off marrying him and preferred the shallow Charles? And yet, she was also furious that Jem had gone off at all. How could he justify taking this risk with his life, gambling with their happiness?

And he'd lost the bet.

Katy walked up to the woods behind her cottage, fuelled by frustrated rage. Within the private embrace of the trees, their branches tinged with the tender green of breaking leaf buds, she allowed herself to let go. Her knees buckled under her. She pummelled her fists on an unsuspecting ash tree begging it to explain to her why this had happened. She slid down on to the carpet of last year's leaves and sobbed until she was exhausted.

Eventually she fell asleep on the soft woodland floor. When she woke up it was twilight and she had a raging thirst. There was a large stream at the bottom of the valley. She and Jem had often walked there on a summer's evening. Katy stood up and picked out the twigs from her hair and then stopped, as she remembered it no longer mattered what she looked like. Jem would never see her again.

How dare he leave her?

Tears threatened once more and she ran to the little river, trying to escape her confused jumble of grief and anger.

Kneeling on its mossy banks, Katy scooped up the cold water, washed her face with it and then drank from her cupped hands. The water was cool and fresh. It soothed her. She lay back against the soft grass, listening to the river splashing gently along on its way to the sea. Daffodils studded the bank and their splash of bright yellow was offset by spikes of white ramson garlic whose flowers gave off a pungent perfume. Jem had loved the tender green leaves cooked in a pie or a soup.

Oh, Jem, Jem, how could he be gone?

She was glad no-one knew where she was. It was a secret glade, a private spot. She needed to be alone to absorb this monumental, horrible fact of Jem's death.

The soft spring night stole in. Still Katy lay by the stream, listening to it babble on. If she stayed here forever and never saw anyone again, never saw that dreadful letter again, maybe it wouldn't be true? Jem would come walking home again, smiling in his cheerful, steady way and everything would be as it was before. She curled up into a ball, hugging her legs with her arms, willing her world to remain unchanged.

She remembered Jem holding Florence and dangling her plump little legs in the stream, only last year. Florence had giggled and squirmed in delight.

The stream's gentle cadence continued to play its sibilant song in her head. She wanted to enter the river, to submerge under its silky caress. Katy started to slide down the bank. She stretched out her arms. She wanted to touch the water, to lie under it, to let it carry her to the ocean, to drift forever...

At first, she didn't hear her name being called. The sound penetrated gradually, as if through a fog.

"Katherine! No, don't!"

Who was that shouting at her? The voice was still distant. It was probably a dream. Katy paid it no heed but continued slithering into the stream. She didn't mind the cold. She was already numb. Her hair started to unpin itself in the water. It became river fronds. Slowly, little waves stroked her face. She welcomed them into her mouth, her nose, and closed her eyes, longing for sleep.

Suddenly she was rudely hauled up out of the water. As she was lifted up air, not water, rushed into her mouth and nose making her cough out the beautiful river that had soothed her. What was happening? She opened her eyes at last and looked into blazing blue ones.

A full moon silvered the face staring at her. She had no idea to whom it belonged or even where she was anymore.

"Katherine, oh, Katherine! What have you done?" Lionel said.

Katy felt very faint and shut her eyes to stop the moon spinning around the sky. She fell back into the dreamlike state she'd succumbed to under the water.

She felt delicate fingers brush the hair from her face just like the stream flowing over it. Loving fingers. Jem! Jem was alive! She kept her eyes closed, not wanting to break the spell. He laid her on the grassy bank. She felt his warm breath on her face. When he kissed her, she opened her mouth, feeling life pouring back into her. Jem wasn't dead after all!

Katy flung her arms around him and kissed him back with all the love in her heart. Those loving hands held her face tenderly, wiping away her warm tears as they flowed.

"Katherine, it's alright, I'm here," he whispered. "Oh, my love, I have you safe, I'll keep you safe forever, my darling."

Katy smiled and opened her arms wide in invitation. She wanted to welcome Jem back into the land of the living. Warm lips, living skin. Still here! Still breathing. Thank God! But this kiss felt different from Jem's. Jem smelled of earth and the clean sweat of hard labour. This male fragrance was exotic, complicated and intoxicating. Katy's head span in confusion. She was dizzy with excitement. Once again, she felt under the spell of a fever. She was not ill - her bones did not ache this time. No, they hummed with life. Her blood fizzed in her veins. Her mind withdrew still further into deep recesses she could not rationally reach.

When Lionel cried out her name again, Katy opened her eyes and saw, not Jem's brown eyes but turquoise blue ones, alive with desire. She shut the image out and kept her eyes screwed tight. Who was this? He was stroking her body, whipping up her senses into a frenzy and caressing her lips with his own. Her skin responded to his touch, becoming warm and tingling. It had been so long since she had felt like this. A shiver shot through her frame and her mind blanked out again. Then a deep velvet blackness blotted everything out.

CHAPTER THIRTY SIX

Lionel lay next to the woman he loved and gazed on her body in disbelief that he had violated it. How could he have done such a thing? But she had kissed him back with such fervour, such passion he could not stop his own. Now Lionel felt bewildered at his betrayal. He had succumbed to the basest of desires with a woman who appeared to be out of her mind. He must stay true to his calling and stop, before things became completely out of hand. He felt ashamed that he had taken advantage and kissed her. But those lips had tasted of honeyed heaven.

Enough!

Lionel stared at Katy, forcing his mind to grapple with the situation and quell his body's urgent prompting before he crossed the ultimate boundary, beyond those sublime kisses. He must think. How had she ended up here by the river anyway? Why had she tried to drown herself in the first place? She was still lying there with eyes shut, in a stupor. A half smile played on her lips.

"Katherine? Katherine, my dear. Please wake up. Let me help you."

Katy did not respond. Lionel felt he was in a dream, one that was rapidly becoming a nightmare. He had been wandering aimlessly in the woods, following the little river at the foot of the hill that overshadowed the valley. He had been thinking of Katy the whole time, as had become his habit. He was hoping to wear himself out with walking so that he might sleep through the night for once. To find her sliding into the water, sinking under it, passively drowning; completely disturbed him. He had only meant to rescue her.

She groaned. "What is it my darling?" he said, stroking her hair.

"I'm cold," she muttered, under her breath. Her eyelids fluttered but did not open.

"Of course! You must be freezing." Lionel touched her clothes and found them soaking wet.

"We must get you home and dry, Katherine," Lionel said.

Even as he said it, he remembered that this was the second time she had been in this state. Last time, she had been grieving for her lost daughter. Had something precipitated this attempt at, well, must he call it suicide? Galvanised now, realising he must not waste a precious second, he gathered her up in his arms, kissed her once and strode as quickly as his burden allowed back towards the village. Katy remained inert and unconscious.

It was past midnight by the time they reached Katy's cottage and the village lay deep in slumber. Glad of the cover of darkness, Lionel went around to back of her house and opened the door, relieved to find it unlocked in the country way.

There was no fire to warm her, but he wouldn't call Sally Fenwick this time. It was too late, and he was far too compromised.

With the last of his strength, he carried Katy up to her bedroom. The bed was unmade. He remembered no-one had been living here for weeks. He laid her down and found some sheets and blankets in a cupboard nearby. He felt Katy's feet. Ice-cold. She needed warming up.

Lionel was at a total loss on how to manage the situation. Katy's dress was sodden and her skin clammy and wet. If he let her remain in them, she would surely get pneumonia a second time. And this time she might die even though it was spring now. What should he do? Lionel baulked at removing her soaking things and exposing her body while she was inert and unconscious. Could he trust himself not to be further tempted if he saw her naked? To take the kiss he'd enjoyed at the riverside to its natural, glorious conclusion? He had no answer to that. Katy started to shiver, and goose-pimples crept up her arms.

Lionel decided this was an emergency, and normal rules did not apply.

Swallowing hard and taking a firm grip of the desire dancing in his veins, he gently stripped her of all her wet clothes and towelled her down with the reverence he normally kept for the altar. The more he revealed of her young and slender body, the more reverential he became. His earlier lust was transcended by her beauty. He felt in awe of it; of her. Katy was as sacred to him as the holy crucifix. Once she was dry, he covered her tenderly with the sheets and blankets and took her clothes downstairs to air on the backs of the chairs.

There was kindling and old newspapers by the bedroom grate. He found it easier to light than the big old range downstairs and soon had a fire crackling away. It lit the room with a flickering glow, so he drew the curtains. He needed no audience tonight.

He looked at Katy. The fire showed her face white and her lips a little blue. He kissed them and found them cold. Too cold.

Not again! Thought Lionel, please God, don't let her be so ill again. He put a couple of logs on the fire to bank it up and placed the fire guard across it. The room still felt chilly and a little damp. There was only one thing for it.

Lionel took off his own clothes and climbed into bed next to Katy who was now sleeping deeply. Her body felt delicious against his warm skin; delightfully cool, like satin. He didn't dare stroke it. He might wake her and his own desire. He laid next to her letting his blood heat warm hers. He stayed there studying every line, every curve of her face, as it rested peacefully next to his. From time to time, he touched her lightly and was relieved to find she had warmed up and seemed to be breathing normally.

It astonished him that here he was, lying next to this graceful young woman, skin to skin. Their breath mingled in the intimacy of the pillow. Lionel wanted to dissolve into her. He longed to wrap his arms about her, to lay his body on top of hers and merge together in the deepest embrace of all. He indulged in this tantalising fantasy until he fell asleep.

He woke a few hours later to find the dawn poking its nose into their secret nest. The short spring night was over.

He gazed at Katy. Her eyelashes brushed her peachy skin with dark sweeping lashes. Her skin was warm now as it should be. He detected no fever except his own. He was a man of the cloth, he must remember that. The devil snapped at his bare skin, daring him to resist the ultimate temptation. He would not let that evil consume him now. Even under the most irresistible, seductive lure of the body of the woman he adored lying right next to his, he would not let the darkness triumph.

He was no sinner, no, not he.

Lionel got out of the bed as carefully as possible. He covered Katy's sleeping form with the blankets to exclude any draught and dressed quietly. The fire had gone out, but the room wasn't so cold now. Already the sun promised warmth.

After checking her once more and satisfying himself that she was still sleeping normally, he dragged himself away and went downstairs. He must not be found here. He must get home before the village woke up to find him in Katy's home. He checked around the parlour to make sure he'd not left a trace of his presence and was distracted by an opened letter on the table. He glanced at it in passing; then, seeing it looked official, he picked it up.

He had to squint to read it in the grey half-light of dawn, but the writing was clear enough. Even so, Lionel had to re-read the official form several times before the enormity of its contents could sink into his whirling brain.

So that was why she was drowning in the river.

Jem was dead.

But that meant - surely that meant - that Katy was free? Free to marry again. She could be his - openly, securely, truly – his *wife*! God had done this. God meant them to be together. Could this be divinely inspired fate? God would condone his actions because she was already free. He had not lain next to another man's wife after all!

He tried to be true to his calling, tried to feel remorse for Jem's young death but his joy blotted it out. He would ask her to marry him today. She might not remember what had happened by the river. If so, he would not remind her that he had already nearly taken what was not yet rightfully his. She'd been out of her mind and now he knew why. Poor Katherine. So many bereavements. He would take care of her now. He would keep her safe always. He could protect her. Give her a home worthy of her beauty.

Ah, her beauty! His beautiful Katherine.

A cockerel crowed in one of the village gardens. Lionel looked up from the letter and saw that soon the sun would be above the valley roofs and shining right into Katy's parlour. He seized his hat and went to the back door, shutting it softly behind him.

With stealthy, quiet steps he tip-toed past the backs of the terraced cottages and, looking furtively right to left, stepped into the main road. He crossed it with his head down and kept his footsteps light. Gaining the narrow lane that rose up the valley side to the vicarage, Lionel broke into a sprint. Panting by the time he reached it, he let himself in through his own front door. Still on tiptoe, he crept upstairs and stole into his bedroom, where he collapsed on to his bed.

But even this wouldn't do. He tore off his soiled, damp clothes and threw them on to their usual chair. Grabbing his nightgown, he put it on, and clambered under the bedclothes. He lay there, gazing at the ceiling, not seeing the ornate plaster, but Katy's face.

He remembered lying next to her in the double bed. He'd never known such ecstasy. He longed for more.

When Mrs Hoskins came in two hours later with his morning tea, Lionel was fast asleep, in his own bed and nightgown, just the way she had found him every morning since he had arrived in her village.

CHAPTER THIRTY SEVEN

Katy stretched out in the bed. She couldn't remember the last time she had slept so well. She yawned, opened her eyes and sat up. Smoothing her hand down her body, she was shocked to find it bare. She checked herself all over, astonished to find not only was she back in her own cottage bedroom but she really was without any nightgown. She always slept in a nightgown except when she and Jem had made love.

With that recollection, Katy's world collapsed in on her.

Jem.

There *was* no Jem.

A chill crawled over her exposed skin. She could not bear to stay alone in her marriage bed a moment longer. She got up and finding no clothes in the room, wrapped a blanket around her naked flesh. Her mind wouldn't function. She could not fathom why she was here like this. She needed to see that wretched British Army form again.

Maybe it had all been a dream after all.

Katy caught up the blanket and tied it round her middle, covering her shoulders as best she could. She stumbled down the narrow stairs and opened the door into the parlour. Sure enough, the hated piece of paper still sat, mute but emphatic, on the table. She sat in front of it and read it again. Its bold print stated the facts, coldly and resolutely, on the page.

It was true.

Jem, her darling Jem, was really gone.

Forever.

He was never coming back.

She looked out of the window at the familiar village street. All she saw was Jem coming and going to work, always smiling, always reliable, always on time. Katy gripped the table edge. She felt faint again. And sick. Just like when she was carrying Florence. Who was also gone.

Katy almost choked on her tears then; they arrived in such a torrent. She threw herself across her green chenille cloth and gave in to utter despair.

She cried until she was spent, then cast about for something to wipe her face with. Reaching out blindly, she picked up what seemed to be a cloth, blew her nose into it and wiped her streaming eyes. She placed it back on the table and looked at it. Gradually her eyes focussed, and Katy realised it wasn't a cloth. It was a glove. A man's glove. The kid leather looked expensive. It did not belong to some menial worker on the estate. This was the glove of a gentleman.

It was a slate grey colour and finely stitched. Her tears had soaked it. She picked it up and wiped it on her blanket. She looked inside and saw the letters 'L W' stitched into the lining.

Her mind was still fuddled and reluctant to compute. Who had those initials?

The sun slanted bright morning rays into the room. Katy blinked at its brash hello. It shone right into her eyes, so she shut them to ward off the unwelcome glare. An image brushed across her mind. An image so bizarre, she tried to shake her head free of it.

She must be imagining it. The vicar? With her? She remembered a vague sensation of water on her face and then someone kissing it. 'L W' - Lionel White - and she'd woken up naked. How could this be happening? What *was* happening?

There was a loud rap on the front door. Katy jumped out of her skin. She couldn't be found like this! Where were her clothes? She looked about the room and saw them draped over the fireside chairs. She got up to fetch them, then turned, in answer to someone tapping insistently on the parlour window.

It was Lionel White – 'L W'.

She needed an explanation of that glove, those dim memories. She let him in.

"Katherine, Katherine, my darling. You are well! I'm so relieved." Lionel rushed towards her, arms held out.

"I don't understand," Katy said, backing off, "I'm not your darling. Your glove is here and how did I get home?"

"I found you, Katherine, dearest. I found you by the river. You were, um, upset. I didn't realise why until I brought you home and found the army's notice about Jeremy. I, I'm so sorry."

Katy looked at the official form and back at Lionel. She was desperately trying to make sense of the situation. "You brought me home?"

"Yes, you had sort of fallen in the river."

"Sort of?"

"Katherine, you were drowning."

Then Katy remembered. She had wanted to drift away. To join Jem and Florence.

She nodded and sat back down at the table, drawing her blanket tighter around her.

Lionel was silent, waiting for his cue.

Katy's furrowed brow cleared. "Reverend White, why was I without any clothes when I woke up?"

"You were soaking wet, Katherine. I didn't know what to do. You had been so ill before I didn't want that to happen again. It was too late to call Mrs Fenwick or your mother, so I took the liberty of, um, removing them and putting you to bed. I lit a fire in the room too, to warm you up."

His tone was pleading. She'd never heard him so humble before. "You had no right to do that."

Katy was surprised to see Lionel blush to the roots of his golden hair. Why was he so uncomfortable? Well, he'd probably never seen a woman naked before. Katy felt too exhausted to be embarrassed. She doubted she'd ever care about anything again. Still, she had to know what else might have happened. Last night was still a blank. Her heart flipped over at possibilities that now presented themselves with a shock.

She looked at Lionel. "When you undressed me last night, what else did you do, vicar?"

"I, um, I lit a fire, I told you." Lionel shifted uneasily and went to sit by the cold range.

"You lit a fire and put me to bed. And that was all?"

"Of course. I stayed a little while just to check on you. You had got very cold by the river in the woods. Do you remember being by the river?"

Katy thought back. Slowly she pieced events together aloud. "I left the manor yesterday afternoon. I'd had enough of Lady Smythe and I came home here to find that communication about Jem. I didn't know what to do so I ran up to the woods to cry in private. I think I must have fallen asleep and when I woke up it was getting dark. I was thirsty so I went to the river for a drink. I didn't want to come home, I know that. I wanted to sleep forever. I do recall being in the water and then, oh!"

"What else do you remember, Katherine?" Lionel looked as white as his surname.

"You! We – you, oh, God! I thought you were Jem and you, you touched me and then... How could you? How could you take advantage of me like that? At such a time? And you a Reverend?"

"Katherine, I couldn't stop myself. You see, dearest, I love you. I've loved you for so long. I think of nothing but you." Lionel got up and knelt before her. "Katherine, Katherine, listen to me, please, you must listen."

Katy put her hand over her mouth and bit her fingers till they hurt.

"Katherine, I know you've had a shock with the news about Jem. But when you've got over that, when you are quite well again, please, won't you reconsider? I shouldn't have done what I did last night but I couldn't stop. You see, you kissed me back, and so passionately. Well, one thing just led to another, but I don't want to hurt you. I never would hurt you. I just love you so much. Please,

Katherine, tell me you understand. Give me leave to hope?"

Katy found her voice then. "Hope? Hope? What have I to hope for? I'll give you no hope, you filthy beast. Get out of my house, you thieving hypocrite! Call yourself a man of God? Where are your morals? Where is your integrity, Preacher? You'd better listen to your own preaching! How dare you strip me naked? How dare you force yourself upon me when I wasn't capable of refusing you?"

"But Katherine, Katy, I…"

"Don't you dare call me Katy. Jem was the only man I'd let call me that, or his darling, or make love to me. Get out I say, get out! I never want to see you again!"

And Katy shoved him in the chest towards the door with all her strength. Clutching her blanket with one hand and pushing Lionel with the other, they reached the door.

"Katherine, please. You must understand! I know I was wrong, but it just happened."

"Get out! I will not listen to you."

She grabbed the door and flung it wide open onto the street.

Lionel looked outside. Billy Threadwell was walking up the road with letters in his hand. He flushed again.

He put on his hat. "You are upset, Katherine, I understand you've had a shock. Don't get cold standing there like that. Someone might see you."

"See you, more like. That would blow your cover right enough, wouldn't it? You'd better go before your reputation is ruined. After all, you've got to uphold the principles of the church, haven't you? With you a pillar of the community and all."

Lionel stepped smartly over the threshold and Katy slammed the door behind him as hard as she could, then stood looking at the back of the closed door. She was shaking from head to foot like one of her mother's calf's foot jellies. Her mind was whirling with conflicting emotions. How could it be possible that Reverend White loved her? Aware she felt cold despite the anger roaring through her veins, she went back into the parlour and snatched up her clothes from the backs of the chairs. They were still a bit damp, but they'd do. Anything to cover herself up.

She went upstairs, taking a jug of rainwater with her, drawn from the barrel outside. She took off the blanket and threw it on the bed. Katy went to the washstand and looked at herself in the spotted mirror. Even to her own eyes, she looked pinched and worn.

She looked for evidence of Lionel on her body. There were no bruises or marks. It was as if she had dreamt it. How far had he gone? If only she could remember! She almost retched at the thought that she might have given herself to another man when Jem lay dead.

She splashed water from the jug into the china basin and then on her face, patting it dry with the towel from the rail. She wanted to cry it all out and fill the basin with her sorrow but something, some inherent will to live coupled with sustained fury, stopped her. She got a flannel from the cupboard and washed her whole body, especially the private areas. She scrubbed those and rubbed herself dry with harsh vigour. The coal tar soap smelt clean. It was small comfort. She doubted she would ever feel really clean again.

She folded the towel and placed it neatly back on its rail. Then she took up the china basin and brought it down to the scullery where she flung the water as far away as she could and Lionel's trespass with it. Getting fresh water, she rinsed and rinsed the flannel and pegged it out on the line, relieved to see none of her neighbours were in their gardens. She could no more have smiled a hello than flown to the moon. With measured steps, she took the clean basin back to its customary station upstairs.

More than anything, Katy wanted everything in its rightful place.

She walked quietly downstairs and went back to the table where the official form still declared Jem's death a fact. Lionel's glove had gone, she noticed. Good, she wanted no reminders of that traitor. She felt tired and empty. Only her anger felt alive, but she couldn't work out who she was more angry with, Lionel for taking what wasn't his, Jem for throwing his life away, or was it herself she hated right now?

Her stomach rumbled. Her body wanted to live; to carry on - even if she did not. How could she carry on? Or eat? It rumbled again, insistent this time. Katy brushed her hand across her tired face. Maybe, if she did eat something, she might be able to think straight. She went into the scullery and rummaged about.

There was a tin of pineapple at the back of the cupboard, obviously forgotten by the last temporary tenants. It still seemed strange to her that food could be preserved like this. She levered it open awkwardly with the tin opener she found next to it, almost cutting her hands on its sharp, pointed edge. She'd never opened a tin like this one before only the sardines that rolled open their lids by means of a key. She forked a couple of chunks into her mouth, marvelling at their fresh exotic taste. They were sweet but also acid. The unusual flavour surprised her mouth and she screwed it up in distaste, but the sugar gave her strength. Her mind began to whirr again. Before she knew it, she'd absentmindedly eaten the contents of the whole tin.

She could find nothing else to eat but the thought of going to the shop was too nightmarish to contemplate. Katy slurped some rainwater from the jug. Her odd breakfast was strangely satisfying. She smoothed her dress down. It was drying well in the warm sunshine that flooded the scullery. She looked out of the window. Still no Jem in the garden. Neither were there vegetables she could raid or hens laying eggs. The garden looked forlorn and uncared for in spite of the spring sunshine and her erratic efforts to keep the weeds down. She couldn't bear to gaze on it any longer and turned back to the parlour.

Katy unlocked her dresser cupboard with the little key she always carried. All her precious things were kept in that dresser, made with such hope by Jem before their marriage. The packet of his letters sat there staring at her. She took it out and placed it on the table.

She knew Jem's letters and postcards off by heart, but she wanted to read them again and touch each one, just in case she could get the faintest trace of him. Most were short and to the point. All were loving and dog-eared with travel. She sorted them into date order and followed his progress through this hateful killing spree that the Government called 'the war to end all wars'. It would never end for her now.

Jem's words were simple and true. His sincerity shone through each pencilled, wobbly line. He'd never been good with writing. Each letter must have been an effort and composed in conditions Katy could only guess at. He'd never stopped loving her or missing her.

If Jem knew what Lionel had done, he'd have knocked him from this week to next. She still couldn't believe what had happened with Lionel. And yet, compared to the black hole of Jem's death, it seemed of little consequence. She was glad she'd sent him packing and hoped she'd never see him again.

Anger spurted up in her at the futile madness of it all. Suddenly, she brushed all the papers off the table with a swipe of pure fury.

CHAPTER THIRTY EIGHT

Lionel paced up and down his study, tormented by Katy's rejection. He clutched his ruined glove, still wet from her tears, in a tight fist. How could she reject him? He reminded himself she'd just been bereaved, just tried to commit suicide because of her grief and this new shock had come on top of losing her only child. He must give her time. Surely, she'd come around. If not, how could he live without her?

He knelt and prayed. After an hour of fervent entreaty, his God spoke to him.

Write to her. Of course! Lionel leapt up from the floor and went to his desk. Grabbing his fountain pen and some paper, he sat down to compose the most important letter of his life.

For once he did not how to begin. Lionel prided himself on his ability to construct a good letter, a cogent argument. He'd won many a campaign with his skill.

He looked out of the window. The river still burbled away at the bottom of his garden. What a shock it had been to see Katherine floating in it, last night. He must be gentle now. Lionel picked up his pen, chewed it for a while, then began to write. Once he'd begun, the ink flowed smoothly over the vellum paper and covered the page quickly.

He signed it with a flourish and sat back to read it over. Yes, she could not fail to be moved by his humble plea.

He blotted the ink dry and sealed it in a matching envelope. He put his hat back on and checked the time on the grandfather clock in the hall. He must be quick so that he could get back to give the morning service. Lionel stepped up his pace and marched swiftly to Katy's cottage at the bottom of the steep valley. He decided not to knock at the door. He didn't want to upset her again and he was no longer concerned for her health. She had looked very well that morning, wrapped up in her blanket with her cheeks aflame and her eyes blazing.

What a woman.

He slipped the envelope through the letterbox, taking care not to let it clang and alert her to his presence. No point revisiting the angry scene earlier. No, he must give his written words a chance to work their magic.

Feeling confident, Lionel walked briskly back to the church, humming his favourite hymn.

***

Lionel needn't have worried that he'd disturb her, for Katy had already left to visit her parents - and Jem's - to break the dreadful news to them. It was only right to let them know as soon as possible before they heard it from other people. News, especially bad news, had a way of escaping boundaries and spreading itself where it wasn't wanted. She owed them all that duty, but it would be very hard.

Reluctant she might be, but Katy knew that if she delayed, she'd never have the courage to tell them, especially after last night's experience. She would say nothing of that to anyone. The hazy memory didn't seem real to her and she felt deeply ashamed that she'd allowed Lionel that license. It compromised her grief for Jem. She hated Lionel for that. How she could have been so confused? She would never know. Best to forget it. She wasn't hurt, just sullied. Jem's death eclipsed everything else.

The sky had clouded over, but the warmth had not dissipated; if anything, it felt too warm for April. A storm was brewing, for sure. The hill rising to Upper Cheadle had never looked more daunting but climb it she must.

The stout lodge house greeted Katy like an old friend. Its familiar shape comforted her. And how often had she unlatched this cottage door, and stepped into her mother's spotless kitchen to sit and lean her elbows on the scrubbed pine table for a cosy chat? If only today could be like that.

Katy composed herself as she sat down, cradling the cup of tea her mother gave her. She felt hot yet clammy at the same time. She waited until Bert was equipped with his mug and in his favourite chair by the range, legs stretched out in front of him, the better to dry his breeches. He'd just come home from his early stint at the stables and had been caught in a sudden downpour. It had been one of those mornings that starts too bright and always ends in showers. She'd been lucky to miss one, walking up the hill under a sky pregnant with thunder. Steam floated upwards from her father's sturdy legs. Agnes was busy fielding laundry, pastry and children all at once, as if she had three pairs of hands, instead of the single pair given to other mortals.

"So young lady, what were you up to yesterday?" asked Agnes, setting her pastry to chill on the stone windowsill. "Lady Smythe says you've packed in helping with her war effort. And you never come home here last night. If it wasn't for that note you left telling us you was stopping at home, we'd have been that worried."

Katy swallowed the hot tea too quickly and coughed.

"Must be lonely down there in the valley on your own," said her father, as conciliatory as ever.

"Yes, it is a bit," Katy said, still prevaricating.

"This bloody war. I heard a lad from the Ponsonby's estate has died over there now. And at the manor, all Sir Robert does is drink himself into a standstill. I tell you, the heart's gone out of the place." Bert bashed his pipe onto the range too hard and snapped the stem. "Damn." He stared at its broken shaft.

Katy could put the moment off no longer. She drew a deep breath and began, "Mum, Dad. I've got something to tell you," she said into the sad silence, speaking too quickly. She'd better get it over with, before her voice gave way. Everything stilled. Agnes gripped a pile of sheets for support and Bert braced his legs against the fender.

Agnes called to the other children, "Daisy, Jack - take little Emily out into the garden, will you? She could do with some fresh air."

"But Mum, it's raining!" protested Daisy, scooping up her little sister.

"Then play in the barn. Now, please, Daisy!" Agnes said in the voice that brooked no argument. Obediently Daisy took Emily and Jack outside and shut the door.

Katy spoke into the sudden vacuum. There seemed no way she could soften her news or break it more gently.

Her voice did tremble as she blurted out, "I had an official form from Jem's regiment yesterday. He's missing, presumed killed."

Both her parents stared at her in frozen disbelief. Neither could get their breath to interrupt her so she went and stood by the window before the sympathy in their eyes undid her. She couldn't bear to see their shocked faces and turned away to watch the children skip to the barn through the rain.

Agnes dropped the sheets and flew to Bert. He held her while tears flowed unchecked between them.

"Not Jem, I never thought it would be Jem. Charles Smythe – well, he was ever a hothead, and that Adam Fairweather too but I can't believe Jem has gone. Oh Katy!" Agnes turned to hold Katy, but her daughter shook her head and kept holding on like grim death to the windowsill, gazing at the beloved landscape while the April shower washed it clean.

Agnes shook her head. "Poor, poor Jem. Gone. I can't believe it. I must go and see Mary."

"It's a massacre, that's what it is" Bert wrapped his arms tight around his wife.

Katy's own tears began again at the sound of her mother, usually so strong, breaking down. The Wiltshire downs blurred, and their hedges swam together. The thundery shower stopped as suddenly as it had started and the sun broke through, making the raindrops on the lattice window sparkle.

Then she felt her mother's arms around her. Agnes held her tight for a long while, not taking no for an answer. Katy laid her head on her mother's generous bosom and let out her grief in that safe embrace.

Bert stared at the fire as if Jem's face danced in the heat of it. When he looked up, as Katy's crying eased at last, he looked twenty years older. Agnes patted her shoulder, dried her own streaming eyes on her apron and went back to her husband by the fire. Katy leaned against the solid windowsill again; the cold stone a welcome, disinterested witness to her distress. The downs sported a rainbow from the April shower as the purple thunder clouds rolled away into the distance.

"I loved Jem like my own son. I was that glad when you married him, Katy. I wish I'd told him so." Bert did not attempt to wipe his own tears away. He held his shaking wife close again but his eyes rested on his daughter, standing so still with her back resolutely to them.

Sensing his gaze, Katy turned to face them. She felt calmer now, cried out and empty. "Give us another cup of tea, Mum, then I must go and see George and Mary."

"I'll come with you, dear." Her mother put the kettle on the hob. "It'll not be easy. Poor Mary. Oh God, keep our Albert safe."

"I'll come with you too," Bert said. "It'll knock George and Mary hard and I'll not see you do it alone."

Daisy was again charged with the care of her younger siblings after a cold lunch when none of the adults ate much. Bert fetched the little gig and drove his eldest daughter and wife down the hill to Lower Cheadle.

"I'll pull up by the walled garden and see if I can find George first." Bert dismounted from the gig when they were halfway down the hill. Katy and her mother watched

231

his burly frame as he unlatched the garden door and disappeared inside.

"I don't know how I'm going to say this to George and Mary," Katy said.

"No, I don't suppose you do. Not an easy thing to say," replied Agnes. "Just keep it simple, love. That's all you can do."

Soon George and Bert joined them, and poor Larkspur had to pull hard with the four of them weighing her down.

"Come on, girl." Bert rippled the reins along her dappled back.

Katy recalled Charles doing the same to the gentle mare but with such carefree joy on their illicit jaunts such a short time ago. Now he was dead too. Would this war leave no family untouched?

George and Bert were chatting about the weather as if nothing had happened. Katy dreaded telling her father-in-law that his beloved son had died. He'd always been so kind to her, even going against his own wife to champion her, when she'd married Jem.

Too soon, Larkspur delivered them to East Lodge in Lower Cheadle. It was an exact copy of their West Lodge but snuggled into the valley floor on the eastern edge of Sir Robert's estate instead of whipped clean by westerly winds on the hill.

They all clambered down from the gig and entered the lodge house. Mary was preparing George's supper. Onions and carrots gave off their homely smell and a rabbit lay, skinned and ready for the pot, next to them.

"Hello, love!" Mary smiled at her husband. "What brings you home so early? And why, here's Agnes and Bert too! Oh, and Katy."

Katy's heart sank.

"Hello, Mary." Agnes greeted her with a grave face.

Katy was grateful her mother filled the breach and reached for her hand. Agnes gave it a squeeze.

Mary's smile faded. "Please, everyone, sit down. I'll put the kettle on." She placed her big copper kettle on the hob and joined them at the table.

"Thanks, Mary, I'd like to sit down." Agnes chose a chair next to her daughter.

When they were all seated, Katy looked at her in-laws expectant faces and took a deep breath. Agnes still held her hand under the table in a firm, reassuring grip.

"Mary, George - I've some bad news," Katy began.

Mary's hand flew to her mouth and George's eyes never left Katy's face. This was even harder than she'd imagined. Much harder than telling her parents and that had been tough enough. Best to get it over with quickly, same as last time.

She cleared her throat and continued, "It's about Jem. I've had a form from his regiment. They say he's missing, presumed killed, in action."

"No! No! It can't be true!" Mary turned to her husband and they gripped each other.

Katy and her parents withdrew to the hallway to let them adjust to the shock in private. They stood there, silent and uncertain, for a good ten minutes before Mary came rushing over and began to beat Katy with her fists.

"It's your fault! It's all your fault! If he hadn't married you, he would never have gone! He was that miserable. You, with all your wailing and moping, getting a chill and being ill. He was always looking after you. He was never happy after he married you. I never wanted him to wed you! I hate you! I hate you!" Mary's fingers clawed at Katy's face.

Katy threw her hands up to guard against the assault, but Mary's words had already given her a deep wound. George pulled his wife off Katy and took her back into the kitchen. Agnes put her arm around her daughter who stood dry-eyed, her stomach hollow with guilt, staring at her mother-in-law's heaving back as Mary sobbed onto George's broad chest.

233

Bert followed the grieving parents into their kitchen. "George? I think it's best we leave now."

George turned around, looked over his wife's head and nodded. "Yes, Bert. I'll see to Mary. Thank you for coming to tell us, Katy. I'm sorry things have turned out like this."

Mary looked up at that, "Don't be sorry for her. She killed Jem. She did it!"

Agnes stepped in. "That's not fair, Mary. Katy loved Jem with all her heart. She's just as upset as you. All the young men are getting conscripted now. Jem would have had to have gone anyway."

"Come on, Agnes, that's enough now, dear." Bert put an arm around each of them and shepherded his wife and daughter out to the waiting gig. They climbed wearily in. Mary's hysterical wails floated out through the open kitchen window.

"God keep our Albert safe," whispered Agnes, shaking her head.

"Mum, Dad?" Katy said.

"Yes, love?" they said in unison.

"I think I'd like to stay here, in my house again, tonight. I need some time alone. To remember...you know."

"Will you be alright on your own?" Agnes looked very anxious.

Katy nodded.

"Leave her be, Katy knows where we are. This will take a bit of getting used to, for all of us." Bert turned to Katy. "Now listen, Katy. You can get word to us through Martha Threadwell's telephone, remember? I'll only leave you here if you promise me, faithfully mind, that you'll get in touch if you need us. You be sure to come and see us in a day or two, don't mope too long on your own. Promise me?"

234

Katy hugged her Dad and then her mother, before stepping down from the gig. She waved them off. Larkspur plodded up the hill to the West Lodge.

Even the horse looked sad.

CHAPTER THIRTY NINE

Katy entered her home through the back door. She sat quietly for a while remembering the shared times when it had been a happy little house. Then she recollected that, while grief might fill her heart until she thought it might break, it wouldn't fill her belly which was now growling from emptiness. Facing Martha Threadwell was the last thing she felt like doing but she could not put off going to the shop for supplies to last her through her precious couple of days of solitude. As she went to the front door, she found a letter lying on the mat.

It had all been a mistake! This must be another letter from the Army, saying Jem had been found, surely to God?

He was alive; he *had* to be.

She snatched it up and tore open the envelope.

A very different hand covered the posh, heavy paper. She took it to the window to read in the bright sunshine.

My dearest Katherine,

Allow me to express my sincere condolences on the news of your husband, Jeremy. You are obviously very upset at his death, coming so soon after the loss of your little girl.

I was so surprised to find you in the river, dear Katherine, and did not know why you were trying to end your life in this manner. I am so glad I did find you, my dear, or who knows what might have happened? Although you are grieving now, you have much to live for. You are a beautiful and intelligent woman with your whole life before you.

I apologise profusely for my trespass last night. We were both confused and bewitched and I regret my part deeply. And yet, dear Katherine, I am not sorry to have shown my profound love for you. I humbly ask your forgiveness for my earlier forwardness.

Yours truly,
Lionel White

P.S. Please show no-one this letter. A third party would not understand about last night.

Damn right they wouldn't understand. Outrageous man! Here she was, trying to pretend that it had never happened; trying to sweep away the raw fact that she'd kissed another man – or worse - when she'd only just learnt that her husband had been killed! Now, with this stark admission written down in black and white, she could no longer keep up this pretence.

She threw the paper on the table in disgust. If the range had been alight, Lionel need not worry that anyone would see it. It would already be ashes. The cheek of the man! How had he got the gall to admit he had molested her? How could he imagine she would ever want to see him again? How could he stand in the pulpit and preach to honest good people about morality? Hadn't she made it clear this morning that she despised every inch of him?

She'd never been so angry in her whole life. He'd not only stolen her self-respect, he'd now stolen her time of quiet reflection. She was quite sure she would have to relinquish her house back to the estate. It was tied to a worker, not a widow. She wanted to dwell in her married home and remember the good times for a little snatched time alone.

And what the hell was she going to do with this stupid letter? Here was evidence of her sin, let alone his. Where could she leave it? She didn't want to keep it with her, like a soiled rag. She recoiled from even touching it.

It was like one of those grenades she'd read about that could explode into her life and his.

Katy picked it up and shoved it back in its envelope. She took the form from the army about Jem and put them both back in the dresser, locking it tight shut with her key. She just couldn't think about the vicar right now. She locked him out of her mind too and stepped out into the warm spring air. She crossed over the lane to the shop for supplies, regretting it was unavoidable.

For once Martha Threadwell smiled at her. "I was that sorry to hear about your Jem, Katy. I saw the official envelope, see, and knowing you were home sent Billy over with it, but you can rest assured I've told no-one, not one soul. That's for you to do."

When Katy only nodded in reply, Martha took the hint and served her quietly, without the normal acid commentary. "We shall all miss him. You can have these groceries on me."

Mrs Threadwell's pity stuck in Katy's throat. "Thank you, Mrs Threadwell but I can still pay my way, thanks all the same."

"As you like, it was well meant." Mrs Threadwell looked hurt.

"I know, Mrs Threadwell, but Jem wouldn't want me to accept charity."

Katy paid for her few items with a shaky hand and, while waiting for her change, read over the posters about women volunteers. Looking at the pictures of those strong, independent women stopped the flow of tears welling up in her eyes at Mrs Threadwell's kindness.

She went back to her cottage to eat, rest, reflect and get the range going. She slept well, surprisingly well. She had put Jem's pillow lengthways in the big bed. Katy hugged it to her all night and kissed it in the morning. The range was still chugging away when she came downstairs, so she boiled the kettle for tea and fried a couple of eggs for breakfast. All the while, she felt Jem's loving presence. It was a great comfort and Katy had the sense he would never really leave her. The love he'd given her would remain a part of her for as long as she lived.

She spent the day remembering happy times with Jem and Florence. She pictured them both in every tiny detail. How similar they had been, especially their smiles. Florence had had her father's eyes too. Hazel brown with flecks of green, open and sincere; straightforward and loving.

She decided to spring-clean her little house thoroughly. She mopped and dusted it with the tenderness she wanted to give to Florence and Jem. She had no need of spit to wet her duster for her tears flowed freely. No-one disturbed her grieving. By the time dusk fell, Katy felt a lot calmer. Her linen was folded and pressed, the wooden furniture polished until it shone, the floors washed clean and the scullery scrubbed. She'd have a go at the garden tomorrow, tidy it up the way Jem would have done.

She ate some supper and went to bed, tired out from her housework and slept even more deeply in her marital bed. The next day was even warmer and she sweated as she weeded the garden. There was no point keeping the range alight with the weather so hot and she let it fizzle out. She couldn't be bothered to cook anyway. Bread, cheese and water would do to fuel her labours. The physical exercise outdoors did much to ease her sorrow, but she planted no seeds for the future, nor did she think about it. She preferred mindless work to that. Sally and Tom waved and smiled from their garden. Katy didn't invite chatter and they took the hint. By evening, the garden was transformed into a tidy but redundant patch of Wiltshire soil. Its edges clipped, its weeds torn out, but no harvest expected.

It was enough.

It was all she could do.

CHAPTER FORTY

The official news about Jeremy Phipps's premature death reached Lionel via its usual route, forty-eight hours after he'd discovered it privately, when Mrs Hoskins relayed it to him with her usual mournful relish. Martha Threadwell's promise of silence had been kept for a day which was something of a record. Mrs Hoskins, bristling with importance, knocked on his study door and rattled in with the tea tray.

"Have you heard the news, Reverend?" She placed the tray down on his desk and lingered, her eyes popping at the prospect of imparting the bulletin.

"What news would that be, Mrs Hoskins?" Every cell in Lionel's brain was working overtime as it prepared an appropriate answer while knowing full well what the news was going to be.

"It's young Jeremy Phipps, sir. The best lad who ever lived."

"What about him?" Lionel poured his tea and hoped his nonchalant mask was convincing.

It appeared to be, as Mrs Hoskins continued in a breathless, excited rush, "Tragic, that's what it is, nothing short of tragic."

Lionel raised his eyebrows and braced himself.

"He's dead, sir, that's what. Like all them other poor souls fighting in France. It's criminal in my eyes, just criminal."

"I'm very sorry to hear that, Mrs Hoskins. Jeremy was a fine young man." Lionel placed his tea-cup back down on the tray, pleased it didn't spill from an unsteady hand.

Mrs Hoskins actually had a tear in her eye. "He was that. A very fine young man. I don't know what's become of the world, sir. I really don't."

"No, indeed. It's very sad news, on top of so many others. I shall visit his parents today - and his widow, of course."

"Yes, poor Katherine, and with her losing that pretty baby too. Poor thing." Mrs Hoskins dabbed at her eyes and ran out of the room.

The unpleasant duty of visiting the bereaved parents could not be delayed and Lionel, exhausted but still exhilarated by recent illicit events, took himself along to the East Lodge that afternoon.

He'd visited many grieving families since the war had started but Mary and George were far more distraught than any others he'd seen.

"Mr Phipps, may I come in?" Lionel asked George at the door, having knocked several times before it opened.

George Phipps stared at him without any sign of recognition. Jem's father scanned his face but only seemed to register who he was when his eyes fell on Lionel's white dog collar. The older man looked like a trained puppy as he obediently opened the door, bound by convention rather than choice.

"Come in, vicar." George took him with leaden steps into the tiny parlour. East Lodge was always a dark house, being set deep in the valley and overshadowed by trees. Even on this sunny day it was still gloomy inside but not as much as its occupants. Mary sat by the bay window, staring out with unseeing eyes. She did not turn to greet God's representative. Lionel had to be content with her husband's nods and sighs as he gave his condolences.

"I was very sorry to hear about your son, Jeremy, Mr Phipps," Lionel said. A voice from the deepest recesses of his mind, shouted, *'LIAR!'*

He looked across at Mary to see if she'd heard it and was shocked to find her staring at him with unblinking, red-rimmed eyes. Lionel shivered involuntarily.

"We can't take it in, vicar." George shook his head.

"No, it is a big adjustment," Lionel said, ignoring the voice that continued to shrill in his head.

"What is the point of this bloody war anyway?" asked George.

Lionel had no answer.

"There'll be no young men left, at this rate," George said.

"I'm so sorry," was all Lionel could trust himself to say. "If there's anything I can do to help, please let me know." His internal voice said, *'Such as take care of the pretty widow?'* He silenced it with, "Such as a memorial service? A lot of families have found that comforting."

George looked at his wife.

She could have been a statue, carved from marble, so still was she.

George looked back at the vicar and croaked through suppressed tears, "We'll think about it, Reverend."

"Yes, of course, of course. I understand. I'll take my leave then, Mr Phipps." Lionel shook George's hand. He went across to Mary and extended his hand to her. "Mrs Phipps?"

No response. He dropped his hand, nodded to her and left, saying he'd see himself out. Once outside, he strode quickly away from the wooded copse that surrounded the lodge and escaped into the bright sunshine once more. The rays gilded his face and he lifted it up to the brightness.

With his first parish duty fulfilled, it was only right and proper to carry out the second and visit the bereaved widow. Inhaling a deep breath of the warm spring breeze, Lionel set off at a jaunty pace along the well-worn path to Katy's door. He couldn't wait for her response to his letter.

He had to knock several times here as well before Katy opened it.

She was less welcoming than her father-in-law. "What are you doing, back here again? Have you nowhere else to go?"

"May I come in, Katherine?"

"No, you may not," answered Katy, and made to shut the door in his face.

"Katherine! Please don't shut the door on me!" protested Lionel.

"What else do you expect me to do after the other night when I heard Jem was dead?"

Lionel's brain was working over-time, but he still couldn't help noticing how her eyes sparkled in anger. His stomach flipped over.

"Katherine, can't we forget that night ever happened? It was a genuine mistake for which I am very sorry. My concern is only for your welfare."

Mrs Fenwick passed by on the street. She stared at Lionel standing in the doorway.

"Morning, vicar," she called out. "Lovely day. Mornin', Katy."

Neither Lionel nor Katy acknowledged her. Lionel ground his teeth as Sally Fenwick came to a halt, waiting for some response.

"Everything alright, Katy? Did I hear you crying just now? You be coming around a lot too, vicar. Not bad news, I hope?" Sally's eyes were on stalks.

Lionel sighed and turned around to greet the old biddy. "Mrs Phipps *has* had some bad news. Do you mind if I tell Mrs Fenwick, Mrs Phipps?" Lionel looked at Katy.

"I'll tell her myself." Katy stepped out into the street.

Lionel watched as Katy spoke quietly to her neighbour who flapped her hands and then put her apron over her head to shut out the tragedy. Katy patted her back and muttered soothing noises to the older woman. Lionel was lost in admiration at her generosity.

Sally could not be consoled, however. Katy turned to Lionel and virtually spat, "Do you think you could take it upon yourself to escort Mrs Fenwick home, vicar? As part of your parish duties?"

Lionel collected himself and nodded assent. He took Sally by the elbow and around the corner, back to her house behind the terrace. He was relieved to find Tom Fenwick at home.

"Sally's had a bit of a shock, Tom." Lionel handed wife to husband with an eagerness he could not disguise.

"What's happened, vicar?" Tom dashed sleep from his rheumy old eyes.

"Jeremy Phipps has died in the war. Mrs Phipps has just told your wife about it," Lionel said over the top of Sally's increasingly loud wails.

"Oh dear, that's terrible news. Come on Sally, love. Don't take on so." Tom patted his wife's hands.

"Shall I leave you to it, then, Tom?" Lionel said, with more hope than duty in his heart.

"Aye, Reverend, I'll see to her. You get off to young Katy now." Tom shooed him away with his other arm.

"Good idea, Tom, I'll do that right now."

Lionel exited through the Fenwicks' back door which was conveniently situated right next to Katy's. Katy always left her back door on the latch.

Confident his letter would have done the trick, Lionel knocked briefly, just once, lifted the latch and entered her cottage. He walked through the scullery and into the parlour with his heart beating at twice its normal speed.

CHAPTER FORTY ONE

Katy was longing for a cup of tea after sending the vicar packing but that meant lighting the fire again and her meagre stock of fuel was dwindling fast.

She knelt by the range, laying newspaper and kindling on the empty grate. When the back-door latch lifted, she looked up in surprise as the vicar entered. "What are you doing here again? How dare you let yourself in the back way? Who the hell do you think you are?"

Lionel stood towering above her as she knelt on the floor. Her hands, full of kindling sticks, froze in mid-air. How dare he just walk in! Furious, she stood up and faced her trespasser.

"Reverend White, hah – what a joke! I've never met anyone less reverent than you! I want to you leave this minute. I never want to see you again. Do I make myself clear?"

Lionel smiled. "You don't mean that Katherine. You are grieving and upset."

Insufferable! She drew back her hand and brandished the sticks of wood, threatening to hit him. She wanted to kill him.

Lionel stopped her arm with one hand, reached out to her face with the other and touched her lips with his forefinger, surprising Katy into silence. "Katherine, don't."

His voice was serious yet calm. He looked curiously unflustered by her attack. Katy lowered her arm. Her body shook with unspent anger.

"Come, sit down," he commanded.

She sat. Astonishingly, Lionel knelt before her in sublimation.

"Katherine, please listen to me?"

She nodded, not knowing what else to do in this extraordinary situation, still struggling to control the rage shuddering through her.

Lionel's unusual turquoise eyes never left her face as he took her hands in his and, still kneeling at her feet, began the strangest speech she'd ever heard.

"Katherine, I understand why you are angry at me. I took advantage of you in the most despicable way and I'm deeply sorry. You see, I love you, Katherine. I've loved you for a long time. Indeed, I can think of nothing but you. When you responded to me the other night, I could not control my desire at first but believe me, nothing else happened other than a kiss. I did put you to bed and I had to remove your wet clothing, but I did not violate you, Katherine. I did not know then that you had been bereaved and I'm sorry for that. No, let me finish, dearest." He raised a flat palm.

Katy had opened her mouth to protest but his determined air of authority silenced her.

Lionel continued, "What I did was wrong, but I did not take advantage of you. I cannot prove this to you, but you will have to take my word for it. I'm not sure if you remember how it happened exactly but you responded to me so passionately, I could not help kissing you at first but, and you must believe this, it went no further than that." He added in a lower voice, "However much you tempted me, I stayed true to my calling. I was shocked to find you drowning and when you came round, I was so glad you were alive, I couldn't help but kiss you and then, to my joy, you kissed me back. Don't shake your head, Katherine."

"I thought you were Jem. I thought you were my *husband*." Katy's anger was still simmering despite his contrite confession.

"Yes, yes, I understand that *now,* but I didn't know it *then*. You must believe me. I humbly ask for your forgiveness, Katherine. Can you do that? No?"

Lionel paused and smiled. "Not even if I ask you to marry me?"

Katherine's shock at this question quenched her anger. "Marry? You? The vicar?"

"Yes, Katherine. You would be secure for the rest of your life. I could give you a beautiful home. It doesn't have to be here, we could go anywhere. See the world. I could take you to India. I've told you of it often enough and I know you were intrigued, weren't you? We could travel wherever you liked, once the war is over. You would never have to work again, Katherine. And I love you so. You are so beautiful. You're wasted here in this backwater. You deserve so much more. Won't you say yes?"

A heavy silence descended on the small parlour. The mantelpiece clock ticked time into it. Katy gazed at the man at her feet as if for the first time. She took in his golden hair, the chiselled, intelligent face, those scorching blue eyes. Who was he? How could it be that he loved her?

"You need time to think. I will leave you. You've had so many shocks in such a short time. Please, may I visit you again?"

Katy nodded, still too stunned to venture a reply. She was glad when he left. She did not get up to see him out. The door shut softly behind him. She stared back at the spot where he had kneeled and pleaded with her. Him! The Reverend! And he wanted to marry her. She hadn't known she was a widow for more than a couple of days.

Her head threatened to explode, and she pressed it back onto the hard wood of her chair trying to release the tension. Her mind was in a whirl. How could she lose her husband one day and another appear the next? She couldn't comprehend the enormity of it. She clutched her kindling sticks and stared at them stupidly, hoping they might have the answer.

She slid down to her knees and placed the sticks on the crumpled newspaper in the grate. She topped the pile with a couple of logs and put a match to the edifice. The fire roared into life and she shut the door on the inferno, out of habit, to keep the range alight. The flames flickered through the bars the same way they always did and yet her world had turned upside down. She went to the water barrel at the back door and filled the kettle, brought it back and placed it on the stove. She fetched the teapot and spooned black, fragrant leaves into the blue china pot, leaving it to warm on the hearth while the fire got going.

Tea, she still longed for a cup. Tea came from India. Lionel had been there. He'd seen tea plantations growing green and dense on those foreign hills. Hills that she might visit too, if she married him. If she was Mrs White, not Mrs Phipps, who'd never left the Cheadles nor was ever likely to; in fact who had never been anywhere beyond Woodbury. Katy picked up the pot and sniffed the tealeaves. She cradled the teapot like her lost child.

Mostly she felt surprise. All this time Lionel had loved her. While she had assumed his visits to be dutiful, they could now be seen in an altogether different light. She was immensely flattered.

Was that why Jem had left though? Had he seen what she had not? No, she didn't believe so. Jem would have stayed to protect his own. Jem had trusted her. Jem had believed in the establishment of the church and those who wore its cloth.

Jem was dead.

Aspirations conquered by marriage resurfaced. She remembered Lionel's study. She had loved Lionel's study. Possibilities wound their secret paths into her mind and images of Jem's battlefield receded.

CHAPTER FORTY TWO

All that afternoon Katy reverberated from her recent shockwaves. She see-sawed between new horizons and old loves. She was a widow and must fend for herself. She would have to give up her home. She had no child dependent upon her. In fact, she was free and single. It was a bewildering concept.

And now, an offer of marriage: one that offered security, prosperity and most alluring of all, travel. Katy pictured an imaginary India, smelled the spices of that continent, speculated on the vastness of the ocean she must sail to reach it. What did it feel like to be on a boat? What would it be like to be mistress of the vicarage? What would it mean to her parents to be able to offer them security in their old age when Bert was no longer able to work as a coachman? Or if cars like Doctor Benson's replaced the horses and he was no longer needed before then?

What would Jem have advised her to do? How she longed for his carefully thought out wisdom.

Lionel White. Could she spend the rest of her life with him? She could never love him as she had loved Jem or Florence but what was she to do with the rest of her life? Could this be the route to the independence she'd craved? Were any other men going to survive this damn war? Or should she make her way alone through the rest of her life like those brave suffragettes? If so, how could she earn enough to keep herself?

If she married Lionel, she would have enough money for all the clothes she could desire. Any book she wanted to read, any amount of pretty china. She would even have servants to command. What a prospect but what a price.

A soft knock on the front door startled Katy out of her reverie. As if her thoughts had conjured him up, Lionel stood on the threshold, a look of calm enquiry on his face. Katy, despising the arrogance that look implied and yet excited at what it might mean, opened the door after only a fraction of a second's hesitation. Lionel's face relaxed. He smiled and entered.

"Hello, Katherine."

"Good evening, Lionel," replied Katy, tasting his Christian name on her lips and trying to decide if she liked it. "Won't you sit down?"

"Thank you. I would like that."

Lionel sat down in the fireside chair opposite hers. Katy wondered if this was an arrangement she could get used to.

"How are you, Katherine?"

"I am well, thank you. A little tired perhaps. I've been cleaning the place up and the garden, too."

"I can see. Everything looks ship-shape and Bristol fashion."

"Sorry?"

"Oh, it's a saying the sailors use. It just means that everything is as clean as could be. No wonder you are a little tired."

Katy reflected how little she knew of the world beyond the confines of the two Cheadles. How clever of him to hint at it. She wished she had worked out her answer to his offer. She hoped he wouldn't bring it up again.

"Have you had a moment to consider my offer?"

"No, I haven't, Lionel," she fibbed, and felt a thrill of power as his calm mask fell away and he looked quite crestfallen, upset even.

Instead of reassuring him, Katy let the silence stretch between the two chairs, only a yard apart.

Lionel leant forward in his seat, the pleading look back in his eyes. "Does that mean you don't know the answer?"

"I just haven't had time to think about it. I've been thinking about Jem and little Florence, not you. I, I need more time."

"But Katherine. Did it mean nothing to you? I know you are grieving. I didn't come round all day deliberately so that you had time to yourself but did you not think of me at all?"

"Lionel, I've just lost my husband. I'm about to lose my home. It takes time to absorb these things. You, as a vicar serving a community, should understand that."

"I do understand, of course I do. Forgive my impatience. My happiness depends on your answer."

It was fully dark now. Katy got up and lit the oil lamp. She drew the curtains against the street. The world outside receded. Instantly, the room became cosy and intimate. As she moved about the parlour, Katy was aware of Lionel's eyes following her movements. She couldn't think straight, except to feel conscious of his powerful presence, and to keep questioning whether this was a companion she wanted to share her life with. But the question overwhelmed her. The answer would not come.

"Katherine, I must press you. Do you give me leave to hope?"

At last she looked him full in the face. She smiled and watched his eyes light up. Barely believing her own ears, she heard herself say, very softly, "I don't know, I just don't know."

"Does that mean that you might say, yes, one day? Perhaps, when you have got used to your new status? To me?"

"I, I can't say, Lionel. Please, do not press me."

"But you do not say no? You are not saying it will always be impossible then?"

Katy looked at him and then quickly away from the intensity of his stare. She felt out of her depth, frightened of his passion. Lost. He got up and stretched out his hands, reaching out for hers.

"Wait, Lionel!" she commanded. "Please! Sit back down. We cannot tell anyone of this. We must wait, Jem is fresh in his grave, God help him. I need time. We must pretend the other night never happened. Indeed, I can barely remember it at all."

Lionel looked chastened immediately. "You are quite right, of course. I completely understand. I will speak of this to no-one. And I shall never mention my trespass again. But know this, Katherine, even the possibility of you marrying me will sustain me through anything. I shall treasure it privately until you give me word to announce it. Then I shall trumpet my joy to the whole world!"

Katy smiled at his boasting. India beckoned but her heart felt like lead. When Lionel left, she watched him walk over the road and up the opposite hill to the vicarage with a light step and a beaming smile. Her own smile, that she had parked on her face to say goodbye, froze and sat there, immobile, as her eyes stared, unseeing, on to the lamp-lit street.

**

Katy was glad parish business on the neighbouring estate kept Lionel busy and away from Lower Cheadle the next day. It gave her time to contemplate the enormity of the decision ahead of her. She spoke to no-one and did not visit her parents. They all left in her in the peace she craved.

More post arrived. More forms. The army were offering her a widow's pension. As if that could ever compensate for her loss.

She felt very unsure of her future. There was nothing to keep her here. What had she to lose after all? She walked in the woods, secure in the knowledge that Lionel was away and absorbed the beauty of the trees. She paddled in the little stream, astonished to half remember that she had submerged herself under its gentle ripples. Its innocent burbling belied the memory. She walked up the hill, right to the top, and gazed out over the surrounding panorama. How odd to be up here alone without Jem's comforting presence; his solid weight to lean on.

The next morning, another letter hit Katy's doormat. She had come downstairs feeling calmer. The lead-weight of her loss was beginning to integrate into her soul; a burden she would carry for the rest of her life. She no longer expected happiness. She felt different, older.

When she picked up the letter, all her newfound serenity evaporated in an instant. A hand from the grave had written the address. Jem's untidy scrawl scrambled her name across the stained envelope. A cold shiver shook her spine regardless of the warm spring weather. She staggered to the table and slit the envelope open with a trembling finger.

"Arras, ... th April 1917
My dearest Katy,

I think of you so often, my love. Never a day goes by when I don't. Sometimes I wonder why I joined up at all, leaving you at home, all alone. Still, I'm here, and must get on with it.

I've met some good blokes on my travels, and no mistake. Makes it hard if they don't make it, so I keep myself to myself a bit more now and think of you mostly. Just got to keep on going. I see no sense in this hellish war. We don't seem to make no progress, it's just back and forth, pointless really.

I wish I was back home, digging the garden, with you seeing to the hens and making dinner for me. I never did want more than that, Katy, my dearest. It was always enough just to look up and see you smiling back at me. I'm so sorry about Florence. I wish I'd comforted you more. Maybe things would have turned out different, like.

I hope I'll make it back and we can start over again, Katy, my love. I do miss you so, but if I don't make it, I wanted to tell you how much I love you, always have, always will.

Your ever-loving Jem. Xxx"

Jem's voice rang around her head. He'd known his time was up.

Darling Jem. So much love. She could almost feel his big, strong arms around her, holding her safe. And he wished he'd comforted her more. Her! Who had turned in on herself, away from his love. His mother was right. She'd made him miserable. Would he have gone had she loved him more? As much as he deserved?

Her composure broke again, and she cried until her heart felt so wrung out with the pity of it, it pained her.

Sobbing, she wrenched open the dresser door and took out Jem's bundle of letters again. She spread them out on the table. She wiped her face and nose on her night-shift. She couldn't bear it if she smudged one word that Jem had written. She compared this new message to the other letters. They were shorter, more optimistic and all promised his return without question. None had the element of doubt expressed here. How low he must have felt, writing that!

How had he died? She hoped it was clean and quick. Please God, don't let him have suffered a lingering death. She pictured the battlefields, trying to imagine what might have happened. The only images she knew were from the newspapers showing the bleak terrain, devoid of trees and houses; seas of mud scarred only by lines of trenches. Katy shivered.

So many gone now. Even Charles Smythe, with his daft smile and complete disregard for convention, lay under the mud of Flanders with his old rival, her sweet Jem. What a stupid waste. And where was Albert in that living hell?

Katy looked back at the letter, scanning it for any detail she might have missed. She looked again at the date, but it was smudged. Damn! Why did Jem always write in pencil? Katy grabbed the envelope and peered at the postmark. 17th April! But that was later than the official army letter about his death! She snatched up the envelope from the official letter. Yes! It definitely was sent before this latest one from her husband.

What if Jem *wasn't* dead? Why had this letter turned up now?

Katy sat back and studied the two envelopes. A seed of doubt crept into her mind as if Jem's hand was clawing up out of the battlefield mud and clutching at her, holding on to her, holding her back. What if he was still alive?

She read the official form again. The words,

"Missing, presumed killed,"

shouted the question loud and clear. It did not definitely, categorically, say Jem *was* dead.

What was she doing, contemplating promising herself to another man when Jem might still be alive? Galvanised now, her drifting days of mourning swept aside, Katy got up and paced about the parlour, running her hands through her hair. She kept coming back to the letters and staring at those words again, *"MISSING, PRESUMED KILLED."* Only presumed! And there were Jem's loving words, so simple and true, and coming *after* the date of his alleged death.

There was only one thing for it. She must go to France and find out for herself and forget all about letting her

256

restlessness seduce her into marriage with a man she might never love. What *had* she been thinking?

Katy paced up and down her parlour, powered by a thrilling energy that raced through her body. She needed no other man! She would do this alone. If Jem was alive, she'd find him, whatever it took. She ran up the stairs, two at a time and threw on her clothes, schooling herself to think clearly, calmly.

And the more she thought about it, as she went through the mundane chores of washing and preparing food, the more her decision settled on her shoulders. It felt right. Yes, she would go to where Jem had died, or she reminded herself, had *gone missing* and help others like him, if she could.

With the decision made, Katy went to the dresser again. The packet of papers Lionel had given her all those weeks ago still sat there, staring back at her.

War afforded unusual opportunities to a young woman who had never been more than five miles from home and normally never would. Despite the depth of her emotions, she couldn't help but feel intrigued at the prospect of travel and the challenge of training for something new. Unexpectedly, her spine tingled with anticipation, mixed with fear. She felt like a traitor to Jem as the sensation crept through her. How could she feel remotely excited about anything with him gone? And yet, and yet, it would be so good to do something *real* at last. Something to help. To be, finally, somewhere else.

Katy spread all the papers out on the green chenille surface in the light from the window. Carefully she sorted them into categories. Nursing was one pile, factory work another, agricultural labour went with various dogsbody tasks, ranging from refuse collection to bandage making and, horror of horrors, yet more sock making. She certainly didn't fancy working on the land. To Katy, toiling in the fields would be the lowest of the low as an occupation. Munitions factories didn't promise much better. She'd read about an incident where sixty-four women had died in one and they'd turned canary yellow from the chemicals.

No, definitely out of these, nursing was by far the most appealing and would take her nearest to where Jem had been; where he might yet be lying wounded. She determined to join the Voluntary Aid Detachment force and get herself off to London as soon as maybe. Through the sticky treacle of grief, she thought of the long train journey and the challenge of new learning. It salved her sore conscience to picture herself tending to men like her Jem.

Katy walked up the hill to Upper Cheadle to tell her parents her plans. Now she'd made up her mind to it, she couldn't wait to get started.

Agnes and Bert were both at home and greeted her with wan smiles and affectionate hugs.

"Hello, Katy love," Agnes said. "I'm glad to see you, we were beginning to worry. How are you feeling?"

"Not too bad, Mum. I needed those few days to myself. It has given me time to think and I've made my mind up about what to do next."

She had decided to keep Lionel White's proposal to herself as well as the latest letter from Jem. No point complicating things. Why give both sets of parents seeds of hope when there might be no good reason? If she found Jem, if he came home again, it would be nothing short of a miracle but waiting to hear would be torture for the older ones. No, she'd keep this tiny flame secretly alive. She looked out of the window at her favourite view. It gave her the courage she needed to tell her parents about her decision. Taking a deep breath, she looked back at their apprehensive faces. Her father nodded gravely and gave her a thin smile.

"I've decided to go to London to train as a nurse. With Jem killed and, and," she swallowed, "my Florence gone, I've nothing to do and no-one to care for. The days are long and empty, and I want to do something useful. I want to help men like Jem come home safe."

Agnes took her cue from her daughter and summoned all her mighty willpower to pull herself together. "Well, Katy, I think that's a good idea. You won't be in no danger, but you could do a lot to help them poor lads, like your Jem. I can't say as I haven't been worried about you this long while. First it was little Florence and then you was so ill, Katy dear, and lately ..."

She didn't finish the sentence. Katy's eyes flew to her mother's face and her own flushed as pink as the sunset gilding the lattice window to the west. Agnes caught the look, her own eyes full of misgiving. Katy had great respect for Agnes's intuition. Had she guessed one of her secrets? Had anyone seen her with the vicar by the river? There were always poachers about in the woods.

Bert filled the breach. "Katy, I'd be that proud of you if you was helping and that's a fact. You've a good head on your shoulders and it's time it was used. All them books you loved to read as a girl – well - show's you can do learning. I reckon it'll be like a duck to water, if you ask me. Your Jem would have been proud of you." His deep voice cracked over his son-in-law's name.

Katy jumped up and hugged him.

"Careful girl - you'll squeeze the life out of me, and your mother can't do without me now with all these youngsters going off and leaving us to fend for ourselves!"

Katy kissed his whiskery face. "Oh, Dad! Thank you!"

"What you thanking me for, girl? Only saying the truth. You been wasted in service - I always knew it. This bloody war has got to be good for something and now you've a chance to get some real training." Bert's brim-full eyes belied his brave words.

"Nursing ain't easy, mind," Agnes said. "Do you think you've the stomach for it?"

"I can't say I'm not fearful, Mum, but I want to try nursing, if they'll let me in."

259

"That's my girl," said Bert.

Katy walked back down the hill, deep in thought. Telling her parents about her plans and having their blessing had strengthened her resolve. She would call round to the vicarage and tell Lionel her decision. Despite his trespasses and her emotional confusion about him, she felt it only fair. Annoyingly, he was conducting evening service to a faithful few of his congregation. She slid into the back of the church and bent her head as reverently as she could and ignored the fast pace of her heart.

CHAPTER FORTY THREE

Lionel faltered only once during the evening service, when he caught sight of Katy's familiar bonnet at the back of the church. Sensing his own weakness, he left precipitately afterwards and ignored the raised eyebrows from waiting parishioners as he cravenly fled back to the vicarage without giving them his usual parting well-wishes. He was confident that he would have given himself away had he come anywhere near Katy, but when she caught up with him on the path through the churchyard, his heart leapt at the sight of her. There was an enormous yew tree to one side of the graves, and he nodded in its direction. Katy followed him. Her face, though as beautiful as ever, looked set and determined. Lionel's stomach started behaving oddly.

Glancing back at his congregation as they drifted homewards far too slowly, Lionel resisted taking hold of Katy's hand and kissing its palm. It took some discipline to quell the desire. He ducked behind the wide trunk of the yew tree, grateful for its sturdy screen. He clasped his hands behind his back, locking them up before they betrayed him and smiled at Katy when she joined him. He was disappointed when she didn't smile back, and his sense of premonition grew.

She didn't even give him a greeting before launching headlong into the reason she'd sought him out in full view of his other parishioners.

"Lionel, I just wanted to tell you that I'm going away. I've had a letter from Jem that postdates the official one about his death. And then I realised that he's only missing, presumed killed. Lionel, he could still be alive! I cannot promise to marry you until I've found out if he's really been killed. I'm going to the Front to see what I can find out. I've just been to the West Lodge and told my parents. They think it's the right thing to do as well."

Her violet eyes never left his face, but they looked completely uncompromising.

"You're doing what? This is a strange turn of events, Katherine! And what of my offer? Have you given no thought to that in your impulsiveness?"

"Of course, I have but I must do this first before I truly know the answer."

"But you said you'd think about it! You almost promised to marry me! And now, you would rather grub about on a dangerous battlefield than be my wife, is that it?"

"Lionel!"

"Has my love meant nothing to you? Is this just a casual, passing thing to you?"

"No, I'm deeply flattered that you care for me but, don't you see? That just makes it worse. Jem's hardly cold in his grave, if he is dead and God knows where that is - or he might still be alive! I must find out the truth. I already have given you too much and I am ashamed of that."

"Yes, we were rash, you are right. But, Katherine, when we are married, we can be together properly and no one will think it wrong, not even God."

"God? I'm none too sure of him anymore."

"Don't say that. He knows we are meant to be together."

"Does He now? I'm not sure about that either."

Lionel's smile was wiped off his face. "What do you mean? We are going to be married! You will be my wife. You are my wife, in my eyes, already."

"But I still feel I'm Jem's! No, Lionel, I am not ready for this. I need time. I need to be free. To be on my own. I'm going to join the VAD service and do my bit for the war. Then I'll know what to do."

"What? You can't go away! Not now! I am a man of God! I cannot kiss you and not have the blessing of the church."

"So, it's for your soul's sake you want to marry me then, is it?"

"Don't twist my words, Katherine. I love you and I want to marry you so that we can live together, as man and wife, under God and within His community."

"I don't want that right now. I can't do it. I have to be free. I'm sorry. I cannot marry you now. I can't. I have to go away. Please, if you do love me, give me time. Ask me when I come home."

"IF you come home! Damn it, I'm offering you a step up in society! My fellow clergymen would frown on my marriage with you, a servant girl from the manor. I've not mentioned it before, because I didn't want to hurt your feelings, but don't you realise what I'm offering you? Security - travel – *status*?" His face felt hot and the palms he clutched behind his back broke out in sweat. He could control them no longer and broke their clasp.

"Yes, but coming so soon on Jem's death, I don't know myself, Lionel. Now, I beg you, let me go! I cannot take any more!"

Lionel gripped her arm like a vice, but Katy tried to shake off his hand.

"But you don't care for me? Is that it? When I can offer you so much? You've always been above yourself and now, now that I offer you all this, you prefer *war*?"

Rage, such as he'd never experienced, flooded Lionel's chest. This woman, this precious, impossible, village girl was truly refusing him! How dare she? He stared at her, willing her to say more, to show some humility; but no, she stood, resolute and defiant like the equal she believed she was! Had she no idea of the elevation that marriage with him would give her? Lionel could not bear this rejection. Without another word he turned, dropped her arm and strode home.

He could not resist a look back. Katy stood by the yew tree, looking distressed and rubbing the arm he had held. Good. He was far too angry to go back and console her. If she found out how much rejection hurt, it might bring her round. He went inside and banged the door shut. Mrs Hoskins hurried into the hall at the unusual noise, instantly alert at the whiff of drama.

"Anything the matter, vicar?" she said hopefully.

"What? Oh, I have some urgent business to attend to, Mrs Hoskins. I'll be in my study. And I don't want any visitors. None at all – do you understand?"

"Yes, sir." Mrs Hoskins looked excited at the turn of events.

Lionel couldn't bear to look at his housekeeper's avid face. Neither did he trust himself not to betray the turmoil in his head. He went into the study and slammed that door too. Damn it. How had he got himself into this predicament? Was this love or simply lust? He'd been a fool to offer marriage to a woman from the lower orders. He flushed, as he remembered his sacred worship of her naked body. He'd behaved like some wretched lovesick cowhand, not a man in a position of dignity, of responsibility in the community, not like the man of God he truly was. Had she possessed him? Did witches still exist in these enlightened times?

So, she'd rejected him, had she? Well, two could play that game. He couldn't stay here in this stifling, petty, confoundedly claustrophobic little village. He too would go to France. He would not be left here waiting like a faithful dog for her victorious return. He'd go tomorrow at first light and though it gave him physical pain not to see her again, he would not give her the satisfaction. He took the stairs at full pelt and went to his bedroom. He pulled down his suitcase from the top of the wardrobe, trying to force images of Katy's face from his mind with feverish activity.

Then, recollecting she might well call at the vicarage still, he rang for his first line of defence. "Mrs Hoskins, I am leaving to go to London tomorrow on urgent business. I am very busy packing. Can you make quite sure that I have no visitors this evening. None whatsoever – do you understand?"

True to form, Mrs Hoskins' beaky nose could smell trouble from a mile away. "Not even in an emergency, sir?"

"Only in the direst circumstances may I be disturbed." And he added, as an afterthought, "with no exceptions."

"I see, sir." Mrs Hoskins' antennae were bristling. The open cases were obviously not lost on her. "Be you going away for a while then? Sir?"

Futilely Lionel stood in front of the packing in a belated attempt to obscure them from view. He started to prevaricate, "I'm, I'm not sure."

And then drew himself up to his full height. "That will be all, Mrs Hoskins. Thank you." His housekeeper stood her ground. "You may go, Mrs Hoskins."

Mrs Hoskins retreated with palpable reluctance.

As he threw his clothes into his valise and hairbrushes into his vanity case, he reminded himself that he would never see these people again anyway and his hasty rush to the war's front-line would excuse him far more than any clumsy words he might stumble over.

He would write his resignation to the bishop from a distance.

CHAPTER FORTY FOUR

Katy watched Lionel stride away, uncertain whether to follow or not. She hadn't intended to say goodbye on this angry note. Now she would be going away on a misunderstanding. She'd tried to be open and honest, though she hardly knew which way was up, when it came to Lionel White.

Once home, she immediately set about packing. The house was already clean from top to bottom. It did not take long to set things in train for leaving. When the village grapevine vibrated with the news of Lionel's abrupt departure the next morning, Katy felt relieved, not sorry. It was one less thing to juggle. No doubt he'd be back soon, and she could think about his offer in the meantime. It all depended on the outcome of her trip. Jem came first and foremost in her mind; she could think of nothing else.

She wrote a note to her in-laws to let them know she was leaving, but not the underlying reason why, and got Billy Threadwell to deliver it. She couldn't face Mary again.

When Katy put her range out for the last time a few days later – witness to every drama in her short life - her house seemed emptier than ever. Lady Smythe had decreed that the cottage be returned to the estate on Jem's death so that another worker could benefit from living there. Katy, having walked out on Lady Smythe's working party, hadn't a leg to stand on and gave in with as good a grace as she could muster in exchange for a reference. It seemed even Lady Smythe could forgive youthful indiscretions when there was a war on.

All the trappings of Katy's short married life had been packed up and stored in the barn at West Lodge. Her husband, her child, and now her little home. All gone. She had loved them all.

Katy went to the mantle-piece and stopped the clock, so that not even its gentle ticking interrupted the silence. It was the last thing to go so she could keep time for catching the train.

She'd decided against wearing mourning and was dressed in her navy-blue wedding dress, with a simple coat over it and a plain navy hat. She'd had enough of black with Florence. No-one would know her in London and she'd rather not have to explain herself to strangers.

She was early for her father. He was taking her to the train station in style in Lady Smythe's carriage.

Katy locked her door for the last time with very mixed feelings. Memories of Lionel and Jem muddled up in her head and wouldn't be sorted. She gave the key to Bert for safekeeping without the regret she'd expected.

She sat on the box with her Dad rather than give herself airs in the carriage.

He told her it was a wasted opportunity. "Ready then?"

She smiled thinly. Everything about her was thin these days, he told his wife later.

"I'm glad to go, Dad."

He nodded. Sighing, he chivvied the horses into a trot, and they drove the few miles to the station in silence. Katy was grateful for it. She knew how sad her father was and couldn't express her own feelings either. The familiar countryside was a balm to her spirit. Who knew when she would see these beloved fields again? She parted from her father outside the station and kissed him, speckling him with fresh tears. They clung to his whiskers, sparkling in the sunshine like dewdrops.

"Get along with you, Katy dear," he said, gruff with emotion. "You'll miss that train if you hangs about. Make sure you write to us now, won't you? Don't make your mother worry more than she has to."

Words choked Katy's throat and she only managed another wobbly smile before grabbing her bag and climbing down from the high driver's seat. She turned once more, gave him a wave and tried to force the image of his dear features into a memory she could draw upon, wherever she was bound. Then she turned and faced her uncertain future.

**

Katy had never taken the train before and was fearful of not knowing where to get on. The train soon hissed its arrival. She had only just been in time. She hung back to see how other passengers managed opening the heavy doors and jumped on the train through an open one. She looked down at the step, horrified to see the gap between the platform and the little steel fender. What if she caught her heel in it? Feeling panicky, Katy heaved her bag inside the compartment, leaving the door open. She was too terrified to reach out and close it. That would mean leaning out over that horrible gap where the tracks showed so far below.

The station master stomped over and slammed the door shut from the platform, tutting under his breath and glaring at her. Katy glared back and then jumped when he blew his whistle right next to her. Then he was lost in a cloud of steam and smoke as the train jerked back into life and lurched forward. Katy sat back on her seat, grateful to feel the solid connection between her back and the wooden boarded seat of her third-class carriage as the train lumbered into full throttle.

Katy glanced nervously round, glad the carriage wasn't too full. The other passengers remained silent after a brief nod of welcome. Thank goodness she wouldn't have to make pointless, polite conversation.

With a hoot and a hiss of steam, the train pulled out of the station. Katy settled back in her uncomfortably hard seat, trying to get used to the strange movement of the train. A wizened grandmother clicked knitting needles together, its homely sound contrasting with the rumble of the metal wheels. Katy listened to the rhythm of the tracks as the carriage swayed along them. Her other neighbour, a portly gentleman, perused his paper from cover to cover. Every time he turned the pages, he flexed the crackling paper and cleared his throat.

The countryside quickly became unfamiliar and whizzed past at an alarming speed, much faster than any of her father's estate horses could travel. Soon the train chugged into another station. They were near Oxford now and more people, both in and out of uniform, piled in. A most unlikely third-class passenger climbed into their carriage. Unlike Katy, who hugged her corner seat like a limpet keeping her eyes firmly on the passing scenery through the steamed-up window, this girl bounced in and beamed at all the other occupants indiscriminately. Then she sat next to Katy.

"Hello. My name is Ariadne Pennington. Are you bound for London too? I've never known the train so full! First and second class are positively heaving and there's not a seat to be found! And I thought - all's fair in love and war, so I'll try Third. I'm so glad I did – I'm dying to sit down."

The young woman had the face of an angel. Her blonde hair curled into an elegant chignon at the nape of her neck. Her hat was so large she couldn't sit against her train seat while wearing it and threw it carelessly on to the luggage rack above them.

Her china blue eyes twinkled artlessly at each upward face as they all turned like sunflowers to her shining countenance. Full lips of coral parted to reveal pearls of even teeth. Katy smiled back involuntarily despite her sore heart.

Ariadne extended a slim, gloved hand to Katy, her arched eyebrows inviting an introduction.

Katy gripped the small digits in a daze, murmuring, "Katy. Katy Phipps," almost adding, Ma'am.

How strange to be sitting next to someone as aristocratic as Cassandra Smythe in a railway carriage. But these were changing times and war a great leveller. And it seemed this young woman blasted through the social barriers as if they were invisible. The other passengers still carried on staring.

"What a lovely name. So refreshingly simple. I can't tell you how many people stumble over Ariadne! Where are you from Katy?"

"Wiltshire." For the first time in her life Katy became acutely aware of the country burr in her voice.

"Now that's a nice county. And where are you off to?"

"I'm going to try and get into the VAD's in London." Katy wondered why she'd confessed her mission to a total stranger.

"No! Really? What a coincidence – so am I. Well I'll be blowed. Are you nervous Katy? I'm terrified. I have never so much as darned a sock or bandaged a cut and I'm utterly clueless. I'm sure I'll be all thumbs and no fingers. They say the Matrons are ghastly and strict. No fraternising with the soldiers. Have you got a young man, Katy?"

Katy, acutely aware of ears bristling with curiosity from the other occupants of the jolting carriage and eyes surreptitiously glancing at their tête-a-tête, didn't know what to say. Her bereavement was so tenuous, so new, so damn complicated; she could only flush to the roots of her hair. Her tongue cleft to the roof of her mouth where it stuck fast, refusing to operate. She now regretted her lack of mourning dress. Maybe it would have saved embarrassment rather than caused it.

"Ooh, I smell romance!" crowed her new acquaintance.

Katy cringed. Ariadne might look like an angel, but she obviously hadn't yet learnt discretion.

"Is he at the front? Are you terrified for him?" Ariadne's blue eyes searched Katy's hot face.

Tears threatened and she looked away hastily at the countryside flashing past.

"Oops, silly me – always putting my foot in it. Take no notice of me, Katy, no-one at home ever does. There goes

Ariadne - they always say – never looking before she leaps."

She said this to the carriage at large. Their fellow passengers shifted uneasily at the unlooked-for intimacy and reverted to knitting and reading or staring out of the window.

At the next station two young soldiers climbed in. Despite frowns from their knitting companion they joined them in their carriage. They eyed Ariadne with naked admiration but looked too awed by her cut glass accent and elegant outfit to venture anything remotely verbal.

Ariadne didn't pause for long. Katy wished she would shut up.

"Well, look how far we've come already," Ariadne declared, nodding at the roofs of London sprawl that now dissected the green fields.

Even Katy could join in at the wonder of being so close to London and feel a thrill of adventure. Row upon row of houses jostled together, connected by lines of washing so close to their train it was bound to be covered in sooty smuts. Thousands of chimneys spewed coal smoke over the roofs.

"I've never been to London before," she volunteered, apprehension making her both bold and honest. "Have you – um - Ariadne?"

"Bless you! I come practically every week to shop and lunch with the dreaded Aunts. Have to keep them sweet because they pay me an allowance, having no children of their own but it's tedious work, I can tell you. Have you really never been before?"

Katy shook her head, spellbound by this window on another, easier, if dirtier, world.

"What fun. I can show you around if we ever get any leave. I don't suppose we shall but if we do, we'll make the most of every second." Ariadne smiled, showing her dimples.

Katy smiled tentatively, unsure whether this would turn into a penance or a pleasure and was glad when the train finally drew to a halt with an exhausted wheeze.

"Here we are then." announced Ariadne unnecessarily. "Oh Lord! Where's my hat? Ah, here it is. Oh, now I've lost my hat pin."

Katy pointed to Ariadne's hat-pin. It was hiding behind the magnificent ostrich feather that was curling into the eye of a bemused young soldier.

"Darling girl. How clever of you."

Ariadne almost took his eye out before he got anywhere near a battlefield when she settled the vast concoction over the golden curls with an extravagant wave of the long, bejewelled hat pin.

"Steady on, Miss!" protested the young combatant, "Don't kill me before I've left home."

Instead of being cross he carried her bags for her off the train.

Out they all tumbled on to the platform and immediately became swept up in the hurly burly of a country at war. All was noise and confusion and Katy had no idea in which direction to go. Ariadne seized her by the hand and marched her firmly to the exit. Screens obscured another platform to one side, but it was obvious that much activity was bustling away behind it.

"What's that?" asked Katy, once her breath had returned.

"Oh, don't look, darling. It's the poor wounded boys. We'll have to deal with that before long but not yet, not today."

Katy could hardly drag her eyes away from the hospital train disgorging what seemed like thousands of wounded soldiers, some on stretchers, some walking with bandages around their heads, arms or legs. All looked white and worn and grubby. Stupidly, she craned her neck to seek Jem.

"Come on, Katy. Not today." Ariadne nodded imperiously at the guard as they went through the barricade and onto the crowded pavement. "What a crush! Let's call a cab and get out of here."

Before she knew what she was about, Katy was bundled into a horse-drawn cab and had parted with a few of her precious coppers with an abandon she could never have managed in her native Wiltshire.

Throughout the short taxi ride through more traffic than Katy had ever seen Ariadne never stopped talking.

It was a relief to get to the teaching hospital. Katy stared at the yellow London bricks that supported its ornate turrets and towers. Once inside the huge carbonised walls, its air of austerity and discipline after the disorder of London streets, calmed Katy's flustered mind in spite of the impending interview with Matron. They sat in the tiled corridor and smelled the antiseptic cleanliness. Nurses in immaculate uniforms, their hair encased in caps of starched white linen, clipped past them with brief, important smiles. Ariadne finally hushed her wittering and they waited in silence.

Soon it was Katy's turn to be interviewed. An elderly secretary read out her name from a list and stared at her over her glasses with bright-buttoned eyes. She opened the wainscot door to Matron's office and waved her in.

The room was lit by a tall window and looked very tidy, sparse even. Matron Ennesley was a spare woman with long, thin fingers that flicked quickly over the papers on her laden, leather-bound desk. The smell of pine disinfectant drifted in from the corridor.

"Who have we here? Ah, Katherine Phipps?"

Katy nodded, not yet ready to trust her voice.

Matron regarded Katy over her pince-nez with the minimum of confidence. "And you are a married woman?"

"Widowed, Ma'am."

"Forgive me, but I must ask how your husband died." Matron stared directly at her.

"Fighting in France, Ma'am. Missing in action, the army form said." Saying it out loud made her new status much too real.

A flicker of compassion passed as quickly as it had come across Matron's lined and tired face. "No children? How long were you married?"

"Three years, Ma'am. No children," Katy said, unwilling to share her other bereavement with this severe stranger.

"Well that's all rather singular." Matron gave her another hard look from her steel-grey eyes.

Katy felt this to be a cruelly apt term for her current state but didn't dare comment.

Matron sifted through the papers on her large desk. "Excellent references from Lady Smythe."

If she only knew the depth of grovelling it had taken to get the old dame to write them.

"Ah yes, I know her daughter, I believe she's a FANY. Do you know something of the work – the hardships involved?"

Katy nodded her silent consent, reluctant to acknowledge her ignorance or lie outright.

"And you're not on a mission to find your husband's dead body, I hope?"

The lines might crinkle the skin around them but Matron's eyes pierced Katy's heart like a scalpel. Brutal woman. Katy swallowed the lump that obscured her vocal chords but still only managed a negative shake of the head.

"Hmm. We don't normally accept married women even if they are widows. Or those who haven't first studied with the Red Cross."

Or who are working class, you mean.

Matron shook her head. "I'm sorry Mrs, um, Phipps - you haven't the experience with the Red Cross that is relevant. You need to have undergone First Aid Training with them prior to your application and we simply haven't the resources to train you up here. I suggest you enrol in the WAAC."

She handed Katy her papers back. They hung suspended in mid-air between them. "The WAAC?"

Matron sighed, pushing the papers towards Katy as if she wanted to push her away too.

"The Women's Auxiliary Army Corps, Mrs Phipps. Much more suitable for you."

"Where do I find them? I don't know London at all." So, the snobby cow didn't want her then? The rejection was like a slap in the face.

Matron Ennesley demonstrated her efficiency. "I can't abide waste. We need all the women recruits we can get so you need the right placement. We don't want you going home to darn socks. Here you are."

She quickly wrote out the address for Katy and gave her brief instructions on how to get to the WAAC Enrolment Office. Before she could think of a reply Katy was outside in the corridor and the next candidate had been shown into Matron's office.

Ariadne was agog. "How did you get on Katy? Was she terrifying?"

Katy nodded and sat down next to her new friend. Mute with disappointment, she handed Ariadne the slip of paper with the WAAC enrolment address on it.

"What's this? Have we got to go there as well?" Ariadne stared at the neat handwriting.

Finding her voice at last Katy said, with her soft Wiltshire accent betraying the reason why, "She didn't want me, Ariadne. Haven't done the Red Cross Training, see."

"No? Well neither have I! Maybe I won't get in either. Will you wait for me, darling?" she added, as her name was called. Katy agreed to wait, not really knowing what else to do.

275

Ten minutes later Ariadne returned, looking flushed and flustered. "Well I say, poor show. She wouldn't have me either, Katy. I'm with you for the WAAC."

"Why? Was it the training?" asked Katy, secretly very glad.

"Yes, yes, that was it."

It was months later that Ariadne revealed that she would have been allowed in to the VAD regardless of her own lack of first aid training. She added that when she queried her friends' rejection and heard, to her absolute disgust, that Katy hadn't been the "right sort of gal", she'd thought twice about her own application. She told Katy that when she realised that even in these desperate times the ruling classes stuck to their own, she had become incensed and told Matron she had decided to offer her services elsewhere.

Ariadne marched Katy out of the antiseptic hospital and, taking her by the hand, climbed into another horse-drawn cab. She gave the driver the WAAC office address then sat back, looking wreathed in self righteous indignation.

Katy squeezed her hand in gratitude. Drawn by the cacophony of noise from the street, she stared out of the window. Motorised omnibuses, painted bright red and sporting two floors, jostled with emaciated horses dragging carriages. Street-sellers and paperboys shouted out their wares.

Katy had never seen so many people in her life. Beggars cringed in doorways mewing at well dressed, well fed citizens who barely noticed them. Katy didn't realise she was sitting with her mouth wide open until she sneezed at the dust the streets spewed out.

CHAPTER FORTY FIVE

The Women's Army Auxiliary Corps accepted both Katy and Ariadne into their ranks without questions about their social status. The interviewing panel, housed in the big old Victorian mansion they eventually found, was intimidating but fair and composed of three middle-aged women in khaki uniforms who looked much too tired and careworn to worry about such things.

Katy was relieved that her references and medical inspection passed the scrutiny of the selection board. Being rejected by Matron Ennesley had made her more determined to be accepted rather than less and she gave her answers clearly and confidently. They were lucky that they were interviewed immediately, and Katy and Ariadne signed their forms of allegiance in happy abandon.

They giggled as they stripped off in neighbouring cubicles for the doctor. Ariadne was bright pink with embarrassment, but Katy couldn't have cared less. Having had and lost a baby she could afford to leave self-consciousness at the door and submitted to the prodding and poking with indifference. Katy kept remembering that Jem had been through this and that every stage of her induction into the women's army took her one tiny step nearer to where he'd been; to where a miracle might help her find him.

"We are sound in wind and limb then." Ariadne still looked flushed even with her clothes back on. They were given their orders and told their conditions.

Katy was thrilled they were to be paid 24 shillings a week but not surprised when half of it would be taken back again for their food. "It's always one rule for the rich and another for the likes of us, well, me."

"But we'll be doing our bit, Katy, that's the point. We're not joining the WAAC to get rich." Ariadne gave a firm nod of her ruffled hair.

"Quite right, I stand corrected." Katy gave her a mock salute. They were delighted to find that their accommodation at a base in Surrey and the uniform, with its daring calf-length skirt, were free. As there were no official ranks everyone was graded purely on their own merits.

"What that's a refreshing change to the rigid old system I was used to when I was working in domestic service."

Ariadne was silent. Katy was reminded that she probably had servants of her own at home and was too nice to say so.

By early evening they were heading for Aldershot and their new living quarters, clutching their identity papers and two train tickets.

"I'm glad we got fed before we had to catch the train. This day is endless." Ariadne flopped back on her train seat, having again thrown her luggage up on the rack along with her hat.

Katy was too tired to worry about the gap between the platform and the train step this time and climbed in wearily, having jostled the crowds like a seasoned traveller at the noisy station. "Is it far to Aldershot?"

"No, not far at all. We'll be there by bedtime and, frankly, that's all I'll be fit for." Ariadne stifled a yawn with her gloved hand.

"I've not had time to see much of London and it's too dark now." Katy stared out of the window as the train moved off. "I've longed to be here so often, but I feel all I've seen are train platforms and officials.

"Tell you what, Katy. We'll come up to town again if we get a day off and I'll take you out for tea. We'll make a treat of it. Who knows what our training will be like? The promise of a treat in the offing might be just the thing to get us through."

They both dozed until the guard shouted out, "Aldershot! The next station is Aldershot!"

It was a short walk along a quiet, moonlit lane to the base camp, but their bags felt like lead by the time they arrived. Katy found the peaceful countryside soothing after her hectic day in the capital and smiled when an owl hooted hello.

"Gosh, it really does look like an army camp." Ariadne gazed at the row upon row of wooden huts that stretched through the wooded encampment. A few had lights glowing from their windows, but many were already shrouded in darkness. Lanterns hung from makeshift posts making glowing pools of yellow on the sandy ground.

"The huts look like soldiers standing to attention, don't they?" Katy swopped hands on her suitcase for the hundredth time.

"As long as there are two empty beds inside one of them, I no longer care."

They knocked on the door of the office inside the perimeter fence. A boot-faced woman in uniform checked their papers. "You're late arriving," she said, without a smile.

"Nice welcome," whispered Ariadne out of the corner of her mouth, as they followed her to their hut.

"There's two beds in here you can have," said the sergeant. "It's past lights out, so just get into bed as quickly and as quietly as you can. The washhouse is opposite but don't take too long over it. The other girls are tired, and we start bright and early in the morning."

Katy and Ariadne nodded sleepily.

In the rudimentary, smelly washhouse Katy confided, "I'm just doing what my mum calls 'a lick and a promise' tonight."

"Oh, Katy, I really feel I've joined the army now. I mean - latrines – ugh!" Ariadne wrinkled her dainty nose.

Katy laughed. "You'll get used to it. Come on, let's lay our weary heads down. I have a feeling tomorrow is going to be another busy day."

279

Every day was busy after that. They felt like real soldiers as they marched up and down in drills and learned to salute. Katy found the humdrum routine and fatigue of her training days acted as a balm to her confusion and gave her no time to remember her recent losses. She was used to hard work from her years working under Lady Smythe's beady eye and her stamina gradually returned, with the regular work and physical exercise demanded of the regime.

Ariadne, on the other hand, was overwhelmed with tiredness. Her hands flaked and chapped with the new demands upon them. She complained that they were never out of water so her expensive hand cream never had a chance to soak in and rescue the red skin before they were plunged into soapy suds or peeling yet more piles of potatoes.

The khaki uniform felt very military - as did the drilling and mandatory sports. Katy had never played hockey in her life before and was amazed to find she was good at it. She loved working in a team, sprinting down the wing and whacking the hard ball across to the centre forward for her to slam it into the goal. She forgot all about her sorrows on the sports field when completely engrossed in a tackle. It was fun and fun was a novelty to a girl who had worked since she left school at thirteen.

As she stretched her body in new ways and found it responded, her mind was also undergoing something of a revolution. Long evening chats with Ariadne and the other recruits expanded her political horizons too.

One evening they sat outside their hut with some of the other girls and a fierce debate sprang up about suffrage. Opinions were surprisingly divided.

"I don't agree with a militant approach to suffrage, but I do believe that women are the equal of their fellow man, although I'd rather not dress like one. This army jacket is very unflattering." Ariadne tightened her belt to demonstrate.

The others laughed.

Katy said, "I know women need to get male political attention, but do you think that force-feeding was really worth it? I think they are amazingly brave."

"I can't imagine anything worse," said another girl, whose plumpness spoke for itself.

Katy, once ignited, discovered she felt a mighty passion about it.

The gentle Ariadne quailed before it and said she wondered what she'd started. "I think it's just as well the suffragette movement has ceased operations for the duration of the war, Katy. That gleam in your eye is quite alarming."

Katy laughed then added, more seriously, "I can't believe that Emily Davison ran under a horse like that. My goodness, she must have felt very strongly about women's votes to do that." Talking amongst these other women from all walks of life certainly had got her thinking, far more than just reading about these events in the newspapers second-hand.

The weeks flew by and mostly they just flopped into bed at the end of a long, exhausting day. Ariadne remained determined to fulfil her promise of showing Katy some of the delights of London when, finally, they were allowed an afternoon off.

Katy laughed when she got on the train. "I was terrified the first time I got on the train to London when I left home. Now I really feel like a soldier, ready for combat."

"Yes, Katy, I think we've both toughened up under Sergeant Morris's regime. Look, my hands don't peel anymore, though they are rough and red. Never mind. Let's enjoy today. I can't wait to introduce you to my brother, Edward."

Katy smiled, marvelling at being included. A year or two ago she would have been washing the floor for a girl like her new friend but here they were, side by side, dressed in khaki bound for an afternoon's pleasure together.

They started proceedings in a Lyons teashop and arrived in style in a motorised taxi-cab, a novelty in itself. Ariadne ordered all sorts of extravagances; tinned peaches and cream and a long glass of soda and lime while Katy scanned the menu in forensic detail to shave her bill to the minimum. With teacakes at a penny each and a pot of tea at tuppence, even Katy could let go and fill up. It was a welcome change from the rushed and drab regulation dinners. The windows of the café were misted up with condensation as the tea urns steamed away and various lids were lifted off pots of this and that. A cheerful clatter buzzed about the place and the two girls ate their sugary treats with gusto.

Ariadne squealed in delight when a handsome young man in uniform stole up behind her and put his hands over her eyes, declaiming, "Guess who!"

"Edward, Eddie – is that you?" Ariadne twizzled round and hugged her assailant.

"Too soon, dear heart, you knew me at once." The young man hugged her back, laughing.

"Of course, I did, dear. Katy, this is my brother Edward. Edward – Katy Phipps." Ariadne seemed delighted to be introducing them.

"Pleased to meet you, Katy," Edward had the tiniest suspicion of hauteur though he shook hands heartily.

"Pleased to meet you, sir," mumbled Katy, acutely aware of his sense of superiority and its refreshing absence in his sister.

Ariadne looked at her brother and for once her countenance cast a shadow. "Edward, you're wearing uniform. You're just a baby and you've signed up!"

"Of course, I have. We all have to do our bit. And I'm certainly not a baby – you're only three years older than me after all."

"Three years – more like three hundred after the training we've had. Oh, Eddie dear, do come back safe, won't you? Where are you posted to?"

"Haven't got my postings yet but I'm attached to the Oxfordshire regiment. Don't worry, sis, I'll be back to plague you yet. Got to give the old Hun a taste of his own medicine you know."

"I suppose you're right, Edward. Now, sit down and have some of this yummy tea. We've just discovered these delightful ices – they're out of this world."

"And melting fast I see," smiled Edward. He pulled up a chair, with only the slightest hesitation, next to Katy who concentrated fiercely on pouring herself a cup of tea with face averted.

Ariadne looked from one to the other and frowned. "Edward do try the strawberry – it's quite divine. Katy, won't you try a little too?"

"No, thanks. I'm happy with my tea." Katy didn't attempt to disguise her country voice. She sipped her tea delicately. The china was thick and clunky. At least she knew she had bone china at home even if it was now shrouded in newspaper and boxed up in the lodge house barn.

Edward gave a little quick smile at Katy then turned away to glance across at the door when it opened for a new customer.

"Well blow me down. There's our padre. I say, Reverend White! Over here."

Edward got up and walked to the door where a tall man with golden hair so unfashionably long it curled onto his white dog collar stood, commanding the room. His blue eyes torched across the restaurant to the table at which Edward pointed with his peaked cap.

CHAPTER FORTY SIX

Lionel felt trapped. Another party pushed past him to the door and were making a lot of fuss putting on coats and hats between him and the only exit. He froze on the threshold. Katy was the very last person he would have expected to see in a London Lyons teashop, let alone fraternising with one of his officers.

Seeing Katy, sitting so demurely across the room, was like a stab to his heart which had begun to hammer loudly in his chest. Sweat prickled under his starchy collar and broke out in sticky, embarrassing pools on his palms. He felt confused. Lionel hated feeling confused above all things. He prided himself on his single-mindedness and clear-cut view of the world. If he could have found a deep hole, he would have gladly jumped as far into it as he could. Katy's rejection of his marriage proposal still smarted. He would never forgive that humiliation.

Before he could collect himself, Edward Pennington had a friendly but firm hand on Lionel's rigid arm and propelled him to the table where his sister and Katy still sat. Lionel was used to public scrutiny, but it was normally from an adoring congregation and tinged with respect. He glanced around the room, horrified to be the centre of attention on this awkward occasion, as if everyone knew his real relationship to the young woman sitting so quietly opposite him. He wanted to run straight out of the crowded café and never look back, but instead plonked down on the chair proffered by the persistent Mr Pennington.

Edward said, "This is my sister, Ariadne, and her, um, friend, Katy Phipps. They're training as WAAC's you know – to look after us lads over there."

"How do you do?" Ariadne swept her arm out in invitation. "Care to join us for tea? We've finished our ices and are greedily ready for muffins now. They're awfully good – Eddie darling – call the waitress for another pot, there's a dear."

At this invitation, Lionel started up, saying, "No, no please – don't order for me – I was meeting someone and must get another table. Pleased to meet you both."

He got up clumsily and knocked his chair over with a clatter. His unusual colouring and height had already gained him unwelcome attention. Now all the other diners looked across at his evident embarrassment.

"Oh, I say, steady on," said Edward. "Can't you wait for your friend with us? We'd be delighted and we don't bite you know."

Katy, to his annoyance, seemed to manage her discomfort rather better. Discreetly she sat as if made of stone, giving nothing away. He was very aware that he had not acknowledged her or even admitted their acquaintance. He didn't know what to do. Rarely had Lionel been at a loss for words. The anger that had precipitated his move back to London re-surfaced and prevented coherent thought. Again, he felt that Katy was in charge, just as she had been when she rejected him. Why did this woman have this effect?

Edward smoothed the moment out by calling over a waitress and ordering more tea and muffins, egged on by his hospitable sister. They prattled on artlessly together after the waitress had left with their order. They talked of home and their parents in a seamless display of good manners.

It gave Lionel the respite he needed to regain his composure to some degree. Katy impressed him, as she always had, by not losing hers. He parked a social smile on his well-chiselled face even managing to nod at appropriate pauses in the ceaseless flow of inanity between the siblings. Katy amazed him by being able to pour another cup of tea. Her hand was steady while his shook under the table.

The familiar act reminded Lionel poignantly of the first time he'd really noticed her in her little cottage with the absurdly delicate blue china, as refined as Katy herself, in

285

that obscure backwater. Being back in London, mixing with a social set more akin to his own, had made him doubt his infatuation with her, to question if it had been love at all.

Katy's khaki uniform made her look older, drawn. And still his heart turned over at the sight of her. She looked more vulnerable than ever. And yet, the last time he'd seen her in that cottage, she'd come at him with sticks like a banshee. You'd never guess it now as she sipped her tea with her little finger extended. He didn't know what to make of her, where to place her in the ordered scheme of things. She stirred him up. It wasn't a comfortable sensation.

Ariadne's voice floated across and cut into his reverie. "Reverend White - you were a vicar in Wiltshire before this, Edward tells me. Why - that is where dear Katy comes from! Have you two not met before?"

Lionel was so startled at this interrogation he didn't know what to say. How could this relationship ever be explained away? It was all so complicated. An awkward silence followed her innocent question.

To fill it, Lionel blurted out, "No, I've never met this young lady before in my life."

It was too emphatic. Too stark. He regretted his words the moment they left his lips. He took refuge in his tea cup. The china was thick and clumsy, unlike Katy's, and his finger slipped in the handle, so his mouth missed its edge, making him cough and splutter as the hot tea went down the wrong way.

Why had he said that? He could have kicked himself. He chanced a peek at Katy. She sat, still calm and quiet, and unlike his fumbling slurps of tea continued to sip hers with elegant precision. Lionel felt furious, mostly with himself but also, irrationally, with her composure. He'd been shown up by a village girl. Would he feel less incensed if she had said yes to his proposal and he was introducing her to these cultured people as his wife? Or

286

would he be ashamed of her country accent, her drab clothes? Lionel could hardly keep his seat, he felt so agitated.

***

Katy sipped her tea. The action calmed her. It was her only defence. What was Lionel playing at? The encounter was unfortunate and unexpected, but he didn't have to denounce her like that. The last time they'd met he'd wanted to marry her! Perhaps being in London had brought him to his senses. Katy felt used and slighted and very, very angry.

Edward shuffled uneasily and Ariadne looked quickly at her friend to see if there was offence given by the brusque reply.

Edward attempted to soften the blow. "Big county Wiltshire, what? Excellent regiment there I've heard. Good hunting too. I say Ariadne - Pa's finally talking about getting a motor you know. He said he'd look into it when I get back from active service. I shall have to stay alive now."

"Oh, of course you will. No doubt about it, Ed dear," Ariadne's polite mask slipped, and she dabbed at her eyes with her standard issue handkerchief.

The tinny doorbell clanged, and another customer entered. A tall, elegant woman of about twenty-five stood imperiously in the doorway. With poise and no sense of hurry, she surveyed the entire café in one slow, sweeping glance, studying each table in turn. Her sangfroid drew all eyes. She didn't appear in the least put out. Her jet-black hair was swept up under an enormous wide-brimmed hat. Fox fur draped elegantly over one expensive silk shoulder. Kid leather kitten boots pointed out from under the dove grey coat. Katy was surprised there wasn't a round of spontaneous applause. The dreamy blue eyes alighted on Lionel's blond locks – easy to pick out in any crowd. He was one of the few diners not to turn and stare at the beauty, as his back was turned to the doorway. However, the tall brunette made her stately way directly to his shining golden head with unerring confidence.

A dove grey glove touched him ever so lightly on his shoulder. Lionel glanced up and gave his first genuine smile of the afternoon.

His relief was palpable to more than Katy. "Cynthia! You're here at last."

"Don't be cross, darling," the vision drawled. "The taxi took ages – there was a roadblock, you know." Cynthia arched her pencilled brows in enquiry as she took in the other members of Lionel's tea table.

"Um, this is Edward Pennington and his sister, Ariadne."

Cynthia shook hands with them graciously.

"And this?" She nodded condescendingly at Katy.

"Oh, this is their friend – Katy – what was it?" Lionel said, as if he'd never met her before!

His rudeness unlocked Katy's control. "Mrs Phipps to you, sir."

"Ah yes, didn't quite catch it before. Shall we go, Cynthia?"

He stood up, mumbled some thanks and turned his back on them all, whilst cupping Cynthia's elbow in a possessive grip. They left immediately. The doorbell jangled, signalling their haughty departure.

"Well, I ask you! How rude was that?" remarked a disgusted-looking Ariadne, squeezing Katy's hand in heartfelt sympathy.

"Rum fellow that," corroborated her brother.

"And he a parson. Just goes to show how hypocritical the church can be! Poor Katy – he was horrid to you. I hate snobs."

Katy smiled, reluctant to answer in case the whole story spilled out. She agreed with Ariadne's quick grasp of Lionel's character. Hmm, he was a lot more horrid than her friend could ever guess. And who was this Cynthia? Lionel had professed his deep love for Katy, had offered marriage though he thought it beneath him. Was he totally shallow – a flirt?

"Still, more muffins for us, hey girls?" Edward smiled at Katy with genuine warmth.

Ariadne beamed at him.

They polished off the muffins together and Katy ate heartily. Her appetite had spontaneously, miraculously, returned as soon as Lionel left. All she felt now was anger. It warmed and sustained her through that strange teatime. She laughed with the duo – maybe a little too much and too loudly but she didn't cry. And she was proud of that.

Katy felt completely spent when they got back to their digs after another ride on the late train. She felt more tired than if she'd worked a double shift and hadn't slept for a week.

Back in her wooden dormitory, she brushed her hair in a half-hearted fashion and slumped onto her narrow bed. The other girls were out for the evening at one of the regular amateur dramatic shows. Katy was glad of the unusual solitude.

She got out her little tin of keepsakes from under the bed. Lionel's letter still lay under the pile of coins she kept there. She took out the little key from her pocket and unlocked the tin. The quality writing paper crackled as she extracted his letter and opened up the single sheet. Katy re-read Lionel's declaration as if for the first time and from an entirely different perspective. Then, slowly, deliberately, she tore the page into tiny strips and, placing them in the enamel wastepaper bin in the corner of the wooden hut, struck a match and burnt the tiny fragments. She opened the nearby window wide to let the smoke out and sat back on a nearby bunk to watch the flames.

She was still staring at the bin long after the acrid smoke had spiralled up from the embers and out through the window when Ariadne popped her golden curls around the door.

She was clutching two piping hot mugs. "Cocoa?"

Katy grinned at her friend and, quickly shutting the window, hurried across the room to help her with the drinks. They sat cross-legged under the covers to keep warm and sipped the sweet, comforting hot chocolate in deep, appreciative slurps.

"I remembered who she was, you know," broached Ariadne.

Katy was relieved to see she hadn't noticed either the open window or the smoky bin.

"Who?"

Ariadne said, with the merest hint of a twinkle, "The lovely Cynthia of course."

"Oh, her." Katy blew on her hot drink to cool it.

"All these airs and graces, darling – it's all new money you know. Her surname is Forbes and Daddy has made a packet from this ghastly war – he's in armaments and has an ammunitions factory in deepest Essex. Only someone newly elevated would condescend in that crass way."

"I see," was all Katy said, reticent lest she say too much. The floodgates, once opened, might well produce an unstoppable tide of risky and ill-advised secrets. Best keep them locked away. Ariadne hesitated, looking unsure if Katy's apparent lack of interest hid hurt feelings or boredom.

"Beastly war. Beastly guns. Beastly Cynthia. Didn't like her beau much. What an odd man. And he of the cloth, too."

"No, I didn't like him either." How could she tell Ariadne she might have married him?

"Nice coat though." Ariadne sighed. "I do love dove grey – it was truly elegant, I'll give her that, just to be fair." She spluttered laughter into her mug.

Katy tried hard to join in, but it was an uphill struggle. She would never go to church again or listen to another sermon as long as she lived. Never trust another man; never give her kisses away.

Ariadne didn't press her further. Katy was grateful for her friend's sensitivity. She guessed that Ariadne took her silence to be due to hurt pride that she'd been snubbed. If only she knew the truth! Ariadne took herself off to bed, leaving behind the glow of companionship.

Katy blessed her new friend, whose warmth and support she had come to value deeply. Apart from that lifeline of camaraderie, there now seemed to be only endless work, service and sacrifice to look forward to. Right now, that seemed preferable to love with all its exhausting, confusing complications. Even her enquiries about Jem's Wiltshire regiment had been rebuffed by every authority she'd written to. Everyone was too busy or too far removed from a simple WAAC recruit to be bothered to find out if he was alive or dead but the hope of finding him never faded.

The other women came back into the dorm, dispelling any chance of introspection. They were laughing and joking after their evening of fun.

"Hello, Katy," said her bedside neighbour, Betty. "Have fun in London? You missed a treat tonight, mind. Enid did a corking imitation of Charlie Chaplin. She was billing and cooing to Gladys Riley. I don't know how she's ever going to wash off that painted moustache, neither."

Katy smiled back. "I wish I stayed with you lot, now."

CHAPTER FORTY SEVEN

A couple of weeks later Katy and Ariadne stood at the dockside, ready to board the boat for Dieppe and onward travel to the northern coast of France. The British army had its base, the British Expeditionary Force popularly known as the BEF, in a huge encampment near the town of Étaples. At the docks, miserable bunches of wounded men shuffled off the returning train. Groans emanated from stretchers and ambulances – some astonishingly driven by women – unloading endless numbers of gaunt and grey soldiers. A miasma of defeat and fatigue hung over the busy quayside.

The small group of new WAAC girls were quiet as they boarded. Katy marvelled at the strange movement of the boat under her. She'd always pictured the sea as turquoise blue - the colour of Lionel's eyes - but today it was grey, with little white flecks of foam cresting each wave and a raw wind whipping across the deck. The girls played cards in the lounge to pass the time. Drizzle dripped down the thick, rimy windows. It wasn't at all how Katy had imagined. As they neared France, they trooped up on deck, bracing themselves against the keen sea breeze. They all fell silent, as the land crept nearer, and the rain lifted to reveal the French coastline.

"It's so beautiful," Katy said. "It's hard to imagine a war happening in such a lovely place."

Ariadne pressed her hand with her newly roughened one. "I know."

The girls huddled together for reinforcement as they contemplated the reality of what lay ahead for them all.

"Why do men fight at all?" asked one of their new friends, to no-one in particular.

"You know I don't really understand what this war is all about?" Ariadne said.

"It's the Gerries isn't it?" said another raw recruit, solidly made and plain-speaking, from Yorkshire farming stock. "They're just too greedy – they want all of Europe under their heels."

"I can't think about all that politics." Ariadne gripped the wet rail on the side of the boat. "It just makes me want to give up. I simply can't afford to feel like that if I'm to carry on and look after the poor blighters."

Katy nodded in silent agreement. If Jem had died for nothing it would be unbearable. But if he was alive, how the hell was she going to find him? As the bulk of France loomed towards her Katy realised, for the first time, the impossibility of her quest. She felt tiny, insignificant and thoroughly daunted, gazing at this huge foreign country. Was her husband's body lying in that soil somewhere? Was he starving in some prison camp? Or still fighting and facing bullets? Was there a letter at home saying it had all been a mistake? Maybe he was heading back to Wiltshire, wounded and needing her care like all those poor boys at the dockside.

Twilight and scudding spring clouds shrouded the coast and details of the shoreline became more indistinct as their boat approached, rather than less. The steady drizzle returned and drove them back inside. Katy felt it was a kindness not to see too much too soon and was grateful for the night's cloak.

***

"Goodness," Katy said, as they looked around them on their arrival in Étaples, "I never realised how enormous the camp would be, did you?"

"Not at all." Ariadne looked just as flabbergasted as Katy felt.

The sheer scale of operations at the Étaples base camp overwhelmed them. A vast city of tents spread out for miles. Their sergeant had given them leave to explore around the base for an hour before turning in for bed.

"Oh, look!" Ariadne nodded towards her left. "A canvas cinema. Well, of all the things."

"There's the hospital tent over there." Katy pointed at the huge canvas expanse, marked with a red cross. "Isn't it gigantic?"

"Yes, and there's not just one. There must be six at least just for this section. Just shows how many wounded there must be. Oh, I hate this war."

Light spilled out of the open flap at the front of the large tents, shining a yellow beam on the ever-present mud. Duckboards provided essential paths between the brown, sucky sea of wet soil.

"What's that strange, sweet smell?" Ariadne's nose wrinkled in distaste.

"It's strongest near the hospital. I have a nasty feeling it's gangrene. Disgusting, isn't it?"

"Let's turn back towards the sea."

They followed the tang of the salt; its clean taste cut through the fetid air.

"Have you noticed that all the men seem to be, sort of, blank faced?" whispered Ariadne, as they walked back from the vast beach past a queue of soldiers waiting to go into the Mess tent.

"Yes, it's as if they are puppets, without real feelings. It's a bit spooky." Katy shivered.

"Come on, I hear there's cocoa before bed and I could do with warming up."

They linked arms and went back to their quarters. The flimsy canvas rippled in the sea breeze and they clutched their enamel mugs to them for warmth. Their narrow beds felt cold and damp despite the season.

Ariadne got out of bed to retrieve her socks. "Can't get my feet to warm up. I think I'll put my jumper on too."

"I think I might stay fully dressed entirely." Katy patted her new dungarees with affection. "I never thought I'd take to wearing trousers but, do you know, I'm fond of them already. So much more practical."

"Yes! If my mother could see me in them – she'd have a fit!" Ariadne clambered into her bed.

"Mine too and as for Lady Smythe – well she'd die on the spot at girls wearing trousers. Her daughter is in the FANY, you know, and she'll be wearing them too, posh jodhpurs, I expect. I wonder where she is stationed?"

"What's her name? I might know her from all those dreary country weekends. Gosh, that all seems a long time ago now."

"Cassandra Smythe."

"Lord, yes. She's been to ours a couple of times. I can't see her driving ambulances. She always seemed a bit horsey, between you and me."

Katy laughed. "She certainly preferred horses and champagne to reading books, I know that. She thought me a complete bluestocking because I was always in the library with my nose in a book every chance I got."

"Jolly good for you, I say. My father always says that intelligence is defined by a curious mind. He always nagged us to read more. Can't say I minded, actually." Ariadne yawned and shut her eyes.

Sergeant Morris called, "Lights out!" The dark night stole their confidences.

A few whispers murmured round the canvas dormitory for a while but soon the long journey took its toll, and all was quiet.

All around them cannon-fire rumbled continuously, more subdued than in the daytime but also more obvious, as the chatter and activity died away. Occasionally Katy could hear a train chugging past. Now and then she could hear motor engines and assumed they were ambulances toiling through the mud bearing their human cargoes.

She doubted it would ever be really quiet here. She turned awkwardly in the narrow camp bed and tried to forget where she was. She resolutely ignored the lump that threatened to block the airways in her throat.

Images of her little cottage down in the dip of the valley, once so despised and now fondly recalled, flashed across her mind. She pictured little Florence lying on the grass of their tiny lawn with Jem digging in the garden nearby. Katy could almost feel the warmth of the sun on her face before she finally surrendered to slumber. She smiled in her sleep as the distant thunder of guns transmuted into the sound of the wind in the trees protecting her Wiltshire home.

CHAPTER FORTY EIGHT

"Trust us to get potato peeling to do," groaned Ariadne. "Look at my poor hands, I've hardly any skin left again, just when I'd got them back to normal."

"You'll get used to it." Katy attempted a smile to cheer up her friend even though she didn't feel that cheerful herself. They had been assigned to the catering corps and been moved out of the dormitory hut into a canvas tent further away.

Katy's hands were accustomed to being busy and she found the work easier to bear. Emptying slops and washing thousands of plates was familiar if tedious work but Ariadne looked appalled at the drudgery and living conditions.

One morning, as the sun shone colour into their monochrome world, Ariadne bounced into the Mess tent grinning from ear to ear. "I've had a word with old Morris and we're to be promoted into serving in the canteen. No more porridge pan scraping. No more potato peelings."

"Thank God for that," Katy said.

At least ladling out hot soup and stews would keep them warm. It also gave them a chance to meet the other people on the camp. Katy was astonished to see Cassandra Smythe on her first morning as she doled out bacon and eggs.

"Katherine Beagle, as I live and breathe." Cassandra kissed her warmly on both cheeks, French style.

"No - three kisses for you, Katherine dear. That's what the Frenchies do for real friends."

Katy flushed with pleasure and embarrassment, remembering how Cassandra had witnessed her kissing her brother, Charles, while wearing her dress and in Cassandra's own bedroom. Oh, the shame of it. What a long time ago it all seemed.

"Hello, Miss Smythe. My name's Phipps now, actually. How are you?"

"Sorry, but never mind surnames here, Katherine, we're all friends in this ghastly war. Call me Cass, like everyone else."

Katy was astonished at this. Cassandra had always been very aloof when they were girls and acutely aware of their class differences.

A queue was forming for the bacon that Katy was dishing out.

"Listen, can you get five minutes to chat later?" asked Cassandra. "I'll pop back in half an hour. We're hanging round waiting for the next train this morning and I'd love to catch up on all the Cheadlely gossip."

Sergeant Morris was approaching. Katy nodded and quickly started serving the next in line, mouthing "Ten o'clock!"

At ten she met up with Cassandra in her FANY dormitory. She never thought she'd be envious of a Nissen hut, but it was far preferable to canvas. Different standards for the toffs, same as ever. Cassandra greeted her warmly and offered her a cigarette. Katy declined, having not yet got the ubiquitous habit.

"Sure?" asked Cassandra, lighting up.

"Yes, thanks."

"You'll be smoking like the rest of us soon," Cassandra inhaled deeply. "It's the flies you see. They're drawn to all the bodies."

Katy stared at this new Cassandra.

"So, what's new in Cheadle then?"

"Well, um, not much." Katy felt so strange to be chatting to Miss Cassandra of all people.

"Oh, come on, Kate. There's always gossip in the Cheadles. I want details. All the little titbits – you know – who's married, who's courting who. Any babies born – you know the sort of thing."

Katy tried to remember. Lately she had mostly been trying to forget the recent past and skip back a year to happier times. Probably the more recent gossip revolved around herself, but she certainly wasn't going to tell Cassandra about that.

"Well, your mother, Lady Smythe, has set up a working group for knitting socks for the soldiers," she began hesitantly.

"God! I know about that. Mother's letters arrive with the regularity of wounded soldiers to the hospital over there and you'd think she was running the entire war through her efforts. No, don't tell me about my bloody mother. What about your family?"

"My family?" This was a subject upon which Katy had never been questioned by any of the Smythes. "Well, my brother, young Albert, he's at the front – at Passchendaele. My Dad's finding it hard without the other gardeners – all the young ones are fighting – or dead."

Cassandra nodded, lighting her next cigarette from the stub of the old one. "Yes, Charles copped it too. Damn fool. And I lost some other dear friends before him. That's what made me sign up for the FANY's. Mother went a bit mad as if it hadn't happened and poor old Pa looked like a kicked puppy. I was glad I'd got away."

"Yes, I heard about your brother – I'm sorry."

"Do you know what, Kate? I'm really glad you had that fling with him. You know, that halcyon time a couple of years ago – before you were married? At least he was happy then."

"It wasn't a fling exactly. That moment you found us was the only time he ever touched me," Katy said, glad to put the record straight, on this score at least.

"No - really?" Cassandra raised her eyebrows.

"Yes, looking back on it now, it all seems rather innocent and silly. I'd always known I would marry Jem really, but I was so young. I wanted to travel – to see the world - and Charles made me feel I was special."

"I'll bet he did. I learnt later he'd got some other young girl into trouble at Oxford and that's why he'd been sent down. She was a girl just like you and he'd taken advantage. At least he had fun in his short life." Cassandra shook her head wearily.

Kate looked at Cassandra with new eyes. "But didn't you mind me wearing your dress?"

"I can't say I wasn't surprised, of course, but even at the time I thought I'd have done the same in your shoes. And now – God! Kate, I've seen so much death and misery." Cassandra stopped and lit yet another cigarette. She drew on it deeply. "It all seems pretty unimportant now and I'm just glad you had a moment of glory with Charles. You did make a pretty pair." Cassandra laughed, a little hysterically. "Anyway, what about your bloke – Jem isn't it?"

Katy looked at the glowing end of Cassandra's cigarette and said calmly, "Killed, well, missing presumed killed, so as good as. I've tried tracing his body whilst I've been here but without success. Couldn't even get started with the bureaucracy."

"No! Oh Kate, I'm so sorry. And didn't you lose your little girl too? Mother mentioned it in one of her lengthy missives." Cassandra let her cigarette dangle in her hand.

"Yes, typhoid." Katy still couldn't say much on the subject of little Florence.

"Oh, God, I'm so sorry – me and my big mouth. Listen, how are you finding it in the catering department? Must be pretty bloody boring peeling spuds and serving up endless splodges of scrambled eggs."

"It's not too bad. I'm used to hard work." Katy was glad she'd changed the subject.

Cassandra looked out of the window at the relentless rain; the morning sun had long disappeared. Then she turned back to Katy and smiled.

"Don't suppose you fancy learning mechanics, do you? I remember you being a bit of a bookworm at home when we were younger so you must have a brainbox and you were always fixing things for us. Lord knows I could never be bothered with education much, but I always rather admired you, you know?"

Katy was astounded for the second time that morning. That Cassandra had even noticed her was a revelation.

"Thing is, the ambulances take a hell of a bashing in this dreadful mud and they're always breaking down. There aren't enough blokes to go round as mechanics and us FANY's are all busy driving the beasts but you could be trained up, if you've a mind to it? What do you say?"

In the distance the next train grumbled into view.

"Come on, hurry up, Kate, I've got to go and meet that train. Wouldn't you like to learn something new? At least get some skills out of this almighty mess?"

Katy thought for thirty seconds. "Yes, I'd really like that. Could you do with two recruits though? My friend Ariadne loathes the kitchen work and she's a bright spark if ever there was one."

"Two for the price of one? You bet. Right, see me tonight about seven o'clock by the ambulance sheds. I'll introduce you to Edna – our chief mechanic - and she can show you the ropes. I'll get Edna to have a word with your sergeant. What's her name?"

"Sergeant Morris – and a right battle-axe."

"No problem, I'll swing it for you. A bientôt!" Cassandra swung her legs down and slapped her driver's cap on her head before leaving the tent to brave the slashing rain.

Katy waved to Cassandra's retreating back. She looked like a man in her leather pilot's blouson jacket and her long legs swinging along in jodhpurs.

Katy smiled and walked back to the Mess Tent.

"Private Phipps! Don't stand their gossiping a moment longer. There are men to be fed. Come on, fall in at the double." Sergeant Morris stood in the tent flap, looking like thunder.

Katy decided that she'd leave it to Cassandra to tell Sergeant Morris about her plans and hurried past her senior officer.

Ariadne was not as thrilled as she'd hoped when Katy told her about the offer.

"Mechanic? For ambulances?" She stared open-mouthed at her friend.

Katy nodded, her initial excitement crumbling. "I'm going to do it anyway. It'll be a way to learn new skills. I'm certainly not learning anything new here in catering. If anything, it's worse than being a domestic servant."

Ariadne's face softened. "Of course, you want to learn something new, darling. It's just a bit daunting, that's all. I've always had two left hands."

"I don't know the first thing about cars myself. My Dad's always stuck with horses for the manor but there again, I never thought I'd see Cassandra driving an ambulance. Come on, Ariadne, say yes."

"You make it very hard to refuse, Mrs Phipps." Ariadne gave her a quick hug.

Edna, the chief engineer, despite being as aristocratic as Cassandra and all the other FANY's, was also a bluff northerner who didn't suffer fools gladly. She made Ariadne nervous, but Katy couldn't wait to start working on the engines and learning how to keep them oiled and repaired.

Ariadne struggled on their first day when Edna began by teaching them some theory about the ambulance design. "I'm sorry, Edna, I think four cylinders are four too many for me to understand. I think I'd be happier washing the ambulances down and filling them with petrol."

"That's the worst aspect of the job." Edna shook her head at Ariadne's delicate frame. "Don't you realise that infection from the men's wounds makes swabbing down the insides of the ambulances a singularly unpleasant and smelly task?"

"I'd still rather do that, Chief." Ariadne looked quite determined.

"On your own head be it, then. How about you, Kate?"

"I'd rather have my head stuck in an oily engine than in blood and gore."

Edna nodded. "Me too. Alright, Private Pennington, you're dismissed for now."

Ariadne gave a relieved smile and made a bee-line for the Mess Tent. Edna turned back to Katy with a grim smile. "I hope Private Pennington knows what she's letting herself in for. The insides of these ambulances can be swimming in blood and guts sometimes."

"She'll be fine. Ariadne is made of sterner stuff than you might think from her looks."

"She'll need to be. Right, we've no time to waste. We desperately need an engineer and I don't care what rank you are or whether you belong to the WAAC, VAD or FANY, so long as you can hold a wrench."

"Lead the way, Chief."

"These ambulances are based on the American Ford T Model, Kate, better known as the 'Tin Lizzie'." Edna lifted the hinged bonnet. "The wooden frame makes it light to lift by a handful of soldiers if it gets stuck in the mud."

"Does that happen often?"

"You've a lot to learn, Kate." Edna's weariness showed through her brusqueness. "Her top speed is forty-five miles per hour and the engine is water-cooled through the four cylinders, here, here and here."

"I see." Katy listened, concentrating hard.

"But we don't have just Tin Lizzies. This one is a Rover, affectionately known as 'Gutless Gert'. I expect you can work out why."

Katy laughed and stroked the filthy chassis with affection; she felt strangely drawn to the metal monster. By the end of the training session she was itching to get to grips with all the pistons and valves and felt she had a good idea of the ambulances' inner workings.

Katy remembered how she was the only one to manage the contrary range in her little cottage and felt a rush of excitement at the prospect of mastering the mechanics of these cars. Her instincts proved correct and she genuinely came to enjoy the work.

"At least we are spared the worst of it," Ariadne said to Katy's rear end one day when her head was in the depths of an engine.

"Don't you count sluicing the ambulances down then?" came the voice from within.

"I'd rather sluice down the blood and gore than have to drive them to the train station like Cassandra with the poor men moaning and crying for their mothers."

Katy withdrew her head and looked at Ariadne, nodding sadly. To protect her golden locks, Ariadne had swathed them in a rough turban, cut from a dress she had brought with her and never had time to wear. A big smear of grease drew a line across her face from eye to jaw.

Cassandra strolled up, smoking as usual. "That ambulance ready yet, Arry?"

Cassandra jerked her head in the direction of the train station. "Another load of cargo is due to arrive after lunch. Word is, every jalopy is needed for this one. God, if my mother could see the state of these boys after they've been over the top. She still thinks it's like the song and Tipperary is a place for heroes. Tell that to the kid who's coughing up his lungs after being gassed. I had one last night simply screaming for his mother. He'd lost both his legs. The stretcher bearers got him into the ambulance, but we all knew it was a waste of time. He was dead by the time we arrived at the station. At least the screaming stopped."

Katy squeezed Cassandra's hand, leaving an oily mark. Neither woman noticed.

304

"It's the shell-shocked men I can't bear to look at," Ariadne said. "The way they twitch so uncontrollably, poor things. And jump out of their skins at the slightest noise."

Katy carefully poured oil into the engine of the ambulance she was working on, and nodded, "I know. Will they ever recover?"

"Do you know, my mother was boasting about giving her only son to 'The Cause' in her last letter? As if it was noble. Like a ruddy Spartan – come home victorious or on the back of your shield. I'll bet she's crowing to her cronies and trying to outdo them. But they have no idea how messy it all is." Cassandra sighed and coughed on her own tobacco smoke.

"Yes, I'm glad I'm working on inanimate engines not nursing living – or rather dying – men as a VAD, which was what I thought I wanted to do." Katy screwed the cap back on the oil can. "I've heard some men are putting coins into their wounds to make them septic enough to get back to England with a Blighty wound."

"God, they must be desperate." Cassandra lit another fag.

Katy nodded. "Who can blame them? Arry, can you help me lift this tyre off?"

The tyres were heavy on the ambulances, made of solid rubber. It always took two of them to shift them. Katy put a jack under the chassis and levered the body of the ambulance higher before removing the nuts that held the tyre in place. She cleaned the mud off the axel before greasing it and replaced the tyre with the help of Arry's extra muscles. Tightening the last nut with a spanner, she stood back to admire her handiwork.

Their supervisor, Edna, came up. "Nice work, girls. We want everything ship shape. Lots of wounded fellers coming in later. Not a good reason to be so busy. Katy, have we got plenty of washers, do you know?"

305

"Yes, Edna. I ordered another batch from Supplies. They should have arrived on the last boat." Katy wiped her spanner with an old rag.

"Good work, Kate. Knew I could rely on you." Edna hurried off.

CHAPTER FORTY NINE

Jem thought the journey would never end. They were alive, yes, but barely. They marched clumsily along with no formation; their only bond with their fellow prisoners being the will to survive. Men fell by the wayside only for their mates to drag them up by the jacket and stumble on again. Rests were infrequent and short. Even then, the ground upon which they lay was cold and hard and afforded little respite. Lips became chapped and raw and boots chafed. They had marched like this for two miles, Jem estimated. Captain Harry Mountford lay on a stretcher, carried by two German stretcher-bearers who looked so tired they hardly cared what nationality they bore to their dugouts. If a man fell down and couldn't get up for a few minutes, they would lay the stretcher down and wait patiently for him, like donkeys, until he could go on again. Not for the first time, Jem thought how daft it was that human beings killed each other when Germans, Russians, French and British were all just people after all. He felt a glow of shared humanity as he watched them pick up their burden again and plod on, regardless of race. He wondered if they were conscientious objectors like many British stretcher bearers. These men worked as deep in the firing line as any soldier and were just as brave; more so really, for many were bullied and labelled as cowards by their compatriots.

He managed to catch up with Harry a few times. Most of the time Harry was unconscious but, just once, he opened his eyes and said, "Jem, where are we going?"

Jem shook his head. "I don't know, Harry. It looks like we're prisoners. There are German wounded amongst us, so I think we're heading for a First Aid post."

Harry shut his eyes and bit his lip.

Jem tried to reassure him. "I'm sure we're in good hands, old fellow."

Harry smiled at him without mirth. "Yes, Jem, I'm sure we are," he muttered through gritted teeth.

Jem's own wound was hurting too. He held his shattered arm across his chest with the other. The tourniquet had stopped the bleeding hours ago, but his lower arm felt strangely numb. He decided he couldn't think about that now and concentrated on placing one foot in front of the other with a single-minded attention that his would have impressed his camp sergeant.

Jem fell into some sort of walking rhythm and left his feet to sort themselves out. He looked about him with interest at the German side of these futile battles. Trees stood blasted by shells and were now just denuded upright poles, their tops and branches ripped to rags. Where French women had once chatted over sweeping brooms, rubble now cascaded into untidy heaps and roof tiles lay scattered about in a chaotic jumble. Sometimes it was hard to pick out the road with the junk from three years entrenched fighting littering its edges. Rotting corpses of horses lay next to empty shell cases, heaped together, equally spent and useless.

Much of the road was featureless and the flat landscape afforded little variety. Now and then a little hill would rise ineffectually above the rest of the plains. Someone else stumbled again and Jem felt a hand on his shoulder, feeling for his neck and arm. He winced from the pain and turned angrily to see who could possibly inflict this extra suffering on him.

"Sorry, lad," he said to the blinded youth clinging to his woollen rough jacket. "Hold on tight, can't be far now. The road is flat hereabouts. Just keep marching on and we'll get there. Lean a bit on me too, if you like."

"Thank you, sir. I can't see a bloody thing with this bandage on. Do you think they'll take it off me when we get there?" said the sightless youth.

"Yes, of course they will and then you'll see again, I'm sure."

The boy pointed his face in the wrong direction and smiled, gripping Jem's shoulder more firmly. Pain shot through Jem's wounded arm above the tourniquet, but he couldn't let go of it to move the lad's arm across to his good one.

They marched on.

He reckoned it would have been lunchtime in a saner world when they finally arrived at the German first aid post. The Germans had large tents for the wounded men, similar to the ones they'd seen in the British camp and they lay around them in various states of disorder and injury.

Jem sat down on the ground next to where Harry's stretcher had been laid. "As you have two hands, sir, do you think you could light up for us?"

Harry, very grey now, still squeezed out a smile and took the fag packet from his friend. Three matches were wasted before he lit the cigarette. He put it in his mouth and lit Jem's from his own. Jem took it and drew on it deeply. It was some comfort, but it wasn't lunch.

The long afternoon was drawing in by the time they were seen by a tired German doctor. Clean bandages were put on them and the bullet in Harry's thigh was extracted perfunctorily. He cried out with the pain, but the German medic was mercifully quick. He had no time to be otherwise. Harry was despatched to a makeshift ward.

The German doctor shook his head over Jem. "The elbow is shattered. Ach, Ach," he said, as he cut off the jacket arm. He left the tourniquet on. "Quickly you must to hospital go for surgery. I cannot do it here."

He nodded to the nurse who bandaged Jem up efficiently and filled out a form that she tucked into his top pocket. She pointed to the dormitory where Jem found Harry fast asleep. The beds were just off the floor and made of chicken wire, covered in filthy blankets.

Jem's arm was throbbing now, and the bandages felt too tight. He dozed fitfully until morning. Harry slept like a top.

All they got for breakfast was a slice of black rye bread and a mugful of brown liquid. The German orderlies called it 'kaffee'. Harry swore it never been near a coffee bean in its life. German soldiers indicated with rifle butts they should board an ambulance. Jem climbed in, feeling lightheaded and frustrated he couldn't help Harry who, once again, suffered the tortures of the stretcher.

There was no window in the back of the ambulance to see where they were headed. They smoked as they jolted along the rutted road. It staved off the hunger though Jem was feeling too feverish to be aware of his lack of food. Harry was looking a lot more cheerful without the bullet in his thigh.

"I wonder where we're off to this time. I've lost track of where we are. I suppose we're still in Frogland – on a frogmarch?" He laughed at his own joke, but Jem could only raise a thin smile.

An hour later they disembarked once more, and this time found they had arrived at a proper hospital – one with bricks and mortar.

"I can't remember the last time I saw an actual building still standing," Harry said, as he bounced along on the stretcher through the grand portals. "Think this must have been a hotel – and a rather good one at that," he added approvingly, as the orderlies carried him up the ornate marble staircase.

Jem was concentrating on ignoring his nausea. He left Harry lying on a hospital bed, stroking the clean sheets in deep appreciation and looking out of the tall French windows on to the cobbled square below.

Jem was taken to be seen immediately by the medics. The doctor anaesthetised him before he could get his bearings or discuss what was being done to him.

The next day Jem woke up to see Harry sitting next to his hospital bed. "Good morning, Lance Corporal Phipps. Glad you could make it."

Jem's tongue resembled leather. Gingerly, he licked his lips. They felt like sandpaper. Harry gave him a sip of water.

"I never thought I'd think water was the best drink possible." Jem lay back on the pillow from the effort.

"War brings many surprises Jem," Harry said, looking sober.

Jem shut his eyes against the morning light. The silence sat comfortably between them. Jem concentrated on other sensations. He smelled antiseptic through the sickly stench of gangrene. He heard clanging trolleys and a boy crying quietly somewhere to his left. Was it the young man who had clutched blindly to his shoulder? His arm thronged with pain. "How long have I been here, Harry?" he asked, still with eyes tight shut.

"Since yesterday."

"Why don't I remember yesterday after we got here?"

"They had to operate on your arm, Jem," Harry said, his voice solemn.

"Oh." He would have to open his eyes and look soon.

"Harry?"

"Yes?"

"Would it be better if I kept my eyes shut?"

"Depends."

"On?"

"Whether you think ignorance is bliss?"

"Who is crying? Is it that lad with the bandage over his eyes on the march?"

"No, Jem, he didn't make it. Bled to death when they took the bandage off. Shrapnel."

Jem swallowed. "Could I have more water?"

"You will have to open your eyes to drink it," Harry said, picking up the glass.

"Yes. What will I see, Harry?"

"Do you want me to tell you or would you rather have a look?" Was the unwelcome reply.

"I suppose it would be fairer to look."

"Yes. Water first?"

Jem shook his head. Using all his resolve, he prized his eyes open against his better judgement and looked at his wounded arm – or where it should have been. He shut his eyes again. "Have we only got water? Nothing stronger?"

"Nothing stronger, no," Harry said quietly.

"Right. Water then."

Jem opened his eyes and took the glass from Harry. He sipped and then gulped the liquid down. He knew he could have been the blinded boy. He knew he might not have got this far, but right now he felt sick. Harry only just got out of the way in time when Jem retched over the side of the bed.

A German Sister of Mercy came striding up and silently cleaned up the mess, sluicing her mop in a bucket of strong disinfectant with disapproving vigour.

Harry had to get up out of her way and made great play of twirling his new crutches in a mock bow to her. It didn't endear him to her, but it bought Jem some time to digest the loss of his arm before conversation resumed.

Once the nurse had clanged off with her metal bucket and dripping mop, her back bristling with hostility, Harry sat back down next to Jem's bed.

"Want to talk or have a bit of peace?"

"Peace! If we had that, the world would be a different place," Jem said, flushed and angry. He looked down the ward at the other patients. There were young men in bandages round their heads, others with cages over where their legs used to be, groaning men with gut wounds and quiet men too ill to do anything but die.

"Did they tell you anything about my arm?"

"No, but the doctors will come round later today, that bloke opposite told me. You can ask them then," Harry said.

"Krauts, of course."

"Yes, but still doctors."

"Huh." Jem felt rage well up inside him as he thought of all the things he could never do again. Couldn't dig, couldn't plant, couldn't chop wood or bring the logs in, couldn't dance with Katy or hold her properly.

"I think I need some time to myself, if it's all the same to you, sir."

"Righto, understood. I'll see you later." Harry hobbled off to his own bed at the other end of the ward.

They were to look back on their time at the German hospital with something akin to affection, though neither man would have believed it at the time. The food they had was decent, if not plentiful, and their medical care was as good as if they were German soldiers, for which they were truly grateful. Jem learnt to play cards one-handed for the second and final time and the days were tranquil and calm.

Six weeks later, they were back in a lurching freight train, heading deeper inland and across the border into Germany itself. The weather worsened the further they went. Rain fell in sheets across the unfamiliar landscape and they got drenched on the few occasions they were allowed out of the truck to relieve themselves. They huddled in the dark and fetid train compartment, bedded down on straw like cattle. The only comfort was the heat from the bodies of other prisoners. After a few miserable days of shunting along like this, they disembarked to a prisoner of war camp, somewhere in the depths of their enemy's country. They had seen few people on their quick functional stops on the journey but those they had seen were shockingly emaciated and obviously starving. It was some preparation for their treatment at the camp. Thanks to the professional care they had received at the German hospital their wounds were healing well and had knitted together. Even Jem's stump had formed a scar under the bandages.

Tired, dirty and disorientated, they disembarked on to a parade ground surrounded by rows and rows of flimsy looking wooden huts. Wire fences enclosed the compound and armed guards greeted them. It resembled the base camp at Étaples in its uniform drabness but on a much smaller scale. Those who could stamped their feet and blew on their hands for warmth, as they waited in line for directions from their captors.

The German soldiers in charge of the camp were mostly older men, presumably too old to be sent to fight at the front. All of them looked gaunt and hungry but, when they met their fellow prisoners, the German guards looked positively prosperous by comparison.

Jem and Harry were sent to Hut Five. Thankfully most of the prisoners were British and could tell them about the conditions as they huddled around the skimpy log stove in the centre of the bare wooden room. Bunks ran along each wall and a thin blanket lay on each of them. There were no pillows or mattresses. The men already there were hollow-eyed and more desperate for news from the Front than eager to tell of camp rules and routines.

Introductions were rushed through and the men clustered round the miserably small fire exchanging information hungrily.

"How are we doing then? Have we got the bastards beat yet?"

"Where did you get wounded? Which battles have you been in?" The questions rained as hard as the water drumming on the tin roof.

Harry asked, "Don't you get letters from home here?"

"Nah, never a one. Ain't nobody knows we're here," said one cockney bloke, called Mike. He drawled, "Why hurry with the news, mates? We've got all the time in the world to hear it. Might as well make it last, if you ask me."

Sensible advice is usually ignored, as it was on this occasion. All the new arrivals were horrified at the state of

314

the inmates. They heard how they were made to load ammunition on to the freight trains that came in regularly.

"But that's against international law!" Harry said, full of indignation.

A Scottish man, called Bill, laughed – a dry harsh sound. "International law doesn't count for much here, laddie. We do what we're told to do and that's that. They'll shoot you soon as look at you, if you don't."

"Do you get any Red Cross Parcels?" asked Jem, without much hope.

"Nah, we ain't never been registered, see? Don't suppose the Red Cross knows we're here either," said Mike.

And so it proved. The wet summer became a wetter autumn. The winter was interminable and the depth of the cold beyond their British experiences. Even Bill said he had never felt so frozen in the highlands of Scotland. Spring brought respite from the weather and some welcome variation to the diet of black bread – three meagre slices per day – and cabbage soup. They joked that the cabbage was missing in the winter months. Men caught dysentery in the summer and bronchitis in the winter. As their numbers diminished with this natural wastage, more prisoners arrived. Jem and Harry became as avid as their predecessors for news. Red Cross Parcels eventually found their camp, but they never were registered individually.

Had it not been for this food arriving, Jem wondered if they would have survived. Sometimes the Germans raided it first but mostly they could share out the cans of corned beef, cake and biscuits between them. Harry had assumed command of their hut despite his youth and rations were shared with scrupulous fairness. Sometimes books came with the food. A lot of the men scoffed at that – they would have preferred cheese to learning, but Harry grabbed them first, and snatched them up as if they were the most delicious chocolate. His enthusiasm rubbed off on Jem and his world, tiny and narrow and harsh in reality,

315

expanded into imaginary realms he had only heard Katy discuss before. Now he understood her ravenous appetite for literature and thought of her with an even deeper respect and longing. When – if - he got home, he would buy her a new book every month.

Then the winter bit into Jem with a vicious attack of influenza. All around the camp, men were succumbing to the infection. All his thoughts of home jumbled together as he tossed and turned with fever on his hard, dirty bed. His stump throbbed even more than the rest of his body. He was wracked with pain. He saw Harry's anxious face floating above him and heard the other men's subdued voices, heavy with misgiving, as they stood at the foot of his bed.

Their grey faces loomed over him until they merged together into an even greyer cloud that turned into smoke. Their muttered forebodings morphed into the screams and shouts of the battlefield and filled up his ears. He saw his old comrades dying again; smelt the blood-streaked mud filling his mouth, blocking his airways. Jem felt like he was falling back into the crater, falling, falling, falling. He couldn't breathe. He was drowning in the filthy water. In his mind, he tried to claw back up the steep slope of the crater. His fingernails dug into the mud, but it was too soft. The wet clay squelched between his fingers. He could get no hold on it.

He slithered back down, and the cold water claimed him.

CHAPTER FIFTY

Life in the WAAC blurred into one long round of work for Katy. Trips into Étaples broke the monotony a little but it was hard to be cheerful when witnessing such endless slaughter. Katy took real pride in her ambulances and her proficiency at coaxing the reluctant engines into life brought her respect and admiration. If an engine proved problematic, it was Katy the other mechanics called for.

All through that summer of 1917, they struggled to keep up with the volume of casualties passing through the camp on their way back to Britain. The cemetery expanded over several fields.

One hot August day, when Katy was struggling with an engine that had overheated, gushing hot steam into the sunshine as if in protest of never getting a holiday, Cassandra brought news.

"God, I'm so hot!" Katy said.

"Well, I'd avoid the showers if I were you," Cassandra said.

"Why?" Katy stood back from the scalding steam issuing from the radiator.

"There's been a bit of a hoo-hah. Some Australian private was struggling to shower off in the canvas Heath Robinson showers, lost his temper and swore at a British officer who had turned off his water supply during his ablutions."

"So what? Those showers are enough to make anyone swear!" Katy ran her greasy hand around her sweaty neck.

"The officer didn't think so. Dragged him off to the punishment compound for it but when the poor man resisted a bunch of his fellow Aussies rushed to his assistance."

"Oh, dear, I bet that didn't go down too well."

They thought no more of it and Katy got on with mending the ambulance's cracked radiator but there was more to the story, as Katy heard in the Mess that evening.

317

She felt really angry when she marched back to her tent after supper.

Katy told a shocked Ariadne, "You know that poor Aussie cut off in his prime in the shower?"

"Hmm, what about it?" Ariadne was trying to get clean using their primitive washing basin.

"You know his friends tried to help him and four of them were court-martialled?"

"Have you heard the verdict then?" asked Ariadne, flannel in mid-air.

"Death by firing squad."

"Oh, God, no! Isn't there enough of that to go around without condemning men here? He only swore for goodness sake!" Ariadne's flannel remained suspended in front of her face.

"I know – it makes you lose heart, doesn't it? But three of them apparently have had their sentences commuted."

"What about the fourth?" Ariadne returned the flannel to the enamel basin.

"His name's Jack Braithwaite – another Australian and a bit of a naughty boy – keeps getting into trouble. Well, he won't anymore – they *are* going to shoot that poor bugger," and Katy shook her head, disbelieving her own words.

"Well, no wonder the men stare in that weird way they do. They're damned if they fight and damned if they don't." Ariadne wrung out her flannel and scrubbed her face with unnecessary force.

Katy nodded. She brushed her dark hair and looked at herself in the makeshift mirror. The tiny glass circle reflected back a worn countenance. The long curls had gone some time ago and a short bob now framed her face. A young face still but, like so many of her peers, deep sadness loomed from world-weary eyes.

The summer heat, along with the flies Cassandra had so accurately prophesied, slowly ebbed away and Katy soon realised that dust was immensely preferable to mud for getting about. Ariadne and Katy chatted over cocoa one unusually balmy September night.

"You know, Ariadne, the way the men still look blank – like on the day we came? In fact, I think it's getting worse since that shower incident." Katy sipped the thin, faintly chocolate-tasting brew.

"Yes, it never seems to get any better does it?" Ariadne put her empty mug down and lay back on her bunk to puff on a Woodbine. "I've heard that the men would rather go back to the front than stay here and go through the retraining in the Bullring. I mean why put them through marching at the double across those windswept dunes? What's it going to achieve?"

Katy nodded. She slipped off her socks and rubbed her weary feet. "I know. I think it's nothing short of cruel, because your feet just sink into the sand – it's twice as hard as on firm ground. They have enough to contend with in the mud in the trenches."

"I think they should let them rest here – not make it worse."

Katy sighed. "Do you fancy going into Étaples tomorrow – we've got the afternoon off, remember?"

"It's a bit of a dump, if you ask me, but what else is there to do? It would certainly be nice to get away from this dreary camp."

Katy nodded. "Even to sit at a table within four solid walls would be a novelty. I never want to see canvas again if this war ever comes to an end."

The next morning the girls set off to walk across the estuary. Low tide came at just the right stage of their few hours' leave, so they took the short cut across the streaky mud flats. Katy's heart lifted a little. Anything to save some energy was welcome.

As it was a Sunday, she felt entitled to some time off. They had a meal in the local estaminet. Madame was used to them now and shooed off any soldiers, French or British, who dared to leer at them. Ariadne and Katy strolled back gently, lubricated by the local red wine, linking arms as they sang some songs and pretended they were on holiday. The military policeman on the bridge smiled at them indulgently as they caroused passed the little fishing village.

"By the light of the silvery moon," they crooned and skipped along the dusty road. Their revelry was curtailed by shouts coming from the bridge they had just left. Ariadne and Katy stopped and turned to look back.

The policeman who had smiled at them, now showed a different face to a young New Zealander in uniform. They could hear shouts, "Halt! I'm arresting you as a deserter."

"Now look, mate," said the soldier, "I'm not deserting, but you can't cross a river when it's high tide. I had to use the bridge. I cut it a bit fine, like and missed the tide, see, so I came across here to avoid being called a bloody deserter."

"You know this bridge is out of bounds!" The policeman jabbed the man in the ribs with his gun.

"Here, get off me! I haven't done anything wrong."

Other policemen came over at the sound of the argument and hauled the offender off.

They watched from a safe distance, until another military policeman started walking rather menacingly towards them too.

"I think caution is the better part of valour." Ariadne grabbed Katy's arm.

"I don't think there's anything we can do anyway," agreed Katy and they turned around and continued walking, more quickly this time, back to the base.

"Isn't that just typical," Katy said. "Those military police are such bullies. They let us go across the bridge – I mean, what's the difference?"

"The poor young man. Isn't it enough that they give their lives fighting? They're just hounded here. I hate it. Why can't they just leave them alone?"

"All that power goes to their heads – it's the same with the Bullring trainers. They're all brutes too. I wonder sometimes if they make it so awful here to stop the men staying here and swinging the lead. I mean who'd want to linger?"

Katy was relieved when they heard that the young New Zealander, Gunner Healy, was released after a large crowd of angry protesters had gathered round the lock-up, next to the bridge where the young soldier had been arrested. The camp was full of the story by night-time.

Cassandra told them about it between puffs of the ever-present cigarette. "Apparently, even though they released old Healy, the men wouldn't back down. They started scuffling with the police at the bridge."

"Huh, rather them than me," Katy said.

"Yes, their reputation rather goes before them, doesn't it? Anyway, over a thousand of the blokes chased them into town, raided the office of the Base Commandant, pulled him out of his chair, no less, and carried him on their shoulders through the town!"

"No! What a nerve." Katy was pleased to hear the tables had been turned for once.

"I don't give much for their chances when they're rounded up." Ariadne shook her head.

The camp was abuzz with tension with sporadic demonstrations breaking out everywhere. By Wednesday, despite reinforcements, another group of about a thousand men broke out of the camp and marched into Étaples again. This time however, four hundred officers and men of the Honourable Artillery Company arrived, armed with wooden staves. When some cavalry also arrived on horseback to assist them, most of the mutineers backed off and only three hundred determined souls got through to the town. They didn't get far and were arrested there.

Cassandra reported the latest development over lunch the next day. "I've heard on the grapevine that the powers that be have decided to relent somewhat since the mutiny."

"Oh yes?" Ariadne laid her fork down to listen.

Katy smiled at her friend, knowing how much her tender heart had been bruised over the incident.

"Yep. It seems that a minute particle of common sense has finally penetrated. The square-bashers have been told to ease up, word is, and put the men under a bit less pressure." A wide grin spread across Cassandra's tired face.

"Hallelujah!" Katy said. "Perhaps they've finally realised that laying down your life for your country is punishment enough."

CHAPTER FIFTY ONE

Despite the tangible relief felt in the camp that summer when the Americans arrived to support the allies, the aftermath of the earlier court martial about the swearing in the shower incident hung over them. On October 29th 1917, the remaining rebel was shot by firing squad.

Ariadne was particularly incensed about it. "I despair of the whole bloody British Army. I really do."

"Let's give the poor sod a private send off, then," Katy said.

They drank a toast to Private Braithwaite in their tent, ending up finishing the bottle and sleeping fully clothed in untidy heaps on their beds.

Katy's mouth felt like straw the next morning and she wasn't amused when Cassandra woke them, far too early, by bursting into their tent and shouting, "Hey! Wake up you sleeping beauties."

"Tea! I will listen to nothing until I have a scalding hot mug of tea," grumbled Ariadne from the depths of her tumbled bed linen.

"Wassertime?" muttered Katy, refusing to turn over.

"Eight o'clock, you lazy layabouts. Time to get up."

Further groans emanated from the camp-beds. "Right, tea it is. I'll go and put the stove on." Cassandra stomped out to wrestle with the camp stove.

Soon they were clutching their enamel mugs and blinking in the autumn sunshine.

When no response was forthcoming from her chatter, Cassandra said, "The best cure for a hangover I know is a big plate of greasy fry up. Come on, let's go to the chow hall. And we'll have another large pot of tea with it."

They tottered off to the mess tent without needing to dress as they'd slept in their clothes anyway.

After her second mug of tea, Ariadne, whose melancholic mood could not be shifted after the news about the firing squad, said, "It seems so pointless to me, us helping to save all these young lads in the hospital, just for officers to order the death of another. I can't get past it."

The other two had seen enough mutilated young men to simply nod soberly in agreement.

But somehow the death of Private Braithwaite felt like a turning point and this was mirrored by a victory of the allied troops in Ypres. When twelve thousand of them had been killed in Passchendaele for a few yards of territory on the first day of the new assault it had felt like a wasted effort but a second attempt, through pouring rain, had resulted in the allies holding the town of Ypres, or Wipers as everyone called it.

But Katy's brother, Albert, was lost there.

Katy felt Albert's death like a punch in her solar plexus. For days she worked feverishly on the ambulances but dropped screws, over-tightened nuts and wrenched bolts until Edna snapped at her.

"Katherine Phipps! You're doing more harm than good. Whatever is the matter with you, girl?"

Ariadne stepped in. "Her brother's been killed, Edna. At Passchendaele."

Edna clapped Katy on the back. "Sorry to hear that, Katy, very sorry."

Katy couldn't stand her sympathy. She dropped her oil can, not caring that it oozed its precious oil over the yard and ran to the privacy of her tent. All the grief for Florence and Jem welled up in this new sorrow that she now felt for her devil-may-care brother. She punched the pillow with anger and then sobbed into it until it was soaked.

Agnes sent numerous letters:

"I'm that proud of you Katy, my girl but I've lost one and don't want to lose another. Your father misses you too. Why can't you come home for a holiday, even if you has to go back? We've got rationing now. Makes the war seem a lot more real. Good job we've a good garden and

plenty of veg or I don't know what we'd do. I hope you've got enough to eat, my girl."

But Katy resisted. She grieved for her brother and remembered his funny grin and stubborn spirit with a lump in her throat, but his death felt unreal. Even his token rebellion of smoking illicit cigarettes looked so innocent from here. She had lost so much already and here, in this no man's land that wasn't France and certainly wasn't England, all seemed to be a grey hinterland of grim death. She could have gone to visit Ypres to see his little cross, but she didn't. She knew what it would look like – there were now millions of them scattered around northern France. What would be the point? It wouldn't bring Albert back.

Just before Christmas, the camp was jubilant when it was announced that British forces had liberated Jerusalem from the Turks, after over six hundred years of being ruled by them. Less good to hear was news from Ariadne's family about more Zeppelin air-raids over London, killing civilians.

"Seems no-one's safe wherever they are." Ariadne looked up from the page upon which her mother's letters were so elegantly written.

They got through another winter somehow and all three women refused leave.

"I don't think I could return if I went home and had a bath and a decent meal. I couldn't wrench myself back here once I'd tasted home comforts again." Cassandra spoke for all of them.

When Queen Mary adopted the WAAC by becoming their patron in April 1918, Katy felt honoured to join in the parade to commemorate the occasion, but the futile marching ceremony irritated her. After the formality of the parade she desperately wanted to escape and suggested a walk on the beach to blow the cobwebs away. Ariadne and Cassandra caught her mood.

"Dare you to swim." Cassandra grabbed her swimming costume.

"It will be freezing," Ariadne said, but rummaged for her own costume. Their chief, Edna, came with them and even overtook them as they ran down to the beach.

"Just look at those daffodils!" cried Ariadne, pointing at the great yellow swathes of daffodils waving them on their way at the side of the coastal path.

"Beautiful," Cassandra said, not stopping in her crazy, careering run towards the dunes.

Katy shuddered to a halt, gasping for breath, and took in the sight. The heavy headed blooms bobbed and danced in the warm breeze, nodding hello. Katy felt they were telling her that life will go on whatever ugliness men inflict on each other. Nature would cover over the mud and the slime of the trenches and beautify it again. A tiny flicker of hope tickled Katy's stomach. She snapped off a stem and smelt its raw spring fragrance. The pale ivory flower had a yellow stamen, sticky with pollen. The aroma wasn't delicate like a rose, but strong and vigorous, full of the promise of a new year. Katy tucked it into her blouse and ran to catch up with her friends.

Although only April, Cassandra declared the day was warm enough and dared them to swim with her. Katy wriggled out of her heavy uniform and slipped on her swimsuit, ignoring the goosepimples that broke out on her body in a raised rash.

"My God, it's so cold!" shouted Ariadne, as they splashed into the waves.

"Come on, if we all hold hands, we can brave it together," Cassandra said.

Laughing and gasping as the cold sea slapped their legs, they ran through the salty shallows.

Katy laughed away the shock as her body heat plummeted. The sun sparkled on the blue-green waves. I feel happy in this moment, she thought. I shouldn't do, when so many of our young men have died but right now, right this second, I feel young and alive. She smiled at her friends and they laughed back.

Ariadne shrieked as Cassandra dropped her hand and splashed sea water on them both, ignoring Edna's pleas to observe rank. Katy waded away from her, as best she could through the undertow. She plunged under the next big wave and ducked her head under it, basking in the floating sensation as the briny water supported her. She could think of nothing else. No screaming wounded men, no spluttering engines, no aeroplanes dropping bombs, no vast rows of silent crosses, just the primordial, life-giving sea.

CHAPTER FIFTY TWO

"Our dear friend the Hun's at it again," Cassandra said, one late spring morning. The weather continued kind and the welcome sun actually had some warmth in it. There were no fewer casualties than before but at least the mud had receded a little.

"Well, I wish he'd bugger off," Katy said, struggling with a recalcitrant nut firmly fixed to a rusty bolt. "He's always taking pot shots at the bridge over the river. Keeps me awake at night sometimes – most inconsiderate. Ouch!" She sucked her thumb after bashing it on the edge of the wheel.

"Here, let me try." Ariadne's slender arms now boasted some useful muscles.

Katy selected a long spanner and together they grasped its handle and heaved off the reluctant nut. Just as the nut released its hold on the mud-encrusted bolt, an enormous explosion rent the air. All three girls instinctively dived under the body of the ambulance. As they lay there, clutching each other's hands, the ground underneath them trembled and shook with the force of the blasts.

"What the hell's happening?" asked Katy.

Cassandra poked her head out a fraction. "It's pandemonium out there. The whole Canadian section seems to be on fire." She scuttled back under the chassis.

"They're nearest the river," shouted Ariadne. "The damn Bosch must be bombing the bridge."

"I shouldn't think there will be a bridge or anything else left standing," shrieked Katy at the top of her voice, as German bomber planes swooped overhead.

Further discussion proved impossible and the three women huddled together, holding each other so tightly, they became one curled up ball sheltering against the bombardment. It felt like they lay there forever. After a little while Ariadne pointed to the sheds questioningly but both Katy and Cassandra shook their heads and clung on for dear life where they were. From underneath the chassis of the ambulance they could see the legs of other people running chaotically in every direction, with some crumpling to the ground as they were hit.

Katy's instinct was to rush out and drag people under the ambulance with them, but it would have been futile. She found it sickening to see the destruction and not be able to prevent it.

Cassandra ventured another peek and her mouth dropped open as an enormous star shell burst over the St John's Hospital tent. She ducked hurriedly back under the ambulance.

Cassandra made the sign of the cross with her fingers to indicate the hospital had been hit and then pointed both her thumbs down to the ground. The other two shook their heads in disbelief. They knew how many wounded men lay there like sitting ducks.

Eventually the bombing stopped. "Is it safe to get out?" asked Katy.

"Not until we hear the planes leaving," Ariadne said. The welcome whine of the engines fading away was soon overlaid by screams and roaring flames all around them. The girls looked at each other, nodded, and crawled out from under their sturdy refuge.

"If our ambulance had been hit, it would have gone up like a torch." Ariadne nodded towards the petrol tank. "I'd just filled it up to the brim with petrol."

Hands on hips to steady herself, Katy looked about her. It was bedlam. All that could be seen of the Canadian quarter were huge flames and pillars of smoke rising from what used to be the St. John's hospital.

"Quick! Get in the ambulance and let's drive over there to see if we can help." Cassandra climbed in behind the wheel.

"Let me get that bolt back on safely first. As Arry said, she's got plenty of petrol." Katy grabbed the spanner back. "We'd better not get too near the flames."

They jumped in the ambulance and raced off. They couldn't have got near the bombsite if they'd tried, so extensive were the fires.

Instead Cassandra parked the ambulance as near as she could and one of the British majors barked out, "Wait there and I'll organise some passengers for you. Take any wounded to the hospital near the British HQ. Once you've offloaded, come back for more."

"Yes, sir." Katy saluted the officer. "Look - Cassandra - you wait with the ambulance while Ariadne and I collect the wounded and bring them over to you. You load them up and drive to British HQ and we'll round up some more."

Ariadne and Katy walked towards the flames. The heat was horrendous, and they choked back the smoke. Burnt and wounded men were stumbling about. Nurses were trying to calm them but were obviously shaken too. All afternoon they ferried casualties to the sorting stations normally reserved for front line soldiers brought in from the battlefields. This time the battlefield had come to them. They worked hard through the night and the other hospital staff worked well past their fatigue levels as they tried to cope with the numbers affected.

The next morning, when only charred embers and twisted bedsteads remained, they learnt that three hundred and sixty people had perished including nine other WAAC girls. Nurses who had remained with their immobile patients had died alongside them. One bomb had dropped next to the graveyard and dead and live bodies were catapulted up into the air, mixing together in a grisly dance of death.

At the funeral a few days later, thousands of serving men and women mourned their comrades. Just to provide four soldiers to each cheap plywood coffin took nearly a thousand men carrying them to their mass graves. The nonchalant sun shone down, as flags were briefly draped over each one, before they were lowered into the French earth, now so used to receiving such numbers of interred souls. No-one could think of anything to say. All was numbness. Bugles heralded speeches and faces turned towards their leaders, quietly hoping for guidance.

A gentle breeze flapped at the nurses' white headdresses. There were many of their own among the dead. Two nurses received Military Medals for their bravery and officers intoned prayers over the camp on the warm spring air. The occasional bouquet splashed colour among the khaki and brought fragrant reminders of English summer gardens in this grey, flat world.

And then, a young minister stood up and cleared his throat before addressing them. Katy's heart, already low from witnessing the mass funeral, sank still further. Lionel's golden hair fluttered in the wind. He stood head and shoulders above the officers surrounding him and his voice carried easily through the spring air. His blue eyes surveyed the crowd and he seemed to embody their grief within his tall frame.

Many heads bowed in prayer, but more looked up at him, initially nodding in response to his clear diction.

"It is God's will and God's will is good."

His strong voice reached each member of the gathered troops. A soldier next to Katy muttered, "And may your God go with you, except you only go as far as the camp's edge."

Katy turned quickly to look at him. The anger plainly writ across the young soldier's face shocked her to the core. She turned back to listen, stunned to find Lionel here. She'd had no idea.

Lionel declaimed further. "War is a noble discipline that purges men of selfishness. By its pity and terror men are brought nearer to God. We are all born sinners in the sight of God. Let us pray for victory, over our fallen comrades. They have died that the glory of God may be made manifest."

Katy noticed that more heads were bowed than uplifted now. When the service was over, she turned to the soldier next to her and asked him what he'd meant.

"These ruddy chaplains! They tell us to pray to God – what God would have this happen? None of 'em ever goes to the front and sees what it's really like. Well, the Roman Catholics do, fair play, but that feller - up there with his combed locks and his clean clothes – he ain't never been seen where it's lively."

His friend agreed. "Aye, pompous git, I'd like to purge his selfishness alright. I don't suppose his fingernails have dirt in them. The biggest adventure he ever gets is to go to town to buy ciggies for the chaps and write sob stories to their mothers when they've copped it. Very brave, I don't think."

"Come on, mate, let's leave it and get back to duty. What else is there?"

Katy stayed behind after most of the mourners had trooped off. Thousands of servicemen swarmed back to the base like a flock of starlings connected by some invisible cord of sorrow.

Lionel's height and colouring distinguished him easily from the universal khaki. When most of the others had dispersed, Katy approached him without fear but with plenty of curiosity. She took off her cap so he might recognise her and ran her fingers through her short, bobbed hair.

Lionel was nodding gravely as he listened to a couple of senior officers deep in conversation. How could he look so involved and self-important when he could only have been here a few short months? Kate went straight up to the clutch of powerful decision-makers. She felt no awe of men whose decisions had wasted youth so extravagantly. She failed to see why she should admire such useless strategists.

"Good morning, Reverend White." She spoke very directly to him and looked at Lionel's blue eyes through her own, clear, de-scaled ones.

Lionel looked irritated, embarrassed - even more than he had beside the sneering Cynthia in the little Lyons tea shop. Katy felt a thrill of triumph in his discomfort. Those soldiers at the funeral had seen through him straight off. They could see him for what he really was. Pity it had taken her so long.

"Excuse me, Brigadier and Major. I have some pastoral work to attend to," Lionel said, with a little bow of deference to the army officers.

"Of course, Reverend. Duty first," said the Major he'd been talking to, who stared at Katy.

Katy smiled at each one in turn and enjoyed seeing them shuffle their feet, discomforted by her stare. She stood her ground and kept on looking at them, wanting them to sense the disgust she felt.

Lionel detached himself from the medal bedecked group and cupped his hand under Katy's elbow. She crossly shook it off, aware that the officers were still watching. If they speculated on this show of intimacy, if it compromised Lionel, she wouldn't be sorry.

"Katherine! You're the last person I expected to see here."

"I'll bet."

Lionel searched Katy's face as if to discover who she had become. Katy smiled at him with her eyes but not her heart.

"How are you keeping, Katherine?"

They fell into step, walking away from the senior officers and out of their hearing.

"Well enough, considering the circumstances. How about you?" Katy deliberately didn't use his title.

"I'm well, thank you," he replied, looking increasingly ill at ease.

"And what are you doing in Étaples, Lionel?"

"Oh, chaplain's duties, you know."

"Ever go to the Front then?"

"Well, I, um. God's voice is needed everywhere, you know."

"Yes, I'm sure it is. That was a fine speech about the glory of war you just gave."

Lionel inclined his head in acknowledgement of the compliment. "I'm obliged to you, thank you. One does one's poor best, you know."

"It must be hard to find the words to convey such a quantity of loss. What do you do in the field when the men die, Lionel?" Katy was determined to get the bottom of what the soldiers had said about him.

"Well, um, you do what you can, you know."

"Do you?" Katy stopped walking and turned to face her former admirer.

The sun shone directly onto his face, blinding him but affording her a fine view of some new wrinkles he was sporting. He'd trimmed his moustache. Katy thought that unfortunate. It had detracted attention from his little chin.

She smiled at him again, "And what do you think your God makes of the numbers of young men dead in this 'great' war, Lionel? Does He deem it a worthwhile sacrifice?"

Lionel screwed up his eyes against the sunlight and then looked away from her. Katy waited patiently for his reply which, when it came, just about matched her expectations.

"God works in mysterious ways, Katherine."

She promptly replied, "His wonders to perform, no doubt."

Lionel reached out for her hand. She ignored it.

"Katherine, you look different. Your hair is so short, and your skirt is too! I hardly knew you."

"Well, it is me, all the same, just older and wiser."

334

"And still beautiful. Katherine, seeing you again, I, I realise I feel the same way about you. Have you thought about my offer at all?"

"After you snubbed me in London? And went off with that fashion plate? Cynthia, wasn't it?"

"She's an old family friend. We grew up together. It didn't mean anything. I feel for no-one as I feel for you, Katherine. Please, look at me?"

Katy looked at him. She saw a man who had still not fought for his country, who only had fine words but no real courage; a man who had taken advantage of a woman stricken by grief.

"You know, Lionel – I'd rather never look on you again for the rest of my life. You're a coward and a thief, one who stole my self-respect. I despise you."

Lionel looked deeply shocked but remained silent and Katy found herself bored.

"Well, fascinating as this is Reverend White, I must away to sluice down a few more ambulances covered in young men's entrails. Good day to you."

Katy brushed her hand through her bobbed hair and marched briskly away, her short, straight skirt allowing her long legs to swing freely. She felt like sprinting as far away from God's reverent representative as she could, but she wouldn't give him the satisfaction of thinking she was running way when she felt more like slapping him.

***

Lionel stood like a sentinel watching her retreat from view until the canvas city swallowed her up. He knew, in that moment, that she was lost to him forever. The modern young woman striding so confidently away from him was a different creature to the one who had kissed him in a wooded glade under a full moon. Had she not been out of her mind with grief, he doubted he would even have that memory.

Katy brought out the pagan in him and suffocated the Christian. She would forever remain a goddess of womanhood to him and he would treasure the sensual memory of that night for the rest of his life.

His heart felt wrung out and painful in his chest. He longed to run after her and hold her back but that look in her eyes told him it would have been a waste of time.

A little worm of doubt crept into his mind. He suspected it might be relief that she'd slipped away, out of his reach. Could such a working-class girl really have risen to the challenge of a vicar's wife, with all the tea parties it entailed? Lionel shook his blonde head.

Katy wasn't even a speck in the distance now. The sea of tents had swallowed her up. She had walked into her future.

Lionel turned back and faced his own.

CHAPTER FIFTY THREE

Katy did not run in to Lionel again. The camp chaplains kept themselves to themselves and rarely appeared amongst the other servicemen and women in the day to day routine. She was relieved not to bump into him and learnt, after discreet enquiries, that he'd asked for a transfer back to England. What a surprise.

German prisoners of war began to pile up around the camp. They were stationed in makeshift tents in the woods on the periphery. Most of them were a sorry sight, emaciated and as hungry as a pack of wolves. Some had enough energy to be angry and hostile. All of them looked exhausted and relieved to be out of it at last.

Ariadne was seconded to be a translator for the German prisoners. She was a fluent speaker in both German and French, thanks to her excellent private education.

"Can't think why they didn't get you doing translation work before. Wouldn't you have preferred a nice cosy office job at HQ all along, Ariadne?" asked Cassandra, one day over lunch in the Mess Tent.

"Because I made sure not to tell them. I wanted to work with dear Katy here." Ariadne attempted a weary smile.

Katy hugged Ariadne fiercely. "You are such a good friend, Ariadne." Her voice sounded muffled against Ariadne's oil stained dungarees. "In all this mess that has been the most marvellous thing, but you shouldn't have stayed here doing this manual work, just to be near me."

"Wouldn't have missed it for the world, dearest girl." Ariadne wiped a tear away, leaving another grease stain on her thin cheek.

"But you're not really cut out for this rough work, Ariadne, are you? Come on, be honest – a nice cushy number in a warm office with officers admiring the English roses in your cheeks has got to be better than wielding a wrench," Cassandra said.

"It's certainly true I'm not the best mechanic in the British army," laughed Ariadne. "And I have to say, girls, wearing a proper skirt again would be heavenly!"

"No doubt the men will think so too." Cassandra clapped her on the back. "And no more engine grease – I can't believe that won't be an improvement? Now Katy here positively glories in the stuff, don't you, Kate?"

Katy nodded and grinned. "There is something about getting an engine to run smoothly that I find really satisfying, I must say. And I prefer trousers any day. If this war ever ends, I'd like to keep on with something mechanical. I shall have to find something to pay my way, with Jem gone."

All her attempts to trace Jem had failed and she had resigned herself to his death. When it was one amongst so many, searching for him had felt increasingly hopeless.

She so rarely mentioned Jem that the other two looked at her quickly and then at each other.

"You alright, Kate?" asked Cassandra.

"Yes, of course, but I shall miss my dear Arry."

"Darling Kate, I shall still be bunking with you. You never know, I might get some privileges – perhaps filch a few extra ciggies and rations off the boys if I'm at HQ." Ariadne patted her arm affectionately.

"Sounds good to me. How do you feel about working with the Huns though?" Cass was always on the cadge for cigarettes. Her fingers were quite yellow with nicotine.

Ariadne looked thoughtful, as she often did these days. "They are all men under God, aren't they? They too have wives at home like you, Kate. Children too, and mothers. We are all just people. This crazy war is waged by politicians and the reason for it is a mystery to me but, in a way, I'd like to get to know some of the German men – see if they *are* monsters - or like us, just people who are confused and scared and worn out."

Kate nodded. Ariadne talked like this a lot nowadays. The bubbly young woman she'd met on the train to

London had aged more than any of them. Cassandra appeared to be stronger for her war experiences. She talked of men being loaded into her ambulance as if they were buns on a tray going into the oven, because the Red Cross ambulances had acquired the nickname of Hot Cross Buns. Kate knew that Cass had cried and ranted against the mass killing of young men when she first came to Étaples and that Cassandra's seeming callousness was simply a defence mechanism. They'd all had to find a way to cope with the daily onslaught on their sensitivities. She wondered how Ariadne would cope with a closer association with an enemy that finally seemed to be losing, inch by gory inch, in this endless entrenched fight.

After her transfer, Ariadne became even more quiet and introspective. She told Katy of the malnutrition amongst the German troops and the high level of illness. They had been suffering from a nasty form of influenza and Ariadne was convinced this was due to their poor diet.

"You should see them, Katy," she would report, as they peeled off their boots before climbing wearily into their narrow, makeshift beds. "They are so thin, my dear! And so grateful for the better food they get here. We might moan about the stodgy puddings and watery soups that the Mess serves up, but they tell me it's very heaven after their thin pickings. They are literally ravenous when they first get here. Some of them are mere boys – striplings still green about the gills and do you know – they are the ones who seem to be getting this 'flu. They go down like flies – and so quickly too! One minute they are fine and then they're really ill – or worse." Ariadne shuddered.

Katy was at a loss for words to comfort her. She could not forget who had killed her husband and brother and couldn't feel quite as charitable as her kind-hearted friend.

One evening Ariadne came back even more tired than usual. Katy had laboured through a long day herself with a rush for ambulances after a major battle at Ypres had brought a fresh load of wounded men through the base camp on their way back to Britain or the hospitals.

A German soldier had given Ariadne a carved cross. "Look Katy – it's beautiful. See the workmanship on the edges."

Katy took the cross unwillingly from Ariadne. "How can they still believe in a just and fair God, when they've killed so many of their fellow men? I've heard their officers shouting at them and you don't need to be an interpreter to get the gist. I've heard they are more frightened of their commanders than of us bumbling Brits."

"Oh, Katy, you are right, but they are good men, decent men most of them." Ariadne coughed and ran the back of her hand across her forehead. "Their officers are trying to inspire discipline amongst them."

"Huh! Bit late for that." Katy remained unconvinced.

"Maybe you're right." Ariadne seemed very sleepy. She yawned and lay back on her little cot. "Oh, my head hurts."

Katy looked at her more closely. Ariadne had hollows under her eyes, and they bore dark, bruised shadows. She looked flushed and seemed restless. Memories of little Florence flashed across Katy's mind. She leaned across the narrow gap between their camp beds and placed her palm on Ariadne's forehead. Ariadne didn't even open her eyes. And her forehead was hot enough to boil their camp kettle. Katy quickly withdrew her hands and washed them with lots of soap in the canvas-slung enamel basin. She dried her hands and looked at her friend, determined not to let her slip away from life, as her other dear ones had.

Ariadne had fallen instantly asleep.

Katy marched straight off to Cassandra's Nissen hut. "Cass?" Cassandra was making inroads into a bottle of whisky with another woman in the FANY unit.

They were playing cards and a haze of smoke billowed above the makeshift table.

340

"Not now, Kate, crucial moment."

"I'll have to interrupt you, Cassandra, something important has come up."

Cassandra turned around, squinting her eyes through the smoke issuing from the fag at the corner of her mouth. She looked red-faced too, but Katy guessed it was from the whisky, not any fever. There was only an inch left in the bottle.

Cassandra was still staring at her through one eye. "Well, Mrs Phipps? What's so important that you are going to make me lose my only pair of silk stockings to Mary Hatherington here?"

A year ago, Katy wouldn't have had the nerve to disrupt a game of anything between two such aristocratic young women and would have quailed with embarrassment at the prospect.

"It's Ariadne. She has a fever. I think it might be this wretched 'flu that the Gerries have kindly brought to us."

"As if shells and bullets weren't enough," Cassandra said, hurrying on her jacket. "Let's get her over to the French hospital. I hear they are the only ones who have the least idea how to tackle it."

"I'm not sure we should move her though, Cass. She's sound asleep and very hot."

They strode back to the tent at a brisk pace.

Ariadne was asleep but didn't look restful.

Katy felt her forehead again and looked up at Cassandra's anxious face.

She shook her head. "Roasting alive," was her verdict. "Let's wait until she stirs naturally and then transport her. Could you bring the ambulance over, Cass, and I'll gather her things together?"

"Righto. I'll pop into the Frenchies' hospital tent and make sure they have a spare bed on the way back. I've heard they're the best at dealing with this wretched influenza. At least the numbers of wounded have diminished with the Wipers lot despatched off home now."

341

Katy nodded and turned back to her flushed friend. Ariadne was tossing from side to side on her camp-bed, as much as anyone could in such a confined space.

An hour later Ariadne was ensconced in a hospital bed and lay pink and hot, against the white sheets. She looked very small. Dr Valnet himself, the respected resident doctor, instructed the nurse to drape the bed in net, sprayed with essential oils of eucalyptus and lavender. The aromas smelt reassuringly antiseptic to Katy's sensitive nose and she felt a slight relaxation of her heightened tension.

"She's in good hands," she said to Cassandra.

The nurse shooed them away. "Allez y. Elle reste ici très tranquille. Ne vous inquiétez pas. Do not disturb yourselves, we will look after her."

They trooped off, feeling at a loss without a task so Katy set to changing some tyres. Cassandra even gave a hand, so worried was she. An anxious few days ensued through which Katy remained relentlessly active.

Katy and Cassandra became closer while Ariadne's life hung in the balance. They were only allowed a peek around the tent flap of the hospital and a brief report in broken English for news as a daily sop to their anxiety.

Cassandra taught Katy poker. It stopped them thinking too much, during the long evenings of waiting. Katy, already mistress of the brave face, relieved her former mistress of the coveted silk stockings, once she had the hang of the game. When she would wear them and who for, she knew not.

After a worrying week, the French matron came to them as they tentatively sidled round the hospital entrance and stood there - both of them looking anxious and careworn.

"Oh, God, it's the Matron. That can't be good." Cassandra squeezed Katy's cold hand.

Katy swallowed hard and gripped a nearby table for support.

"Bon soir," said Matron, solemn as a judge.

The two women gripped each other's hands until the knuckles showed white. "Bon soir, Matron," they chorused in a whisper.

"Your friend, Madamoiselle Ariadne?"

Katy nodded, dreading the next sentence.

"She is doing well. She is over the worst and she will live. Monsieur le Docteur Valnet, he is very pleased wiz her."

Katy and Cassandra turned and hugged each other, tears falling freely and disregarded.

Matron allowed herself a smile. "Mes enfants – tout va bien. All is well."

"Can we see her?" asked Cassandra.

"No, not yet. In a few days perhaps, not now," said Matron, still smiling.

"And she really will be alright?" asked Katy.

"Oui, mes petites, tout va bien. Restez tranquilles, don't worry," and Matron patted Katy's hand.

"Oh, thank you Matron, thank you so much!" and Katy kissed her roughened cheeks.

Matron beamed at the French gesture. Cassandra followed suit and the two younger women departed in a cloud of relief.

Ariadne recovered only slowly and remained in the hospital for another two weeks. They were allowed visits by then but had to wear gauze masks sprayed with eucalyptus oil, as directed by Dr Valnet, to protect themselves against infection from other cases.

The influenza was fast becoming an epidemic. Ariadne remained a shadow of her former self and acquiesced quietly when instructed to go home to England to convalesce. Katy and Cassandra could not argue against it. Their dear friend, once the epitome of English beauty with her peach skin and rosy cheeks, was now an invalid – thin to the bone and as pale as the moon.

They took her to the dockside themselves. Cassandra lifted her into her ambulance as if she was made of the finest porcelain. Katy had packed her bags for her and filched cake from the mess cook to sustain her for the journey though she knew Ariadne would only pick at it - her appetite was tiny now.

"Don't wait outside by the railings once you're on the boat, Arry dear," implored Katy, "but go straight to your cabin and keep warm. We'll be much happier knowing you're safe inside than waving you off while you're on deck and getting chilled."

"Yes, you must be sensible, Arry," added Cassandra, looking stern but with tears in her eyes.

Ariadne gave them her huge smile. It made her hollow eyes look even more enormous in her thin face. Her teeth looked much too big for her. Katy shivered despite the summer sun.

"I promise to be a good girl. Don't fret, little mothers," Ariadne said with a wan smile.

"Soon you'll be with your own mother. She'll be that glad to see you, I'm sure." Katy thought guiltily of hers, whose letters still formed a steady stream of pressure to return home.

"Yes, and I will be glad to see her. I've had enough war and adventure to last me a lifetime. I'm longing to be home again. Edward will be there too. We'll be a sorry pair – me a convalescent and him with his shell shock."

"At least you will both be alive. Your mother will be grateful for that," Cassandra said. "So many of the boys in my ambulance didn't make it."

"Ay, and you can mend together, brother and sister helping each other along," Katy said, thinking of Albert.

Ariadne pressed their hands affectionately. "Yes, we are the lucky ones. You have both lost your brothers."

They hugged in turn and Ariadne turned and wobbled unsteadily up the gangplank. A young officer supported her elbow with his one remaining arm. She gave him a weak, thankful smile.

A single tear fell like a dew drop from Cassandra's nose and she wiped it roughly away with her sleeve. "Come on, Kate, I need a drink."

Katy nodded and they turned away, for neither could bear to see the boat off.

CHAPTER FIFTY FOUR

As the autumn drew on it became clear that the allies were gaining the upper hand. More and more starving German soldiers amassed round the camp and feeding them became a priority. They were obviously malnourished, and no amount of German army discipline could compensate. They had lost their fighting spirit because of it and, when the Hindenburg line fell breaching German defences, it marked the beginning of the end of the war.

Cassandra was transferred to the American base at Nevers to drive the Model T Fords there. A month later, Katy received a letter from her old employer.

Cassandra wrote:

Nevers, 10th October 1918

Dear Katy,
I have big news! These Americans waste no time, I can tell you! I've fallen in love with one of them. He's an officer and his name is Douglas Flintock. He's from Boston, Massachussetts, in the good old U S of A."

Katy wondered what Lady Smythe would make of an American in the family and read on.

"Mother will be horrified of course that he's
a) not a Ponsonby, so our marriage won't swell her little empire by joining the two neighbouring estates together and
b) he's not a blue-blooded English aristocrat. There's only one Ponsonby left at Winterton, I

believe, and he's got an enormous nose and two left feet!

Douglas is of course tall, handsome and altogether wonderful. He has two sisters, Cheryl and Rose, and they are helping with the war effort at home. Douglas's father is a lawyer and rather important over in America. Douglas was glad to get away and do his own thing in the war."

Let us hope he survives it then, thought Katy and felt a glow of pride that here she was servicing ambulances in the thick of it and not still hiding at home like Douglas's sisters. Cassandra signed off in a flurry of haste to get back to her American beau.

Although pleased for her friend, Katy felt even more bereft after reading Cassandra's happy news and heard about the victories as they piled in with a hollow heart.

When the armistice was announced at the eleventh hour on the eleventh day of November 1918, she took herself off to the beach at Étaples and let the scudding wind scald the tears from her face. The rest of her life stretched before her and how empty it looked.

A cold easterly wind had sprung up. It whipped the sand into scurries of pale clouds of quartz. The pallid November sun teased them into sparkling diamonds. Katy sat on the dunes, the spiky grass darning her dungarees with its sharp needles. She shifted her seat unconsciously, only vaguely aware of the discomfort.

She missed her friends. Her mind slid back to April when they had come down to this same beach, past huge drifts of butter yellow daffodils when the sun had had some warmth in it. She remembered that fleeting moment of happiness when they had run through the surf, splashing each other and shrieking in forgetful delight. She smiled at the memory.

She supposed they would be celebrating back at the camp and indeed at home. Katy's mind slipped further back in time. Her sleepy Wiltshire village and its silly, petty rivalries between hill and valley seemed so distant, so remote. A golden past in retrospect, filled with the usual ordinary family dramas of births, deaths and domestic triumphs. Small disasters that had seemed mountainous at the time.

It all looked so tiny from here. Jem featured in all the rose-coloured memories. She pictured him digging the first potatoes of summer and bringing them in to her tiny, lean-to kitchen. The little creamy tubers would still be covered with damp, fertile soil and the fresh mint crushed between his big hands would smell sweet and true, just like the wide, satisfied smile on his face.

Katy took in a deep breath, hoping for a whiff of that fragrant summery herb. Instead she inhaled salt air – swept clean and devoid of fecund earth. It cut her like a razor and blew away her soft memories.

Katy ran down to the sea's edge and screamed with the seagulls. She wanted to tear down the blue sky and rip the white clouds from it. Her short hair, now cropped like a page-boy's, blew into her eyes and the sea air invaded her lungs with ferocious cold. She ran into the blast of the gusty wind, still screaming, still crying; into the surf; gasping as a big wave tumbled into her boots. She kept running through its frothy edge. Her sodden feet became numb but only when her mind followed suit, did she stop. She had run half the length of the long beach. Katy came to a halt, panting for breath, her feet still submerged in the sucking tide. She could hardly breathe but at least she could feel no emotion.

The sun withdrew its meagre autumnal warmth and sulked behind clouds now grey with rain. Katy became aware of how very cold and wet she was and dragged her leaden feet away from the cleansing foam. She plodded back up the beach, sand clinging to her wet boots and making them heavier than ever. She even thought about taking them off entirely and running barefoot back to camp but the barbed wire, often concealed in the dunes, made her hesitate.

She was so tired, so utterly tired. Sick and tired of the whole miserable drama. The overwhelming colossal tragedy of all these young men, yes and women too, wiped out. Working at the base camp, through which most of the army was processed, could not spare anyone from the scale of the losses.

Katy fell on her knees on to the damp strand. She rolled into a ball, and hugged herself, as if she were her own lost baby.

A stream of soldiers ran onto the beach from the crest of the dunes. They shouted and cheered and threw their hats in the air. Katy sat up and ran her hand through her chaotic hair.

The soldiers cascaded down onto the beach in a flood of euphoria.

"Hello, darling. Cheer up!" said one of them with a grin that stretched from ear to ear.

"Here, have this. Don't you know we won the war?" said his friend.

They laughed. The first soldier blew her a kiss and shoved a bottle of red wine into her hand. The two men ran on past her towards the sea. The wine was half drunk already and a seam of saliva round its neck gleamed; wet and slimy. She threw it away in disgust. It left a dark red stain like blood on the sand before quickly seeping away. Katy stamped on the red mark and then buried it with clean, fresh sand before walking slowly back to her quarters.

CHAPTER FIFTY FIVE

Peace brought Katy a new role. The ambulances still ferried men to the port for debarkation and she still had to service them when necessary but there was also a huge amount of paperwork to be done to discharge thousands of men from the army. Soldiers were being converted back into civilians and most of those serving in France had to pass through Étaples for this procedure. So Katy had to divide her time between maintaining the ambulances and wading through yards of discharge papers.

Queues of veterans waited patiently in line in the Nissen huts that served as offices. Most were smiling and smoking as they stood there, waiting their turn. A few were quiet and withdrawn with only their haunted eyes revealing their histories.

Katy had little time to study them. The queues were literally endless. Her hand ached with writer's cramp from long hours of laboriously writing out the names, dates of birth and military history of the sea of faceless men.

Their jokes about girls in trousers were funny at first.

"We shall have to watch our backs when we get home, boys," they would josh. "These girls will be catching up with us."

"Yes, and be after our jobs, I dare say," was their fellows' frequent, guarded response.

Katy answered back at first. "We've fought as hard a war as you, haven't we?" But she soon gave up when the men showed real fear, and sometimes animosity, at the perceived threat to their manly livelihoods.

By Christmas the procedures had become mechanical. Despite the warmth of the office headquarters, Katy longed to be back in the ambulance sheds, fixing hoses and polishing chrome. She found the form filling tedious in the extreme and the same old jokes even more so. She tended to keep her head down, her short hair tucked behind her ear and her roughened, oil-stained hands moving swiftly across the pages in a vain attempt to expedite things and get to the end of the everlasting queue of demob happy men.

She was writing "Lieutenant Peter Hopkins, Yorkshire Regiment," when the hairs on the back of her head began to prickle. The small of her back had been aching for days from sitting on her hard wooden chair and she sat up and stretched, flexing her tired spine and rubbing her hand across the back of her tingling neck.

As she did so, she looked up and saw a tall, thin soldier staring at her so intensely, it sent a shock right through her.

The young man suddenly broke ranks.

"Oi! Wait your turn, Corporal," shouted an officer from another table.

The babble of chatter in the room hushed to silence. The soldier appeared not to hear the senior officer and walked, ever so slowly, towards Katy.

Locked in his stare, she barely registered that he only had one arm.

Katy went completely cold. The tingling that had begun with the hairs on the back of her neck now spread all over her trembling body. Barely realising what she was doing, she stood up shakily, gripping the edge of the wobbly deal table for what little support it could give.

Jem walked towards her, oblivious of the interested looks of everyone present in that huge room. It was as if each person held their breath, as husband and wife approached each other for the first time in years. Katy held out both her hands but only found one reaching out in return.

Jem's image blurred in front of her as she whispered his name. She sidestepped the table as his mouth started, ever so slowly, to curl upwards. Her tears ran down his face when their lips met, and his arm pulled her to him. He was so thin.

When they pulled away to look deep into each other's eyes to try and believe what they saw, the whole room erupted into enormous shouts and cheers as people realised what was happening.

Katy could hardly hear herself think through the noise and spontaneous applause. Neither could let go of the other but grinned and hugged and grinned again. In that moment Katy had never felt more love for anyone in the world, not Florence, not dear Albert, not even her parents. Her Jem, she had her Jem back! Back from the bloody dead! She laughed hysterically and he laughed with her.

"Look at you, Katy Phipps, with your trousers and short hair."

"Oh, Jem, you're so thin. Oh, I love you! Love you, love you!"

"What are you doing in France?"

"What happened to your arm?"

All these questions were quickly scotched when half a dozen men picked up first Katy, then Jem and balanced them on their shoulders. The men marched out of the hut, parading the couple in front of astonished groups of bored, waiting men.

"For they are jolly good fellows, for they are jolly good fellows, for they are jolly good fellows...and so say all of us!" they chorused.

Soon hundreds of soldiers were joining in, tossing their unwanted army caps in the air and wiping tears of joy on their rough khaki sleeves.

When they finally realised that Katy was shaking from head to foot like a jelly, they eventually put them down in the Mess Tent. Officers came rushing in to see what all the fuss was about and promptly ordered champagne for the reunited couple and beer for everyone else. This went down very well and Jem and Katy were plonked on the table in the centre of the room and toasted roundly by officers and soldiers alike.

"I can't hardly hear myself think, let alone talk to you," shouted Jem.

Katy nodded. There were so many questions and so much to catch up on. But it hardly mattered. They kissed and hugged and laughed and cried. Champagne effervesced inside Katy's stomach, but it was no match for her own bubbles of joy.

Eventually Captain Harry saved them. He got one of his men to lift him on to the table next to them and laid his crutch down using Jem's familiar shoulder for support. He quickly picked it up again when he couldn't make himself heard and used the crutch like a hammer as if he was a judge in court.

Slowly, the noise simmered down.

Katy turned her face to the young man who, with the poise of a much older one, spoke for them all.

"Listen everybody!" he cried, "This here is Jeremy Phipps, Lance Corporal of the 2nd Battalion of the Wiltshire Regiment." Enthusiastic clapping was stopped by Harry's raised palm.

"And this, I believe is his wife, Katherine Phipps."

Katy blushed as big cheers erupted at this confirmation of her happy situation.

"Jeremy has saved my life at least twice and probably more, with his constant cheerful resourcefulness with whatever the enemy could throw at us. Jem was the best soldier to have at your side in battle and led his men with great courage and bravery. He was a tower of strength during our imprisonment in Germany and I only have my leg here because of his quick thinking when I was wounded and his constant care afterwards. I can truly say that if it wasn't for him, I probably wouldn't be here at all and going home tomorrow.

"But enough of me. This moment is about this married couple here. I don't know Katy yet but Jem has talked about her constantly, so I feel I do already. Never was there a more loving husband and now I have met her, I can see why. What a beauty, eh lads?"

A huge cheer went up at this point, making Katy squirm, but when she saw that all eyes continued to gaze at the trio on the table tops and none were dry, Captain Harry's face blurred as her own eyes had also filled up.

"Now, I suggest we leave 'em to it! What do you say? I reckon they've a bit of catching up to do! Come on lads, let's carry 'em off to their quarters and leave them to get to know each other again," shouted Harry.

Amongst rather more raucous cheering, vociferous offers of broad shoulders surged forward as once more Katy and Jem were carried away by the crowd. This time they were deposited at Katy's private little tent, awarded through courtesy of her long service, and following her pointed, breathless directions.

Katy worried that Jem's thin shoulders might collapse under all the friendly slaps but eventually all the soldiers dispersed in a swarm, back to the tent and the beer.

Harry left last, after shaking Katy's hand. Before he went, she pulled him to her and kissed him soundly on both cheeks, too choked with emotion for words. He hugged them both, popped two bottles of champagne inside the tent flap, smiling sweetly. Then he saluted them smartly and limped after the other men.

At last, Katy could turn to wonder at her husband. She grabbed his hand and pulled him inside the tent, clutching a champagne bottle in the other. With fluttering hands, she clattered some mugs together and poured out the fizzing liquid. Froth cascaded over the rims, as they clinked the enamel cups and drank it straight down.

"To you, Mr Phipps."

"And to you too, Mrs Phipps."

Giggling, they collapsed on to Katy's camp bed which promptly fell apart under their combined weight. They laughed until their sides ached and hugged and rolled together like puppies while the world melted away.

CHAPTER FIFTY SIX

When Katy didn't turn up for work the next morning, the British Army didn't disturb her. She and her husband were given unofficial leave for twenty-four hours and left in glorious isolation. With so much to tell each other and so much loving to catch up on, they had very little sleep.

"How did you lose your arm, Jem?" was the first thing Katy wanted to know.

"Being shot twice didn't do it any good and, despite my efforts with a tourniquet, the German doctors decided I'd be better off without it."

"German doctors!"

"Yes, and damn good they were too. I would have died, had they not amputated, Katy."

Katy lifted his sleeve and kissed his stump. Her tears cleansed the wound.

Jem stroked her short hair. "You had an amputation yourself, Katy. I used to love letting your hair down."

"Too much bother," she said, looking back up at him. "I chopped it off during my training. I couldn't be doing with drying it for hours. Jem, I lost something else while you were away," she added, her voice soft and low.

Jem made a play of checking her arms and legs, "Seem to be all present and correct." He laughed.

"This isn't funny, Jem."

Her heart had begun to knock against her ribcage. She had to tell him about Lionel. She couldn't have that trespass festering like an untended wound between them.

Jem sat up on one end of the uncomfortable, broken camp bed. He looked back at Katy, sitting at the other, as solemnly as she could have wished.

Katy took a deep breath. Her eyes never left her husband's face while she told him what had happened the night she'd heard he'd died.

"I'd come down the hill from the manor so carefree and happy. I'd decided to enrol as a nurse in the VAD and try

355

and join you here at the front. I didn't know then that I wouldn't get in but that's another story. I found the letter about you in our cottage when I got home. I went a bit mad, Jem. I'm ashamed of it now but, at the time, it was just unbearable."

Jem put his one arm out to hug her, but she held him away. "No, Jem, dearest, I must finish this."

"Go on then, love, if you must."

"I must," she said, her voice almost a whisper now. "I went to the river, at the bottom of the woods where we used to take our little Florence."

"I remember."

"I'd fallen asleep in the woods and I was thirsty when I woke up so I went to drink from the river. Then I dozed off again. Jem, I don't know how to tell you the next bit."

"Go on, Katy."

"I slid into the river. I wanted it to carry me away – to you – and Florence."

Jem wouldn't let her push his arm away then, so Katy carried on, holding his hand and forcing her eyes to gaze on his young, tired face.

"The next thing I knew, someone was lifting me out of the river."

"Thank God for that!"

"You might not think so when you know what happened next, Jem dear."

"But if it kept you safe?"

"Safe, in that I was alive, maybe; but not safe in another way."

"Who was it?"

"Lionel White, the vicar."

"Oh, the vicar, well, that's alright then." Jem squeezed her hand.

"You would think so but it wasn't, Jem. It wasn't alright at all. He, um, he took advantage of me. I must have fainted and passed out and when he started kissing me, I thought it was you, back from the dead. Jem, please believe me, I thought it was you, and God forgive me, I kissed him back."

Katy scanned Jem's face. It had been thin and tired and now looked old as well, but she couldn't give up. She must tell him everything even if it meant she lost him.

"Was that all? A kiss don't signify much, Katy, not after all I've been through."

This was hard and getting harder by the minute. "No, Jem, that wasn't all. I thought it was you, see, and I loved him back. Not *him*, I didn't know it was him; all the time I thought it was you. You see, I'd nearly drowned and fainted and I, well, I wasn't myself." It sounded lame even to her ears.

"You mean, you made love with him, with the vicar, with Lionel White?"

"No, I didn't make love to him, but I passed out and he took me home and put me to bed. When I woke up, I was naked," and finally, she dropped her head.

Jem lifted her chin with his fingers. They were as tender as Lionel's had been that moonlit night. Her face came up but not her eyes. She could not look at her husband for shame.

Softly, he said, "What happened next?"

"I don't honestly know. I only pieced it together the next day. I woke up in our cottage bedroom alone and I don't know how I got there. He came round after I woke up. He'd left his glove. He told me he loved me but hadn't violated me and later said that, because you were dead, we were free to marry."

"And what did you do, Katy? What did you say? Look at me!"

"I chucked the bugger out!"

Jem roared with laughter then. Katy could not believe her ears. Her eyes flew to his.

"Oh, Katy. I love you so much!"

"How can you say that when I betrayed you? I even thought I *might* marry him at one point and then the

357

strangest thing of all happened. I got another letter from you, after the one that said you were dead, after Lionel asked me to marry him. It was as if you were calling me from the grave. I knew then I had to try and come and find you. But when I got to France, there were so many deaths, it was just impossible. Now you're here and alive, I can hardly believe it, or that you will ever forgive me."

"Katy, if you'd seen what I have seen. What men do to each other - the death, the destruction, the mutilation of people, land, horses, houses, villages. The wasteland. You mistook me for another man. You kissed him because you thought he was me. How can I think that a betrayal?"

"Jem, oh, Jem, I can't believe you are not angry or jealous."

"I didn't say I wasn't jealous. If I ever clap eyes on that bloody vicar, I'll skin him alive. Tell me, Katy, what did you say when you threw him out?"

Katy's skin tingled with warmth as she remembered the scene. "I told him he was a hypocrite and a coward. He was here, you know, at the base camp when it was bombed. He made this pompous speech and afterwards I told him I never wanted to see him again. I told him I despised him."

"Of course, you did, that's my girl! Katy, I'm not angry, I'm proud of you. Listen, I've killed men in this cursed war. Probably good men too; men with children and wives. Women like you have been raped all across Europe. Children killed. And what for? All those young soldiers, just boys some of 'em. Gone. But we're here, Katy. You and me – we're *alive*! It don't matter about the blasted vicar. Come here. Let me hold you, as best I can, that is. I'm never going to let you go, Katy. Not now, not ever. We're both a bit broken but we're alive. We're together again and that's all that matters."

Katy wrapped her body around his, laid her weary head against his shoulder and let her tears flow free.

Only when they got ravenously hungry and all the champagne was drunk, did they emerge from their tent the next day and totter into the Mess Tent for a feed. The knowing winks and elbow nudges were a small price to pay for being together again. The next few days were spent going through the formalities of endless form-filling.

"There's nothing the British army likes better than reams of pointless paper, Jem," Katy said, as they signed form after form. "Believe me, I know."

They just had time to scribble telegrams to their respective families before getting on the boat for their journey home.

"Do you think we'll be home in time for Christmas?" asked Jem, as he slung their baggage on to the rack above the wooden benches in the boat that would take them back to Britain.

"Of course. We just need to get the train to Paddington, and we'll be home tonight."

They scrabbled across London hand in hand, snatching a hot pasty each from a street seller near the station. Katy hailed a Hansom cab after they disembarked from the Dover train as if she'd lived in London all her life. She didn't even think about the crowds pushing this way and that when they got to Paddington. All she could feel was Jem's hand in hers. Just the one hand but it was warm and throbbed with life even if it was wasted and thin.

"Oh, Katy, will you just look at those green fields," Jem said, over and over, as they got nearer to their Wiltshire home. They sat as close as decency allowed in the train compartment. Side to side, bodies melting together through their khaki uniforms, connected as if they were skin to skin. Greener and greener were the fields that rushed by even though it was winter.

"They've ploughed there already, look," Jem said, as they whisked through the chalk downlands.

"I love that soft brown colour. It has the look of doves about it and look how softly the land curves here. I thought

359

I'd never see colour again after the grey base camp. I never want to see canvas again."

Jem laughed and hugged her close. Katy ignored their fellow passengers and kissed him full on the mouth, saving deeper kisses for later after one of them coughed very loudly.

Jem was astonished to be greeted by Cassandra at their local station.

"Kate, how wonderful to see you back in Blighty. And Jem, yes, I remember you now. Chuck over your suitcases and I'll bung them in the back of the motor."

In a weird changeover of roles, Cassandra slung their suitcases into her new car, acquired when she had returned home a month earlier and held the door open for them to climb onto its luxurious rear upholstery. Cassandra clambered into the driver's seat and, tooting wildly, drove off – looking like some mad, gender-defying chauffeur in her leather jacket and the jodhpurs she still stubbornly espoused.

Jem looked across at Katy, his eyebrows raised in enquiry, but Katy was too busy diagnosing a mechanical problem to listen to him. "Cass?"

"Yes?"

"There's something wrong with this engine. It's mis-firing."

"Do you reckon? This old Sunbeam does cough a bit. Been sat in the garage doing nothing all through the war."

"Definitely mis-timing. I'll have to take a look at it when we get back."

"Righto, you're the expert, after all."

"Expert?" Jem said.

"Best bloody engineer on the base, your Katy." Cassandra swerved round a bend far too fast.

Jem gripped the handle of the door and shouted back, "A woman of many talents, my wife."

"Absolutely!" Cassandra drew up in front of Cheadle Manor with a flourish and a loud toot of her horn.

At this signal the heavy front door swung wide open and Mr Andrews, the butler, stood aside to reveal a rakish looking young man of about twenty-five and, behind him, most of the staff of the manor.

"Douglas, you made it!" Cassandra bounded up the steps and kissing the younger man soundly on the mouth.

"Sure, I did, honey, drove all the way. Hey - is this the famous engineer and her war hero?"

"Yes, darling. This is Jem Phipps and his wife, Kate."

They stepped inside the big hall and saw, to their amazement, most of the population of both Cheadle villages, all decked out in their best winter clothes and wearing their biggest smiles of welcome.

Christmas lanterns lit the hall and sprigs of holly nodded above the portraits of past Smythes. Cassandra's ancestors stared down from their dark oily canvases, oblivious to the joyful welcome that greeted the two war refugees.

Lady Smythe came forward first. She deigned to shake Jem's hand and astonished Katy by kissing her on both cheeks with misty eyes. Their parents were there too and, uninhibited by their fellow villagers, embraced them warmly, nearly squeezing the life out of them and universally declaring them both to be far too skinny and needing feeding up.

Mary Phipps forgot her dislike of her daughter-in-law when she saw her care of her wounded son, miraculously returned to life. "Jem, my Jem! Let me touch you so I know you're real."

George clapped his son on the back and shook his good hand. "Jem lad, I've never been happier to see anyone in my whole life."

Agnes couldn't wait to jump in and kiss them both. "Katy! You're that thin and you've cut all your hair off! But I've never seen a bonnier sight."

Bert held Katy's hands in his. "Welcome home, my girl. It's good to see you again. And Jem, too. I can't tell you how much it means to us to have you home safe. We thought you was lost, like our Albert, and now you are found."

Sir Robert ordered that his best sherry be brought out and the maids scurried round with trays of titbits for ballast, hardly knowing whether to treat the prodigal couple as gentry or staff. Even Mrs Andrews and Mrs Biggs beamed at them and shook their hands. Mr Andrews, who'd obviously had a few swigs of sherry already, tottered about with a silly smile pasted on his face that never moved, even when he tripped over his own two feet. Mrs Threadwell and Mrs Hoskins shook Katy's hands and dabbed their eyes in unison; their usual double act, for once, entirely benign.

Jem managed to laugh about balancing a sausage roll and a glass of sherry with only one hand and his parents tried not to wince at the joke.

Somehow, Cassandra had tracked down both Captain Harry and Ariadne and persuaded them to attend the welcome home party. It was Katy's turn to be amazed when Ariadne came out of the library, still frail, but obviously getting on famously with Captain Harry upon whose arm she leant despite his needing the other for his stick.

Such delightful moments were had then as their new friends were introduced to their families and hugs and kisses crossed the class divide. Cassandra looked quite radiant when she introduced the others to her American fiancé. Lady Smythe seemed to approve of him without qualification despite his Bostonian drawl.

When the older generation felt the need to sit down and collect their breath with all the excitement, the younger still had some energy to spare. Cassandra wound up the old gramophone and put on some American jazz music. The young people danced ad lib to the strange new intoxicating sound while their elders shook their heads in mock and, in some cases, real horror.

Katy revelled in Jem's uneven embrace. The sherry and the music swam together in her mind. Beloved faces beamed at her as she whirled round the drawing room. A room she used to dust and polish, in which she was now one of the guests of honour.

She closed her eyes, wanting the moment to last forever, knowing it couldn't but thankful, so thankful, to be home.

THE END

"Excellent novels with a well rounded and strong central female character. You do need to read all the books, but they are all good so go for it and enjoy."

**Daffodils is also available as an
AUDIOBOOK
Narrated by the author**

Book One of The Katherine Wheel Series

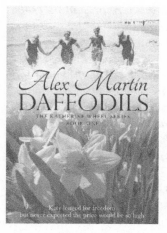

Katy dreams of a better life than just being a domestic servant at Cheadle Manor. Her one attempt to escape is thwarted when her flirtation with the manor's heir results in a scandal that shocks the local community.
Jem Beagle has always loved Katy. His offer of marriage rescues her, but personal tragedy divides them. Jem leaves his beloved Wiltshire to become a reluctant soldier on the battlefields of World War One. Katy is left behind, restless and alone.
Lionel White, just returned from being a missionary in India, brings a dash of colour to the small village, and offers Katy a window on the wider world.
Katy decides she has to play her part in the global struggle and joins the war effort as a WAAC girl.
She finally breaks free from the stifling Edwardian hierarchies that bind her but the brutality of global war brings home the price she has paid for her search.

"Impressively well-researched and vividly imagined."

"A fantastic story which was written beautifully. I have not read many books based around WW1 and this was just right. The characters have some hard times and I found myself in tears at times, but overall, the story was told in a way I could relate to and understand. Highly recommended for fans of historical fiction."

"Probably one of the best books I've read of this genre. Took me to the First World War as never before. Will certainly read the second with great anticipation. Only chose it because of the price and picture on the front but what a find and such a treat !!!"

"Daffodils is an extraordinary story of commitment and enduring hope which teaches us the power of resilience, integrity and true honor. This book was a deeply emotional experience that managed to reach the inner core of my being. This is such a powerful story! Highly recommended."

Daffodils is also available as an audio book, narrated by the author

Book Two of The Katherine Wheel Series

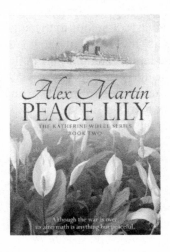

Although the war is over, its aftermath is anything but peaceful

After the appalling losses suffered during World War One, three of its survivors long for peace, unaware that its aftermath will bring different, but still daunting, challenges.

Katy trained as a mechanic during the war and cannot bear to return to the life of drudgery she left behind. A trip to America provides the dream ticket she has always craved and an opportunity to escape the straitjacket of her working-class roots. She jumps at the chance, little realising that it will change her life forever, but not in the way she'd hoped.

Jem lost not only an arm in the war, but also his livelihood, and with it, his self-esteem. How can he keep restless Katy at home and provide for his wife? He puts his life at risk a second time, attempting to secure their future and prove his love for her.

Cassandra has fallen deeply in love with Douglas Flintock, an American officer she met while driving ambulances at the Front. How can she persuade this modern American to adapt to her English country way of life, and all the duties that come with inheriting Cheadle Manor? When Douglas returns to Boston, unsure of his feelings, Cassandra crosses the ocean, determined to lure him back.

As they each try to carve out new lives, their struggles impact on each other in unforeseen ways.

"Daffodils' sequel Peace Lily is as enthralling and fresh as its predecessor."

"Great follow on book. Couldn't put down till finished."

Book Three of The Katherine Wheel Series

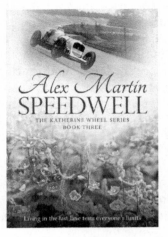

Living in the fast lane tests everyone's limits

Katy and Jem enter the 1920's with their future in the balance. How can they possibly make their new enterprise work? They must risk everything, including disaster, and trust their gamble will pay off.

Cassandra, juggling the demands of a young family, aging parents and running Cheadle Manor, distrusts the speed of the modern age, but Douglas races to meet the new era, revelling in the freedom of the open road.

Can each marriage survive the strain the new dynamic decade imposes? Or will the love they share deepen and carry them through? They all arrive at destinies that surprise them in Speedwell, the third book in the Katherine Wheel Series.

"I really enjoyed the stories. Read all three books in the series while on holiday. Her writing style makes for comfortable reading. Her characters are credible and in the main her story lines are unpredictable and powerfully descriptive."

"A fascinating set of characters weave their magical story through a daring enterprise just after the end of the Great War. The story travels from humble but daring beginnings in a small Wiltshire village with Katy and Jem and takes us to Boston in the USA and back."

Book Four of The Katherine Wheel Series

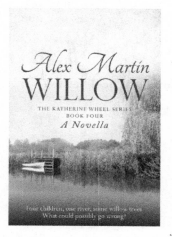

Willow is a short novella that bridges the generational gap. Book Four in The Katherine Wheel Series may be small, but it packs in many surprises for the children of Katy and Jem, and Douglas and Cassandra.

"This is a very well written and descriptive novella with the children and the idyllic countryside setting, well observed and portrayed. You feel you are there experiencing it first-hand. It draws you into a totally believable world, perfect material for a film or a Sunday evening drama series."

"This tale brings to life their distinctive well-rounded characters; the dialogue distinguishes each child's voice and fits exactly into the era it represents. The descriptive narrative sets the scene perfectly and moves the plot along in gripping speed."

The stifling heat of a midsummer's day lures four children to the cool green waters of the river that runs between Cheadle Manor and The Katherine Wheel Garage.
Al captains the little band of pirates as they blithely board the wooden dinghy. Headstrong Lottie vies with him to be in charge while Isobel tries to keep the peace and look after little Lily.

But it is the river that is really in control.

Lost and alone, the four children must face many dangers, but it is the unforeseen consequences of their innocent adventure that will shape their futures for years to come.

Book Five of The Katherine Wheel Series

Two sisters, divided by love and war, must each fight a different battle to survive

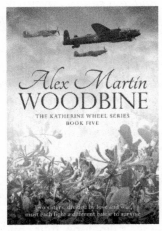

Lottie, her sister Isobel and Al, the man they both love, are on the brink of adulthood and the Second World War in Woodbine, the fifth book in The Katherine Wheel Series. Trapped and alone in occupied France, Lottie must disguise her identity and avoid capture if she is to return and heal the bitter feud over the future of Cheadle Manor.

Back in England, Al is determined to prove himself. He joins the Air Transport Auxiliary service, flying aeroplanes to RAF bases all over the country. Isobel defies everyone's expectations by becoming a Land Girl. Bound by a promise to a dying woman, she struggles to break free and follow her heart.

"Great story - this is a real family saga through the important milestones of the 20th Century. It's all here. Love, hate, life, death, war and peace. Woodbine takes us through the second world war with real insight into people's lives. I especially enjoyed Lottie's time in France and the scenes in the Normandy farmhouse are very evocative. Looking forward to the next, and final, chapter to see how everything comes together."

"Woodbine is fifth book of the brilliant Katherine Wheel series and, having read and enjoyed all four of the previous books I was looking forward to this one. I was not disappointed; Alex Martin has once again brought to life the characters that I followed all that time and, I have to say, I've been riveted by the historic detail to the background of the stories. It is obvious that the author researches extensively to portray the atmosphere of each era – and succeeds again with Woodbine."

"This is Book 5 in the series and carries on with the next generation of Katy and Cassandra, both ladies from different spectrum of the social classes have a deep and abiding friendship. Now their children are grown and are now encountering WWII. Surprises of inheritance, a love triangle, and the turmoil of a world war. I've read all the previous books and would advise a reader to start with the first book so that they get the full impact of these two families. Well written, well researched."

IVY

Book Six in The Katherine Wheel Series

Two sisters, each caught in a trap in World War Two, must escape to find their true destiny

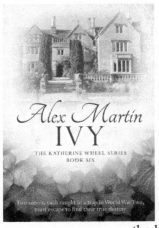

All the disparate threads of this epic saga are seamlessly woven together in Ivy, the sixth and final book in The Katherine Wheel Series.

Drawn into the Resistance in Occupied France, Lottie's strengths and endurance are tested to the limit.

Home-loving Isobel, torn between love and duty, must set herself free if she is ever to find happiness.

Flying planes for the Air Transport Auxiliary frequently puts Al in danger but securing the woman he loves proves much more challenging.

Cheadle Manor once lay at the heart of the lives of Lottie, Isobel and Al, but World War Two has broken every bond tying them to their safe haven. Can they ever come home and be together again?

"5.0 out of 5 stars A majestic Series finale: a perfectly paced drama, full of tension, mystery,

I love this beautifully woven story of Ivy, the impressive conclusion of the Katherine Wheel Series. It is so easy to visualise how it could have felt being Lottie in wartime occupied France. She has to draw on her huge courage to face some very scary exploits, whilst her friends there also risked their lives to help bring freedom to Europe. It's such a satisfying read, as the array of interesting characters pull us into into life from their perspective in France as well as rural England through their own adventures. Gripping at times, I really wanted to know how things would turn out for everyone - the families and friends in Wiltshire, her friends in France - and especially Lottie herself. The ending is excellent!
romance and compassion."

Alex Martin's debut book is based on her grape picking adventure in France in the 1980's. It's more of a mystery/ thriller than historical fiction but makes for great holiday reading with all the sensuous joys of that beautiful country.

Every journey is an adventure. Especially one into the unknown.

The shocking discovery of her lover with someone else propels Roxanne into escaping to France and seeking work as a grape-picker. She's never been abroad before and certainly never travelled alone.

Opportunistic loner, Armand, exploits her vulnerability when they meet by chance. She didn't think she would see him again or be the one who exposes his terrible crime.

Join Roxanne on her journey of self-discovery, love and tragedy in rural France. Taste the wine, feel the sun, drive through the Provencal mountains with her, as her courage and resourcefulness are tested to the limit.

The Twisted Vine is set in the heart of France and is a deeply romantic but suspenseful tale. Roxanne Rudge escapes her cheating boyfriend by going grape picking in France. She feels vulnerable and alone in such a big country where she can't speak the language and is befriended by Armand le Clair, a handsome Frenchman. Armand is not all he seems, however, and she discovers a darker side to him before uncovering a dreadful secret. She is aided and abetted by three new friends she has made, charming posh Peter, a gifted linguist; the beautiful and vivacious Italian, Yvane; and clever Henry of the deep brown eyes with the voice to match. Together they unravel a mystery centred around a beautiful chateau and play a part in its future.

"The original setting of this novel and the beauty of colorful places that Roxanne visits really drew me in. This book was a lot more than I'd expected, because aside from the romantic aspect, there's a great deal of humor, fantastic friendship, and entertaining dialogue. I strongly recommend this book to anyone who likes women's fiction."

"This is a wonderful tale told with compassion, emotion, thrills and excitement and some unexpected turns along the way. Oh, and there may be the smattering of a romance in there as well! Absolutely superb."

<u>The Rose Trail</u> is a time slip story set in both the English Civil War and the present day woven together by a supernatural thread.

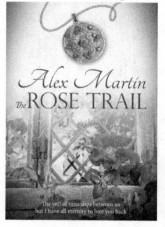

Is it chance that brings Fay and Persephone together? Or is it the restless and malevolent spirit who stalks them both?
Once rivals, they must now unite if they are to survive the mysterious trail of roses they are forced to follow into a dangerous, war torn past.

"The past has been well researched although I don't know a lot about this period in history it all rings so true – the characters are fantastic with traits that you like and dislike which also applies to the 'present' characters who have their own issues to contend with as well as being able to connect with the past."

"A combination of love, tragedies, friendships, past and present, lashings of historical aspects, religious bias, controlling natures all combined with the supernatural give this novel a wonderful page-turning quality."

" I loved this book, the storyline greatly appealed to me and the history it contained. Fay has always been able to see spirits. The love of her life is Robin, whom she met when she was 11 at school. She trains to become an accountant and purely by chance meets up with an old school friend. The book develops into an enthralling adventure for them both as they slip back and forth in time."

All Alex Martin's stories are available as ebooks as well as paperbacks and make great gifts!
Alex writes about her work on her blog at
www.intheplottingshed.com
where you can get your FREE copy of Alex Martin's short story collection, 'Trio', by clicking on the picture of the shed.
Constructive reviews oil a writer's wheel like nothing else and are very much appreciated on Amazon or Goodreads or anywhere else!

Alex Martin, Author

Facebook page:
https://www.facebook.com/TheKatherineWheel/
Twitter handle: https://twitter.com/alex_martin8586
Email: alexxx8586@gmail.com

Made in the USA
Monee, IL
05 August 2021